George John Romanes, Ethel Duncan Romanes

The Life and Letters of George John Romanes

George John Romanes, Ethel Duncan Romanes

The Life and Letters of George John Romanes

ISBN/EAN: 9783744782104

Printed in Europe, USA, Canada, Australia, Japan

Cover: Foto ©Raphael Reischuk / pixelio.de

More available books at **www.hansebooks.com**

THE
LIFE AND LETTERS

OF

GEORGE JOHN ROMANES

M.A., LL.D., F.R.S.

WRITTEN AND EDITED BY HIS WIFE

LONGMANS, GREEN, AND CO.
LONDON, NEW YORK, AND BOMBAY
1896

LIBERIS NOSTRIS

RECORDATIO

PATRIS DESIDERATISSIMI

MEMORIA JUSTI CUM LAUDIBUS

PREFACE

Is writing my husband's life I have tried, so far as it was possible, to let him, especially in matters scientific, speak for himself.

For the purpose of his biographer it is unfortunate that my husband lived in almost daily intercourse for parts of many years with more than one of his most intimate friends. Hence there are no letters to several people with whom he was in the habit of discussing scientific, philosophic, and theological questions.

The letters relating to his work will, I hope, interest any one who cares for biological science. Whatever may be the exact place which shall be assigned to him, by those who come after, in the great army of workers for Science, this much may be said: that no one ever served in the cause of Science with more passionate and whole-hearted devotion, more entire disinterestedness—

All for Love, and nothing for Reward.

I have to acknowledge the kindness of many who have put letters at my disposal. I cannot sufficiently express my thanks to Mr. Francis Darwin for generously allowing me to print portions of the correspondence which for seven or eight years was one of the chief pleasures and privileges of my husband's life. I must also thank my brother and sister-in-law, the Dean of Christ Church, Professor Poulton, Professor Schäfer, Professor Le Conte, Mr. Thiselton-Dyer, and others for like permission.

And I must express my most sincere gratitude to the Rev. P. N. Waggett, to Professor C. Lloyd Morgan, and to my cousin Mrs. St. George Reid (late of Newnham College, Cambridge), for their constant help and advice.

To Mrs. Reid I owe more than I can well express. Her scientific knowledge and ability have been simply invaluable, and have been used with ever-ready and ungrudging generosity and kindness.

There are other aspects of my husband's life which are interesting, but again I think he has told his own story, and it is needless for me here to speak of what, to some extent, he has laid bare—of mental perplexity and of steadfast endurance and loyalty to Truth. It may be that others, wandering in the twilight of this 'dimly lighted world,' may be stimulated and encouraged and helped to go on in patience until on them also dawns that Light. If this be so it will not be altogether in vain that he bore long years of very real and very heavy sorrow.

E. R.

Oxford: 1895.

CONTENTS

ILLUSTRATIONS

GEORGE JOHN ROMANES

CHAPTER I

BOYHOOD—YOUTH—EARLY MANHOOD

BOYHOOD. 1848–1867

GEORGE JOHN ROMANES was born at Kingston, Canada, on May 20, 1848, the third son of the Rev. George Romanes, D.D., then Professor of Greek in the University of that place.

The Professor had come out to Canada some years previously, and, after a short experience of work in country parishes, had settled down to teach Greek to the *alumni* of the little University.

Dr. Romanes was descended from an old Scottish family settled since 1586 in Berwickshire: he had been educated at the High School and University of Edinburgh, and was an excellent classic and learned theologian, with views of a strictly 'Moderate' type. From him his distinguished son inherited the sweetness of temper and calmness of manner which characterised George John Romanes through life, and which earned for him amongst his friends the playful sobriquet of 'The Philosopher.'

Dr. Romanes married, after his arrival in Canada, Miss Isabella Gair Smith, daughter of the Rev. Robert Smith, for many years parish minister of Cromarty. Mrs. Romanes was connected with several old Highland families, and was a thorough Highlander. Handsome, vivacious, unconventional, and clever, she was in all respects a great contrast to her husband, who, as years went on, seems to have lived mainly the life of a student, and to have left the care of mundane things to his wife. Three sons and two daughters were born. Of these, only two, the eldest son and youngest daughter, now survive.

In 1848, the inheritance of a considerable fortune relieved Dr. Romanes from any necessity to continue the duties of his chair, and the family returned home, wandering about for a few years and finally settling in 18 Cornwall Terrace, Regent's Park. There was a good deal of continental travel during these first years after their return, and as he grew into boyhood George Romanes spent several months at various times in Heidelberg and other German towns, and the family performed a journey from Nice to Florence in a delightful and now bygone fashion, travelling with a vetturino.

Probably the beauty of the scenery, the fascination of travel, and the charm of the beautiful surroundings exercised an unconscious influence over the boy, and did something to rouse the poetic sense which was to be so great an element in his life. Otherwise there seems to have been little or no sense of pleasure in the art treasures or the historic associations of Italy, and at no time of his life did he ever care for pictures in anything like the same degree as he loved poetry or music.

After the family settled in London, George Romanes was sent to a preparatory school near his own home. Two of his schoolfellows became in after life intimate friends. These were Francis Paget, the present Dean of Christ Church, and his brother, Henry Luke Paget, now Vicar of St. Pancras, London.

An attack of measles put a stop once and for all

to his preparatory school career, and the idea of a
public school was never entertained.

He was educated in a desultory and aimless fashion
at home, and was regarded by his family as a shocking dunce.   Parts of two years were spent in Heidelberg, and here he picked up some German, and had a
few lessons on the violin, and saw as he grew up
something of student life in Germany.   Music was
always a perfect passion with George Romanes, and if
a little wholesome discipline had been exercised, the
boy might have become a very good musician.

Heidelberg and the days at Heidelberg represented
to the younger Romanes the 'golden age.'

They lived in an old house outside the town, surrounded by woods, and here the children, George and
his younger sister, roamed about to their hearts' content, making collections and keeping pets, like the
born naturalists they were.   Shockingly idle children
but marvellously happy ones, and in the peculiar 'let
alone' system of their household, they grew up, neither
of them remembering any reproof, far less any punishment, nor any attempt to make them learn lessons
or carry on studies for which they were not inclined.
A long interval of years separated the brothers, now
only two in number,[1] and the younger brother and
sister were looked on and treated as children long
after they had emerged from childhood.

The father and mother seem to have attended
Presbyterian and Anglican churches with entire im-
partiality, but the younger members of the family preferred the English church, and were confirmed in it.
Religion was a potent influence with the boy in quite
early years, and there grew up in him a purpose of
taking Holy Orders, a purpose which met with no encouragement from either of his parents.

If of intellectual achievement he gave as yet no

---

[1] Robert, the second son, died in childhood.

promise, at least there were the signs of a singularly pure and unselfish nature which seemed to grow and develope with the growing years. All through his life he was peculiarly tender, gentle, and unselfish, and his younger sister describes a little scene of how, while a children's party was going on downstairs, George found her upstairs alone and miserable, suffering from some odd childish misery of nerves, unable to go down, and yet hating to be alone; how he at once soothed and petted her, sat by her the whole evening, telling her stories and successfully driving away her unhappiness. The most characteristic bit appears at the end. This sort of unselfish conduct was so usual, that his little sister really forgot to thank him, nor did it occur to her till long after that there was anything unusual in his willingness to sacrifice a whole evening's amusement to what most boys would have regarded as mere fancifulness, only deserving a due amount of severe teasing.

During these years the Romanes family spent their summers at Dunskaith, on the shores of the Cromarty Firth. Here George Romanes had his first lessons in sport at the hands of Dr. Brydon, the well-known survivor of the fatal retreat from Cabul, 1842.[1] He soon became an ardent sportsman and excellent shot, and not until his fatal illness began did he ever fail to keep August 12 and September 1 in the proper way.

When George Romanes was about seventeen, he was sent to a tutor to read in preparation for the University, his mother having suddenly awakened to the fact that he was nearly grown up and not at all ready for college. One of his fellow pupils was Mr.

[1] Dr. Brydon resided on a small but beautiful property overlooking the Cromarty Firth, and, after his death, Dr. Romanes rented the place from its owners, who were distant cousins of Mrs. Romanes, in order that 'George might have some shooting.'

Charles Edmund Lister, brother of the present owner
of Shibden Hall, Halifax. With Mr. Lister he formed
a friendship destined to be only broken by Mr. Lister's
premature death in 1889. This friendship had important results for George Romanes. He had been intended for Oxford, and his name had been entered at
Brasenose College, but Mr. Lister was to go to Cambridge, and he easily persuaded his friend to follow
him.

In October 1867 George John Romanes entered
Gonville and Caius College, Cambridge.

CAMBRIDGE. 1867-1873

Most men feel that their University life is one of
the most marked phases of their career. Even to
those who come up from a public school, with all the
prestige and with all the friendships, the sense of
fellowship, the hundred and one influences, the cus-
toms of a great school 'lying thick' upon them, realise
more and more, as time goes on, how great a part
Oxford or Cambridge plays in their lives; how it is
in their University life they make their intellectual
choice, and receive the bias which, for good or for evil,
will influence their whole life.

And to this raw boy, fresh from a secluded and
somewhat narrow atmosphere, plunged for the first
time into a great society, brought for the first time
under some of the influences of the then 'Zeitgeist,'
into contact with some of the leaders of thought,
entrance into the University was the beginning of an
entirely new life.

He entered Cambridge, half-educated, utterly un-
trained, with no knowledge of men or of books. He
left it, to all intents and purposes, a trained worker
and earnest thinker, with his life work begun—that
work which was an unwearied search after truth, a

work characterised by an ever-increasing reverence for goodness, and, as years went on, by a disregard for applause or for reward. His Cambridge life was happy; he made several friends, chief of whom was Mr. Proby Cautley, the present rector of Quainton near Aylesbury.

He enjoyed boating, and once narrowly escaped drowning in the Cam.[1]

At first George Romanes fell completely under Evangelical influences, at that time practically the most potent religious force in Cambridge. He was a regular communicant, and it is touching to look at the little Bible he used while at Cambridge, worn, and marked, and pencilled, with references to sermons which had evidently caught the boy's attention. He used to attend meetings for Greek Testament study, and enjoyed hearing the distinguished preachers who visited the University.

But of the *intellectual* influences in the religious world of the University he knew nothing. F. D. Maurice was still in Cambridge, but he seems to have repelled rather than to have attracted George Romanes, nor did he ever come under the influence of Westcott, or of Lightfoot, or of Hort.

And, when the intellectual struggles began, he seems in early years to have owed very little to any Christian writer, Bishop Butler alone excepted.

His summers were spent in Ross-shire, and there is no doubt these months were of great use to him. He was perfectly unharassed so far as pecuniary cares or family ambition were concerned, and he had abundant time to think. Years afterwards, Mr. Darwin

---

[1] His younger sister records an old experience of hers. At the time of her brother's accident she was travelling in Spain with her father and sister, and one day was taken suddenly ill, became slightly delirious, and expressed great anxiety on George's account. Afterwards, on comparing notes, it was found that the time of his accident coincided with that of her illness.

said to him : ' Above all, Romanes, cultivate the habit of meditation,' and Mr. Romanes always quoted this as a most valuable bit of advice. His intellectual development was rapid in these Cambridge years, and it is not improbable that his slowly growing mind had not been ill served by being allowed to mature in absolute freedom, although he himself bitterly regretted and, through his whole life, deplored the lack of early training, and of mental discipline.

Through these early Cambridge years he still cherished the idea of Holy Orders, and with his friend, Mr. Cantley, he had many talks about the career they both intended to choose. They spent a part of one long vacation together, and occupied themselves in reading theology—such books as ' Pearson on the Creed,' Hooker's ' Ecclesiastical Polity,' Bishop Butler's ' Analogy,' and in writing sermons. Some of Mr. Romanes' are still extant, and are curious bits of boyish composition—crude, unformed in style, and yet full of thought, and showing a remarkable knowledge of the Bible.

He seems to have been, for the rest, a bright, good-tempered, popular lad, always much chaffed for absent-minded mistakes, for his long legs, for his peculiar name ; and he certainly gave no one the faintest idea of any particular ability, any likelihood of future distinction.[1] Some slight chance, as it seemed, turned his attention to natural science ; one or two friends were reading for the Natural Science Tripos, and George Romanes ceased to read mathematics and began to work at natural science, competing for and winning a scholarship in that subject.

Eighteen months only remained for him to work for his Tripos, and it is not surprising that he only

[1] Mr. Cantley writes : ' I have never seen Romanes, under the greatest provocation, out of temper. Always gentle, always kind, never overbearing . . . never forgetful of friends.'

obtained a Second Class. In the Tripos of 1870, in the same list among the First-Class men, Mr. Francis Darwin's name appears.

Mr. Romanes had gone but a little distance along the road on which he was destined to travel very far. He had up to this time read none of Mr. Darwin's books, and to a question on Natural Selection which occurred in the Tripos papers he could give no answer.

By this time he had abandoned the idea of Holy Orders, perhaps on account of the opposition at home, perhaps because of the first beginnings of the intellectual struggles of doubt and of bewilderment. He began to study medicine, and made a lifelong friendship with Dr. Latham, the well-known Cambridge physician, of whose kindness Mr. Romanes often spoke, and to whom he dedicated his first book, which was the Burney Prize for 1873. But he also began to study physiology under the direction of Dr. Michael Foster, the present Professor of Physiology at Cambridge, to whom she owes her famous medical school, at that time in its very early beginnings.

Science entirely fascinated him ; his first plunge into real scientific work opened to him a new life, gave him the first sense of power and of capacity. Now he read Mr. Darwin's books, and it is impossible to over-rate the extraordinary effect they had on the young man's mind. Something of the feeling which Keats describes in the sonnet 'On Looking into Chapman's Homer' seems to have been his :

> 'Then felt I like some watcher of the skies
>   When a new planet swims into his ken;
> Or like stout Cortez when, with eagle eyes,
>   He stared at the Pacific   and all his men
> Looked at each other with a wild surmise
>   Silent, upon a peak in Darien.'

About the spring of 1872 Mr. Romanes began to show signs of ill-health. He was harassed by faintness and incessant lassitude, but struggled on, going up to Scotland in the summer and beginning to shoot, under the belief that all he wanted was hard exercise. At last he broke down and was declared to be suffering from a bad attack of typhoid fever. He had a very hard struggle for life, and owed a great deal to Dr. Latham, who from Cambridge kept up a constant telegraphic communication with the Ross-shire doctors. It was a long and weary convalescence, beguiled in part by writing an essay on 'Christian Prayer and General Laws,' the subject assigned for the Burney Prize Essay of 1873.

Much of this essay was dictated to one or other of his sisters, and it is a curious fact that his first book and his last should have been on theological subjects. Both were written when he was struggling with great bodily weakness, and in these months of early manhood he showed the same almost pathetic desire to work, the same activity of thought which he displayed more than twenty years later in the last days of his life.

The essay was successful, and its author was more than once claimed as a champion of faith on the strength of it.

It is a very hard bit of reading, and of course has to some extent the drawback of a prize essay, a work written not simply to convince the public, but to impress examiners. It is full of knowledge and of intellectual agility, but is perhaps needlessly difficult in style. His success was absolutely unexpected by his family, and made him very happy, as the following letters show, written in the first glow of success.

To Mrs. Romanes.

18 Cornwall Terrace.

My dearest Mother,—Your letter of surprise and rejoicing has been to me one of the best parts of the result. All the letters of congratulation which are now coming in mention you : ' How delighted your mother will be,' &c. ; and it is a great thing for me to find that you are so. Without appreciative sympathy success soon palls ; but the two combined go to make up the best happiness.

I went to Cambridge yesterday to get the manuscript, and as there happened to be a congregation in the afternoon, I also took my degree. I saw all my friends, who were overflowing with delight. Indeed, I never before realised how great the competition is, for I never had an opportunity of knowing how the successful man is lionised. The Caius dons especially are up in the air about it, as this is the first time in the history of the college that one of its members has got the Burney ; so that, as Ferrers writes to me, ' when the same year produces a Senior Wrangler and a Burney Prizeman, the college may be said to be looking up.' I was invited to breakfast with the Professor of Divinity (who is the principal adjudicator), and I found him very pleasant indeed. Afterwards I went to the Vice-Chancellor, from whom I got the well-remembered ' pages ' (but now with Prize I. written across them) ; and lastly, to the third adjudicator, the master of Christ's. They all said more in praise of the essay than I would care to repeat, but, to tell you the simple truth, I was perfectly astonished. For example, ' In the history of the Burney Prize there have only been two equals and no superiors.'

The Vice-Chancellor told me that there was another essay well deserving of a prize which was written

by a man of whom I dare say you will remember I
said I was most afraid, viz., Mr. ———.   I knew
him very well when we were undergraduates, and
three years ago he obtained the Trinity Scholarship
in Philosophy, open to all competitors, and ended
up eighteen months ago by graduating as Senior of
the Moral Science Tripos.   It is a great satisfaction
to me that the man who was universally admitted to
be the best of the Cambridge metaphysicians should
have written, and that, notwithstanding, the decision
should have been given unanimously in my favour.

To James Romanes, Esq.

18 Cornwall Terrace : April 21.

My dearest James,—I am sure you will be as much
pleased with the result of my labours as I am myself.
I remember so well our speculating upon the probable
chances of success, and how low we set them down.
Had I known for certain that ——— was going to
compete, I think I should have given up altogether.
His essay does seem to have been extraordinarily
good, and yet he cannot get a second prize, because
the foundation requires that every penny of the
interest shall go to the first man.   As this seems
rather hard lines for ———, I have to-day written to
the Divinity Professor offering to share the prize
money, on condition that the University recognise
——— as a prizeman.

The extraordinary thing about the whole affair is,
not so much the award, as the opinion which the
adjudicators entertain of the work.   I do not know how

it is that, stranded on a sandbank and in a half dead-
and-alive state, without thinking I was doing anything unusual, I should have written the prize essay.
But I don't care how it is so long as it is so, as ——
writes, ' You certainly have achieved a great success,
handicapped as you were in so many ways.' This,
of course, relates to the award ; but, as I said before,
what surprised me most is that I should not only be
first, but such a good first. The praise given by each
of the adjudicators separately, in as strong terms as
it is possible in donnish phraseology to convey it, was
very gratifying to me, especially as pronounced in the
studiously dignified manner of the Vice-Chancellor.

I hope soon to see you and tell you more about
the whole thing ; for one of the best parts of it is,
that ' if one member be honoured, all the members
rejoice with it.'

Ever your loving Brother,
GEO. J. ROMANES.

During his convalescence Mr. Romanes finally
abandoned the idea of a profession and resolved to
devote himself to scientific research.

It was about this time that a letter of his in
' Nature ' (see ' Nature,' vol. viii. p. 101) attracted
Mr. Darwin's attention, and caused him to send a
friendly little note to the youthful writer.

Probably Mr. Darwin had little idea of the effect
his letter produced on its recipient, who was then
recovering from his long illness. That Darwin should
actually write to *him* seemed too good to believe. It
was a great encouragement to go on with scientific
work.

Up to 1873 or 1874 Mr. Romanes had been working, when at Cambridge, in Dr. Michael Foster's laboratory, and was a member of that band who formed the nucleus of what was destined to be the famous physiological school of Cambridge. Side by side with Mr. Romanes were working Mr. Gaskell, Mr. Dew Smith, and others now well known for their work and achievements.

In some ways Mr. Romanes suffered from not remaining at Cambridge and becoming a permanent member of the band.

It is impossible not to feel that had he stayed on at the University he would have devoted himself more and more to strictly experimental work and less to what may be called philosophical natural history. Some will regard his removal as a misfortune, and others as a happy accident, but the might-have-beens of life are never very profitable subjects for speculation.

In order to be with his now widowed mother, he returned to London, and made his home with her and his sisters. They spent their summers at Dunskaith, and Mr. Romanes embarked on researches on the nervous system of the Medusæ. He began also to work in the physiological laboratory of University College under Dr. Sharpey and Dr. Burdon Sanderson. Both he regarded as masters and friends, and perhaps, next to Mr. Darwin, Dr. Sanderson was the scientific friend George Romanes most valued and loved, although it is impossible to overrate what he owed to Cambridge, and to those early longings for biological study which were inspired by Dr. Foster

As has been said, a letter in ' Nature ' attracted Mr. Darwin's notice, and somewhere about 1874 he invited Mr. Romanes to call on him.

From that time began an unbroken friendship, marked on one side by absolute worship, reverence, and affection, on the other by an almost fatherly kindness and a wonderful interest in the younger man's work and in his career. That first meeting was a real epoch in Mr. Romanes' life. Mr. Darwin met him, as he often used to tell, with outstretched hands, a bright smile, and a ' How glad I am that you are so young!'

Perhaps no hero-worship was ever more unselfish, more utterly loyal, or more fully rewarded. As time went on, and intimacy increased, and restraint wore off, Mr. Romanes found that the great master was as much to be admired for his personal character as for his wonderful gifts, and to the youth who never, in the darkest days of utter scepticism, parted with the love for goodness, for beauty of character, this was an overwhelming joy.

In a poem written about 1884 Mr. Romanes has expressed something of what he felt for Mr. Darwin, and in this he has poured out his ' hero-worship ' in terms which were to him the expressions of simple truth.

It is interesting to look over the long series of letters from 1874 to 1882 and notice how the formal ' Dear Mr. Romanes ' drops into the familiar ' Dear Romanes,' and the letters become more and more affectionate, intimate, personal.

About this time also Mr. Romanes made many other scientific friends, Professor Schäfer, Professor Cossar Ewart, Mr. Francis Darwin, Dr. Pye Smith, Professor R. Lankester, Professor Clifford, Dr. Lauder Brunton, and many more ; and as his work became known it is pleasant to see with what kindness of welcome the new recruit was welcomed to the scientific army by such men as Professor Huxley, Sir John Lubbock, Sir Joseph Hooker, Mr. Busk, Mr. F. Galton, and Mr. Spottiswoode, then President of the Royal Society.

Just at that time there was a set of rising young

biologists who all seemed destined to do good work, and it is melancholy to look back and to see ' how of that not too numerous band a number have been taken from us in the prime of life, Garrod, Frank Balfour, Moseley, H. Carpenter, Milnes Marshall, Romanes.' [1]

At Dunskaith a little laboratory was fitted up in an adjoining cottage, and here during the summer Mr. Romanes worked constantly for some years, diversifying his labours by shooting. It was in his country home also that he began those series of observations on animals which he worked up into the ' Animal Intelligence ' of the International Scientific Series, perhaps the most popular of his books. The terrier Mathal was his special companion, and he observed various traits of her intelligence which are recorded in ' Mental Evolution in Animals,' pp. 156, 157, 158. It was also at Dunskaith that he began his first attempts at verse making, but for some years these did not come to much.

His scientific work at Dunskaith led to a paper communicated to the Royal Society in 1875, and entitled ' Preliminary Observations on the Locomotor System of Medusæ.'

This paper the Royal Society honoured by making it the Croonian Lecture, an honour awarded to the best biological paper of each year.[2]

Mr. Romanes had worked for two years, or rather two summers, very constantly and very strenuously on the Medusæ. He set himself to try and discover whether or not the rudiments of a nervous system existed in these creatures. Agassiz had maintained it

---

[1] Prof. E. R. Lankester in *Nature*, May 1894.

[2] But he also communicated a paper to the Royal Society entitled, ' The Influence of Injury on the Excitability of Motor Nerves.' Of this paper Professor Burdon Sanderson says that the observations were made with great care, and that the new facts recorded have been fully confirmed by later observers. This work was done at Cambridge.

did, others considered his deductions premature, and Huxley, in his 'Classification of Animals,' summed up the much-debated question by saying that 'no nervous system had yet been discovered in Medusæ.'

Microscopically, it had already been shown that in some forms of Medusæ there are present certain fine fibres running along the margin of the swimming bell, from their appearance said to be nerves, but in no case had it been shown that they functioned as such. Thus it was to solve this question, whether or not a nervous system, known to be present in all animals higher in the zoological scale, makes its first appearance in the Medusæ, that Mr. Romanes entered upon a long series of physiological experiments, first on the group of small 'naked-eyed' Medusæ, and then on the larger 'covered-eyed' form, the latter division containing the common jelly-fish. These names, 'naked-eyed' and 'covered-eyed,' are given to the two groups on account of a difference in their sense organs, which are situated on the margin of the umbrella or swimming bell, and are protected by a hood of gelatinous matter in the 'covered-eyed' forms, so called in contradistinction to the 'naked-eyed' group, where the hood is absent.

Romanes first carefully observed the movements of the Medusæ, which, it will be remembered, are effected by the dilatation and contraction of the entire swimming bell, and he found that if, in the 'naked-eyed' group, the extreme margin of this swimming bell be excised, immediate, total, and permanent paralysis of the whole organ took place. This result was obtained with every species of this group which he examined; he therefore concluded that in the margin of all these forms there is situated a localised system of centres of spontaneity, having for one of its functions the origination of impulses to which the contraction of the swimming bell is, under ordinary circumstances, exclusively due. This deduction was confirmed by the behaviour of the severed thread-like portion of the margin, which continued its rhythmical contractions quite unimpaired by its severance from the main organism, the latter remaining perfectly motionless. In the 'covered-eyed' forms Romanes found that excision of the margin of the umbrella, or rather excision of the sense organs or marginal bodies, produced paralysis; in this case, the paralysis was of a temporary character, as in the great majority of cases contractions were resumed after a variable period. From this series of experiments he was led to believe that in the 'covered-eyed' Medusæ the margin is the *principal*, but not the *exclusive*, seat of spontaneity, there being other locomotor centres scattered throughout the general contractile tissue of the swimming bell.

Having demonstrated the existence of a central nervous system capable of originating impulses, Romanes had yet to prove the identity of this nervous tissue of the Medusæ with that of nervous tissues in general: therefore, he next proceeded to test whether it was also capable of responding to external stimulation by light, heat, electricity, &c.

As regards appreciation of light, he was able to prove conclusively for at least two species of the 'naked-eyed' forms that as long as their marginal bodies remained intact they would always respond to luminous stimulation, and would crowd along a beam of light cast through a darkened bell jar in which they were swimming; if their marginal bodies were removed, they remained indifferent to light. With regard to the 'covered-eyed' forms, he obtained sufficient evidence to induce him to believe they possessed a visual sense localised in their marginal sense organs.

The effects of electrical stimulation agreed in all

respects with those produced on the excitable tissues of other animals. He next experimentally investigated in the jelly-fish the paths along which the nervous impulses must pass in their passage from the locomotor centres, where they originate, to the general contractile tissues of the animal.

The results of these experiments led him to infer the existence of a very fine plexus of nerve fibres, in which the constituent threads cross and re-cross one another without actually coalescing. This conclusion, which he arrived at from purely experimental grounds, was some years afterwards confirmed by minute histological research.

Finally, the effect of various poisons, chloroform, alcohol, &c., was tried, and the striking resemblance of their action on the nervous system of the Medusæ with that which they exert on that of higher animals supports the belief that nerve tissue when it first appears in the scene of life has the same fundamental properties as it has in higher animals.

This piece of work was important, as the facts threw light, as Professor Sanderson has said, on elementary questions of physiology relating to excitability and conduction, and it was a characteristic of Mr. Romanes that in all his work, of whatever kind, he was always searching for principles. The minutest detail never escaped his attention if it appeared at all likely in any way to throw light on some biological or psychological problem. Only a trained scientific worker can appreciate the amount of labour these Royal Society papers represented. In 1875 he gave a Friday evening lecture at the Royal Institution on his work on Medusæ.

He was also at this time working on the subject of 'Pangenesis,'[1] and a series of letters to Mr.

---

[1] The following extract from 'An Examination of Weissmannism,' pp. 2, 3, will possibly explain the theory of Pangenesis, which assumes:

1. That all the component cells of a multicellular organism throw off

Darwin and to Professor Schäfer may interest some
readers.

18 Cornwall Terrace, Regent's Park, N.W.:
January 14, 1875.

Dear Mr. Darwin,—I should very much like to
see the papers to which you allude. *A priori* one
would have thought the bisecting plan the more
hopeful, but if the other has yielded positive results,
in the case of an eye and tubers, I think it would be
worth while to try the effect of transplanting various
kinds of pips into the pulps of kindred varieties of

inconceivably minute germs, or 'gemmules,' which are then dispersed
throughout the whole system.

2. That these gemmules, when so dispersed and supplied with proper
nutriment, multiply by self-division, and, under suitable conditions, are
capable of developing into physiological cells like those from which they
were originally and severally derived.

3. That, while still in this gemmular condition, these cell-seeds have
for one another a mutual affinity, which leads to their being collected
from all parts of the system by the reproductive glands of the organism:
and that, when so collected, they go to constitute the essential material of
the sexual elements—ova and spermatozoa being thus aggregated packets
of gemmules, which have emanated from all the cells of all the tissues of
the organism.

4. That the development of a new organism out of the fusion of two
such packets of gemmules is due to a summation of all the developments
of some of the gemmules which these two packets contain.

5. That a large proportional number of the gemmules in each packet,
however, fail to develop, and are then transmitted in a dormant state to
future generations, in any of which they may be developed subsequently,
thus giving rise to the phenomena of reversion or atavism.

6. That in all cases the development of gemmules into the form of
their parent cells depends on their suitable union with other partially
developed gemmules which precede them in the regular course of
growth.

7. That gemmules are thrown off by all physiological cells, not only
during the adult state of the organism, but during all stages of its development. Or, in other words, that the production of these cell-seeds depends
upon the adult condition of parent cells, not upon that of the multicellular organism as a whole.

c 2

fruit ; for the homological relations in this case would be pretty much the same as in the other, with the exception of the bud being an impregnated one. If positive results ensued, however, this last-mentioned fact would be all the better for ' Pangenesis.'

You have doubtless observed the very remarkable case given in the ' Gardener's Chronicle ' for January 2—I mean the vine in which the *scion* appears to have notably affected the *stock*. Altogether vines seem very promising ; and as their buds admit of being planted in the ground, it would be much more easy to try the bisecting plan in their case than in others, where one half-bud, besides requiring to be fitted to the other half, has also to have its shield fitted into the bark. All one's energies might then be expended in coaxing adhesion, and if once this were obtained, I think there would here be the best chance of obtaining a hybrid ; for then all, or nearly all, the cells of the future branch would be in the state of gemmules. I am very sanguine about the buds growing under these circumstances, for the vigour with which bisected seeds germinate is perfectly astonishing.

Very sincerely and most respectfully yours,

GEO. J. ROMANES.

P.S.—I have been to see Dr. Hooker, and found his kindness and courtesy quite what you led me to expect. Such men are rare.

April 21, 1875.

In returning you ——'s papers, I should like to say that the one on ' Inheritance ' appears to me quite destitute of intelligible meaning. It is a jumble of the same confused ideas upon heredity about which I complained when you were at this house. How in the world can 'force' act without any material on which to act? Yet, unless we assume that it can, the whole discussion is either meaningless, or else assumes the truth of some such theory as 'Pangenesis.' In other words, as it must be 'unthinkable' that force should act independently of matter, the doctrine of its persistence can only be made to bear upon the question of heredity, by supposing that there is a material connection between corporeal and germinal cells—*i.e.* by granting the existence of *force-carriers*, call them gemmules, or physiological units, or what we please.

Lawson Tait says (p. 60)—'The process of growth of the ovum after impregnation can be followed only after the assumption either expressed or *unconsciously accepted* of such a hypothesis as is contained in Mr. Darwin's "Pangenesis;"' and it is interesting, as showing the truth of the remark, to compare, for example, p. 29 of the other pamphlet—for, of course, 'Pangenesis' assumes the truth of the persistence of force as the prime condition of its possibility. If ever I have occasion to prepare a paper about heredity, I think it would be worth while to point out the absurdity of thinking that we explain anything by vague allusions to the most ultimate generalisation of science. We might just as well say that Canadian institutions resemble British ones because force is persistent. This doubtless is the ultimate reason, but our explanation would be scientifically valueless if we neglected to observe that the Canadian colony was founded by British individuals.

The leaf from ' Nature ' arrived last night. I had previously intended to try mangold-wurzel, as I hear it has well-marked varieties. The reference, therefore, will be valuable to me.

Before closing, I should like to take this opportunity of thanking you again for the very pleasant time I spent at Down. The place was one which I had long wished to see, and now that I have seen it, I am sure it will ever remain one of the most agreeable and interesting of memory's pictures.

With kind regards to Mrs. Darwin, I remain, very sincerely and most respectfully yours,

GEO. J. ROMANES.

To Professor E. Schäfer.

Dunskaith. Ross-shire.

My dear Schäfer,—I am glad to hear that your rest has been beneficial, and also about all the other news you give.

I should like to have your opinion about the meaning of the following facts.

In Sarsia gentle irritation of a tentacle or an eye-speck causes the *polypite* to respond, but not the bell (stronger irritation, of course, causes both to respond); this seems to show that there are nervous connections between the eye-specks and the polypite. By introducing cuts between former and latter, these connections may be destroyed—the tolerance of the tissue to such sections being variable in different cases, but never being anything remarkable. So far, then, the matter seems favourable to the nerve-plexus theory.

In another disc-shaped species of naked-eyed Medusæ with a long polypite, which I have called *Tiaropsis indicans*, from its habit of applying this long polypite to any part of the bell which is being injured, the *localising* function of the polypite is destroyed as regards any area of bell-tissue between which and the polypite a circumferential section has been introduced. In other words, the connections between the bell and the polypite, on which localising function of the latter depends, are exclusively radial. But not so the connections between the bell and the polypite, which render it possible for the one to be aware that something is wrong *somewhere* in the other. For if the whole animal be cut into a spiral with the polypite at one end, irritation of the other end of the spiral, or any part of its length, causes the polypite to sway about from side to side trying to find the offending body. And here it is important to observe that wherever a portion of one of the radial tubes occurs in the course of the spiral, irritation of that portion causes a much stronger response on the part of the polypite than does irritation of any of the general bell-tissue, even though this be situated much nearer to the polypite. This seems to show that the nervous plexus, if present, has its constituent fibres aggregated into trunks in the course of the nutriment tubes.

Thus far, then, I should be inclined to adopt the nerve-plexus theory. But lastly, we come to another species with a very large bell and a very small polypite. Irritation of margin or radial tubes causes the animal to go into a violent spasm, but irritation of the general muscular layer only causes an ordinary locomotor contraction. On cutting the whole animal into a spiral, and irritating the extreme end of several marginal strips, the entire muscular part of the spiral goes into spasm. On interposing a great number of interdigitating cuts in the course of the spiral, there is no difference in these results. Now the question is, What is the nature of the tissue that conducts impressions from the ganglionic tissue to the muscular, making the latter go into a spasm? A spasm is as different as possible from an ordinary contraction, and will continue to pass long

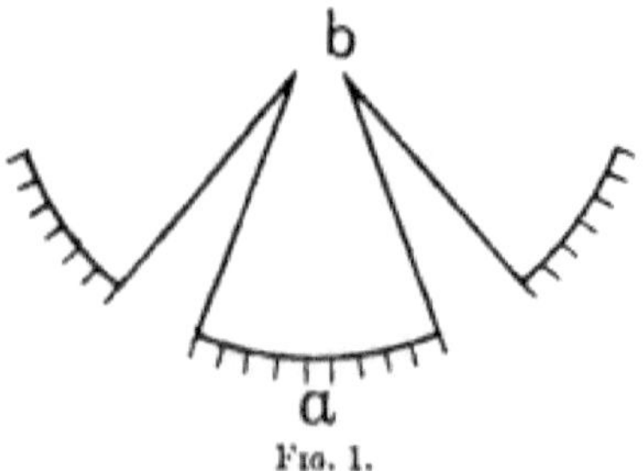

Fig. 1.

after the ordinary contractions have been blocked by severity of section. It is scarcely possible to suppose a nerve-plexus here—the tolerance towards section being so great, although it varies in different cases. Besides, suppose this to be a segment of animal cut as represented. On irritating margin at *a* all the bell goes into a spasm, and it is evident that whatever the nature of the conductile tissue, all the connections must pass through the tract of tissue at *b*. Yet on irritating that tract no spasm is given. I cannot understand this on any view as to the nature of the conductile tissue.

Altogether, then, this part of the inquiry is very perplexing. Other parts are definite enough. All the poisons, for instance, yield very definite results, which are in conformity with their actions elsewhere.

I have had no time to do anything at the histology as yet. Would it be worth while for me to send you various species in a little sea water? They would arrive in a tolerably fresh condition, but would require to be examined at once. I might try sending some in spirit and others in chromic acid. I have made a few preliminary experiments with the galvanometer on Sarsia, placing one electrode on the margin and another on the muscular sheet, but without any decided results. I also tried placing a Sarsia in one beaker and simple sea water in another, connecting by means of the electrodes, but no disturbance was observable.

June 4.

I am working very hard just now, as there are so many irons to keep hot at once. It is too soon yet to see the results of spring grafting on the many plants I have operated on, and I have not had time to do anything with animals since I left London.

The Medusæ have now come on in their legion, and occupy my undivided attention. The results so far have proved as definite as they are interesting and important. The following is a summary of the principal.

All genera of naked-eyed yet examined become immediately and permanently paralysed (except polypite) upon excision of margin, but not so with the covered-eyed.

The organism thus mutilated responds with a single contraction to a nip with the forceps, also to various chemical stimuli. The chain of ganglia do the same, and further resemble the mutilated organism in contracting once to both make and break of direct or of induced shock. They differ, however, in one important particular: the severed margin retains its sensibility to the induced shock much longer than to the direct, while with the necto-calyx the converse is the case—the latter responding vigorously to make and break of direct current after it has ceased to be affected by even interrupted current with secondary coil pushed up to zero (one cell).

A strange and, so far as I am aware, an unparalleled phenomenon is sometimes manifested by *Sarsia* after removal of ganglia. It only happens in about one case out of ten, and *never* except in response to either chemical or electrical stimulation. A bell quite paralysed, and which may have responded normally enough to stimulation for a number of times, suddenly begins an active shivering motion, which may last from a minute to half an hour. This motion is totally different from anything exhibited by the animal when alive, and after ceasing never recommences without fresh stimulation. The shivering appearance, I think, is due to the various systems of muscles contracting without co-ordination, but why it should take place in some cases and not in others, I am quite unable to determine.

Irritability of bell to shocks increases progressively from centre to circumference, and is greatest when electrodes are placed on marginal canal. Also a similar progressive increase is observable on approaching one of the *radial* canals, and is greatest when electrodes are placed on one of these. (I may observe that however neat a person's fingers may be it would be simply impossible to conduct these and other observations of the same nature without a mechanical stage. The electrodes must be needle-points passed through cords, the latter being supported by a copper wire fixed to the stage, and therefore moveable with it; and I defy anybody to get the electrodes into the field, and at the same time upon the marginal canal, unless they all move together.)

Sarsia stands an astonishing amount of section without losing nervous conductibility. For instance, the whole organism may be cut into a three-turned spiral,

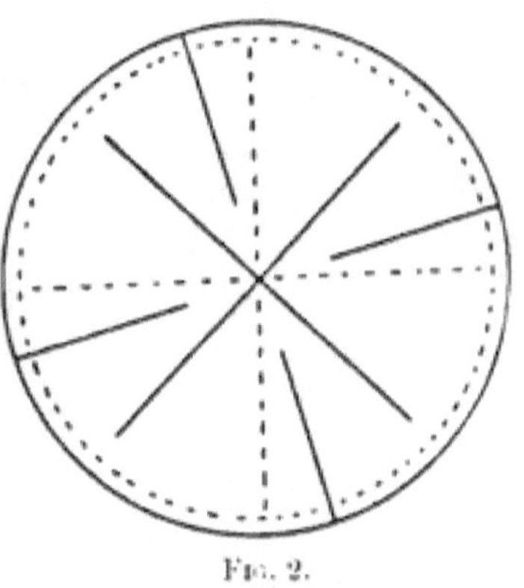

Fig. 2.

and on irritating the end, the whole contracts; yet a moment's thought will show how trying this mode of section is to nervous connections. As the animal may be cut, as in the following diagram, which represents the whole organism in projection—the dotted lines being the canals, and the thick ones the cuts—on now irritating any part of the animal, the whole contracts, but the co-ordination power is lost, both in spontaneous contraction and for those in response to stimuli.

If the entire margin be cut out in a continuous piece save a small portion to unite it with the bell, and if the distal end be now irritated, a main of contraction runs along the entire severed part till it arrives at the small united part, when the whole bell contracts. I should like to try whether under such circumstances the margin would be thrown into a state of electrotomus, but only having one cell I am not able to make out this point satisfactorily.

The severed margin continues its rhythmical contractions for two or three days. I am now trying the effect of different chemical stimuli, and if you can suggest any further line of experimentation, of course I shall be very pleased. Only, if you can think of anything which might be tried and which is not mentioned in this letter, please write soon, as the Sarsia will not last much longer, and they are the best adapted for my purposes.

I remain, very sincerely yours,
GEO. J. ROMANES.

P.S.—I should have said that neither gold nor silver brings out any nervous tissue.

Medusa muscle is not doubly refracting, but then none that I have here seen is striated, and unstriated muscle is not doubly refracting anywhere, is it?

Dunskaith: June 24.

Many thanks for your long and suggestive letter. The poisons also are most acceptable. I have waited before writing to try effect of the latter, but the weather has been so stormy that no jelly-fish could be got.

The most interesting observations I have made since writing before are the following. Unmutilated Sarsia in a dark room seek a beam of light thrown into the bell-jar containing them, and this as keenly as do moths. But when the so-called eye-specks are cut out, the animal no longer cares for light.

I have only come across two species of luminous Medusæ—both, I believe, as yet undescribed—and in these the light is emitted from the margin alone, and, with electrical stimulus, is strictly confined to the intra-polar regions, being strongest at the two poles.

There is no doubt at all about the muscular nature of the fibres we saw. In the larger kinds of Medusæ (the covered-eyed) these fibres are much coarser, and are clearly seen to be arranged in concentric bundles, having four or five fibres in each bundle. Alternating with these bundles, and about the same width as these, are strands of undifferentiated protoplasm. These strands are not spontaneously contractile, although their dimensions are altered by the contraction of the muscular branch on each of their sides. No part of the tissue is doubly refracting in the fresh state. Is there any way of treating it with a view of bringing out this property if latent, so to speak? The peculiarity is not due to the *transparency* of the tissue, for I find that the muscular fibre of the transparent osseous fish *Leptocephalus* is as doubly-refracting as could be wished. There are no signs of striæ, but Agassiz

says that in some of the Mediterranean species striæ
are well marked.   But if both striated and unstriated
fibres are elsewhere doubly-refracting, it does not, I
suppose, much signify whether or not the muscles of
Medusæ are striated—so far, I mean, as the peculiarity in question is concerned.

I wish you would say what you think about this
peculiarity in relation to a subject that I have been
working up.   You no doubt remember that in ——'s
paper that we heard read, he said that the snail's heart
had no nerves or ganglia, but nevertheless behaved
like nervous tissue in responding to electrical stimulation.   He hence concluded that in undifferentiated
tissue of this kind, nerve and muscle were, so to
speak, amalgamated.   Now it was principally with
the view of testing this idea about 'physiological
continuity' that I tried the mode of spiral and other
sections mentioned in my last letter.   The result of
these sections, it seems to me, is to preclude, on the
one hand, the supposition that the muscular tissue of
Medusæ is merely muscular (for no muscle would
respond to local stimulus throughout its substance
when so severely cut), and, on the other hand, the
supposition of a nervous plexus (for this would
require to be so very intricate, and the hypothesis of
scattered cells is without microscopical evidence here
or elsewhere).   I think, therefore, that we are driven
to conclude that the muscular tissue of Medusæ,
though more differentiated into *fibres* than is the
contractile tissue of the snail's heart, is, as much as
the latter, an instance of 'physiological continuity.'
(Whether or not the interfascicular protoplasmic

substance before spoken of is the seat of this physiological continuity is here immaterial.) Dr. Foster
fully agrees with me in this deduction from my experiments, and is very pleased about the latter, thus
affording additional support to his views. But what
I want to ask you is, supposing the interfascicular
substance to have no share in conducting stimulus
(and I have no evidence of its presence in Sarsia),
and hence that the properties of nerve and muscle
are united in the contractile fibres of Medusæ—supposing this, do you think that the peculiarity you
observed in the molecular conformation of this tissue,
considered as muscular, is likely to have anything to
do with this peculiarity in its function?

I know you do not like theory, so I shall return
to fact. There can be no doubt whatever that the
seat of spontaneity is as much localised in the
margin as the sensibility to stimulus is diffused
throughout the bell. There *must*, therefore, be some
structural difference in the tissue here to correspond
to this great functional difference. Agassiz is very
positive in describing a chain of cells running round
the inner part of the marginal canal. Now, although
I sometimes see a thin cord-like appearance here, I
should not dare to say it was nervous. Gold certainly stains it, but it also stains many other parts
of the tissue, and until I can see *cells* here I cannot
be sure about a *visible* nervous cord. The cord I do
see may be the wall of the marginal canal. I intend
to persevere, however, trying your suggestions, also
osmic acid.

I can get no indications of electrical disturbance

during contraction in the way you suggest—at least not with Sarsia; but I intend to try with some of the larger Medusæ.

Some apparatus is coming from Cambridge to enable me to test for electrotonus and Pflüger's law. I shall apply it to the luminous Medusæ also, whose light, I forgot to say, is seen under the microscope in the dark to proceed not only from the margin alone, but from that particular part of the margin where Agassiz describes his chain of nervous cells.

GEO. J. ROMANES.

From C. Darwin to G. J. Romanes.

Down, Beckenham, Kent : July 18, 1875.

I have been much interested by your letter, and am truly delighted at the prospect of success. Such energy as yours is almost sure to command victory. The world will be much more influenced by experiments on animals than on plants. But in any case I think a large number of successful results will be necessary to convince physiologists. It is rash to be sanguine, but it will be splendid if you succeed. My object in writing has been to say that it has only just occurred to me that I have not sent you a copy of my 'Insectivorous Plants;' if you would care to have a copy, and do not possess one, send me a postcard, and one shall be sent. If I do not hear, I shall understand.

Yours very sincerely,
CH. DARWIN.

Dunskaith, Nigg P.O., Ross-shire, N.B.: July 20, 1875.

My dear Mr. Darwin,—Your letter arrived just in time to prevent my sending an order to my bookseller for 'Insectivorous Plants,' for, of course, it is needless to say that I shall highly value a copy from yourself. At first I intended to wait until I should have more time to enjoy the work, but a passage in this week's 'Nature' determined me to get a copy at once. This passage was one about reflex action, and I am very anxious to see what you say about this, because in a paper I have prepared for the 'B.A.' on Medusæ I have had occasion to insist upon the occurrence of reflex action in the case of these, notwithstanding the absence of any distinguishable system of afferent and efferent nerves. But as physiologists have been so long accustomed to associate the phenomena of reflex action with some such distinguishable system, I was afraid that they might think me rather audacious in propounding the doctrine, that there is such a thing as reflex action without well-defined structural channels for it to occur in. But if you have found something of the same sort in *plants*, of course I shall be very glad to have your authority to quote. And I think it follows deductively from the general theory of evolution, that reflex action ought to be present before the lines in which it flows are sufficiently differentiated to become distinguishable as nerves.

I am very glad that you are pleased with my progress so far.

From C. Darwin to G. J. Romanes.

Down, Beckenham, Kent : Sept. 24.

I shall be very glad to propose you for Linnean Soc., as I have just done for my son Francis. There is no doubt about your election. I have written for blank form. Please let me have your title, B.A. or M.A., and title of any book or papers, to which I could add 'various contributions to "Nature."' Also shall I say 'attached to Physiology and Zoology'? When I have signed whole, shall I send a paper to Hooker and others at Kew; or do you wish it sent to some one else for signature? Three signatures are required. The paper will have to be read twice or thrice when Soc. meets in November. But you could get books out of library or out of that of Royal Soc. by my signature or that of any other member.

I am terribly sorry about the onions, as I expected great things from them, the seeds coming, I believe, always true. As tubers of potatoes graft so well, would it not be good to try other tubers as of dahlias and other plants? I have been re-writing a large portion of the chapter on Pangenesis, and it has been awfully hard work. I will, of course, send you a copy when the work is printed. How I do hope that your fowls will survive! F. Galton was here for a few hours yesterday; I see that he is much less sceptical about Pangenesis than he was.

Dunskaith, Nigg, Ross-shire, N.B., Sept. 29, 1875.

My dear Mr. Darwin,—Many thanks for your kind letter. I am an M.A. and a fellow of the Philosophical Society of Cambridge, but otherwise I am nothing, nor have I any publication worth alluding to. I suppose, however, this will not matter if I am proposed by yourself, Dr. Hooker, and Mr. Dyer. I think there would be no harm in saying 'attached to Physiology and Zoology.' I may read a paper before the Linnean next November on some new species of Medusæ, but I think it is better not to allude to any contributions in advance.

Your letter about Pangenesis made me long for success more even than does the biological importance of the problem.[1] Yesterday I dug up all my potatoes. Some of the produce looked suspicious, but more than this I should not dare to say. By this post I send you a box containing some of the best specimens, thinking you may like to see them. The lots marked A and B are sent for comparison with the others, being the kinds I grafted together. If you think it worth while to have the eyes of any of the other lots planted, you might either do so yourself or send them back to me. Lot C is the queerest, and to my perhaps too partial eye looks very like a mixture. In the case of this graft the seed potato was rotten when dug up

[1] The experiments in graft-hybridisation were to prove that formative material (or gemmules) was actually present in the general tissues of plants and was capable of uniting with the gemmules of another plant and thus of reproducing the entire organism. For if the hybrid, afterwards produced, presents equally the characters of the scion and the stock, then formative material must have been present in the tissues of the scion, and it is demonstrated that the somatic tissues of the scion have exercised an effect on the germinal elements of the stock, inasmuch as it has caused their offspring in part to resemble it. Such facts Romanes considered to be fully in harmony with the theory of Pangenesis, and inconsistent with any theory which supposes that *no* part of the parent organism generates *any* of the formative material.

yesterday, and this may account for the small size of the tubers sent.

I did try dahlias and peonies, but in the former the 'finger and toe' shape of the tubers, with the eyes situated in the worst parts for cutting out clearly, prevented me from getting adhesion in any one case. With the peonies I was too late in beginning. It was also too late in the year when I began Pangenesis to try the spring flowers, but I hope to do so extensively this winter. Next year I shall try grafting beets and mangolds by cutting the young white root into a square shape and placing four red roots all round. In this way the white one will have a maximum surface exposed to the influence of the red ones. I shall also try grafting the crown of the red in the root of the white variety, and *vice versâ*. I have already done this very successfully with carrots—making a little hole in the top of the root, and fitting in the crown like a cork in a bottle.

I shall look forward with great interest to the appearance of the new edition of the 'Variation.' I only wish I had begun Pangenesis a year earlier, when perhaps by this time the graft-hybrid question might have been settled. Perhaps, however, it is as well to have this question once more presented in its *à priori* form, for if it can soon afterwards be proved that a graft hybrid is possible, the theoretical import-ance of the fact may be more generally appreciated.

A day or two ago I saw on a farm near this a beautiful specimen of striping on a horse. The animal is a dark dun cob, with a very divided shoulder stripe coming off from the spinal one on either side.

Each shoulder stripe then divides into three prongs, and each prong ends in a sharp point. All the legs are black as far as the knees (*carpi* and *tarsi*), and above the black part for a considerable distance all four legs are deeply marked with numerous stripes. I can get no history of parentage. If you would like a drawing I can send one, but perhaps you have already as many cases as you want in the ' Variation.'

Very sincerely and most respectfully yours,

GEO. J. ROMANES.

To Professor E. Schäfer.

Dunskaith : Sept. 1875.

My dear Schäfer,—I have to apologise for having left your last letter so long unanswered, but there has really been nothing going on here to make it worth while writing.

I gave my careful consideration to all you said about publishing, and at one time nearly decided to wait another year. But eventually I sent in the paper.[1] It seems to me that the histology can very well wait for future treatment—that its absence is not sufficient justification for withholding the results I have already observed. These results, after all, are the most important ; for they prove that some structural modification there *must* be ; whether or not this modification is *visible* is of subordinate interest. Besides, I do not, of course, intend to abandon the microscopical part of the subject altogether. In my view, inquiry into function in this case must certainly always precede inquiry into structure ; for

---

[1] To the Royal Society.

although, when all the work shall have been collected into one monograph, the histology must occupy the first place in order of presentation, very little way could have been made by following this order of investigation.

I also had to reflect, that if I postponed publication, it would be impossible to expect the R.S. to publish the results *in extenso*,—*i.e.*, I should have to bring out the work through some other medium.

And in addition to all this, there came a letter from Foster preaching high morality about it being the duty of all scientific workers to give their results to others as soon as possible.

As I said before, I thank you very much for the consideration and advice you have given, but I know that you would not like me to feel that the expression of your opinion in a matter with which you are not so fully acquainted as myself should lay me under any obligation to be led by it, after mature consideration seemed to show that the best course for me to follow was the one which I took.

Hoping soon to see you, I remain, very sincerely yours,

GEO. J. ROMANES.

P.S.—I forgot to say that I acted upon your suggestion about the Linnean, and have been proposed by Darwin, Hooker, and Huxley.

From C. Darwin to G. J. Romanes.

Down, Beckenham, Kent : July 12, 1875.

I am correcting a second edition of ' Var. under Dom.,' and find that I must do it pretty fully.   There-

fore I give a short abstract of potato graft hybrids,
and I want to know whether I did not send you a
reference about beet. Did you look to this, and can
you tell me anything about it? I hope with all my
heart that you are getting on pretty well with your
experiments; I have been led to think a good deal on
the subject, and am convinced of its high importance,
though it will take years of hammering before physiologists will admit that the sexual organs only collect
the generative elements.

The edition will be published in November, and
then you will see all that I have collected, but I
believe that you saw all the more important cases.
The case of vine in 'Gardeners' Chronicle' which I
sent you I think may only be a bud-variation, not
due to grafting.

I have heard indirectly of your splendid success
with nerves of Medusæ. We have been at Abinger
Hall for a month for rest which I much required, and
I saw there the cut-leaved vine, which seems splendid
for graft hybridisation.

Yours very sincerely,
CH. DARWIN.

To C. Darwin, Esq.

Dunskaith : July 14, 1875.

I was very glad to receive your letter, having been
previously undecided whether to write and let you
know how I am getting on, or to wait until I got a
veritable hybrid.

In one of your letters you advised me to look up

the 'beet' case, but I could nowhere find any references to it. Dr. Hooker told me that although he could not then remember the man's name, he remembered that the experimenter did not save the seed, but dug up his roots for exhibition. I forget whether it was Dr. Masters, Bentham, or Mr. Dyer who told me that the experiment had been performed in Ireland, although they could not remember by whom. But if the experimenter did not save the seed, the mere fact of his sticking two roots together would have no bearing on Pangenesis, and so I did not take any trouble to find out who the experimenter was.

As you have heard about the Medusæ, I fear you will infer that they must have diverted my attention from Pangenesis; but although it is true that they have consumed a great deal of time and energy, I have done my best to keep Pangenesis in the foreground.

The *proximate* success of my grafting is all that I can desire, although, of course, it is as yet too early in the year to know what the *ultimate* success will be. I mean that, although I cannot yet tell whether the tissue of one variety is affecting that of the other, I have obtained intimate adhesion in the great majority of experiments. Potatoes, however, are an exception, for at first I began with a method which I thought very cunning, and which I still think would have been successful but for one little oversight. The method was to punch out the eyes with an electro-plated cork-borer, and replace them in a flat-bottomed hole of a slightly smaller size made with another instrument in the other tuber. The fit, of course,

was always perfect; but what I went wrong in was not
having the cork-borers made of the best steel; for
after I got about one hundred potatoes planted out,
I found that the inserted plugs did not adhere. I
therefore tried some sections with an exceedingly
sharp knife that surgeons use for amputating, and
the surfaces cut with this always adhered under
pressure. The knife, however, must be set up in a
guide, in order to get the surfaces perfectly flat. Next
year I shall get cork-borers made of the same steel
as this knife is made of, and then hope to turn out
graft-hybrids by the score. Even this year, however,
a great many of my potatoes are coming up, so I hope
that some of the eyes may have struck. I think it is
desirable to get some easy way of experimenting
with potatoes (such as the cork-boring plan), and one
independent of delicacy in manipulation, for then
everybody could verify the results for himself, and not,
as now, look with suspicion upon the success of other
people.

With beans I get very good adhesion of the young
shoots, but the parts which grow after the operation
always continue separate. In some cases I am trying
a succession of operations as the plant grows.

With beetroots and mangold-wurzel of all
varieties, adhesion is certain to occur with my method
of getting up great pressure by allowing the plants
to grow for a few days inside the binding. I have
therefore made grafts of all ages, beginning with
roots only an inch or two long and as thin as threads.

The other vegetables also are doing well, but with
flowers I have had no success. The vine-cuttings

were too young to do anything with this year, but I hear from my cousin, who has charge of them, that they are doing well. They certainly have very extraordinary leaves.

This year I never expected to be more than one in which to gain experience, for embryo grafting, as it has never been tried by anybody, cannot be learned about except by experiments. But as I am a young man yet, and hope to do a good deal of 'hammering,' I shall not let Pangenesis alone until I feel quite sure that it does not admit of being any further driven home by experimental work; and even if I never get positive results, I shall always continue to believe in the theory.

I am very sorry to hear that you 'much needed rest,' and do earnestly hope that you will not work too hard over the new edition of one of the most laborious treatises in our language—a treatise to which we always refer for every kind of information that we cannot find anywhere else.

Dunskaith: November 7.

I have to-day sent you a beautifully successful graft. It is of a red and white carrot, each bisected longitudinally, and two of the opposite halves joined. You will see that the union is very intimate, and *that the originally red half has become wholly white*. The graft was made about three months ago, at which time the carrots were very small, but the colours very decided. I think, therefore, that unless red carrots ever turn into white ones—which, I suppose, is absurd—the specimen I send is a graft-hybrid so far as the parts in contact are concerned. It will be of great importance, as you observed in your last letter, in a case like this, to see if the other parts are affected—*i.e.* to get the plant to seed if possible. This, I suppose, can only be done at this late season with so young a plant by putting it in a greenhouse. Perhaps, therefore, you might pot it, as soon as it arrives, and keep it till I go up. If you do not care, to take charge of it altogether, I can then get a home for it somewhere in the South. It will not require a deep pot, for I see that I have cut through the end of one of the roots. It would be as well, before potting, to cut off the end of the other root also, so that the one half may not grow longer than the other, and thus perhaps assert an undue amount of influence during the subsequent history of the hybrid. If the plant when you get it, or after potting, shows signs of drooping, I should suggest clipping off the older leaves to check evaporation : having found this a good plan with beets, &c.

In the same box with the hybrid there is another carrot. This is for comparison, it having been from the same seed and grafted (upon the crown) at the same time as the originally red half of the hybrid.

I am doubtful about the potatoes I sent. On looking over a number of ' red flukes,' I find some here and there are mottled. At any rate, I shall try other varieties next year, and not say anything about this doubtful case.

I forgot to say that the hybrid carrot is the only specimen of longitudinal grafting which I tried with carrots, having been somewhat disheartened with this method by the persistent way in which beets and mangolds refuse to blend when grafted longitudinally. There have thus been no *failures* with carrots grafted in this way.

If it is not too late, I may suggest that the passage in the ' Variation ' about the deformity of the sternum in poultry had better be modified. I have this year tried some experiments upon Brahma chickens, and find that the deformity in question is caused by lazy habits of roosting—the constantly recurring pressure of the roost upon the cartilaginous sternum causing it to yield at the place where the pressure is exerted. The experiments consisted merely in confining some of a brood of young chickens in a place without any roost, and allowing the others to go about with all the March chickens. The former lot have the sternum quite straight, and the latter lot have it deeply notched.

I write to thank you for the copy of the new edition of the ' Variation ' which I received a few days ago. I am very glad to see that you have thought my views about rudimentary organs worth a place, and that you speak so well of them.

The chapter on Pangenesis is admirable. The case is so strong, that it makes me more anxious than ever to get positive results in this year's experiments. I mean there seems less doubt than ever that such results must be obtainable if one hammers long enough. I did not know that there were so many cases of graft-hybridisation in potatoes. Perhaps it will be better this year to give one's *main* energies to other vegetables.

I find that a German, Dr. Eimer, is on the scent of the jelly-fish, but he does not seem to have done much work as yet. It is arranged that I am to have a Friday evening at the Institution soon after Easter, to tell the people about my own work.

From C. Darwin to G. J. Romanes.

6 Queen Anne Street : April 29, 1876.

I must have the pleasure of saying that I have just heard that your lecture was a splendid success in all ways. I further hear that you were as cool as the Arctic regions. It is evident that there is no occasion for you to feel your pulse under the circumstances which we discussed.

Yours very sincerely,

Ch. Darwin.

To C. Darwin, Esq.

I write to thank you for the slip about graft hybrids, and to say that as yet I have obtained no results myself. This place is too far north to admit of the seeds ripening properly after the plants have been thrown back several weeks by the operation. This applies especially to onions, so next year—the neck of Medusæ having now been broken—I intend to wait in London till all the grafting and planting out is finished. I do not think you will regret my not having followed such a course this year when you come to read the paper I am now writing. I never did such a successful four months' work, and if as many years suffice to answer all the burning questions that are raised by it, I think they will require to be years well spent.

And this makes me remember that I have to apologise for the inordinate time I have kept your copy of Professor Häckel's essay on Perigenesis. Since you sent it I have scarcely had any time for reading, and as you said there was no hurry about returning it, I have let it stand over till this paper is off my hands.

Lankester seems to have doubled up Slade in fine style. I suppose the latter has always trusted to his customers not liking to resort to violent methods. His defence in the 'Times' about the locked slates was unusually weak. 'Once a thief always a thief' applies, I suppose, to his case; but it is hard to understand how Wallace could not have seen him inverting the table on his head. In this we have another of those perplexing contradictions with which the whole subject appears to be teeming. I do hope next winter to settle for myself the simple issue between Ghost *versus* Goose.

Very sincerely and most respectfully yours,

Geo. J. Romanes.

To C. Darwin, Esq.

18 Cornwall Terrace.

Professor Häckel's paper on the Medusæ is called ' Beitrag zur Naturgeschichte der Hydromedusen ' (Leipzig, 1865). Professor Huxley has lent me his copy, but says he wants it returned in a week or two. I ought certainly to have the work by me next summer, so I thought that if you happen to have it

and can spare it till next autumn, I need not send
to Germany for it, remembering what you said when
I last saw you. I should also much like to see the
other paper of Häckel's about cutting up the ova of
Medusæ.

I have an idea that you are afraid I am neglecting
Pangenesis for Medusæ. If so, I should like to
assure you that such is not the case. Last year I
gave more time to the former than to the latter
inquiry; and although the results proved very dispro-
portionate, this was only due to the fact that the one
line of work was more difficult than the other. However, I always expected that the first year would
require to be spent in breaking up the ground, and I
am quite satisfied with the experience which this
work has brought me. I confess, however, that but
for personal reasons I should have postponed Pangenesis and worked the Medusæ right through in one
year. There is a glitter about immediate results
which is very alluring.

From C. Darwin to G. J. Romanes.

I will send the books off by railway on Monday or
Tuesday. You may keep that on Medusæ until I ask
for it, which will probably be never. That on Siphono-
phora I should like to have back at some future time.

So far from thinking that you have neglected
Pangenesis, I have been astonished and pleased that
your splendid work on the jelly-fishes did not make
you throw every other subject to the dogs. Even if
your experiments turn out a failure, I believe that

there will be some compensation in the skill you will have acquired.

P.S.—I have been having more correspondence with Galton about Pangenesis, and my confusion is more confounded with respect to the points in which he differs from me.

About this time Mr. Romanes made the acquaintance of Mr. Herbert Spencer and also that of Mr. G. H. Lewes, and of the wonderful woman known to the outer world as George Eliot, and to a small circle of friends as Mrs. Lewes.

Mr. Romanes was one of the favoured few who were allowed to join the charmed circle at the Priory on Sunday afternoons. He enjoyed the few talks he had with George Eliot, and, amongst other reminiscences, he told a characteristic story of Lewes. One afternoon, when there were very few people at the Priory, the conversation drifted on to the Bible, and George Eliot and Mr. Romanes began a discussion on the merits of the two translations of the Psalms best known to English people—the Bible and the Prayer Book version. They 'quoted' at each other for a short time, and then Lewes, who had not his Bible at his finger ends to the extent the other two had, exclaimed impatiently, 'Come, we've had enough of this; we might as well be in a Sunday school.' Both George Eliot and Mr. Romanes, by the way, preferred the Bible version.

In one of the letters to Mr. Darwin, Mr. Romanes alludes to the question of spiritualism, and his own determination to investigate the question so far as in him lay for himself.

He worked a good deal at spiritualism for a year or two, and he never could assure himself that there was absolutely nothing in spiritualism, no unknown phenomena underlying the mass of fraud, and trickery, and vulgarity which have surrounded the so-called manifestations.

He was always willing to investigate such subjects as hypnotism, thought reading, &c., and in 1880 he wrote an article for the September number of the 'Nineteenth Century,' in which he pleads for a candid and unprejudiced investigation of the facts. The article was a review of Heidenhain's 'Der sogenannte thierische Magnetismus.'

The work on Pangenesis and on Medusæ went on through 1876, and some letters to and from Mr Darwin are here inserted.

From C. Darwin, Esq., to G. J. Romanes

Dear Romanes,—As you are interested in Pangenesis, and will some day, I hope, convert an 'airy nothing' into a substantial theory, therefore I send by this post an essay by Häckel, attacking 'Pan.,' and substituting a molecular hypothesis. If I understand his views rightly, he would say that with a bird which strengthened its wings by use, the formative protoplasm of the strengthened parts becomes changed, and its molecular vibrations consequently changed, and that their vibrations are transmitted throughout the whole frame of the bird. How he explains reversion to a remote ancestor I know not. Perhaps I have misunderstood him, though I have skimmed the whole with some care. He lays much stress on inheritance being a form of unconscious memory, but how far this is part of his molecular vibration I do not understand. His views make nothing clearer to me, but this may be my fault. No one, I presume, would doubt about molecular movements of some kind. His essay is clever and striking. If you read it (but you must not on my account), I should much like to hear your judgment, and you can return it at any time.

We have come here for rest for me, which I much needed, and shall remain here for about ten days more, and then home to work, which is my sole pleasure in life. I hope your splendid Medusæ work and your experiments on Pan. are going on well. I heard from my son Frank yesterday that he was feverish with a cold, and could not dine with the Physiologists, which I am very sorry for, as I should have heard what they think about the new Bill.[1] I see that you are one of the secretaries to this young society. I was very much gratified by the wholly unexpected honour of being elected one of the hon. members. This mark of sympathy has pleased me to a very high degree.

Believe me, yours very sincerely,
CH. DARWIN.

Häckel gives reference to a paper on Pan. of which I have never heard.

I fear that you will have difficulty in reading my scrawl.

Do you know who are the other hon. members of your Society?

From G. J. Romanes to C. Darwin.

Dunskaith, Nigg. Rosshire. N.B.: June 1, 1876.

Many thanks for your long and kind letter. Also for the accompanying essay. It seems to me,

[1] For the Suppression of Vivisection.

from your epitome of the latter, that if Pangenesis is 'airy,' Perigenesis must be almost vacuous. However, I anticipate much pleasure in reading the work, for anything by Häckel on such a subject cannot fail to be interesting.

I am sorry to hear that you 'much needed rest,' and also about Frank. I had hoped, too, that you would have mentioned Mrs. Litchfield.

Having been away from London for several weeks, I cannot say anything about the feeling with regard to the Bill. Sanderson and Foster think it 'stringent,' and so I suppose will all the Physiologists. The former wants me to write articles in the 'Fortnightly,' 'to make people take more sensible views on vivisection;' but I cannot see that it would be of any use. The heat of battle is not the time for us to expect fanatics to listen to 'sense.' Do you not think so?

I am sure the Physiological Society will be very pleased that you like being an hon. member, for it was on your account that honorary membership was instituted. At the committee meeting which was called to frame the constitution of the Society, the chairman (Dr. Foster) ejaculated with reference to you —'Let us pile on him all the honour we possibly can,' a sentiment which was heartily enough responded to by all present; but when it came to considering what form the expression of it was to take, it was found that a nascent society could do nothing further than make honorary members. Accordingly you were made an hon. member all by yourself; but later on it was thought, on the one hand, that you might feel lonely, and on the other that in a Physiological

Society the most suitable companion for you was Dr. Sharpey.

Perhaps a 'secretary' ought not to be giving all the details about committee meetings, but if not, I know you will take it in confidence. It seems to me that you never fully realise the height of your pedestal, so that I am glad of any little opportunity of this kind to show you the angle at which the upturned faces are inclined. I am glad, too, to see from the inscription in Häckel's essay, that he is still doing his best to show that in Germany this angle is fast being lost in horizontality.

As the spring was so backward, the plants at Kew were too small to graft before I had to leave for the Medusæ. But this does not much matter, as I had a lot of vegetables planted down here also, which are doing well. Pangenesis I always expected would require a good deal of patience, and one year's work on such a subject only counts for apprenticeship. If, by the time I am a skilled workman, I am not able to send anything to the international exhibitions, I shall not envy any one else who may resolve to enter the same trade.

I am working hard at the jelly-fish just now, and have succeeded in extracting several new confessions. The nerve-plexus theory, in particular, is coming out with greater clearness. The new poisons, too, are giving very interesting results. I suppose you do not happen to know where I could get any snake poison. The ' Phil. Trans.' seem very long in coming out. I have not yet got the proofs of my paper.

June 6, 1877

I am very glad you sent me the extract from Lamarck, for I had just been to the R.S., hunting up several of the older authors to see whether any mention had been made of the theory before Spencer wrote.

While at Down I forgot my speculations about inter-crossing, and, therefore, although I do not think they are much worth. I send you a copy of my notes. The ideas are not clearly put—having been jotted down a few years ago merely to preserve them —but no doubt you will be able to understand them Do not trouble to return the MS.

I had intended to ask you while at Down if you happen to know whether stinging nettles are endemic plants in South America. The reason I should like to know is, that last year it occurred to me that the stinging property probably has reference to some widely distributed class of animals, and being told— rightly or wrongly, I do not know—that ruminants do not object to them, I tried whether my tame rabbits would eat freshly plucked nettles. I found they would not do so even when very hungry, but in the same out-house with the rabbits there were confined a number of guinea-pigs, and these always set upon the nettles with great avidity. Their noses were tremendously stung, however, so that between every few nibbles they had to stop and scratch vigorously. After this process had been gone through several times, the guinea-pig would generally become furious, and thinking apparently that its pain must have had some more obvious cause than the nettles, would fall upon its nearest neighbour at the feast, when a guinea-pig fight would ensue. I have seldom seen a more amusing spectacle than twenty or thirty of these animals closely packed round a bunch of nettles, a third part or so eating with apparent relish, another third scratching their noses, and the remaining third fighting with one another. But what I want to ask you is this. Does it not seem that the marked difference in the behaviour of the rabbits and the guinea-pigs points to inherited experience on the part of the former which is absent in the case of the latter? If nettles are not endemic in South America, this inference would seem almost irresistible. Dr. Hooker tells me nettles grow there now, but he does not know whether they did so before America was visited by Europeans. Possibly there might be some way of ascertaining.

I have now made a number of grafts at Kew. In about a month, I should think, one could see which are coming up as single and which as double sprouts. If, therefore, Frank is going to work in the laboratory in July, he might perhaps look over the bed (which is just outside the door), and reject the double-stalked specimens. I could trust him to do this better than any one at Kew, and if the useless specimens were rejected, there would afterwards be much less trouble in protecting the valuable ones. But do not suggest it unless you think it would be quite agreeable to him. If he is in town within the next fortnight, I wish he would look me up.

I have deferred answering your letter until having had a talk with Mr. Galton about rudimentary organs. He thinks with me that if the normal size of a useful organ is maintained in a species, when natural selection is removed, the average size will tend to become progressively reduced by inter-crossing, and this down to whatever extent economy of growth remains operative in placing a premium on variations below the average at any given stage in the history of reduction.

I think I thoroughly well know your views about natural selection. In writing the manuscript note, so far as I remember, I had in view the possibility which Huxley somewhere advocates, that nature may sometimes make a considerable leap by selecting from single variations. But it was not because of this point that I sent you the note; it was with reference to the possibility of natural selection acting on organic *types* as distinguished from individuals—a possibility which you once told me did not seem at all clear, although Wallace maintained it in conversation.

I do not myself think that Allen [1] made out his points, although I do think that he has made an effort in the right direction. It seems to me that his fundamental principle has probably much truth in it, viz. that æsthetic pleasure in its last analysis is an effect of normal or not excessive stimulation.

Very sincerely and most respectfully yours,

Geo. J Romanes.

[1] Mr. Grant Allen.

From C. Darwin, Esq.

Down, Beckenham, Kent: August 9.

My dear Romanes,—I have read your two articles in 'Nature,' and nothing can be clearer or more interesting, though I had gathered your conclusions clearly from your other papers. It seems to me that unless you can show that your muslin (in your simile) is rather coarse, the transmission may be considered as passing in any direction from cell or unit of structure to cell or unit; and in this case the transmission would be as in Dionæa, but more easily effected in certain lines or directions than in others. It is splendid work, and I hope you are getting on well in all respects. The Mr. Lawless to whom you refer is the Hon. Miss Lawless, as I know, for she sent me a very good manuscript about the fertilisation of plants, which I have recommended her to send to 'Nature.'

As for myself, Frank and I have been working like slaves on the bloom on plants, with very poor success; as usual, almost everything goes differently from what I had anticipated. But I have been absolutely delighted at two things: Cohn, of Breslau, has seen all the phenomena described by Frank in Dipsacus, and thinks it a very remarkable discovery, and is going to work with all reagents on the filaments as Frank did, but no doubt he will know much better how to do it. He will not pronounce whether the filaments are some colloid substance or living protoplasm; I think he rather leans to latter, and he quite sees that Frank does not pronounce dogmatically on the question.

The second point which delighted me, seeing that half of the botanists throughout Europe have published that the digestion of meat by plants is of no use to them—(a mere pathological phenomenon as one man says!)—is that Frank has been feeding under exactly similar conditions a large number of plants of Drosera, and the effect is wonderful. On the fed side the leaves are much larger, differently coloured, and more numerous—flower stalks taller and more numerous, and, I believe, far more seed-capsules, but these not yet counted. It is particularly interesting that the leaves fed on meat contain very many more starch granules (no doubt owing to more protoplasm being first formed), so that sections stained with iodine of fed and unfed leaves are to the naked eye of very different colour.

There, I have boasted to my heart's content; and do you do the same, and tell me what you have been doing.

Yours very sincerely,
CH. DARWIN.

From G. J. Romanes.

Dunskaith, Ross-shire: August 11, 1877.

I was very pleased to get your long and genial letter, which I will answer *seriatim*.

The ' muslin ' in the hypothetical plexus seems to be very coarse in some specimens and finer in others —the young and active individuals enduring severer forms of section than the old. And in exploring by graduated stimuli, areas of different degrees of excitability may be mapped out, and these areas are pretty large, averaging about the size of one's finger-nails. I am rather inclined to think that these areas are determined by the course of well-differentiated nerve-tracts, while the less-differentiated ones are probably more like muslin in their mesh. But the only reason why I resort to the supposition of nerve-tracts at all is because of the sudden blocking of contractile waves by section, and the fact that stimulus (tentacular) waves very often continue to pass after the contractile ones have been thus blocked.

I am sorry I made the ungallant mistake about Miss Lawless, but I had no means of knowing. If I had known I should not have written the letter, because I am almost sure the movements of the Medusa were accidental, and my pointing out this source of error may be discouraging to a lady observer.

I remember thinking you were too diffident about the bloom, but I suppose that is the advantage of experience; it keeps one from forming too high hopes at the first.

The rest of your letter contains glorious news. Cohn, I suppose, is about the best man in Europe to take up the subject, and although I cannot conceive what else he can do than Frank has done already, it is no doubt most desirable that his opinion should be formed by working at the problems himself.

The other item about the effects of feeding Drosera is really most important, and in particular about the starch. I have heard the doubts you allude to expressed in several quarters, but this will set them all at rest. It was just the one thing required to cap the work on insectivorous plants. What capital work Frank is doing!

I have nothing in the way of 'boasting' to set off against it. The year has been a very bad one for jelly-fish, so that sometimes I have not been able to work at them for several days at a time. The most important new observation is perhaps the following.

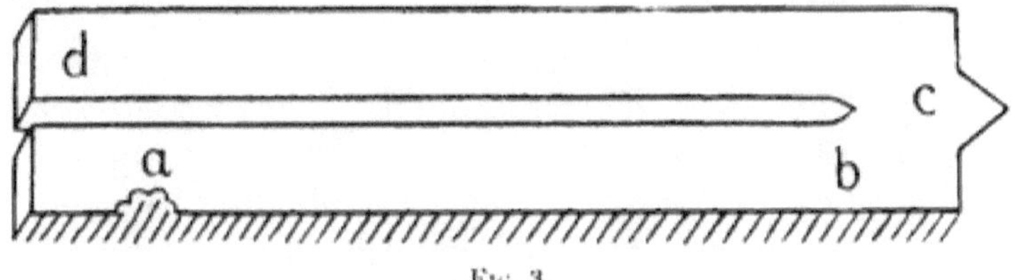

Fig. 3.

Suppose a portion of Aurelia to be cut into the form of a pair of trousers, in such a way that a ganglion, *a*, occupies the bottom of one of the legs. Usually, of course, contractile waves starting from *a* course along to *b*, and thence round to *c* and backwards to *d*. But in one specimen I observed that every now and then the exact converse took place—viz. the contractile wave starting at *d* to course to *c*, *b*, and *a*. On now excising the ganglion at *a* both sets of contractile waves ceased —thus showing that even in the case where they started from *d* it was the ganglion at *a* which started them. This power on the part of Medusoid ganglia to discharge their influence at a distance from their own seat I have also observed in other forms of section, and it affords the best kind of evidence in favour of nerves.

On the days when I could get no jelly-fish I took to star-fish. I want, if possible, to make out the functions of the sand-canal and the aviculæ; but as yet I have only discovered the difficulties to be overcome. I had intended to make a cell to cover the calcareous plate at the end of the sand-canal, and to fill the cell with dye, in order to test Siebold's hypothesis that the whole apparatus is a filter for the ambulacral system; but Providence seems to have specially designed that no substance in creation should be adapted for sticking to the back of a starfish.

The aviculæ are very puzzling things. I am sure Allen is wrong in his hypothesis of their function being to remove parasitical growths; for, on the one hand, parasites are swarming around them unheeded, and on the other, they go snapping away apparently at nothing. It is more easy, however, to say what they are not than what they are.

I went a few days ago to see the vine. It is now five feet high and vigorous, but I believe spring is the proper time for grafting.

With best thanks for your 'boasting' and good wishes, I remain very sincerely and most respectfully yours,

Geo. J. Romanes.

From C. Darwin, Esq.

Down: June 4.

Sir Joseph Fayrer supplied me with cobra poison. It is very precious, but I have no doubt that by explaining your motive he would give you a little, and your best plan of applying would be through Lauder Brunton.

Your letter has made me as proud and conceited as ten peacocks. I am inclined to think that writing against the bigots about vivisection is as hopeless as stemming a torrent with a reed. Frank, who has just come here, and who speaks with indignation on the subject, takes an opposite line, and perhaps he is right; anyhow he had the best of an argument with me on the subject. By the way, I think Frank has made a fine discovery, but I won't say what, for fear it should break down. It seems to me the Physiologists are now in the position of a persecuted religious sect, and they must grin and bear the persecution, however cruel and unjust, as well as they can.

I shall be very glad to hear what you think about Häckel; perhaps I have shamefully misrepresented him. About the other subject (never mentioned to a human being) I shall be glad to hear, but I fear that I am a wretched bigot on the subject.[1]

Yours very sincerely,
CHARLES DARWIN.

The rest has done me much good. We return on the 10th. My daughter is certainly better a good deal, but not up to her former poor standard.

From G. J. Romanes to C. Darwin, Esq.

Dunskaith, Nigg, Ross-shire: June 11.

We had a good laugh over some parts of your letter. I have not, as yet, had time to read any of Häckel's book.

[1] Spiritualism.

I am delighted to hear about the discovery, and hope, if it turns out well, to have my stimulated curiosity satisfied with regard to it. If it is as interesting as the observations about the seeds, people will think Frank a very lucky fellow to hook so many good fish in such a short time.

Not having heard his arguments about the article-writing, I am still strongly of your opinion, and, being besides ill able to afford any time just now, I shall not bother with it. When I think that in this one county (Ross, and still more in Cromarty) there are more rabbits expressly bred every year for trapping than could be vivisected in all the physiological laboratories in Europe during the next thousand years, it seems hopeless to reason with people who, knowing such facts, expend all their energies in straining at a wonderfully small gnat, while swallowing, as an article of daily food, such an enormously large camel.

From C. Darwin, Esq.

Down: August 10.

Dear Romanes,—When I wrote yesterday, I had not received to-day's 'Nature,' and I thought that your lecture was finished. This final part is one of the grandest essays which I ever read.

It was very foolish of me to demur to your lines of conveyance like the threads in muslin, knowing how you have considered the subject, but still I must confess I cannot feel quite easy. Every one, I suppose, thinks on what he has himself seen, and with Drosera, a bit

of meat put on any one gland on the disc causes all
the surrounding tentacles to bend to this point ; and
here there can hardly be differentiated lines of conveyance.   It seems to me that the tentacles probably
bend to that point whence a molecular wave strikes
them, which passes through the cellular tissue with
equal ease in all directions in this particular case.
But what a fine case that of the Aurelia is !

Forgive me for bothering you with another note.

Yours very sincerely,

C. DARWIN.

From G. J. Romanes to C. Darwin, Esq.

Dunskaith, Ross-shire, N.B.: August 13, 1877.

I thought you had given me quite enough praise
in your first letter, but am not on that account the
less pleased at the high compliment you pay me
in the second one.   The ending up was what the
people at the Institution [1] seemed to like best.

Pray do not think that I have yet made up my
mind about the ' muslin.'   On the contrary, the more
I work at the tissues of Aurelia the more puzzled I
become, so that I am thankful for all criticisms.   If
Aurelia stood alone, I should be inclined to take your
view, and attribute blocking of contractile waves in
spiral strips, &c., to some accidental strain previously
suffered by the tissue at the area of blocking.   But
the fact that in Tiaropsis the polypite is so quick and
precise in localising a needle prick, seems to show
that here there must be something more definite

[1] He had just lectured at the Royal Institution.

in the way of conducting tissue than in Drosera, although I confess it is most astonishing how precise the localising function, as described by you, is in the latter. In 'Nature' I did not express my doubts, but it was because I feared there may yet turn out to be a skeleton in the cupboard that I kept all these more or less fishy deductions out of the R.S. papers. Further work may perhaps make the matter more certain one way or another. Possibly the microscope may show something, and so I have asked Schäfer to come down, who, as I know from experience, is what spiritualists call 'a sensitive '—I mean he can see ghosts of things where other people can't. But still, if he can make out anything in the jelly of Aurelia, I shall confess it to be the best case of clairvoyance I ever knew.

I am very glad you have drawn my attention prominently to the localising function in Drosera, as it is very likely I have been too keen in my scent after nerves ; and I believe it is chiefly by comparing lines of work that in such novel phenomena truth is to be got at. And this reminds me of an observation which I think ought to be made on some of the excitable plants. It is a fact not generally known, even to professed physiologists, that if you pass a constant current through an excised muscle two or three times successively in the same direction, the responses to make and break become much more feeble than at first, so that unless you began with a strong current for the first of the series, you have to strengthen it for the third or fourth of the series in order to procure a contraction. But on now reversing the direction of the current, the muscle is tremendously excitable for the first stimulation, less so for the second, and so on.   Now this rapidly exhausting effect of passing the current successively in the same direction, and the wonderful effect of reversing it, point, I believe, to something very fundamental in the constitution of muscular tissue.   The complementary effects in question are quite as decided in the jelly-fish as in frog's muscle; so I think it would be very interesting to try the experiment on the contractile tissues of plants.   But there are so many things to write about that I am afraid of 'bothering you,' and this with much more reason that you can have to be afraid of 'bothering' me.

Aurelia is, as you say, 'a fine case,' and I often wish you could see the experiments.

Very sincerely and most respectfully yours,

GEO. J. ROMANES.

The leading Physiologists felt the importance of co-operation and of alliance, and a society entitled the Physiological Society was formed of which Mr Romanes and Professor Gerald Yeo were the first honorary secretaries.

In 1876 Mr. Romanes made his first appearance at the British Association; he recounts his experiences in the following letter.

To Miss C. E. Romanes.

British Association, Glasgow : Monday, 1876.

My dearest Puffin,—I have received all your letters, and had a good laugh over them ; it is evident

F

that I must get back soon to pilot the way. We shall indeed have a jolly time.

I have just got out from the section room, and my work is over. I had a splendid audience both as to number and quality.

When I had finished, all the great guns had their say, Professor Häckel leading off with a tremendous eulogium on the work, laying special stress on the great difficulty of conducting an inquiry of the kind, and complimenting me highly on the success obtained. Sanderson then made a long speech, and then Stirling and Balfour, &c.

The latter stated it as his opinion that my investigation is the most important that has as yet been conducted in any department of invertebrate physiology. The discussion was then cut short by the president to leave time for the other papers, my own exposition having taken so long. I replied briefly.

Shortly after this, Mr. Romanes delivered a lecture on the Evidences of Organic Evolution, which he reprinted in the ' Fortnightly,' and afterwards worked up into a little book called ' The Scientific Evidences of Organic Evolution.' About this lecture Mr. Darwin wrote :—

Down.

My dear Romanes,—I have just finished your lecture. It is an admirable scientific argument and most powerful. I wish that it could be sown broadcast throughout the land. Your courage is marvellous, and I wonder that you were not stoned on the spot. And in Scotland! Do please tell me how it was received in the Lecture Hall. About man being made like a monkey (p. 37) is quite new to me; and the argument in an earlier place on the law of parsimony admirably put. Yes, p. 21 is new to me. All strikes me as very clear, and considering small space you have chosen your lines of reasoning excellently.

But I am tired, so good night!

C. DARWIN.

The few last pages are awfully powerful in my opinion.

Sunday Morning.—The above was written last night in an enthusiasm of the moment, and now this dark, dismal Sunday morning I fully agree with what I said.

I am very sorry to hear about the failure in the graft experiments, and not from your own fault or ill-luck. Trollope, in one of his novels, gives us a maxim of constant use by a brick-maker, ' It is dogged as does it!' and I have often and often thought this is the motto for every scientific worker. I am sure it is yours if you do not give up Pangenesis with wicked imprecations. By the way, G. Jäger has just brought out in ' Kosmos ' a chemical sort of Pangenesis, bearing chiefly on inheritance.

I cannot conceive why I have not offered my garden for your experiments. I would *attend* to the plants, as far as mere care goes, with pleasure, but Down is an awkward place to reach.

C. D.

(Would it be worth while to try if the ' Fortnightly ' would publish it?)

To this Mr. Romanes replied:

18 Cornwall Terrace : Dec. 2, 1877.

It was most kind of you to write me such a long and glowing letter. In one way it is a good thing that all the world are not so big-hearted as yourself—it would make young men awfully conceited. Yet I value your opinion more than the opinion of anybody, because in other things I have always found your judgment more deep and sound than anybody's. However, I will go to Huxley next Saturday for an antidote, as it is quite true what he said about himself at Cambridge, that he is not given to making panegyrics.

On the whole, as I have said, I was surprised how well it was taken. And still more so in Yorkshire last week—where I was lecturing at Leeds and Halifax on Medusæ, and took occasion to wind up about you and your degree. I was perfectly astonished at the reception you got among such popular audiences. What a change you have lived to see! If ever human being had a right to cry ' *Vici* '—but you know it all better than I do.

About the grafts, I thought it most natural that you should not like the bother of having them done at Down, when there are such a multitude of other gardens belonging to do-nothing people. But as you have mentioned it, I may suggest that in the case of onions there is a difficulty in all the gardens I know—viz., that they are more or less infested with onion worms. If, therefore, you should know any part of your garden where onions have not grown for some years, I might do the grafts here in pots, and bring the promising ones to plant out at Down in May. Seed could then be saved in the following autumn. All the other plants could be grown in the other gardens, and well attended to.

That is a very interesting letter in 'Nature.' What do you think of Dr. Sanderson's paper in the same number, as to its philosophy and expression? I have sent a letter about animal psychology which I think will interest you.

With kind regards to all, I remain, very sincerely and most respectfully (this is a bow which I specially reserve for you, and would make it lower, but for the fear of making myself ridiculous),

GEO. J. ROMANES.

P.S.—I fear Mr. Morley would think my lecture too long, and not original enough for the 'Fortnightly.'[1]

Early in the year 1878, a great sorrow fell on the Romanes family. The elder of the two sisters, Georgina, died in April, and to her brother, her junior by two or three years, her loss was very great. She was a brilliant musician, and had done much to prevent her young brother from becoming too entirely absorbed in science, and in keeping alive in him the passionate love for music which was always one of his characteristics.

They went much together to concerts, and the house was the centre of a good deal of musical society. Among the many musicians who came and went may be mentioned Gounod. He had a great admiration and liking for Miss Romanes, and used to make her

[1] It was subsequently published in the *Fortnightly*.

sing to him. And also there was Dr. Joachim who with characteristic kindness came in the last days of Georgina's life and played, as only he can play, to her.

From G. J. Romanes to C. Darwin, Esq.

18 Cornwall Terrace : April 10, 1878.

Many thanks for your kind expressions of sympathy. When the sad event occurred I had some thoughts of sending you an announcement; but as you had scarcely ever seen my sister, I afterwards felt that you might think it superfluous in me to let you know.

The blow is indeed felt by us to be one of dire severity, the more so because we only had about a fortnight's warning of its advent. My sister did not pass through much suffering, but there was something painfully pathetic about her death, not only because she was so young and had always been so strong, but also because the ties of affection by which she was bound to us, and we to her, were more than ordinarily tender. And when in her delirium she reverted to the time when our positions were reversed, and when by weeks and months of arduous heroism she saved my life by constant nursing—upon my word it was unbearable.[1] The blank which her death has created in our small family is very distressing. She always used to be so proud of my work that I feel that half the pleasure of working will now be gone—but I do not know why I am running on like this. Of course it will give me every pleasure to go to Down before leaving for Scotland. If you have no preference

[1] He refers to the attack of typhoid fever in 1873.

about time, I suppose it would be best to go when you return home in May, as the onions might possibly be then ready for grafting. Unless, therefore, I hear from you to the contrary, I shall write again some time between the middle and end of May.

Then came a second appearance at the British Association. Mr. Romanes was asked to deliver one of the evening lectures at the meeting of 1878, which took place at Dublin.

The subject was animal intelligence, and seems to have excited a good deal of attention. The following letters relate to the lecture and to his book on Animal Intelligence :

To C. Darwin, Esq.

18 Cornwall Terrace, Regent's Park. N.W.: June 18.

Very many thanks for your permission to use your observations, as well as for the additional information which you have supplied. If all the manuscript chapter on instinct is of the same quality as the enclosed portion, it must be very valuable. Time will prevent me from treating very fully of instinct in my lecture, but when I come to write the book for the International Science Series on Comparative Psychology, I shall try to say all that I can on instinct. Your letter, therefore, induces me to say that I hope your notes will be published somewhere before my book comes out (*i.e.* within a year or so), or, if you have no intention of publishing the notes, that you would, as you say, let me read the manuscript, as the references, &c., would be much more important for the purposes of the book than for those of the lecture. But, of course, I should not ask to publish your work in my book, unless you have no intention of publishing it yourself. I do not know why you have kept it so long unpublished, and your having offered me the manuscript for preparing my lecture makes me think that you might not object to lending it me for preparing my book. But please understand that I only think this on the supposition that, from its unsuitable length, isolated character, or other reason, you do not see your way to publishing the chapter yourself.

From C. Darwin, Esq.

Down: June 19.

My dear Romanes,—You are quite welcome to have my longer chapter on instinct. It was abstracted for the Origin. I have never had time to work it up in a state fit for publication, and it is so much more interesting to observe than to write. It is very unlikely that I should ever find time to prepare my several long chapters for publication, as the material collected since the publication of the Origin has been so enormous. But I have sometimes thought that when incapacitated for observing, I would look over my manuscripts, and see whether any deserved publication. You are, therefore, heartily welcome to use it, and should you desire to do so at any time, inform me and it shall be sent.

Yours very sincerely,

CHARLES DARWIN.

From G. J. Romanes to C. Darwin, Esq.

18 Cornwall Terrace : June 21, 1878.

I am of course very glad to hear that you have no objection to letting me have the benefit of consulting your notes.

Most observers are in a frantic hurry to publish their work, but what you say about your own feelings seems to me very characteristic. Like the bees, you ought to have some one to take the honey, when you make it to give to the world—not, however, that I want to play the part of a thieving wasp. I will send you my manuscript about instinct (or the proofs when out), and you can strike out anything that you would rather publish yourself.

I shall not be able to begin my book till after the jelly-fish season is over. This will be in September or October ; but I will let you know when I want to read up about instinct.

With very many thanks, I remain, yours very sincerely and most respectfully,

GEO. J. ROMANES.

The Palace, Dublin : August 17, 1878.

Your letter and enclosure about the geese arrived the day after I left Dunskaith, but have been forwarded here, which accounts for my delay in answering, for I only arrived in Dublin a few days ago.

I am sorry to hear about the onions, and can only quote the beatitude which is particularly applicable to a worker in science, Blessed is he that expecteth nothing, for he shall not be disappointed.

But I am still more sorry to hear of your feeling knocked up. I meet your son here, who tells me about you.

Yesterday was the evening of my big lecture, and I send you a copy as well as a newspaper account. (The latter was in type before delivery, and so no 'applauses,' &c. are put in.) The thing was a most enormous success, far surpassing my utmost expectations. I had a number of jokes which do not appear in the printed lecture, and I never saw an audience laugh so much. The applause also was really extraordinary, especially at some places, and most of all at the mention of your name at the grand *finale*. In fact, it was here tremendous, and a most impressive sight to see such a multitude of people so enthusiastic. I expected an outburst, but the loud and long-continued cheering beat anything that ever I heard before. I do not know whether your son was there, but if so he will tell you.

Hooker, Huxley, Allen, and Sir W. Thomson, Flower, D. Galton, and a lot of other good men were present, and had nothing but praise to give, Captain Galton going so far as to say that it was the most successful lecture he had ever heard. So I am quite conceited.

Ever your devoted worshipper,
GEO. J. ROMANES.

From C. Darwin, Esq.

August 20, 1878.

My dear Romanes,—I am most heartily glad that your lecture (just received and read) has been so

eminently successful. You have indeed passed a
most magnificent eulogium on me, and I wonder
that you were not afraid of hearing 'Oh! oh!' or
some other sign of disapprobation. Many persons
think that what I have done in science has been
much overrated, and I very often think so myself;
but my comfort is that I have never consciously done
anything to gain applause. Enough and too much
about my dear self. The sole fault that I find with
your lecture is that it is too short, and this is a rare
fault. It strikes me as admirably clear and interesting. I meant to have remonstrated that you had
not discussed sufficiently the necessity of signs for
the formation of abstract ideas of any complexity,
and then I came on to the discussion on deaf mutes.
This latter seems to me one of the richest of all the
mines, and is worth working carefully for years and
very deeply. I should like to read whole chapters
on this one head, and others on the minds of the
higher idiots. Nothing can be better, as it seems to
me, than your several lines or sources of evidence,
and the manner in which you have arranged the
whole subject. Your book will assuredly be worth
years of hard labour, and stick to your subject. By
the way, I was pleased at your discussing the selection of varying instincts or mental tendencies, for I
have often been disappointed by no one ever having
noticed this notion.

I have just finished *La Psychologie, son présent
et son avenir*, 1876, by Delbœuf (a mathematician
and physicist of Belgium), in about one hundred
pages; it has interested me a good deal, but why I

hardly know; it is rather like Herbert Spencer; if you do not know it, and would care to see it, send me a post-card.

Thank Heaven we return home on Thursday, and I shall be able to go on with my humdrum work, and that makes me forget my daily discomfort.

Have you ever thought of keeping a young monkey,[1] so as to observe its mind? At a house where we have been staying there were Sir A. and Lady Hobhouse, not long ago returned from India, and she and he kept three young monkeys, and told me some curious particulars. One was that the monkey was very fond of looking through her eye-glass at objects, and moved the glass nearer and further so as to vary the focus. This struck me, as Frank's son, nearly two years old (and we think much of his intellect!), is very fond of looking through my pocket lens, and I have quite in vain endeavoured to teach him not to put the glass close down on the object, but he will always do so. Therefore I conclude that a child just under two years is inferior in intellect to a monkey.

Once again I heartily congratulate you on your well-earned present and I feel assured grand future success.

Yours very truly,
Ch. Darwin.

P.S. 28th.—Can you spare time to come down here any day this week, except Saturday, to dine and

---

[1] Mr. Romanes carried out this suggestion, or rather his sister, Miss C. E. Romanes, did; she kept a monkey for observation for several months, as is recorded at p. 484 of 'Animal Intelligence.'

sleep here? We should be very glad indeed if you can come. If so, I would suggest your leaving Charing Cross by the 4.12 train, and we would send a carriage to Orpington to meet you, and send you back next morning. In this case let us have a line fixing your day. It will be dull for you, for none of my sons except Frank are at home.

The extraordinary modesty, the absolute simplicity, the fatherly kindness, which breathe in this letter, cannot but give some idea of what Mr. Darwin was and why he was so much loved.

Dunskaith, Ross-shire: August 29, 1878.

My dear Mr. Darwin,—I only returned here yesterday and found your letter awaiting me.

Your letter has made me as proud as Punch, and as you have such a good opinion of the line of work, I think I shall adopt your plan of working up the subject well before I publish the book. The greatest difficulty I had in writing the lecture was to make it *short enough*, but it will be splendid to be able to spread oneself over the whole subject in a book. I was at one time in doubt whether it would be better to spend time over this subject or over something more purely physiological, but of late I had begun to incline towards the former, and your opinion has now settled mine.

I have not previously heard of the book by the Belgian physicist, and should much like to read it. I have already such a number of your books that I fear you must sometimes miss them; but I can return any of them at a minute's notice.

I had thought of keeping a monkey and teaching its young ideas how to shoot, and wrote to Frank Buckland for his advice as to the best kind to get, but he has never answered my letter. The case about the lens is a capital one.

I have such a host of letters to answer, which have accumulated during my absence, that I must make this a short one. Your 'congratulations' are of more value to me than any of the others, and I thank you for them much.

Ever your devoted disciple,
GEO. J. ROMANES.

P.S.—Science is not a world where a man need trouble himself about getting more credit than is due.

From C. Darwin.

Down : Sept. 2, 1878.

My dear Romanes,—Many thanks for your letter. I am delighted to hear that you mean to work the comparative psychology well. I thought your letter to the 'Times' very good indeed. Bartlett, at the Zoological Gardens, I feel sure, would advise you infinitely better about hardiness, intellect, price, &c., of monkeys than F. Buckland, but with him it must be *vivâ voce*.

Frank says you ought to keep an idiot, a deaf mute, a monkey, and a baby in your house!

Ever yours sincerely,
CH. DARWIN.

Dunskaith, Ross-shire, N.B.: Sept. 10, 1878.

My dear Mr. Darwin,—Having been away for a week's deer-stalking in the hills, I have only to-day received your letter together with the book. Thank you very much for both, and also for the hints about Espinas and Bartlett. I am glad you thought well of the letter to the 'Times.' In a book I shall be able to make more evident what I mean.

Frank's idea of 'a happy family' is a very good one; but I think my mother would begin to wish that my scientific inquiries had taken some other direction.

The baby too, I fear, would stand a poor chance of showing itself the fittest in the struggle for existence.

I am now going to write my concluding paper on Medusæ, also to try some experiments on luminosity of marine animals

Ever sincerely and most respectfully yours,

GEO. J. ROMANES.

In addition to other scientific and purely philosophical work, Mr. Romanes had, even while writing his Burney Prize, entered on that period of conflict between faith and scepticism which grew more and more strenuous, more painful, as the years went on, which never really ceased until within a few weeks of his death, and which was destined to end in a chastened, a purified, and a victorious faith. His was a religious nature, keenly alive to religious emotion, profoundly influenced by Christian ideals, by Christian modes of thought. As time went on he felt, like all philosophically minded men, the impossibility of a purely materialistic position, and as he

pondered on the final, ultimate mysteries, on[1] ' God,
Immortality, Duty,' he arrived very slowly, very
painfully, but very surely, at the Christian position.

But these years were, to him and to many, years
of peculiar and of extraordinary difficulty. Roughly
speaking, the time between 1860 and 1880 was a time
of great perplexity to those who wished to adhere to
the faith of Christendom.

It is impossible to exaggerate the influence which
Mr. Darwin's great work has had on every department of science, of literature, and also of art.
Thirty-six years have passed away since the publication of the ' Origin of Species,' and we have lived to
see that again *tempora mutantur, nos et mutamur in
illis.* Now we see that a man can fully accept the
doctrine of evolution, and yet can also believe in a
personal God and in the doctrines which logically
follow on such a belief. But it was not so at first.
To many on both sides the new teaching seemed to
threaten destruction to Theism, at least to Theism as
understood either by Newman or by Martineau.

Again, in philosophy Herbert Spencer seemed to
many to have constructed a lasting system of philosophy, a system sufficient to account for all things in
heaven, in earth, and under the earth. And German
criticism seemed to many to be rapidly destroying
the credibility of the early documents of Christianity.

Many a noble soul made shipwreck of its faith,
nor is this disaster wonderful. For popular theology
had made many unwise, many untenable claims, and
the ground had to be cleared before the battle could
be fought out on its real issues. There were some
who, amidst all the strife of tongues, kept their heads,
remembered bygone storms, and did not lose their
courage, their whole-heartedness, but they were few,

----

[1] Cf. F. Myers's ' Essay on George Eliot,' Modern Essays, p. 269.

and were not over much heard or heeded.' For the
most part, those on the Christian side adopted the
line taken by the Bishop of Oxford in his review of
Mr. Darwin's 'Origin of Species' in the 'Quarterly
Review,' and in his famous speech at Oxford during
the British Association of 1860.

Certainly the outlook now is more encouraging
than it was twenty years ago.

It has been well and eloquently said by one than
whom none is more qualified to speak on this subject:
'It is quite certain that this scientific obstacle has
been, in the main, removed. In part, it has been
through the theologians abandoning false claims, and
learning, if somewhat unwillingly, that they have no
" Bible revelation " in matters of science; in part, it
has been through its becoming continually more
apparent, that the limits of scientific " explanation " of
nature are soon reached; that the ultimate causes,
forces, conditions of nature are as unexplained as
ever, or rather postulate as ever for their explanation
a Divine mind. Thus, if one " argument from design "
was destroyed, another was only brought into pro-
minence. No account which science can give, by
discovery or conjecture, of the method of creation,
can ever weaken the argument which lies from the
universality of law, order, and beauty in the universe
to the universality of mind. The mind of man looks
forth into nature, and finds nowhere unintelligible
chance, but everywhere an order, a system, a law, a
beauty, which corresponds, as greater to less, to his
own rational and spiritual intuitions, methods, and
expectations. Universal order, intelligibility, beauty,
mean that something akin to the human spirit,
something of which the human spirit is an offshoot

---

[1] Cf. 'Life and Letters of Dean Church.' p. 154.

[2] 'Buying up the Opportunity,' a sermon by the Rev. C. Gore,
preached before the University of Oxford, and published by the S.P.C.K.

and a reflection, is in the universe before it is in
man.

'Or, again, a prolonged period of controversy and
reflection has resulted in making it fairly apparent
that no scientific doctrine or conjecture about the
dim origins of the spiritual life of man can affect
the argument from its development and persistence.
It has developed and persisted, as one of the most
prominent features of human life, solely on the
postulate of God.   And is it not out of analogy with
all that science teaches us to imagine that so important, continuous, and universal a development of
human faculty could have arisen and persisted unless
it were in correspondence with reality?

'In fact we may almost say that the obstacles to
belief on the side of science were gone when once it
was admitted that God Who has revealed to us His
nature and ours, and made this revelation in part
through an historical process and in the literature of
a nation, has yet, and for obvious reasons, given us
no revelation at all on matters which fall within the
domain of scientific research.

'A similar removal of obstacles must be claimed
in the region of historical criticism. There, again,
it has become apparent that, whatever turns out true
about this or that Old Testament narrative, no
question really vital to the Christian religion can be
said to be at stake in this field; while in the region
of the New Testament the most sifting criticism has
had a result emphatically reassuring. The critical
evidence justifies, or more than justifies, the belief of
the Church which is expressed in her Creeds.'

But this has been a hard-won fight for most—

> 'Friends, companions, and train
> The avalanche swept from our side.' [1]

and no one felt the strain, the positive agony of soul,

[1] 'Rugby Chapel, M. Arnold.'

in greater degree than did George Romanes. Step
by step he abandoned the position he had maintained
in his Burney Prize, with no great pauses, rather, as
it seems, with startling rapidity, and with sad and with
reluctant backward glances he took up a position of
agnosticism, for a time almost of materialism. He
wrote a book, published in 1876, which was entitled
'A Candid Examination of Theism.' It is almost
needless to discuss the work, as it has been dealt
with by its author in his posthumous 'Thoughts on
Religion.' It is an able piece of work, and is
marked throughout by a lofty spirit, a profound sadness, and a belief (which years after he criticised
sharply) in the exclusive light of the scientific method
in the Court of Reason.

His education had been on strictly scientific
lines, and the limitations of thought produced by
such education are clearly seen in that essay;
'limitations' which the philosophical and the
metaphysical tendencies of his mind soon led him
to overstep.

The reaction against the conclusions of the essay
set in far sooner than has been at all suspected.
Perhaps the first published mark of reaction is the
Rede Lecture [1] of 1885.

Yet anyone who reads carefully the conclusion of
the 'Candid Examination' [2] will see the note of 'longing and thirsting for God.'

---

[1] Now republished in a book called 'Mind and Motion.'

[2] And forasmuch as I am far from being able to agree with those who
affirm that the twilight doctrine of the 'new faith' is a desirable
substitute for the waning splendour of 'the old.' I am not ashamed to
confess that with this virtual negation of God the universe to me has lost
its soul of loveliness: and although from henceforth the precept to 'work
while it is day' will doubtless but gain an intensified force from the
terribly intensified meaning of the words that 'the night cometh when no
man can work.' yet when at times I think, as think at times I must, of
the appalling contrast between the hallowed glory of that creed which

There are many who abandon belief for various reasons, and who in various methods stifle regret and call in stoicism to their aid. There are those who really care very little about the 'ultimate problems,' and who find the world of sense quite enough to occupy them. And there are souls who seem to be constantly crying out in their darkness for light, the burden of whose cry seems to be: ' *Fecisti nos ad te, Domine, et inquietum est cor nostrum donec requiescat in te.'* These last have within them the capacity for holiness, the capacity for a real and tremendous power to witness for the truth, to do and to suffer *pro causa Dei.* To this class George Romanes belonged. By nature he was deeply and truly religious, and interested and absorbed as he was in science, it is no exaggeration to say he was just as keenly interested in theology, that is to say, in the deepest and ultimate problems of theology. By the questions which divide Christians he was not greatly attracted, and he never could see any reason for the bitterness which exists between *e.g.* Roman and Anglican.

This is anticipating. In 1878 he had touched the very depths of scepticism, and he would have rejected the idea of a possibility of return, and would have rejected it in terms of unmeasured regret.

A letter from Mr. Darwin is interesting.

once was mine, and the lonely mystery of existence as now I find it, at such times I shall ever feel it impossible to avoid the sharpest pang of which my nature is susceptible. For whether it be due to my intelligence not being sufficiently advanced to meet the requirements of the age, or whether it be due to the memory of those sacred associations which to me at least were the sweetest that life has given, I cannot but feel that for me, and for others who think as I do, there is a dreadful truth in those words of Hamilton, philosophy having become a meditation not merely of death but of annihilation, the precept *know thyself* has become transformed into the terrific oracle to Œdipus—

' Mayest thou ne'er know the truth of what thou art.'

Down: December 5, 1878.

My dear Romanes,—I am much pleased to send my photograph to the future Mrs. Romanes.

I have read your anonymous book—some parts twice over—with very great interest ; it seems admirably, and here and there very eloquently written, but from not understanding metaphysical terms I could not always follow you. For the sake of outsiders, if there is another edition, could you make it clear what is the difference between treating a subject under a ' scientific,' ' logical,' ' symbolical,' and ' formal ' point of views or manner? With regard to your great leading idea, I should like sometimes to hear from you verbally (for to answer would be too long for letters) what you would say if a theologian addressed you as follows :

' I grant you the attraction of gravity, persistence of force (or conservation of energy), and one kind of matter, though the latter is an immense admission ; but I maintain that God must have given such attributes to this force, independently of its persistence, that under certain conditions it develops or changes into light, heat, electricity, galvanism, perhaps even life.

' You cannot prove that force (which physicists define as that which causes motion) would inevitably thus change its character under the above conditions. Again I maintain that matter, though it may in the future be eternal, was created by God with the most marvellous affinities, leading to complex definite compounds and with polarities leading to beautiful crystals, &c. &c. You cannot prove that matter would necessarily possess these attributes. Therefore you have no right to say that you have " demonstrated " that all natural laws necessarily follow from gravity, the persistence of force, and existence of matter. If you say that nebulous matter existed aboriginally and from eternity with all its present complex powers in a potential state, you seem to me to beg the whole question.'

Please observe it is not I, but a theologian who has thus addressed you, but I could not answer him. In your present ' idiotic ' state of mind, you will wish me at the devil for bothering you.'

Yours very sincerely,
CH. DARWIN.

18 Cornwall Terrace, Regent's Park : Sunday, Dec. 1878.

My dear Mr. Darwin,—Many thanks for your portrait—not only from myself but also from the ' future Mrs. Romanes.'

I am glad that you think well of the literary style of the book on Theism. As regards the remarks of the supposed theologian, I have no doubt that he is entitled to them. The only question is whether I have been successful in making out that *all* natural cases must reasonably be supposed to follow from the conservation of energy. If so, as the transmutations of energy from heat to electricity &c. all take place in accordance with law, and as the phenomena of polarity in crystals &c. do the same, it follows that neither these nor any other class of phenomena

' He was engaged to be married.

afford any better evidence of Deity than do any other class of phenomena. Therefore, if all laws follow from the persistence of force, the question of Deity or no Deity would simply become the question as to whether force requires to be created or is self-existent. And if we say it is created, the fact of self-existence still requires to be met in the Creator.

Of course it may be denied that all laws do follow from the persistence of force. And this is what I mean by the distinction between a scientific and a logical proof. For in the last resort all *scientific* proof goes upon the assumption that energy is permanent, so that if from this assumption all natural laws and processes admit of being deduced, it follows that for a scientific cosmology no further assumption is required; all the phenomena of Nature receive their last or ultimate *scientific* explanation in this the most ultimate of scientific hypotheses. But now *logic* may come in and say, ' This hypothesis of the persistence of force is no doubt verified and found constantly true within the range of science (*i.e.* experience), so that thus far it is not only an hypothesis but a fact. But before logic can consent to allow this ultimate fact of science to be made the ultimate basis of all cosmology, I must be shown that it *is* ultimate, not merely in relation to human modes of research, but also in a sense absolute to all else.'

But the more I think about the whole thing the more am I convinced that you put it into a nutshell when you were here, and that there is about as much use in trying to illuminate the subject with the light of intellect as there would be in trying to illuminate the midnight sky with a candle. I intend, therefore, to drop it, and to take the advice of the poet, ' Believe it not, regret it not, but wait it out, O Man.'

G. J. R.

I return the papers, having taken down the references. The books I shall return when read, but honey-mooning may prolong the time.

Mr. Romanes married, on February 11, 1879, Ethel, only daughter of Andrew Duncan, Esq., of Liverpool, whom he had met at the house of her cousin and guardian, Sir James Malcolm, of Balbedie and Grange, Fifeshire.

From 1879 to 1890 Mr. Romanes resided in 18 Cornwall Terrace, which his mother gave up to him, and these eleven years were perhaps the brightest and most fruitful of his life.

It is difficult to give any just idea of the extreme happiness and pleasantness of the home life and of outward circumstances; happiness which only seemed to increase as years went on. He grew more boyish, more playful, and seemed to have an endless capacity for enjoyment, for friendship, for happiness of the best and purest kind.

He greatly enjoyed society, and had full opportunities for seeing the kind he liked best, the cream of the intellectual world of London, and perhaps one may be allowed to say that no one was ever more unspoilt by success, by popularity. He seemed to grow more simple, more single-hearted each year.

The amount of work he did was very considerable. His books, 'Animal Intelligence,' 'Mental Evolution in Animals,' 'Mental Evolution in Man,' 'Jelly-Fish and Star-Fish,' 'Darwin and after Darwin,' 'An Examination of Weismannism,' represent an enormous amount of reading and thought ; and besides all these, there was experimental work in University College and in his own laboratory in Scotland, and a succession of important articles in reviews, chiefly the ' Nineteenth Century,' ' Fortnightly ' and ' Contemporary ' Reviews, and ' Nature.' [1]

It would be quite absurd to deny that Mr. Romanes liked a fair and free fight, and there was a good deal of scientific controversy, but he was absolutely incapable of anything but fairness, and never imported into private life any quarrel in print. He had plenty of stiff fights, chiefly with Mr. Thiselton-Dyer, Professor Lankester, and Mr. Wallace, but the first two were always his friends, and with the latter he had a very slight acquaintance. The following letter, though it belongs to a later date, will show his feelings on the subject of controversy :

Christ Church, Oxford.

Dear Professor Meldola,—I trust that our differences—and *disagreements*—as presented in ' Nature,' will not disturb our relations in private. Anyhow, I send the inclosed circular, which I am addressing to English biologists, and hope you will testify to your desire for ' facts ' by signing the memorial.

Yours truly,

GEO. J. ROMANES.

He lectured a good deal in provincial towns, and gave several Friday evening discourses at the Royal Institution. Lecturing, even in days of failing health, was always a pleasure, never a burden to him. The following letter is a mock triumphant description of a lecture in Glasgow, written purely to amuse his wife, and provoke some mock depreciatory remarks.

[1] He was elected to the Fellowship of the Royal Society in 1879.

Now for my news. Everything was splendid, much the best thing in the way of lecturing that I have done since Dublin,[1] and I was so sorry that you were not there.

First of all we had a dinner given by my host in my honour, the guests being all the chief men in the University, including Professor Caird [2] and the biggest of all big swells, Sir W. Thomson.[3]

The dinner was to me highly interesting, as I talked nearly all the time to Sir William, who is a wonderful psychological study.

We then went to the lecture, where Sir William took the chair, and introduced me to the audience with such a glowing oration that it would have startled you. (It quite astonished me.) The audience being thus led to suppose that I was one of the brightest of all bright lights, received me very warmly; I got enthusiastic, discarded my notes, and swam along in the most magnificent style even for me, which, you know, is the highest praise I can bestow upon myself. I spoke for an hour and a half; at the end the people applauded so, I felt really awfully sorry you were not there. There seems to be a cruel fate preventing you from witnessing my performances

The vote of thanks was proposed by Professor McKendrick. I was met by another storm of applause; I began to feel quite overcome. But I said

[1] The Brit. Assoc. Lecture, 1878.
[2] The present Master of Balliol.   [3] Now Lord Kelvin.

a few words with all becoming humility, and then Sir William summed up.

Here is an affectionate outburst to his mother, written about this time:

> 'When thou art feeble, old, and grey,
> My healthy arm shall be thy stay,
> My mother.'

When. But you are not yet either so feeble, old, or grey as to make me imagine that you have lost a needful prop in the absence of your 'peerless son!' And I am sure you are not more proud of him than he is of you. With your eyes as bright as the bright starlight, and your face as ruddy as the morning, I am glad you are *my* mother.

In 1881 Mr. Romanes was at Garvock, Perthshire. And he was for a short time also at Oban, working with his friend Professor Ewart on *Echinodermata*, and their joint paper was made the 'Croonian Lecture.'[1]

This was the last bit of work on marine zoology, excepting a trifling research on the smelling power of anemones, at which he worked with Mr. Walter Herries Pollock, who had been tempted to make a temporary excursion from the paths of literature into the walks of science. They contributed a joint paper to the Linnean Society on indications of smell in Actinia, and it is greatly to be feared, such is the frivolity of literary men, that Mr. Pollock regarded the whole affair as a very good joke.

The following letters describe the work of the years 1880 and 1881. The summer of 1879 and 1880 had been spent at Westfield.

---

[1] His book entitled 'Jelly-Fish, Star-Fish, and Sea Urchins,' gives a full account of Mr. Romanes' researches on these primitive nervous systems.

From G. J. Romanes to C. Darwin, Esq.

By this post I return you Häckel's essay on Perigenesis. Although I have kept it so long, I have only just read it, as you said there was no need to return it at any particular time.

To me it seems that whatever merit Häckel's views may have in this matter, they certainly have no claim to be regarded as *original*; for I cannot see that his 'Plastidules' differ in anything but in name from Spencer's 'Physiological Units. Why he does not acknowledge this, it is difficult to understand. Anyhow, the theories being the same, the same objections apply; and to me it has always seemed that this theory is unsatisfactory because so general. As you observe in your letter, everyone believes in molecular movements of some kind; but to offer this as a full explanation of heredity seems to me like saying that the cause, say, of an obscure disease like diabetes, is the persistence of force. No doubt this is the ultimate cause, but the pathologist requires some more proximate causes if his science is to be of any value. Similarly, I do not see that biology gains anything by a theory which is really but little better than a restatement of the mystery of heredity in terms of the highest abstraction. Pangenesis at least has the merit of supplying us with some conceivable carriers, so to speak, of the modified protoplasm from the various organs or parts of the parent to the corresponding organs or parts of the offspring, and the multiplication of gemmules seems to me to avoid a difficulty with which Perigenesis (as stated by

Häckel) is beset, viz. that atavism sometimes occurs over too large a gap to be reasonably attributed to what remains of the original 'stem-vibrations' after their characters have been successively modified at each 'bifurcation.' But it would be tedious to enter into details. Perigenesis, in my opinion, is 'more simple' than Pangenesis, only because its terms are so much more general.

P.S.—I forgot to tell you, when we were at lunch, that the seed of the grafted beets is ready for sowing; also that the vine is now four feet high, and so, I should think, might be grafted next spring.

From C. Darwin, Esq., to G. J. Romanes.

Down: February 3, 1880.

I will keep your diagram for a few days,[1] but I find it very difficult now to think over new subjects, so that it is not likely that I shall be able to send any criticisms; but you may rely on it that I will do my best.

I am glad you like Guthrie's book. If you care to read a little book on pure instinct, get Fabre, 'Souvenirs Entomologiques,' 1879. It is really admirable, and very good on the sense of direction in insects. I have sent him some suggestions such as rotating the insects, but I do not know whether he will try them.

Yours very sincerely,

CHARLES DARWIN.

[1] Diagram for a lecture on 'Mental Evolution.'

From *G. J. Romanes to C. Darwin, Esq*

February 6, 1880.

I have to thank you very much for your two letters, and also for the enclosures from ———, which I now return. The latter convey exactly the criticism that I should have expected from ———, for while writing my essay on Theism I had several conversations with him upon the subject of Spencer's writings, and so know exactly what he thinks of them. But in none of these conversations could I get at anything more definite than is conveyed by the returned letters. In no point of any importance did he make it clear to me that Spencer was wrong, and the only result of our conversation was to show me that in ——— opinion it was only my ignorance of mathematics that prevented me from seeing that Mr Spencer is merely a ‘word philosopher.’ Upon which opinion I reflected, and still reflect, that the mathematicians must be a singularly happy race, seeing that they alone of men are competent to think about the facts of the cosmos. And this reflection becomes still more startling when supplemented by another, viz. that although one may not know any mathematics, everybody knows what mathematics are : they are the sciences of number and measurement, and as such, one is at a loss to perceive why they should be so essentially necessary to enable a man to think fairly and well upon other subjects. But it is, as you once said, that when a man is to be killed by the sword mathematical, he must not have the satisfaction of even knowing how he is killed. Of course, in a general way I quite understand and agree with —— that Spencer has done but little service to science. But I believe that he has done great service to thinking, and all the mathematicians in the world would not convince me to the contrary, even though they should all deliver their judgment with the magnificent authority of a ——.

Coming now to the diagram, I am much obliged to you for your suggestions. The 'Descent of Man,' with all its references upon the subject, and also your paper on the 'Baby,' were read, and the results embodied in the diagram, so I am very glad you did not take the needless trouble of consulting these works. By 'Love' I intend to denote the complex emotion (dependent on the representative faculties) which, having been so lately smitten myself, I am perhaps inclined to place in too exalted a position. But you did not observe that I placed 'Parental Affection' and 'Social Feeling' very much lower down.

In my essay I carefully explain the two cases of Drosera and Dionaea as being the best hitherto observed for my purpose in establishing the principle of discrimination among stimuli, as a principle displayed by non-nervous tissues.

April 22, 1880.

As soon as I received your first intimation about Schneider's book I wrote over for it, and received a copy some weeks ago. I then lent it to Sully, who wanted to read it, so do not yet know what it is worth. I, together with my wife—who reads French much more quickly than I can—am now engaged upon all the French books on animal intelligence which you kindly lent me. I am also preparing for my Royal Institution lecture on the 7th of May. I will afterwards publish it in some of the magazines, and, last of all, in an expanded and more detailed form, it will go into my book on Animal Intelligence.

I went to see —— the other day on Spiritualism. He answered privately a letter that I wrote to 'Nature,' signed 'F.R.S.,' which was a feeler for some material to investigate. I had never spoken to —— before, but although I passed a very pleasant afternoon with him, I did not learn anything new about Spiritualism. He seemed to me to have the faculty of deglutition too well developed. Thus, for instance, he seemed rather queer on the subject of astrology! and when I asked whether he thought it worthy of common sense to imagine that, spirits or no spirits, the conjunctions of *planets* could exercise any causative influence on the destinies of children born under them, he answered that having already 'swallowed so much,' he did not know where to stop!!

My wife and baby are both flourishing. I noticed that the latter, at four days old, could always tell which hand I touched, inclining its head towards that hand.

From C. Darwin to G. J. Romanes.

September 14, 1880.

We send you our best thanks for your magnificent present of game. I have not tasted black-game for *nearly half a century*, when I killed some on my father-in-law's land in Staffordshire.

I hope that you are well and strong and do not give up all your time to shooting. Pray tell Mrs. Romanes, if you turn idle, I shall say it is her fault, and being an old man, shall scold her. But you have done too splendid work to turn idle, so I need not fear, and shall never have audaciously to scold Mrs. Romanes. But I am writing great rubbish. You refer to some Zoological station on your coast, and I now remember seeing something about it, and that more money was wanted for apparatus, therefore I send a cheque of 5*l*. 5*s*. just to show my goodwill.

Yours very sincerely,

CH. DARWIN.

We went to the Lakes for three weeks to Coniston, and the scenery gave me more pleasure than I thought my soul, or whatever remains of it, was capable of feeling. We saw Ruskin several times, and he was uncommonly pleasant.

To C. Darwin, Esq.

18 Cornwall Terrace: November 18, 1880.

Very many thanks for your kind assistance and expressions of approval. It was stupid of me to forget your article in ' Nature ' about the geese. I now quite well remember reading it when it came out.

Focke's book is just the very thing I wanted, as it supplies such a complete history of the subject. If I do not hear from you again. I shall keep it for a few days to refer to when the proof which I have sent to press shall be returned with my historical sketch added.

I have now nearly finished my paper on the physiology of the locomotor system in Echinoderms. The most important result in it is the proof, both morphological and physiological, of a nervous plexus, external to everything, which in Echinus serves to co-ordinate spines, feet, and pedicellariæ in a wonderful manner. By the way, I remember once talking with you about the function of the latter, and thinking it mysterious. There is no doubt now that this function is to seize bits of seaweed, and hold them steady till the sucking feet have time to establish their adhesions, so assisting locomotion of animal when crawling about seaweed-covered rocks.

November 5, 1880.

I was sorry to hear on my return from Scotland that I had missed the pleasure of a call from you, and also to hear from Mr. Teesdale to-day that you had returned to Down, owing, he fears, to the alarming condition of Miss Wedgwood. I trust, however, that her state of health may not be so serious as he apprehends.

On my way South I stayed for a couple of days at Newcastle, to give two lectures on Mental Evolution, and hence my absence when you called. I stayed with Mr. Newall, who has the monster telescope, and 'as good luck would have it, Providence was on my side,' in the matter of giving us a clear sky for observing, rather a rare thing at Newcastle.

You will be glad to hear that our season's work at the 'Zoological station' has been very successful. A really interesting research has been conducted by Ewart and myself jointly on the locomotor system of Echinoderms, he taking the morphological and I the physiological part. When next I see you I shall tell you the principal points, but to do so in a letter would be tedious.

I think it is probable that Mivart and I shall have a magazine battle some day on Mental Evolution, as I think it is better to draw him in this way before finally discussing the whole subject in my book.

18 Cornwall Terrace : November 13, 1880.

I am grieved to hear from Mr. Teesdale that his fears were only too well founded. Although I had not myself the privilege of Miss Wedgwood's acquaintance, I know, from what I have been told by those who had, how greatly your household must feel her loss.

I should not, however, have written only to trouble you with expressions of sympathy. I desire to ask you one or two questions with reference to an article on Hybridism which I have written for the 'Encyclopædia Britannica,' and the corrected proof of which I send. It is in chief part an epitome of your own chapters upon the subject, and therefore you need not trouble to read the whole, unless you care to see whether I have been sufficiently clear and accurate. But there are two points on which I should like to have your opinion, both for my own benefit and for that of my readers. First, I think it is desirable to append a list of the more important works bearing upon the subject, and if I make such a list I should not like to trust to my own information, lest I should do unwitting injustice to some observing writers. If, therefore, you could, *without taking any special trouble*, jot down from memory the works you think most deserving of mention, I think it would be of benefit to the reading public.

From C. Darwin, Esq.

Down: November 14, 1880.

My dear Romanes,—Many thanks for your kind sympathy. My wife's sister was, I fully believe, as good and generous a woman as ever walked this earth.

The proof-sheets have not arrived, but probably will to-morrow. I shall like to read them, though I may not be able to do so *very* quickly, as I am bothered with a heap of little jobs which must be done. I will send by to-day's post a large book by Focke, received a week or two ago, on Hybrids, and which I have not had time to look at, but which I see in Table of Contents includes full history of subject and much else besides. It will aid you far better than I can; for I have now been so long attending to other subjects, and with old age, I fear I could make no suggestions worth anything. Formerly I knew the subject well.

Kölreuter, Gärtner, and Herbert are certainly far the most trustworthy authorities. There was also a

German, whose name I mention in 'Origin,' who wrote on Hybrid Willows. Naudin, who is often quoted, I have much less confidence in. By the way, Nägeli (whom many think the greatest botanist in Germany) wrote a few years ago on Hybridism; I cannot remember title, but I will hunt for it if you wish. The title will be sure to be in Focke.

I quite agree with what you say about Passiflora. Herbert observed an analogous case in Crinum.

November 15, 1880.

I have just read your article. As far as my judgment goes it is excellent and could not be improved. You have skimmed the cream off the whole subject. It is also very clear. One or two sentences near the beginning seem rather too strong, as I have marked with pencil, without attending to style. I have made one or two small suggestions. If you can find my account in 'Nature' (last summer I think)[1] about the hybrid Chinese geese being fertile, *inter se*, it would be worth adding, and would require only two or three lines. I do not suppose you wish to add, but in my paper on Lythrum, and I think requoted in 'Var. under Dom.' vol. ii. 2nd edit. bottom of page 167, I have a good sentence about a man finding two vars. of Lythrum, and testing them by fertility, and coming to egregiously wrong conclusion.

I think your idea of reference to best books and short history of subject good. By the way, you have made me quite proud of my chapter on Hybridism, I

---

[1] See *Nature*, vol. xxi. p. 207.

had utterly forgotten how good it appears when dressed
up in your article.   Yours very sincerely,
                                        CHARLES DARWIN.

I have had a hunt and found my little article on
Geese, which please hereafter return.

From G. J. Romanes to C. Darwin, Esq.

18 Cornwall Terrace, Regent's Park, N.W.: December 10, 1880.

I return by this post the book on Hybridism,
with many thanks. It has been of great use to me
in giving an abstract of the history.

I have read your own book with an amount of
pleasure that I cannot express.

One idea occurred to me with reference to luminous stimulation, which, if it has not already occurred
to you, would be well worth trying. The suggestion
suggests itself. How about the period of latent stimulation in these non-nervous and yet irritable tissues?
And especially with reference to luminous stimulation
it would be most interesting to ascertain whether the
tissues are affected by brief *flashes* of light. If you
had an apparatus to give bright electrical sparks in a
dark room, and were to expose one of your plants to
flashes of timed intervals between each other, you
might ascertain, first, whether *any* number of sparks
in *any* length of time would affect the plants at all;
and second, if so, what number in a given time. I
should not wonder (from some of my experiments on
Medusæ, see 'Phil. Trans.' vol. clxvii. pt. ii. pp. 683–4)
if it would turn out that a continuous uninterrupted
series of sparks, however bright, would produce no

effect at all, owing to the plant tissues being too sluggish to admit of being affected by a succession of stimuli each of such brief duration. But if any effect were produced, it would still be interesting to make out whether this interrupted source of flashing light were considerably less effective than a continuous source of the same intensity.

Very sincerely and most respectfully yours,

GEO. J. ROMANES.

Linnean Society, Burlington House, Piccadilly, London, W.:
December 14, 1880.

My dear Mr. Darwin,—I am glad that you think the experiment worth trying. As you say you have not got the requisite apparatus for trying it, I have written to Professor Tyndall to see if he would allow it to be carried through at the Royal Institution.

If I had known you were in town I should have called to tell you about the Echinoderms. My paper on them is now written (70 pages), so I have begun to come here (Burlington House) to read up systematically all the literature I can find on animal intelligence. Hence it is that, having left your letter at home, and not remembering the address upon it, I have to send this answer to Down.

—— is a lunatic beneath all contempt—an object of pity were it not for his vein of malice.

Very sincerely and most respectfully yours,

GEO. J. ROMANES.

18 Cornwall Terrace, Regent's Park, N.W.: December 17, 1880.

My dear Mr. Darwin,—Just a line to let you know that Professor Tyndall has kindly placed at my disposal the apparatus required to conduct the experiment with flashing light.

Frank's papers at the Linnean were, as you will probably have heard from other sources, a most brilliant success, as not only was the attendance enormously large and the interest great, but his exposition was a masterpiece of scientific reasoning, rendered with a choice and fluency of language that were really charming. I knew, of course, that he is a very clever fellow, but I did not know that he could do that sort of thing so well.

I have now got a monkey. Sclater let me choose one from the Zoo, and it is a very intelligent, affectionate little animal. I wanted to keep it in the nursery for purposes of comparison, but the proposal met with so much opposition that I had to give way. I am afraid to suggest the idiot, lest I should be told to occupy the nursery myself.

Very sincerely and most respectfully yours,

GEO. J. ROMANES.

Down, Beckenham, Kent: January 24.

My dear Romanes,—I have been thinking about Pompilius and its allies. Please take the trouble to read on ' Perforation of the Corolla by Bees,' p. 425 of my Cross Fertilisation to end of chapter. Bees show so much intelligence in their acts, that it seems not improbable to me that the progenitors of Pompilius originally stung caterpillars and spiders, &c., in any part of their bodies, and then observed by their intelligence that if they stung them in one particular place, as between certain segments on the lower side,

their prey was at once paralysed. It does not seem
to me at all incredible that this action should thus
become instinctive, *i.e.* memory transmitted from one
generation to another. It does not seem necessary
to suppose that when Pompilius stung its prey in the
ganglion that it intended or knew that the prey would
long keep alive. The development of the larvæ may
have been subsequently modified in relation to their
half-dead instead of wholly dead prey, supposing
that the prey was at first quite killed, which would
have required much stinging. Turn this notion
over in your mind, but do not trouble yourself by
answering.

Yours very sincerely,

CH. DARWIN.

N.B. Once on a time a fool said to himself
that at an ancient period small soft crabs or other
creatures stuck to certain fishes; these struggled
violently, and in doing so, discharged electricity,
which annoyed the parasites, so that they often
wriggled away. The fish was very glad, and some
of its children gradually profited in a higher degree
and in various ways by discharging more electricity
and by not struggling. The fool who thought thus
persuaded another fool to try an eel in Scotland, and
lo and behold electricity was discharged when it
struggled violently. He then placed in contact with
the fish, or near it, a small medusa or other animal
which he cleverly knew was sensitive to electricity,
and when the eel struggled violently, the little animals
in contact showed by their movements that they felt

a slight shock. Ever afterwards men said that the
two fools were not such big fools as they seemed
to be.

STELTES.

From G. J. Romanes to C. Darwin.

18 Cornwall Terrace, Regent's Park, N.W. Sunday, March 1881.

I have got a lot of cats waiting for me at different
houses round Wimbledon Common, and some day
next week shall surprise our coachman by making a
round of calls upon the cats, drive them several miles
into the country, and then let them out of their respective bags. If any return, I shall try them again
in other directions before finally trying the rotation
experiment.

I am also getting the experiment on flashing light
agoing. The first apparatus did not answer, so now
I have invested in a large eight-day clock, the pen-
dulum of which I intend to make do the flashing.

18 Cornwall Terrace, Regent's Park, N.W. : March 24, 1881.

I write to ask you what you think of the following
idea as to a possible method of attacking Pangenesis.
Why not, I mean, inarch, at an early period of their
growth, the seed-vessels or ovaries of plants belonging to different varieties? If adhesion takes place,
the ovary might then be severed from its parent
plant, and left to develop upon the foreign one.

If you think this a possible experiment, now
would be the time of year to try it. Therefore I write
to ask whether you do think it possible, and if so, what
plants you may think it would be best to try it with.

All the cats [1] I have hitherto let out of their respective bags have shown themselves exceedingly stupid, not one having found her way back.

Very sincerely and most respectfully yours,

GEO. J. ROMANES.

From C. Darwin, Esq., to G. J. Romanes.

Down, Beckenham, Kent: March 26, 1881.

You are very plucky about Pangenesis, and I much wish that you could have any success. I do not understand your scheme. Do you intend to operate on an ovarium with a single ovule, and to bisect it after being fertilised? I should fear that this was quite hopeless. If you intend to operate on ovaria with many seeds, whether before or after fertilisation, I do not see how you could possibly distinguish any effect from the union of the two ovaria. Any operation before fertilisation would, I presume, quite prevent the act; for very few flowers can be fertilised if the stem is cut and placed in water. Gärtner, however, says, that some Liliaceæ can be fertilised under these circumstances.

If Hooker is correct, he found that cutting off or making a hole into the summit of the ovarium and then inserting pollen caused the fertilisation of the ovules. This has always stretched my belief to the cracking point. I think he has published a notice on this experiment, but forget where, and I think it

---

[1] Mr. Romanes used to describe with much amusement the ludicrous nature of the experiment as seen by passers-by. He drove in a cab well into the country, released the cats, and mounted the roof of the cab in order to get a good view of the cats speeding away in different directions.

was on ' Papaver.' Dyer could probably tell you about it. Perhaps your plan is to remove one half of the ovarium of a one-seeded plant and join it on to the ovary of another of a distinct var., with its ovule removed; but this would be a frightfully difficult operation.

I am very sorry to hear about your ill success with cats, and I wish you could get some detailed account of the Belgium trials.

Yours very sincerely,

C. DARWIN.

April 16, 1881.

My manuscript on Worms has been sent to printers, so I am going to amuse myself by scribbling to you on a few points; but you must not waste your time in answering at any length this scribble. Firstly, your letter on intelligence was very useful to me, and I tore up and rewrote what I sent you. I have not attempted to define intelligence, but have quoted your remarks on experience, and have shown how far they apply to worms. It seems to me, that they must be said to work with some intelligence, anyhow, they are not guided by a blind instinct.

Secondly, I was greatly interested by the abstract in ' Nature ' of your work on Echinoderms; the complexity, with simplicity, and with such curious co-ordination of the nervous system, is marvellous; and you showed me before what splendid gymnastic feats they can perform.

Thirdly, Dr. Roux has sent me a book just published by him, ' Der Kampf der Theile,' &c.,

1881 (240 pages in length). He is manifestly a well-read physiologist and pathologist, and from his position a good anatomist. It is full of reasoning, and this in German is very difficult to me, so that I have only skimmed through each page, here and there reading with a little more care. As far as I can *imperfectly* judge, it is the most important book on evolution which has appeared for some time. I believe that G. H. Lewes hinted at the same fundamental idea, viz. that there is a struggle going on *within* every organism between the organic molecules, the cells, and the organs. I *think* that his basis is that every cell which best performs its function is as a consequence at the same time best nourished and best propagates its kind. The book does not touch on mental phenomena, but there is much discussion on rudimentary or atrophied parts, to which subject you formerly attended. Now if you would like to read this book, I will send it after Frank has glanced at it, for I do not think he will have time to read it with care. If you read it and are struck with it (but I may be *wholly* mistaken about its value), you would do a public service by analysing and criticising it in 'Nature.' Dr. Roux makes, I think, a gigantic oversight in never considering plants; these would simplify the problem for him.

Fourthly, I do not know whether you will discuss in your book on the 'Mind of Animals' any of the more complex and wonderful instincts. It is unsatisfactory work, as there can be no fossilised instincts, and the sole guide is their state in other members of the same order and mere probability. But if you do discuss any (and it will perhaps be expected of you) I should think that you could not select a better case than that of the sand-wasps, which paralyse their prey, as formerly described by Fabre in his wonderful paper in 'Annales des Sciences,' and since amplified in his admirable 'Souvenirs.' Whilst reading this latter book, I speculated a little on the subject. Astonishing nonsense is often spoken of the sand-wasp's knowledge of anatomy. Now will anyone say that the Gauchos on the plains of La Plata have such knowledge, yet I have often seen them prick a struggling and lassoed cow on the ground with un-erring skill, which no mere anatomist could imitate. The pointed knife was infallibly driven in between the vertebræ by a single slight thrust. I presume that the art was first discovered by chance, and that each young Gaucho sees exactly how the others do it, and then with a very little practice learning the art. Now I suppose that the sand-wasps originally merely killed their prey by stinging them in many places (see p. 129 of Fabre, 'Souvenirs,' and page 241), on the lower and softer side of the body, and that to sting a certain segment was found by far the most successful method, and was inherited, like the tendency of a bull-dog to pin the nose of a bull, or of a ferret to bite the cerebellum. It would not be a very great step in advance to prick the ganglion of its prey only slightly, and thus to give its larvæ fresh meat instead of old dry meat. Though Fabre insists so strongly on the unvarying character of instinct, yet it shows that there is some variability, as on pp. 176, 177.

I fear that I shall have utterly wearied you with my scribbling and bad handwriting.

　　　　My dear Romanes,

　　　　　　Yours very sincerely,

　　　　　　　　Ch. Darwin.

From G. J. Romanes to C. Darwin, Esq.

18 Cornwall Terrace, Regent's Park. N.W.: April 17, 1881.

Your long letter has been most refreshing to me in every way.

I am looking forward with keen interest to the appearance of your book on Worms, and am unexpectedly glad to hear that my letter was of any use.

I should very much like to see the book you mention, and from what you say about sending it I shall not order it. But there is no need to send it soon, as I have already an accumulation of books to review for 'Nature.'

I am very glad that you think well of the Echinoderm work. Several other experiments have occurred to me to try, and I hope to be able to do so next autumn, as also the interesting experiment suggested by Frank of rotating by clockwork (as you did the plants) an Echinus inverted upon its aboral pole, to see whether it would right itself when the influence of gravity is removed.

No doubt I must in my second book deal with instincts of all kinds, complex or otherwise. Your 'speculations' on the sand-wasp seem to me very pithy—excuse the pun suggested by the analogy of the cattle—and I think there can be little doubt that

such is the direction in which the explanation is to
be sought. I also think that the difficulty is mitigated
by the consideration that both the ganglion of the
spider and the sting of the wasp are organs situated
on the median line of their respective possessors, and
therefore that the origin of the instinct may have been
determined or assisted by the mere anatomical form
of the animals—the wasp not stinging till securely
mounted on the spider's back, and when so mounted
the sting might naturally strike the ganglion. But
I have not yet read Fabre's own account, so this
view may not hold. Anyhow, and whatever de-
termining conditions as to origin may have been, it
seems to me there can be little doubt that natural
selection would have developed it in the way you
suggest.

I have now grown a number of seeds exposed to
the flashing light, but am not yet quite sure as to the
result. About one seedling out of ten bends towards
the flashing source very decidedly, while all the rest,
although exposed to just the same conditions, grow
perfectly straight. But I shall, no doubt, find out
the reason of this by further trials. It is strange
that the same thing happens when I expose other
seedlings to constant light of exceedingly dim intensity. It looks as if some individuals were more
sensitive to light than others. I do not know
whether you found any evidence of this.

I have just found that this year again I have
been too late in asking them to send me cuttings of
the vine for grafting. I did not know that the sap
in vines began to run so early.

I remain ever yours, very sincerely and most respectfully,

GEO. J. ROMANES.

From C. Darwin, Esq., to G. J. Romanes.

Down: April 18, 1881.

I am extremely glad of your success with the flashing light. If plants are acted on by light, like some of the lower animals, there is an additional point of interest, as it seems to me, in your results. Most botanists believe that light causes a plant to bend to it in as direct a manner as light affects nitrate of silver.

I believe that it merely tells the plant to which side to bend, and I see indications of this belief prevailing even with Sachs. Now it might be expected that light would act on a plant in something the same manner as on the lower animals. As you are at work on this subject, I will call your attention to another point. Wiesner, of Vienna (who has lately published a good book on Heliotropism) finds that an intermittent light during 20 m. produces same effect as a continuous light of same brilliancy during 60 m. So that Van Tieghem, in the first part of his book, which has just appeared, remarks, the light during 40 m. out of the 60 m. produced no effect. I observed an analogous case described in my book. Wiesner and Tieghem seem to think that this is explained by calling the whole process 'induction,' borrowing a term used by some physico-chemists (of whom I believe Roscoe is one), and implying an agency which does not produce any effect for some time, and continues its effect for some time after the cause has ceased. I believe (?) that photographic paper is an instance. I must ask Leonard whether an interrupted light acts on it in the same manner as on a plant. At present I must still believe in my explanation that it is the contrast between light and darkness which excites a plant.

I have forgotten my main object in writing, viz. to say that I believe (and have so stated) that seedlings vary much in their sensitiveness to light; but I did not prove this, for there are many difficulties, whether time of incipient curvature or amount of curvature is taken as the criterion. Moreover, they vary according to age and perhaps from vigour of growth; and there seems inherent variability, as Strasburger (whom I quote) found with spores. If the curious anomaly observed by you is due to varying sensitiveness, ought not *all* the seedlings to bend if the flashes were at longer intervals of time? According to my notion of contrast between light and darkness being the stimulus, I should expect that if flashes were made sufficiently slow it would be a powerful stimulus, and that you would *suddenly* arrive at a period when the result would *suddenly* become great. On the other hand, as far as my experience goes, what one expects rarely happens.

I heartily wish you success, and remain, yours ever very sincerely.

CH. DARWIN.

Do you read the 'Times'? As I had a fair opportunity, I sent a letter to the 'Times' on Vivisection, which is printed to-day. I thought it fair to bear my share of the abuse poured in so atrocious a manner on all physiologists.

From G. J. Romanes to C. Darwin, Esq.

18 Cornwall Terrace : April 22.

I have left your last letter so long unanswered in order that I might be able to let you know the result of the next experiment I was trying on the seeds with flashing light. I think in the end the conclusion will be that short flashes, such as I am now using, influence the seedlings, but only to a comparatively small degree, so that it is only the more sensitive seedlings that perceive them.

Your letter in the 'Times' was in every way admirable, and coming from you will produce more effect than it could from anybody else. The answer to-day to —— is also first-rate—just enough without being too much. It would have been a great mistake to have descended into a controversy. I thought —— had more wit than to adopt such a tack and tone, and am sure that all physiologists will be for ever grateful to you for such a trenchant expression of opinion.

I have a little piece of gossip to tell. Yesterday the Council of the Linnean nominated me Zoological Secretary, and some of the members having pressed me to accept, I have accepted. I also hear that your son is to be on the same Council, and that Sir John Lubbock is to be the new President.

I have at length decided on the arrangement of my material for the books on Animal Intelligence and Mental Evolution. I shall reserve all the heavier parts of theoretical discussion for the second book—making the first the chief repository of facts, with only a slender network of theory to bind them into mutual relation, and save the book as much as possible from the danger that you suggested of being too much matter-of-fact. It will be an advantage to have the facts in a form to admit of brief reference when discussing the heavier philosophy in the second book, which will be the more important, though the less popular, of the two.

Just then some correspondence had been going on in the 'Times' on the subject of Vivisection, and Mr. Darwin wrote to Mr Romanes as follows :—

Down, Beckenham, Kent : April 25, 1881.

My dear Romanes,—I was very glad to read your last notes with much news interesting to me. But I write now to say how I, and indeed all of us in the house, have admired your letter in the 'Times.' [1] It was so simple and direct. I was particularly glad about Burdon Sanderson, of whom I have been for several years a great admirer. I was, also, especially glad to read the last sentences. I have been bothered with several letters, but none abusive. Under a selfish point of view I am very glad of the publication of your letter, as I was at first inclined to think that I had done mischief by stirring up the mud, now I feel sure that I have done good.

The following letters relate to the portrait of

[1] A letter written at the end of April 1881.

Mr. Darwin which was painted by the Hon. John Collier for the Linnean Society.

18 Cornwall Terrace, Regent's Park, N.W.: May 25.

My dear Mr. Darwin,—When at the Linnean this afternoon, I was told by Dr. M—— that he had obtained your consent to sit for a portrait for the Society. Now, as it appears to me a great favour to ask of you to sit for yet another portrait, the least we can do, if you consent, is to employ a thoroughly good man to paint it. Therefore, if you have not already entered into any definite agreement. I write to suggest a little delay (say of a month), when, as Secretary, I might ascertain the amount of the subscription on which we might rely, and arrange matters accordingly. John Collier (Huxley's son-in-law) told me some time ago that he would dearly like to have you to paint, and I doubt not that he would do it at less than his ordinary charges if necessary. He would be sure to do the work well, and so I write to ascertain whether you would not prefer him, or some other artist of known ability, to do the work, if I were to undertake to provide the needful.

Please give to Mrs. Darwin, and take to yourself, our best thanks for your kind congratulations on the opportune arrival of another baby—just in time to be worked into the book on Mental Evolution. Everything is going well.

Very sincerely and most respectfully yours,

GEO. J. ROMANES.

To C. Darwin, Esq.

18 Cornwall Terrace, Regent's Park, N.W.: July 1.

I have told Collier that he had now better write to you direct at whatever time he intends to make his final arrangements with you as to place and time of sitting. He has just finished a portrait of me, which my mother had painted as a present to my wife. It is exceedingly good, and as all his recent portraits are the same—notably one of Huxley—I am very glad that he is to paint you. Besides, he is such a pleasant man to talk to, that the sittings are not so tedious as they would be with a less intelligent man.

I shall certainly read the 'Creed of Science' as soon as I can. The German book on Evolution I have not yet looked at, as I have been giving all my time to my own book. This is now finished. But talking of my time, I do not see how the two or three hours which I have spent in arranging to have a portrait, which will be of so much historical importance, taken by a competent artist, could well have been better employed.

You will see that I have got into a row with Carpenter over the thought-reading. Everybody thinks he made a mistake in lending himself to Bishop's design of posing as a scientific wonder. Bishop is a very sly dog, and has played his cards passing well. In an article which he published two years ago in an American newspaper, he explains the philosophy of advertising, and says the first thing to attend to is to catch good names.   He has now succeeded well.

Very sincerely and most respectfully yours,

GEO. J. ROMANES.

Down: August 7.

My dear Romanes,—I received yesterday the enclosed notice, and I send it to you, as I have thought that if you notice Dr. Roux's book in 'Nature' or elsewhere the review might possibly be of use to you. As far as I can judge the book ought to be brought before English naturalists.   You will have heard from Collier that he has finished my picture.   All my family who have seen it think it the best likeness which has been taken of me, and, as far as I can judge, this seems true.   Collier was the most considerate, kind, and pleasant painter a sitter could desire.

My dear Romanes,

Yours very sincerely,

CH. DARWIN.

To C. Darwin, Esq.

18 Cornwall Terrace, Regent's Park, N.W.: August 8, 1881.

Many thanks for the notice of Roux's book.   I have not yet looked at the latter, but Preyer, of Jena (who has been our guest during the Congress meeting,[1] and who knows the author), does not think much of it.

I am delighted that the portrait has pleased those who are the best judges.   I saw it the day it came up, and feel no doubt at all that it is far and away the

[1] International Medical Congress.

best of the three. But I did not like to write and venture this opinion till I knew what you all thought of it.

I have been very busy this past week with the affairs of the Congress in relation to Vivisection. It has been resolved by the Physiological Section to get a vote of the whole Congress upon the subject, and I had to prepare the resolution and get the signatures of all the vice-presidents of the Congress, presidents and vice-presidents of sections, and to arrange for its being put to the vote of the whole Congress at its last general meeting to-morrow. The only refusal to sign came appropriately enough from the president of the section ' Mental Diseases.'

We leave for Scotland to-morrow, when I shall hope to get time to read Roux's book, though I shall first review ' The Student's Darwin.'

I remain, very sincerely and most respectfully yours,

GEO. J. ROMANES.

The following letters relate to the burning question of Vivisection :—

Garvock. Perthshire : August 31, 1881.

My dear Mr. Darwin,—It is not often that I write to dun you, and I am sorry that duty should now impose on me the task of doing so, but I have no alternative, as you shall immediately see.

The Physiological Society was formed, as you may remember, for the purpose of obtaining combined action among physiologists on the subject of Vivisection. The result in the first instance was to resolve on a tentative policy of silence, with the view of seeing whether the agitation would not burn itself out. It is now thought that this policy has been tried sufficiently long, and that we are losing ground by continuing it. After much deliberation, therefore, the society has resolved to speak out upon the subject, and the 'Nineteenth Century' has been involved as the medium of publication. Arrangements have been made with Knowles for a symposium-like series of short essays by all the leaders of biology and medicine in this country—each to write on a branch of the subject chosen by himself or allotted to him by the society. In this matter of organising the contributions, the society is to be represented by Dr. Pye Smith, who combines science, medicine, and literary culture better than any other member of our body.

As secretary I am directed to write to all the men whose names are mentioned in a resolution passed by the society in accordance with the report of a committee appointed by the society to consider the subject. Hence these tears.

Of course, your name in this matter is one of the most important, and as the idea is to get a body of great names, it would be a disappointment of no small magnitude if yours should fail. It does not matter so much that you should write a long dissertation, so long as you allow yourself to stand among this noble army of martyrs. Two or three pages of the 'Nineteenth Century' on one, say, of the following topics would be all that we should want :—

'The limits and safeguards desirable in carrying on scientific experiments on animals.'

'Mistaken humanity of the agitation real humanity of vivisection.'

'The Royal Commission and its report.'

Or any other topic connected with Vivisection on which you may feel the spirit most to move you to write.

Any further information that you may desire I shall be happy to give, but please remember how much your assistance is desired.

This is a very delightful place, though not very conducive to work. If any of your sons are in Scotland and should care for a few days' sport with other scientific men on the spree, please tell them that they will find open house and welcome here.

The proofs of my book on Animal Intelligence are coming in. I hope your work on Worms will be out in time for me to mention it and its main results.

Ewart has pitched his zoological laboratory at Oban, so as to be as near this as possible. I shall go down when I can to keep his pot of sea-eggs upon the boil.

I remain, very sincerely and most respectfully yours,

GEO. J. ROMANES.

Down, Beckenham, Kent: September 2, 1881.

My dear Romanes,—Your letter has perplexed me beyond all measure. I fully recognise the duty of everyone, whose opinion is worth anything, expressing his opinion publicly on vivisection, and this made me send my letter to the 'Times.' I have been thinking at intervals all morning what I could say, and it is the simple truth that I have nothing worth saying. You, and men like you, whose ideas flow freely, and who can express them easily, cannot understand the state of mental paralysis in which I find myself. What is most wanted is a careful and accurate attempt to show what physiology has already done for man, and even still more strongly what there is every reason to believe it will hereafter do. Now I am absolutely incapable of doing this, or of discussing the other points suggested by you.

If you wish for my name (and I should be glad that it should appear with that of others in the same cause), could you not quote some sentence from my letter in the 'Times,' which I inclose, but please return it. If you thought fit you might say that you quoted it with my approval, and that, after still further reflection, I still abide most strongly in my expressed conviction. *For Heaven's sake*, do think of this; I do not grudge the labour and thought, but I could write nothing worth anyone's reading.

Allow me to demur to your calling your conjoint article a 'symposium,' strictly a 'drinking-party;' this seems to me very bad taste, and I do hope everyone of you will avoid any semblance of a joke on the subject. I know that words like a joke on this subject have quite disgusted some persons not at all inimical to physiology. One person lamented to me that Mr. Simon, in his truly admirable address at the Medical Congress (by far the best thing which I have read), spoke of the 'fantastic sensuality'[1] (or some such

<hr>

[1] See 'Life &c. of C. Darwin,' vol. iii. p. 210.

term) of the many mistaken, but honest men and women who are half mad on the subject.

Do pray try and let me escape, and quote my letter, which in some respects is more valuable, as giving my independent judgment before the Medical Congress. I really cannot imagine what I could say.

I will now turn to another subject : my little book on Worms has been long finished, but Murray was so strongly opposed to publishing it at the dead season, that I yielded. I have told the printers to send you a set of clean sheets, which you can afterwards have stitched together. There is hardly anything in it which can interest you.

Two or three papers by Hermann Müller have just appeared in ' Kosmos,' which seem to me interesting, as showing how soon, *i.e.* after how many attempts, bees learn how best to suck a new flower ; there is also a good and laudatory review of Dr. Roux. I could lend you ' Kosmos ' if you think fit.

You will perhaps have seen that my poor dear brother Erasmus has just died, and he was buried yesterday here at Down.

Garvock, Bridge of Earn, Perthshire. September 4.

My dear Mr. Darwin,—I hasten to relieve your mind about writing on vivisection, as I am sure that none of the physiologists would desire you to do so if you feel it a bother. After all, there are plenty of other men to do the writing, and if some of them quote the marked sentences in your letter (which I return), with the statement that you still adhere to them, the chief thing will be done—viz. showing again and emphatically on which side you are.

It is not intended to call the article a 'Symposium.' I only used this word to show that they are to be of the same composite kind as those which the 'Nineteenth Century' previously published under this designation.

You letter gives me the first news of your brother's death. I remember very well seeing him one day when I called on you at his house. It must make you very sad, and I am sorry to have written you at such a time.

I have already sent in a short review of Roux's book, but should like to see about the bees in 'Kosmos.' I am trying some experiments with bees here on way-finding; but, contrary to my expectations, I find that most bees, when marked and liberated at one hundred yards from their hive, do not get back for a long time. This fact makes it more difficult to test their mode of way-finding, as the faculty (whatever it is) does not seem to be certain.

Many thanks for sending me the book on Worms so early. As yet I have only had time to look at the table of contents, which seems most interesting.

Lockyer is staying here just now, and has given me the proofs of his book. It seems to me that he has quite carried the position as to the elements being products of development.

Down: October 14.

My dear Romanes,—I have just read the splendid review of the Worm book in 'Nature.' I have been much pleased by it, but at the same time you so over-estimate the value of what I do, that you make me feel ashamed of myself, and wish to be worthy of such praise. I cannot think how you can endure to spend so much time over another's work, when you have yourself so much in hand; I feel so worn out, that I do not suppose I shall ever again give reviewers trouble.

I hope that your *opus magnum* is progressing well, and when we meet later in the autumn I shall be anxious to hear about it.

In a few days' time we are going to visit Horace in Cambridge for a week, to see if that will refresh me.

Pray give my kind remembrances to Mrs. Romanes, and I hope you are all well.

Garvock, Bridge of Earn, Perthshire: October 16, 1881.

My dear Mr. Darwin,—If I did not know you so well, I should think that you are guilty of what our nurse calls ' mock modesty.' At least I know that if I, or anybody else, had written the book which I reviewed, your judgment would have been the first to endorse all I have said. I never allow personal friendship to influence what I say in reviews; and if I am so uniformly stupid as to ' over-estimate the value of all you do,' it is at any rate some consolation to know that my stupidity is so universally shared by all the men of my generation. But your letters are to me always psychological studies, and especially so when, as in this one, you seem without irony intentionally grim to refer to my work in juxtaposition with your own.

The proof-sheets are coming in, and I suppose the book will be out in a month or two. I do not know why they are so slow in setting up the type. But, as I said once before, this book will not be so good (or so little bad) as the one that is to follow.

Ewart and I have been working at the Echinoderms again, and at last have found the internal nervous plexus. Also tried poisons, and proved still further the locomotor function of the pedicellariæ.

I observed a curious thing about anemones. If a piece of food is placed in a pool or tank where a number are closed, in a few minutes they all expand: clearly they *smell* the food.

I am deeply sorry to hear that you feel ' worn out,' but cannot imagine that the reviewers have done with you yet.

The vivisection fight does not promise well. Like yourself, most of the champions do not like the idea.

G. J. ROMANES.

There are many other letters, but care has been taken only to select the most interesting. In 1881 came the last visit to Down, full of brightness. Mr. Darwin was most particularly kind, and gave Mr. Romanes some of his own MSS., including a paper on ' Instinct,' which is bound up with Mr. Romanes' own book, ' Mental Evolution in Animals.' It transpired that Mr. Darwin was extremely fond of novels, and had the most delightful way of offering his guests books to take to bed with them. In fact, Down was one of the few houses in which readable books adorned the guest-chambers.

It came out on this occasion that Mr. Darwin had an especial love for the books written by the author of ' Mademoiselle Mori.' He offered one of his guests

' Denise,' saying it was his favourite tale, or words to
that effect.

Down was indeed one of the most delightful of
houses in which to stay, and that snowy January
Sunday of 1881 was a very real red letter day.

To Miss C. E. Romanes.

18 Cornwall Terrace, Regent's Park, N.W.: July 24, 1881.

My dearest Charlotte,—There have been no letters
from you for two days, so I have nothing to answer.

I did not write yesterday because we were spending the day with Mr. Teesdale, in his house at Down,
and did not get back again till past the post hour.
We went over to pay a call upon Darwin. He and
his wife were at home, and as kind and glad to see us
as possible. The servant gave our names wrongly to
them, and they thought we were a very old couple
whom they know, called Norman. So old Darwin came
in with a huge canister of snuff under his arm—old
Norman being very partial to this luxury—and looked
very much astonished at finding us. He was as
grand and good and bright as ever.

In to-day's ' Times' you will see a letter by ' F.R.S.'
which is worth reading, as are all the productions of
his able pen.

I have been applied to by the Editor of the
' Encyclopædia Britannica' to supply an article on
' Instinct.' This I am writing.

We are all quite well, except that I have had a
cold, which is now going away.

With united love to all, yours ever the same.

GEORGE.

K

One evening Mr. Romanes personally ' conducted ' Mr. Darwin to the Royal Institution to hear a lecture by Dr. Sanderson on ' Dionæa.' A burst of applause greeted Mr. Darwin's entrance, much to that great man's surprise. Earlier in the day he had half timidly asked Mr. Romanes if there would be room at the Royal Institution for him.

In 1882 came the great sorrow of Mr. Darwin's death. The following letters show something of what the loss was to the ardent disciple, the loyal-hearted friend.

To Francis Darwin, Esq.

18 Cornwall Terrace, Regent's Park. N.W. : April 22. 1882.

My dear Darwin,—I did not write because I thought it might trouble you, but I sent some flowers yesterday which did not require acknowledgment.

Even you, I do not think, can know all that this death means to me. I have long dreaded the time, and now that it has come it is worse than I could anticipate. Even the death of my own father— though I loved him deeply, and though it was more sudden, did not leave a desolation so terrible. Half the interest of my life seems to have gone when I cannot look forward any more to his dear voice of welcome, or to the letters that were my greatest happiness. For now there is no one to venerate, no one to work for, or to think about while working. I always knew that I was leaning on these feelings too much, but I could not try to prevent them, and so at last I am left with a loneliness that never can be filled. And when I think how grand and generous his kindness was to me, grief is no word for my loss.

But I know that your grief is greater than mine, and that, like him, I should try to think of others before myself. And I do feel for you all very much indeed. But although I cannot endure to picture your house or your household as the scene of such a death, I can derive some consolation from the thought that he died as few men in the history of the world have died—knowing that he had finished a gigantic work, seeing how that work has transformed the thoughts of mankind, and foreseeing that his name must endure to the end of time among the very greatest of the human race. Very, very rare is such consolation as this in a house of mourning.

I look forward to hearing more about the end when we meet. I feel it is very kind of you to have written to me so soon, and I hope you will convey our very sincere sympathy to Mrs. Darwin and the other members of your family.

Yours ever sincerely,
GEO. J. ROMANES.

After 'Mr. Darwin's Life' appeared, Mr. Romanes writes :—

To Francis Darwin, Esq.

Geanies, Ross-shire, N.B.: November 21, 1887.

Dear Darwin,—In this far-away place I have only to-day seen the 'Times' review, and sent for the book. But from what the review says I can see that all the world has to thank you. Therefore I write at once to say how more than glad I feel that you have carried so great a work to so successful a termination.

K 2

How glad *you* must be that the immense labour and anxiety of it all is over. Do not trouble to answer, but believe in the genuine congratulations of

Yours very truly,
GEO. J. ROMANES.

November 26, 1887.

I write again to thank you—this time for the presentation copy of the Life and Letters. I had previously got one, but am very glad to have the work in duplicate. It is indeed splendidly done.

I send you the enclosed to post or not, as you think best. On reading ——'s letter yesterday it occurred to me that if any answer were required, it might be better for somebody other than yourself to supply it. But I do not know how you may think it best to treat this man, therefore post the letter or not, according to your judgment.

Yours very sincerely,
GEO. J. ROMANES.

Geanies: December 1, 1887.

I have now nearly finished the ' Life and Letters,' and cannot express my admiration of your work. What a mercy it is that you were so wonderfully qualified to do it.

Yours ever indebtedly,
GEO. J. ROMANES.

Mr. Romanes wrote one of the memorial notices in the little volume ' Charles Darwin,' published by Messrs. Macmillan.

Thus closed a very significant and important chapter in his life.

The relationship of disciple to master ceased for

him, no one else exactly held the place Mr. Darwin had held, to no one else did he so constantly refer; and dear as were other friends, notably Dr. Burdon Sanderson, no one stood in the position to Romanes of 'The Master.'

There was no exaggeration in his expressions of grief, or in the verses in which he poured out his soul :—

> 'I loved him with a strength of love [1]
>   Which man to man can only bear
> When one in station far above
>   The rest of men, yet deigns to share
> A friendship true with those far down
>   The ranks : as though a mighty king,
> Girt with his armies of renown,
>   Should call within his narrow ring
> Of counsellors and chosen friends
>   Some youth who scarce can understand
> How it began or how it ends
>   That he should grasp the monarch's hand.'

To all those to whom a great friendship has been given, a friendship, not on equal terms, but one in which the chief elements on one side have been reverence and gratitude, on the other affectionate approval and esteem, to all these fortunate souls these letters and verses will appeal. For it is no small matter in a man's life that he should have had a passionate friendship for a great man, a real leader; and it is a still greater matter that the younger man should have found his confidence, his devotion, his reverence worthily bestowed.

To Francis Darwin, Esq.

18 Cornwall Terrace, Regent's Park, N.W.: January 13, 1885.

Dear Darwin,—I will think over the conversations and write you again whether there is anything that would do for publishing.

---

[1] *Charles Darwin* : a memorial poem.

Meanwhile I send for your perusal some verses which I have written at odds and ends of time since he died. This was only done for my own gratification, and without any view to publishing. But having recently had them put together and copied out, I have sent them to two or three of the best poetical critics for their opinion upon the literary merits of the poem as a whole. The result of this has been more satisfactory than I anticipated; and as one of them suggests that I should offer the verses as an addendum to the biography, I act upon the coincidence of receiving your letter and his at about the same time.

It seems to me there are two things for you to consider: first, whether anything in the way of poetry, however good, is desirable; and next, if so, whether this poetry is good enough for the occasion. The first question would be answered by your own feelings, and the second, I suppose, by submitting the verses to some good authority for an opinion— say one to whom I have not sent them. Only, if the matter were to go as far as this, I should like you to explain to the critic that as it stands the poem is only in the rough. If it were to be revised for publication I should spend a good deal of trouble over the process of polishing, and some of the lines expressive of passionate grief would be altogether changed.

In sending you the MS. I rely upon you not to let the authorship be known to anyone without first asking me, because, although I have published poetry already,[1] it has been anonymous, and I do not want

---

[1] A few stray poems in magazines.

it to be known that I have this propensity. And on this account, if these verses were to appear in the biography, it would require to be without my name, or headed in some such way as 'Memorial verses by a friend.' In this case I should modify any of the lines which might lead to the author being spotted.

Should you decide against admitting them, I do not think that I should publish them anywhere else, because where such a personality is concerned, independent publication (without the occasion furnished by the appearance of a biography) might seem presumptuous even on the part of an anonymous writer.

Yesterday I received a letter from the Frenchman who translated my book on 'Mental Evolution,' asking me to let him know whether he might apply for the translation of the biography. His name is De Varigny, and he does some original work in vertebrate physiology. I think he has done my book very well.

Yours ever sincerely,
G. J. ROMANES.

Can you suggest a subject for a Rede lecture which I have to give in May?

CHAPTER III

LONDON—GEANIES

ONE may now for a short space turn away from the scientific side of Mr. Romanes' life and speak a little of other aspects.

No one was ever a more incessant worker and thinker. If he went away for a short visit, his writing went too; and if in Scotland wet weather interfered with shooting, he would sit down and write something, perhaps a poem, perhaps (as he once said playfully when condoled with on account of heavy rain and absence of books, ' I don't care, I'll write an essay on the freedom of the will ') an article for a magazine.

A great deal of reviewing, chiefly in ' Nature,' filled up some of his time, and he also turned his attention more and more to poetry.

In the postscript of a letter written in 1878 to Mr. Darwin he says: ' I am beginning to write poetry!' and poetry interested him more and more as years went on. Of this, more later.

He much enjoyed society; he ceased to mingle exclusively with scientific and philosophical people, and as time went on he became acquainted with many of the notabilities of the day. And, as has been said, it is impossible perhaps to exaggerate the outward pleasantness of those years.

He was able to devote himself to his work; he had an ever-increasing number of devoted friends both of men and women, and he was intensely happy in his home life.

His children were a great and increasing interest to him, and he was an ideal father, tender, sympathetic, especially as infancy grew into childhood. He shared in all his children's interests, and lived with them on terms of absolute friendship, chaffing and being chaffed, enjoying an interchange of pet names and jokes, and yet exacting obedience and gentle manners, and never permitting them as small children to make themselves troublesome to visitors in any way, or to chatter freely at meals when guests were present.

He had very strong feelings about the importance of making children familiar with the Bible. He used to say that as a mere matter of literary education everyone ought to be familiar with the Bible from beginning to end. He himself was exceedingly well versed in Holy Scripture.

He also thought a good classical training very desirable for boys (and girls also), and had no very great belief in science being taught to any great extent during a boy's school career. Memory, he considered, ought to be cultivated in childhood, and he did not think that the reasoning powers ought to be much taxed in early years. He used to say that Euclid could be learnt much more easily if it were begun later in boyhood. He also much wished that foreign languages should be taught very early in life, and with little or no attention to grammar.

Perhaps a few words of reminiscence from one of his children may not be unwelcome.

MEMORIES.—G. J. R.

I remember that when my father was particularly amused at anything, he used a certain gesture, which, according to the 'Life of Darwin,'[1] must have been precisely similar to that of Darwin, and was probably unconsciously copied by my father. He never used the gesture except when very much tickled at hearing some amusing story; when the climax of the story was reached he would burst into a peal of hearty laughter, at the same time bringing his hand heavily but noiselessly down upon his knee or on the table near him.

When we were at Geanies, our greatest delight was 'to go out shooting with father.' We used to tramp for hours together over turnip and grass fields behind my father and the gamekeeper. We used to enjoy the expeditions so much better if our father was the only sportsman, for then we had him all to ourselves. We were very small then: our ages were ten, nine, and six respectively, but we were good walkers and we never became tired. What little sunburnt, healthy, grubby children we were to be sure! When Bango, the setter, pointed at a covey, we all had to stand quite still while our father walked forward towards the dog. Directly the covey rose we all 'ducked' for safety. I shall never forget the joy and pride we felt when a bird fell, and we ran with shouts of triumph to pick it up. Then the delight of eating lunch under a hedge or in a wood! That was a time of jokes and fun, and we talked as freely and unrestrainedly as we liked about all kinds of subjects. Then came some more tramping in the turnips, and we would journey homewards, a weary but very happy little party. The counting of the

[1] *Life and Letters of Charles Darwin,* by Francis Darwin, vol. i. p. iii.

game would follow, and our pride was very great
when the number of brace was high, for we felt that
we had been helping our father to slay the partridges.
In fact, we thought that Sandy, the gamekeeper, was
a very useless personage when we went out, for did
we not mark as well as, or better, than he did?   And
surely we could carry the game bags; they were not
very heavy even when they were full to bursting!

There was something very beautiful in the respect
and reverence which George Romanes felt for children
and for child-life, and a sonnet 'To my Children'
expresses these feelings :—

> 'Of all the little ones whom I have known
>   Ye are so much the fairest in my view—
>   So much the sweetest and the dearest few—
> That not because ye are my very own
> Do I behold a wonder that is shown
>   Of loveliness diversified in you :
>   It is because each nature as it grew
> Surpassed a world of joy already grown.
>
> If months bestow such purpose on the years,
>   May not the years work out a greater plan ?
> Vast are the heights which form this ' vale of tears,'
>   And though what lies beyond we may not scan,
> Thence came my little flock—strayed from their spheres,
>   As lambs of God turned children into man.'

As has been said, for music Mr. Romanes had an
absolute passion.   A good concert of chamber or of
orchestral music was absolute happiness to him, and
he heard a great deal in these years.   One or two of
his friends were excellent musicians.   To one of these
he once wrote a sonnet, 'To a Member of the Bach
Choir,'[1] and sent it to her in the form of a Christmas
card, producing much pleasant mystification and

[1] Miss M. M. Paget.

laughter when it was discovered from whom the
sonnet came.

To Miss Paget.

18 Cornwall Terrace, Regent's Park : December 27, 1887.

Dear Miss Paget,—If my sonnet gave half as much
pleasure as your note, I am sure we have both the
best reasons to be glad. The letter was as much a
surprise to me as the former was to you, because, far
from seeing the ' ungraciousness ' of yesterday, even
then I thought that my reward was much in excess
of my deserving. But your further response of to-
day has given me a greater happiness than I can tell;
let it, therefore, be told in some of the greatest words
of the greatest man I ever knew. These you will
find in the first nine lines of a letter on page 323,
vol. ii., of the ' Life of Darwin,' and in one respect
you have conferred an additional benefit, for, unlike
him, I did not previously know that my own feelings
of friendship were so fully reciprocated. If you think
that this amounts to a confession of dulness on my
part, my only excuse is that I formed too just an
estimate of my own merits as compared with those of
a friend. All that the latter were, or in this estimate
must ever continue to be, I shall not now venture to
say; for, if I did, the peculiar ethics of the Paget
family (which you have been good enough to explain)
would certainly pound this letter into a pulp. But
there are two remarks which I may hazard. The
first is, that I make it a point of what may be called
æsthetic conscience never to write anything in verse
which is not perfectly *sincere*. The next is, that my

dulness is not so bad as to have prevented me from observing the Sebastian attachment.

Last Christmas I lost my greatest and my dearest friend.[1] This Christmas I have found that I had a better friend than I was aware of. For the seasonable kindness, therefore, of your truly Yule-tide consolation, *gratias tibi ago*.

Ever yours, most sincerely,

G. J. ROMANES.

For some years a delightful society existed in London, known as the 'Home Quartet Union,' the members of which met at different houses and listened to perfect music performed by first-rate artists under perfect conditions.

There were few happier evenings in his life than those spent in such a way.

Of all composers, Beethoven represented to him everything that was highest in art or poetry; for Beethoven, Mr. Romanes had much the same reverence and admiration which he felt for Darwin, and perhaps Beethoven, in other and very different ways, taught him and influenced him much.

He was very catholic in his musical tastes, except perhaps that Italian opera never greatly fascinated him. Wagner's operas, on the other hand, became a great delight, particularly after a visit to Baireuth in 1889, where he saw Parsifal and Meistersinger.

Politics interested Mr. Romanes moderately. He was by nature and by family tradition a Conservative, but he cared very little for parties, and admired great men on whichever side of the House they sat.

Perhaps of all living politicians, the one for whom he had the greatest enthusiasm and respect was

---

[1] The friend referred to on p. 178.

Mr. Arthur Balfour. For him, both as a politician and as a thinker, Mr. Romanes had an unbounded admiration.

EXTRACTS FROM JOURNAL.[1]

Feb. 1881.—Went to Mr. Norman Lockyer. Several people, including William Black, the novelist, were there. After Mr. Lockyer had shown us several experiments in spectrum analysis, a lady asked him 'What is the use of the spectroscope?' Called on Mr. Cotter Morison and saw some beautiful books. He is a wonderfully good talker.

June 1881.—Dinner at the Spottiswoodes'. Mr. Browning was there and talked much about Victor Hugo. He mentioned that when Wordsworth was told that Miss Barrett had married Mr. Browning, he replied, 'It's a good thing these two understand each other, for no one else understands them.'

Garvock. Perthshire : November 5, 1881.

My dearest Charlotte,—I thought you would like the photos, and your letter to-day more than justifies my anticipation. Coming events cast their shadows before, and it will not now be long before you see the former. These are both exceedingly well. I wish you could see little Ethel dancing. It is now her greatest amusement, and she does it with all the state and gravity of an eighteenth century *grande dame.*

Many thanks for your prompt action about the proofs. You did everything in the best possible way, as I knew you would. It is a great blessing you were in London at the time, as the caretaker would be sure to have made some mistake, and time is pressing.

---

[1] It should be explained that the writer of this memoir is responsible for the Journal, but as it was kept for the benefit of both husband and wife a few extracts are given.

The duke has answered me in this week's ' Nature,' and likewise has Carpenter. I have written a rejoinder for next week's issue in a tone which I have tried to make at once dignified and blunt.

I send you a riddle which I have just made. See if you can answer it in your next.

> ' My first is found in Scripture,
>   My second hangs in air,
> My third a thing to all unknown,
>   Yet maps can tell you where.
>
> My whole is neither fact nor thing,
>   A word, yet not a word,
> And if you stand me on my head,
>   I'm bigger by a third.' [1]

Much love from both to both.

Yours ever the same,

GEORGE.

In this Journal constant mention occurs of concerts and of the pleasure given by amateur musical friends. The late Professor Rowe's name often occurs, he succeeded Professor Clifford at University College, and besides his great mathematical attainments he was also a most accomplished musician. He played Schumann especially in the most poetic way.

Journal, Feb. 1882.—Lecture by Professor Tyndall on the action of molecular heat. Triumphant vindication of his own work against Magnus and Tait.

April 2.—Sunday, the 25th, we spent at Oxford, met the Warden of Keble in Mr. F. Paget's rooms, as a year ago we had met Dr. Liddon. Met Mr. Vernon Harcourt at Christ Church.

[1] The answer is the word *six*.

May.—Met Shorthouse, author of 'John Inglesant,' at the F. Pollocks'. He spoke of Mr. Scott-Holland's review of his book. Sir T. Bramwell lectured the other day at the Royal Institution on the making of the Channel tunnel, and was as amusing as usual.

June.—Interesting talk with Mr. J. R. Green. Both J. R. G. and G. J. R. agreed that Herbert Spencer, Professor Huxley, and Leslie Stephen only represented one side of the question, *i.e.* that conduct can only be called moral when it is beneficial to the race, and that the ethical quality of an action is determined solely by its effects as beneficial or injurious. This purely mechanical view of morality deprives morality of what both speakers considered the essential elements of morality as such, *i.e.* the feeling of right and wrong. so that, *e.g.*, ants and bees, according to this canon. have a right to be considered more truly moral than men.

The view taken by J. R. G. and G. J. R. was that the essential element of morality resided in feeling and inclination.

To Miss C. E. Romanes.

18 Cornwall Terrace : June 9.

My dearest Charlotte,—We are all well and lively. Ascot and an 'at home' yesterday ; to-day artists' studios, dinner at the Pagets', and Sanderson's lecture ; to-morrow, College of Surgeons' reception and dinner party of our own ; and next week, one, two, or three engagements for every day. 'Babylon' is in full swing, and I heard yesterday, from the head of the Census department, that for the last ten years it has been growing at the rate of 1,000 per week.

I have only time to write a few lines to thank you and the mother for the very jolly letters received this morning, and to let you know that we are all well.

The reason of my haste now is this extraordinary discovery that has been made in the Botanical Gardens, and which you have probably read about in the 'Times.' Medusæ have been found in swarms in the fresh-water tank of the Victoria Regina Lily. Such a thing as a fresh-water Medusa has never been heard of before, and I want to lose no time in getting to work upon his physiology. You see, when I don't go to the jelly-fish the jelly-fish come to me, and I am bound to have jelly-fish wherever I go.

It would have been very odd if I had been the discoverer, as I should have been had I known that there was a living Victoria Regis, for then I should have gone to see the plant, and would not have failed to see the Medusæ. Only in that case I might have begun to grow superstitious, and to think that in some way my fate was bound up in jelly-fish.

I must get to work soon because all the naturalists are in a high state of excitement, and there has been a regular scramble for priority.

The worst about this jelly-fish is that it will only live in a temperature of 90°, so I shall have to work at it in the Victoria House, which is kept at a temperature of 100°, and makes one 'sweat.' But I shall not work long at a time.

From 1882 to 1890 Mr. Romanes rented Geanies,

a beautiful place overlooking the Moray Firth. It belongs to a cousin of the Romanes family, Captain Murray, of the 81st Regiment. Captain Murray's mother and sisters lived not far away, and the Murrays and Romanes formed a little coterie in that not very populous neighbourhood.

He continued to be an ardent sportsman, and probably his happiest days were those he spent tramping over moors or plodding through turnips in those October days of perfect beauty, which seem especially peculiar to Scotland.

The surroundings of Geanies, without being romantically beautiful, have a charm of their own. There is a certain melancholy and loneliness about the inland landscape round Geanies which appealed strongly to him. It is a place abounding in every kind of sea-bird, and it is almost impossible to describe the weird, uncanny effect which the long endless twilight of the summer, the silence broken by hootings of owls, by the scream of a sea-gull, produce on one.

It is an old rambling house with long passages and mysterious staircases, and, as the children found, endless conveniences for playing at hide-and-seek. The library is a most lovely room, lined with book-cases, and leading into an old-fashioned garden, full of sweet-smelling flowers.

It is impossible to imagine a more ideal abode for a poet, a naturalist, a botanist, a sportsman, than this, his summer home ; and as Mr. Romanes was, to some extent, all four, Geanies was a place of exceeding happiness to him.

Two of his sonnets are dedicated to his dogs, 'To my Setters,' and 'To Countess,' and the following letter will show him as a sportsman.

To Mrs. Romanes.

Achalibster.[1] Caithness: August 14, 1883.

To-day turned out not at all bad after all; and although there was a good deal too much rain I had a glorious time. Bag twenty brace of grouse, one brace plover, one hare, one duck; I could easily have got more, only Bango got so tired in the afternoon that we knocked off at five o'clock, moreover I did not begin till eleven, as I did not wake till ten! So the twenty brace was shot in about five hours. The new setter 'Flora' is a beauty. She is extraordinarily like Bango, but with a prettier face. She is a splendid worker.

Even at Geanies he always 'worked' for some part of the day, and sport, tennis, boating, filled up the rest of his time.

Very often there was a house party, and the evenings were particularly bright—merry talk, games, very amateurish theatricals, learned discussions. Nothing came amiss to the master of the house. He was always a little apt to be absent-minded and dreamy, and his pet name, bestowed on him by the dearest and merriest of all the merry 'Geanies brotherhood' was 'Philosopher.' It stuck, and many people only knew him by that name.

No one ever appreciated a good story more than he, and, as a friend has said, 'his laugh was so merry and so often heard.'

His own jokes were invariably free from any unkindness, and he did not in the least appreciate repartee or epigram, the point of which lay chiefly, if

---

[1] A moor taken in addition to the low ground shooting of Geanies.

not wholly, in unkindness. Many friends enlivened his summer home, and all those who paid a second visit were known as the ' Geanies brotherhood.'

Journal, Geanies, July 26.—Yesterday came the terrible news of Mr. Frank Balfour's sudden death.[1] His loss is irreparable. It is only a month since we met him at Cambridge, looking so well, quite recovered from his recent illness; we were looking forward to his promised visit.

Sept.—Mr. Lockyer, the Bruntons, and the Burdon Sandersons have been here. Memorial Poem to Darwin begun.

Nov. 14, *Edinburgh.*—Met for the first time Mr. and Mrs. Butcher, who were just taking possession of the Greek Chair; also Professor Blackie, who was *himself*, and talked much of the insolence of John Bull.

Jan. 1883.—Dr. Sanderson is elected Professor of Physiology at Oxford.

To this election was due the ultimate change in Mr. Romanes' life in 1890, when he followed Dr. Sanderson to Oxford, attracted mainly by the facilities for physiological research.

On Jan. 2 of this year (1883) his mother died.

Mr. Romanes lectured at the Royal Institution in January, and immediately afterwards went abroad on one of the only two Continental tours he took simply for pleasure. He much enjoyed this Italian journey, and the rhyming instinct woke up in him greatly. He wrote a good deal about this time, and one of his sonnets has reference to this journey—' Florence.'

---

[1] Mr. F. Balfour was killed on the Aiguille Blanche de Peuteret, July 1882.

He also made acquaintance for the first time with a good many well-known novels, read to him during a temporary illness at Florence—the precursor, alas, of many such times of novel-reading. He shared Mr. Darwin's tastes for simple, pure, love stories, and one of the party at Florence well remembers how 'The Heir of Redclyffe' brought tears to his eyes. For this and 'The Chaplet of Pearls,' read to him some years later, he had a great admiration.

Journal, March 28, 1883.—Mr. F. Paget's wedding in St. Paul's, a special anthem by Stainer. The Warden of Keble and Dr. Liddon married them, and the whole service was very impressive.

June.—Mr. Spottiswoode's death has been a terrible blow. Service at the Abbey. We put off our party on June 27th; it seemed improper to have a party, mainly composed of scientific people, the very day after the death of the President of the Royal Society.

12th.—Dinner at the Pagets'. Met Browning,[1] who is entirely on Carlyle's side *à propos* of Froude's recent revelations.

15th.—Went to Professor and Mrs. Allman, at Parkston. He is a most fascinating naturalist of the old type, caring for birds, and beasts, and flowers.

Met Mr. E. Clodd the other night, who alluded to 'Physicus'[2] and the tone of depression in the book. ('Candid Examination of Theism.')

---

[1] Mr. Browning told the same story of the Carlyles at this party which Mrs. Ritchie narrates in *Tennyson, Ruskin, and Browning,* pp. 198, 199.

[2] The *nom de plume* adopted in writing *Candid Examination of Theism.*

This year Mr. Romanes and Professor Ewart set up a small laboratory on the Geanies coast, and the Journal notes:

Professor Ewart could not get the farmhouse he hoped, and this was unfortunate, as he had written to the British Association and invited one or two foreigners to come and work and live in this farmhouse. In vain were the foreigners warned not to come, for one evening in walked a young Dane, who preceded a postcard he had sent announcing his arrival. Very nice, and extremely embarrassed at finding himself in a country house where people dressed for dinner.

However, he got accommodation in the neighbourhood and worked at Ascidians, but the experiment of inviting stray foreign scientists was abandoned.

Sept.—The Allmans, Turners, and Mr. Lockyer have been here, and we have been getting up some private theatricals.

Jan. 1884.—Lecture at the Royal Institution on ' the Darwinian Theory of Instinct.'

To Miss C. E. Romanes.

January 5. 1884.

I am preparing a beautiful surprise for Ethel after she comes down again. The library is to have its end wall papered and panelled, the conservatory is to be painted green, and filled with stands of flowers, and the little room is to have the window filled with stained glass, the walls, ceiling, and doors, beautifully papered and decorated. I expect my book to pay the bills. Is not this a nice idea?

Little Ethel's ideas about writing, by the way, are original. A few days ago she wanted me to play at gee-gee. I said, 'No, Ethel, father is writing.' She asked, 'Writing letters or writing book?' I said, 'Writing book.' Whereupon she made the shrewd remark—'Father not writing to anybody, father can play gee-gee.' So much for her estimate of my popularity as an author.

Journal, April.—Lecture at Manchester; stayed with Professor Boyd Dawkins.

This year Mr. Romanes attended Canon Curteis' 'Boyle Lectures' at Whitehall.

Journal, March 1883.—'G. Lectured at ——. One of the hearers asked whether in the lecturer's opinion man or animals had first appeared on the earth! G. spent a pleasant day at Bromsgrove with the F. Pagets.'

To James Romanes, Esq.

18 Cornwall Terrace, Regent's Park, N.W.: June 1, 1884.

My dearest James.—Little Ethel has just brought me the enclosed letter to send to you. She had written it as far as the up and down lines go, and said it was to tell you how much she loved you, and how sorry she was that she should not see you when she goes to Geanies. She then asked me to tell her how to write kiss. I told her that in letters they write kiss by a cross, and then she made the crosses. She also made me promise to send you the letter at once, without any delay : and as the idea of writing you a letter was entirely her own, I do as I was told. You may take it as a definite expression of the emotions, even though it be not a very intelligible expression of ideas.

She wants to know why you are going away, and whether you will write to her when you are away, and a heap of other questions of the same kind.

We are all well now, and I am just going with the two Ethels to a children's service, which they both enjoy. It is very pretty to hear the little one singing with the other children, which she does perfectly in tune.

They are waiting for me now, so with best love from all,

Yours ever the same,
GEORGE.

In 1885 came the first warnings of ill-health. Mr. Romanes had a short but very sharp illness, and after that year he suffered frequently from gout, which necessitated visits to various foreign 'cures.' He was a perfect travelling companion, he liked to have arrangements made for him, and was never discomposed if anything went wrong, never put out by any of the ordinary mischances of travel. Although he always professed indifference to architecture and art, he would grow quite boyishly enthusiastic over some cathedral, as his sonnets to Amiens, and Christ Church, Oxford,[1] testify, and for sculpture he had a real love.

In May 1885 came the first marked public utterance which showed that Mr. Romanes was now in a very different mental attitude to that in which he wrote his 'Candid Examination of Theism.'

---

[1] See sonnets, *The Bible of Amiens*, and *Christ Church, Oxford*.

He delivered the Rede Lecture at Cambridge, and in it he criticises the materialistic position. (It must be remembered that his anti-Theistic book was published anonymously, and at that time he had no intention of ever referring to it.)

The reaction set in very soon after the 'Candid Examination' was published.

He was severe, as it seemed often to those who knew him best, unduly severe with himself, and often described himself as utterly agnostic when possibly 'bewildered' would have better described him.

Through these years, underneath all the outward happiness, the intense love for scientific work, there was the same longing and craving for the old belief, and before his eyes was always the question, 'Is Christian faith possible or intellectually justifiable in the face of scientific discovery?'

These years between 1879 and 1890 were years of frequent despondency, of almost despair, but also of incessant seeking after truth, and year after year he grew gradually nearer Christian belief.

The letters which follow will be interesting in this place. They arose out of a correspondence in 'Nature.'[1]

To Professor Asa Gray.

May 16, 1883.

Dear Professor Gray,—The receipt of your kind letter of the 1st instant has given me in full measure the sincerest kind of pleasure; for in the light supplied by your second letter communicated to 'Nature' I came deeply to regret my misunderstanding of the spirit in which you wrote the first one, and now you enable me to feel that we have shaken hands over the matter.

[1] See *Nature*, January 25, 1883.

For my own part I am always glad when differences in matter of opinion admit of being honestly expressed without enmity, and still more so when, as in the present case, this discussion leads to a basis of friendship. I therefore thank you most heartily for your letter, and remain yours very truly,

G. J. ROMANES.

P.S.—If you have not already happened to read a book called 'A Candid Examination of Theism,' I should like to send you a copy. I wrote it six or seven years ago and published it anonymously in 1878. I do not now hold to all the arguments, nor should I express myself so strongly on the argumentative force of the remainder, but I should like you to read the book, in order to show you how gladly I would enter your camp if I could only see that it is on the side of Truth.

December 30, 1883.

Dear Professor Gray,—I sent you my papers as a return for those which you so kindly sent to me, and for which I have written to thank you before. I quite agree with your view, that the doctrine of the human mind having been proximately evolved from lower minds is not incompatible with the doctrine of its having been due to a higher and supreme mind. Indeed, I do not think the theory of evolution, even if fully proved, would seriously affect the previous standing of this more important question.

The sorrow is, that this question is so far removed from the reach of any trustworthy answer. Or, at least, such is the sorrow if that answer when it comes

is to prove an affirmative. If it is to be an eternal
sleep, no doubt it is better to live as we are than in
the certainty of a Godless universe. But although
we cannot find any sure answer to this momentous
question, I cannot help feeling that it is reasonable (although it may not be orthodox) to cherish this much
faith, that if there is a God, whom, when we see, we
can truly worship as well as dread, He cannot *ex
hypothesi* be a God who will thwart the strong desire
which He has implanted in us to worship Him,
merely because we cannot find evidence enough to
believe this or that doctrine of dogmatic Theology.

But I do not know why I should thus trouble you
with my troubles, unless it is that the kindness of
your letters has broken through the bars by which
we usually imprison such feelings from the world.
Anyhow, I thank you for that kindness, and hope
you will forgive this somewhat odd requital.

Very sincerely yours,
G. J. ROMANES.

'The desire to worship Him.'

These words are the key-note of the religious
history of the pure and noble character which I am
trying to describe.

The letters, so touching in the momentary breaking
down of reserve, give, as it were, a glimpse of the
inner life, give an indication of the struggle, the perplexity, the sorrow which eleven years later ended in
'Eternal Peace.'

Readers of the lately published 'Thoughts on
Religion' will see how gradually he grew to perceive

the *reasonableness* of the Christian Faith ; he had never doubted the beauty, the moral worth, the attraction of that faith. And with him it was what Dante in his 'Paradiso' puts into S. Bernard's mouth :

> ' A quella luce cotal si diventa,
> Che volgersi da lei per altro aspetto
> È impossibil che mai si consenta.'

And through all these years there was a constant willingness to try to aid other people in their difficulties, to remove stumbling-blocks which hindered others. He was always willing to discuss problems of belief, always perfectly fair and candid, and there were not a few who, since his death, have spoken of the real help which he gave them. He did not drop religious observances; on Sunday in London he usually went to Christ Church, Albany Street, of which the present Bishop of St. Albans was then vicar, and for some years at Geanies he had a short Evening Service for guests and servants who could not drive ten miles to church.

This service, unless a clergyman happened to be staying at Geanies, he conducted himself, and ended it by reading a sermon. He had all his Presbyterian ancestors' love for a good discourse, and serious efforts had to be made to prevent him from reading too long a sermon.

Mozley's 'University Sermons' he liked particularly, and when these were divided, they were tolerated by his audience, who at first considered them much too long. He also read many of Dean Church's sermons.

He first knew the Dean in 1883, and although he only went very occasionally to the Deanery, he was greatly impressed by the striking personality of the great divine and scholar, whom to know was to love. The Dean's beautiful style, his great learning, his intel-

lectual sympathy with perplexities and troubles of heart
and mind, and the indefinable air of distinction which a
great writer stamps on every bit of work he undertakes,
all appealed to Mr. Romanes; and above and beyond
all these, the almost austere loftiness of thought, the
moral heights implied in Dean Church's writings,
seized on the mind of one who, beyond all else,
reverenced personal character and personal goodness.

He really enjoyed reading Dean Church's sermons,
and they exercised much influence on him. For
Newman, on the other hand, he had little liking, and
indeed he never did Newman adequate justice. He
had promised a friend just before his death to read
more of Newman, and discover for himself the great
gifts of that wonderful man, but there was not time.
Only one bit of Newman's writing was dear to him,
'Lead, kindly Light.'

The following letter rose out of a conversation
Mr. Romanes had with Dr. Paget, during one of the
Oxford visits:

The Palace, Ely : June 15, 1886,

My dear Romanes,—I have often and anxiously
thought over the question which you asked me when
you were at Oxford about your boy's education, and
the part which you should take in his religious training: and I would venture, with most true and
affectionate gratitude for your trust, to write a few
lines in partial qualification of what I then said.

I start on the ground of your own wish (for which
indeed I am with all my heart thankful) that your boy's
character should be fashioned after the Christian type
and under the influence of Christ. And I am as anxious
as ever that, even if your own estimate of the evidences

of Christianity should for a long while remain as it is, your children may never, in their later years, feel that you ever taught them anything which you did not believe: on every ground I long to avoid all danger of such a thought crossing their minds. But at the same time I do long that they may be spared to the very last possible moment the knowledge that in the judgment of the mind which they, I hope, will most reverence and love, the bases of their religious trust and hope are uncertain. It is only far on in life, I think, that a man comes to realise either the vast importance of things which are not held with absolute certainty, or the mysterious and complex nature of the act of faith, and the discipline of obscurity, and the way in which real spiritual progress may be going on where the mind seems only to be holding on, as it were, with fear and trembling.

To a boy of sixteen the mere knowledge of uncertainty in his father's mind may drain all the moral cogency out of the whole conception of religion :—the very suspicion of the uncertainty may unnerve him more than the full realisation of the doubt would change his father's aim and hope in doing his duty.

And so, at the risk of paining you—believe me, I would rather have the pain than give it you—and presuming very thankfully on the wish of which you spoke, I would plead that your children might remain as long as possible in ignorance of your uncertainty and anxiety; that they should only know in a general way that the religious influences, the principles of their Godward life which they receive, are given to them by your wish—that you would have them grow

up after that type, with that hope and aspiration;
and I would plead that *for their sakes* you should
suffer the pain, great as it may be, of being reticent
where you long to be ever communicative, ever unreserved. You may be unspeakably thankful some day
that you did so suffer :—and, whatever comes, you will
be sure of your children's deepest love and gratitude,
if ever they should know that this was one of your
acts of self-sacrifice for them.

Please forgive me, dear Romanes, where I have
written blunderingly, or given you unnecessary pain.
I pray God to guide and teach and gladden both you
and yours, and I am

Your affectionate friend,
FRANCIS PAGET.

Geanies, Ross-shire, N.B.: June 24. 1886.

My dear Paget,—I should indeed require to be
made of unduly sensitive material, if either the
extreme kindness of your thought or the most considerate delicacy of your expression could give me pain.
Pain I have, but it is of a kind that is beyond the
power of friends either to mitigate or to increase.

The advice which you give accords precisely with
my own view of the matter, and it is needless to say
that in such an agreement I find no small degree of
satisfaction. Moreover, the principles which it thus
appears to be my duty to adopt are made easy for me.
. . . So that on the whole it does not now appear to me
that in its practical aspects the problem is likely to
prove difficult of solution: although theoretically, or
as a matter of ethics, I do think it is a complex

question whether (or how far) parents should teach dogmas as facts, or matters of faith as matters of knowledge. Happily, however, ethics are to morals very much what shadow is to sunshine; and in seeking to follow the right or the good, instinct is often a better guide than syllogism.

And now, in conclusion, let me endeavour—inadequately as it must be—to express my deep sense of gratitude to you for having so earnestly taken my troubles into your consideration. I assure you that your letter has touched me truly, and that on its account I am more than ever happy to subscribe myself

Your affectionate friend,

GEO. J. ROMANES.

Journal says :—

April 12, 1885.—Went with the Church family to St. Paul's and heard a fine sermon from Dr. Liddon. He spoke very touchingly of Lady Selborne's death, and also alluded to Max Müller's new book.

Have been to Pfleiderer's Hibbert Lectures.[1] We met Pfleiderer the other day, and he described a Sunday in which he had tried to study English religious life. Spurgeon, Parker, and, I think, Stopford Brooke or Haweis, I forget which, he took as samples! Pfleiderer also went to St. Paul's on the day the Bishop of Lincoln[2] was consecrated, and as he got within earshot he heard Dr. Liddon's silvery voice pronouncing his own name *not* with approval.

Geanies, August.—Mr. Cotter Morison is here, and

---

[1] Mr. Romanes remarked *à propos* of Pfleiderer's lecture that St. Paul seemed to be a very hard nut for the lecturer to crack. [2] Dr. King.

is most amusing. Mr. Horsburgh asked two comic riddles: ' Why are men like telescopes and women like telegrams ? '

Men are like telescopes, because they are made to be drawn out and shut up ; and women are like telegrams because they far exceed the *males* (mails) in intelligence.

G. fiddled at an amateur concert at Tain.

Mr. F. Galton is here. He told us an amusing child's question : ' How did sausages get along when they were alive ? '

To Miss C. E. Romanes.

Geanies, Ross-shire : November 7, 1885.

The two Ethels left this afternoon *minus* their luggage and luncheon, which arrived at the station with the dog-cart just as the train was leaving. Pathetic it was to see their hungry eyes looking at the neat luncheon basket from the train windows ! We are all well here. L—— is here. He has now fired his first hundred cartridges, and has nothing to show but a brace of cats which he took a pot shot at in the trees.

November 12.

I am now playing at the last day in the old house, and doing so in the library all by myself. L—— left this morning, and we all leave to-morrow. Gerald now leads me from one room to another, and after opening the door and looking round each says, ' All gone !'

I have somewhat relieved the monotony of my solitary life by buying a horse. This you will no doubt think is a purchase well timed and thus worthy of a philosopher. For six months at least I shall have to pay for his keep, and never have a chance of a single bit of use for him all that time. Yet, strange to say, I think I have made a good bargain.

Nov., Edinburgh.—Dined at Dalmeny. We met Mr. and Mrs. Gladstone, and also Lieutenant Greely, of Arctic fame.

Nov., London.—Dinner with the F. Galtons, and met the Leckys and other nice people. Mr. Galton says the study of statistics fascinates him just as skating on thin ice does some people—it's so perilous.

Returning for a little while to the scientific work of these years, one may say that they were chiefly devoted to the more philosophical side of his work as a naturalist.

'Animal Intelligence,' 'Mental Evolution in Animals,' appeared respectively in 1881 and 1883, and are works designed to prove that the law of evolution is universal, and applies to the mind of man as well as to his bodily organisation.

Mr. Romanes read widely and observed much, and no one less deserved the charge of writing without observing, or of being a 'paper philosopher.' Both these books abound in stories of animals, and are full of interest for anyone caring at all for 'beasts,' quite apart from the special object of the books.

Lecturing and reviewing were, so to speak, pastimes to him, and gave him little trouble. One lecture given at the Royal Institution on ' The Mental Differences between Men and Women ' drew upon the head of the unlucky lecturer a great storm of indignation—why, the writer of this memoir has never been able to discover.

In May 1886, Mr. Romanes read a paper before the Linnean Society on ' Physiological Selection, an additional suggestion on the origin of species.' This paper was the outcome of many years' study of the philosophy of evolution, during which time he had gradually been coming to the conclusion that natural selection cannot be regarded as the sole guiding factor in the production of species, but that there must be some other cause at work in directing the course of evolution.

The theory of natural selection rests on two classes of observable facts: first, that all plants and animals are engaged in a perpetual struggle for existence, there being in every generation of every species a great many more individuals born than can possibly survive; and secondly, that the offsprings, although closely resembling the parent form, do present individual variations. It follows, therefore, that those individuals presenting variation in any way beneficial to them in the struggle for existence will survive as being the fittest to do so, Nature, so to speak, selecting certain individuals of each generation, enabling them not only to live themselves, but also to transmit their favourable qualities to their offspring. If a special line of variation is in some way preserved, there may result a variety so fixed and so distinct from the parent and collateral related forms as to constitute a separate species.

Further, since the environment (*i.e.* the sum total of the external conditions of life) is continually changing, it follows that natural selection may slowly alter a type in adaptation to the slowly changing environment, and if in any case the alterations effected are sufficient in amount to lead naturalists to name the result a distinct species, then natural selection has transmuted one specific type into another.

Mr. Romanes pointed out that the theory of natural selection only accounts for such organic changes as are of *use* to the species—by use signifying life-preserving—that it is, in fact, a theory of the origin and cumulative development of adaptations, whether these be distinctive of species, or of genera, families, classes, &c.

The question then arises, do species differ from species *solely* in points of a useful character, as they undoubtedly should do if natural selection has been the sole factor in their formation? Investigation shows that systematists recognise a species by a collection of characters, the value of a character depending not on its *utility*, but upon its *stability*; in fact, a large proportional number of specific characters, such as minute details of structure, form, and colour, are wholly without meaning from a utilitarian point of view. Investigation further shows that the most general of all the 'notes' of a true species is *cross-infertility*, that is, the infertility of the offspring of two individuals belonging to separate species: this, it was urged, could not be due to the action of natural selection. Lastly, apart from the primary distinction of cross-infertility, and the inutility of so many of the secondary specific distinctions, neither of which can be explained by the action of natural selection, Mr. Romanes was strongly of the opinion that even if a beneficial variation did arise, the swamping effects of free intercrossing would reabsorb it, and so render evolution of species in divergent lines, as distinguished from linear transmutation, impossible. This last difficulty can only be met by assuming that the same beneficial variation arises in a number of individuals simultaneously, for which assumption our present knowledge furnishes no warrant. If natural selection is brought forward as the sole factor in the guidance of organic evolution, then he considered that these difficulties remain insurmountable: if, however, it is regarded as a factor, even the chief factor, then these difficulties vanish, it being consistent, in the latter case, to hold the other factor, or factors, responsible for an explanation of the difficulties in question. It was the object of this paper to suggest another factor in the formation of species, which, although *independent* of natural selection, was in no way *opposed* to it, and might be called *supplementary* to it, and was at the same time capable of explaining the facts, of the *inutility of many specific characters*, the *cross-infertility of allied species*, and the *non-occurrence of free intercrossing*. Very briefly indicated, Mr. Romanes' line of argument is as follows:—Every generation of every species presents an enormous number of variations, of which only the ones that happen to be useful are preserved by natural selection. The useless variations are allowed to die out immediately by intercrossing.

Consequently, if intercrossing be prevented, there is no reason why unuseful variations should not be perpetuated by heredity quite as much as useful ones when under the nursing influence of natural selection. Thus, if from any cause, a section of a species is prevented from intercrossing with the rest of its parent form, it is to be expected that new varieties— for the most part of a trivial and unuseful kind— should arise within that section, and in time pass into new species. This supposition is borne out by the nature of the flora and fauna of oceanic islands, which are particularly rich in peculiar species, and where intercrossing was, of course, prevented with the original parent forms by the action of the geographical boundaries.

However, closely allied species are not always, or even generally, separated by geographical boundaries, and the cross-infertility remains to be explained. The cardinal feature of Mr. Romanes' theory is that the initial step in the origin of species is the arising of this infertility as an independent variation, by which, free intercrossing with the parent form on a common area is prevented, and specific differentiation rendered possible. Innumerable varieties are known to occur which do not pass into distinct species, the reason being that this initial variation, that is, incipient infertility whereby the swamping effects of intercrossing might be obviated, was lacking, and the variations became re-absorbed. That is, given any degree of sterility towards the parental form which does not extend to the varietal form, then a new species must take its origin. Without the bar of sterility, in Mr. Romanes' opinion, free intercrossing must render the formation of species impossible. Mutual sterility is thus the cause, not the result, of specific differentiation. As regards the occurrence of this initial variation, the reproductive system is known to be highly variable, its variability taking the form either of increased fertility, or of sterility in all degrees, and depending on either extrinsic causes (changes of food, climate, &c.), or on an intrinsic cause arising in the system itself.

From the nature of this additional factor at work in the formation of species, Mr. Romanes called his theory 'physiological selection.'

Physiological selection is conceived of as co-operating with natural selection, the former allowing the latter to act by interposing its law of sterility, with the result that the secondary specific characters may be either adaptive or non-adaptive in character.

To Miss C. E. Romanes.

Aix-les-Bains: May 1886.

The Linnean Society paper went off admirably. There was a larger attendance than ever I saw there before. But this may have been partly due to the president (Lubbock) having had a paper down for the same evening. He was considerate enough to withdraw it at the last moment so as to leave all the evening for mine. I spoke for an hour and a half, and the discussion lasted another hour. The paper itself I have brought with me here, and am now putting the last touches upon it.

Probably I shall have to try the rat experiment again, if the young ones show no signs of piebalding. But look at them occasionally to see.

There would be no use in getting the parrot to make a gesture sign at the same time as he makes a verbal one ; for, as you say, he would only show that he can establish an association between a phrase and a thing (whether object, quality, or action), and about this there is no question. The question is whether he can use verbal signs, not only as stereotyped in phrases (when they are really equivalent to only one word), but as movable types, which he can transpose for the purpose of expressing *different* ideas with the *same* words.

He writes concerning a Junior Scientific Society which had a meeting to discuss his theory :

'The meeting was the best fun imaginable, the paper was merely a statement of my theory by a young man who made it very clear. —— got up and expressed disapproval of the theory, but expressly declined to argue, so I had merely to give him some chaff. The young men highly enjoyed it. Afterwards they were enthusiastic in their applause.

'I have no doubt, if I had not been present, the class would have had a very different impression both of me and my theory.'

To Professor Meldola.

Geanies: September 16, 1886.

Dear Professor Meldola,—Physiological selection seems to have brought a regular nest of hornets about my head. If I had known there was to have been so much talk about it at the British Association I should have gone up to defend the new-born. If you were there, can you let me know the main objections that were urged? It seems to me there is a good deal of misunderstanding abroad, due, no doubt, to the insufficiency with which my theory has been stated. In 'studying' the paper, therefore, please keep steadily in view that the backbone of the whole consists in regarding mutual sterility as the *cause* (or at least, the chief *condition*) instead of the *result* of specific differentiation. This is just the opposite view to that now held by all evolutionists, and, I believe, by Darwin himself. (See 'Origin,' pp. 245–246; 'Variation,' ii. pp. 171–175.) Now, if this view be sound, my theory is obviously not restricted to any one class of causes that may induce mutual sterility. Such cases may be either extrinsic or intrinsic as regards the reproductive system; they may be either direct in their action on that system or indirect (*e.g.* natural selection, or use and disuse, &c., producing morphological changes elsewhere, which in turn react on that system); therefore these causes may act either on a few or on many individuals. Yet Wallace does not seem to see this, but argues in the 'Fortnightly' that they can only act on an individual here and there.

I sincerely hope you will give your attention to the subject, because the great danger I now fear is prejudice against the theory on account of people not taking the trouble to understand it. How absurd —   , for example, giving that quotation from 'Origin' in 'Nature,' as evidence of Mr. Darwin's having considered the theory. Read with its context, the passage is arguing (much against the writer's desire) that variations in the way of sterility with parent forms cannot be seized upon (or perpetuated as specific distinctions) by natural selection. But physiological selection says that such variations *do not require to be seized upon by natural selection.* Therefore, so far as the passage in question proves anything, it tends to show that nothing could have been further from the mind of the writer than a theory which would have rendered his whole argument superfluous, and I can scarcely believe that if the theory of physiological selection had ever occurred to him, he would not have mentioned it, if only to state his objections to it, as he has done with regard to so many ideas of a much less feasible character.

I write at length because I value your judgment more than that of almost anybody else upon a subject of this kind, and therefore I should like it to be given with your eyes open. Prejudice at first there must be, but there need not be misunderstanding; and private correspondence shows me that the theory has already struck root in some of the best minds who do understand it. Any explanation, therefore, will be gladly given you by

Yours very truly,
GEO. J. ROMANES.

To F. Darwin, Esq.

Geanies : November 5, 1886.

Dear Darwin,—I am much interested by the enclosed, and therefore much obliged to you for letting me see it. But it would have been made a better 'answer' if it had gone on to say something about the relation of such an experiment (supposing it successful) to the question of originating a species. Some weeks ago I was planning with a friend a closely analogous experiment, but designed to produce a 'family' which would be sterile towards the majority of the parent form, or not only towards one other 'family.' And it seemed to me that if this could be done it would amount to the artificial creation of a new species by conscious selection of a physiological kind.

But, as far as I can gather from the enclosed, the idea seems to be that of experimenting on the conditions leading to sterility ; not that of regarding sterility, however conditional, as itself the condition of specific divergence. In other words, the passage seems to go upon the supposition that sterility is the result and not the cause of specific divergence. But if so, I do not see that it affects the question whether he ever contemplated the latter possibility.

I have just received Seebohm's British Association paper, which, except when it repeats Wallace's objection about the doctrine of chances, elsewhere curiously contradicts all the points in his criticism.

The editor of the 'Fortnightly' tells me that a further delay has arisen in bringing out my reply, on account of Wallace desiring to answer it. For my own part I think that all this fire of criticism at the present juncture is a mistake. As yet the theory is only a 'suggestion,' and, until tested, there can be no adequate data for forming a definite opinion.

Therefore I regret the published opposition—those who are in favour do not publish only because it may tend to choke off co-operation in carrying out the experiments ; and it was for the sake of securing assistance in so laborious a research that I published the suggestion in outline.

I wonder who Catchpole is? His answer in 'Nature' to Wallace won't do.

Yours very truly,
GEO. J. ROMANES.

18 Cornwall Terrace, Regent's Park, N.W.: January 7, 1887.

Dear Darwin,—Some time ago you write that I ought to read a book or paper by Jordan about varieties in relation to sterility. I cannot find any book or paper of his at the L.S. library which treats of this subject ; could you give me the name of his essay?

I am making arrangements for trying whether there are any degrees of sterility to be found between well-marked and constant varieties of plants. But as I have never done anything in the way of hybridising, perhaps you would be good enough to let me know whether the enclosed plan of experimenting represents the full and proper way of going to work. I know that you do not believe in the object of it, but, even supposing it to be a wild goose chase, there would be no harm in your telling me the best way to run. Then, whether the results prove positive or negative, it will not be open for any one to doubt them on the ground of any fault in the method.

Do any objections occur to you *re* my answer to critics in the 'Nineteenth Century'? Of course I might have said more about the swamping effects of free intercrossing (which appears to me the only point in which I deviate at all from the 'Origin of Species'), but it is much too large a subject to be dealt with in a review. My greatest difficulty here is to conceive the possibility of differentiation (as distinguished from transmutation in linear series) without the assistance of isolation in some form or another.

Yours very truly,
GEO. J. ROMANES.

Dear Darwin,—Criticism of an intelligent kind is what I feel most in need of, and therefore it is no merit on my part to like it when it comes.

The point about the combined action of natural and physiological selection is, after all, a very subordinate one, and, as I said in 'Nature' some weeks ago, is the most highly speculative and least trustworthy part of the theory. Moreover, it is the only part that is directly opposed to an expressed conclusion in the 'Origin,' though, even here, the opposition is not real. If natural selection can do anything at all in the way of bringing about sterility with parent forms, it can only do so by acting on the type or whole community (for I quite agree with the reasoning in the 'Origin,' that it cannot do so by acting on individuals); and whether natural selection could in any case act on a type is a question which your father has told me he could never quite make up his mind about, except in the case of social hymenoptera and moral sense of man.

You will see what I mean by 'secondary variations' by looking at page 366 of my paper. It is merely a short-hand expression for all other specific differences save the sexual difference of sterility. My view is that these secondary differences are always sure to arise sooner or later in some direction or another wherever a portion of a species is separated from the rest, whether by geographical or physiological isolation, which, indeed, as regards the former, is no more than you (following Weismann, &c.) acknowledge. Now, to me it seems obvious that Weismann's 'variations' (*i.e.* slight changes in the form of shells) cannot possibly be themselves my 'physiological sports,' although they may very well be the consequences of such a sport leading to physiological isolation, and so to independent variation in two or three directions simultaneously, till afterwards blended by inter-crossing. And my reason for thinking this is that 'Weismann's variations' always arose in crops at enormously long intervals of time. On the mere doctrine of chances it therefore becomes impossible to suppose that each of these variations was due to a separate physiological sport, although it is easy to see how each crop of them might have been so. For, if not, why should they always have arisen in crops, each member of which was demonstrably fertile with the other members of that crop, while no less demonstrably sterile with the original parent form? Therefore, what I see in these facts is precisely what, upon my theory, I should expect to see, viz. first, a 'primary variation,' or 'physiological sport,' arising at long intervals; secondly, closely following upon this, a crop of 'secondary variations' in the way of slight morphological changes affecting two or three different 'strains' simultaneously; and thirdly, an eventual blending of these strains by intercrossing with one another without being able to intercross with the surrounding and (at first) very much more numerous parent form.

But I can now quite understand why you thought these facts were 'dead against' me: you thought that every single slight change of morphology must (on my theory) have had a separate 'physiological sport' to account for it. This, however, most emphatically is not my theory. Physiological isolation I regard as having morphological consequences precisely analogous to those of geographical isolation; and you would not think of arguing that there must be a separate geographical isolation for every slight change of structure—for example, that a peculiar species of plant growing on a mountain top must have had one isolation to explain its change of form, and another isolation to explain its change of colour.

Lastly, if you will look up Hilgendorf's paper about these snails of Steinheim, I think you will find it impossible to suppose that all these little changes (thus arising at long intervals in crops) can have been useful. Or, if you can still doubt, look up the closely analogous but much larger case of the ammonites investigated by Neumayr and Wurtenberger.

What I meant about the sexual system being specially liable to variation is, that it is specially liable to variation in the way of sterility. In other words, changed conditions of life more readily effect variations in the primary functions of the sexual system than they do in general morphology. But at the same time, I quite agree with your view that in the last resort all changes of structure may be regarded as due to variations of this system. And, as you will see by turning to pp. 371–72 of my paper, important capital is made out of this doctrine.

Now about making too much of the inutility of specific characters; if I do so, it is erring on the side of natural selection; for it clearly follows from this theory that, if there are any useless structures at all, they ought to occur with (greater?) frequency among species, where (as?) yet natural selection has not had time to remove them. But I cannot think I have here unduly favoured natural selection. For although there are not a few instances of apparently useless structures running through even an entire class (as the ‘Origin’ remarks), these are not only infinitely less numerous than apparently useless structures in species, but are also very much more rarely trivial.

Now the latter fact, coupled with that of the greatly wider range of their occurrence, appears to me intensely to strengthen ‘the argument from ignorance,’ *i.e.* to give us much more justification for believing that they are now, or once were, of use.

For in the case of species, the '*once were*' possibility is virtually excluded.

A propos to this point, I do not believe that any-one yet has half done justice to natural selection in respect of its action subsequent to the formation of species—at least, not expressly. But I must shut up.

I should greatly like to see Jordan's paper. Sir J. Hooker and Professor Oliver have sent me references to literature, but neither of them mention this.

Why my answer to Wallace has not appeared in this month's 'Fortnightly' I am at a loss to understand. The editor bullied me with letters and telegrams to have it ready in time, till I laid everything else aside, and sent him back the proof on the 15th.

This new theory roused the public interest (so far as the scientific public were concerned) and produced much criticism.

There is a scientific orthodoxy as well as a theological orthodoxy 'plus loyal que le roi,' and by the ultra-Darwinians Mr. Romanes was regarded as being strongly tainted with heresy.

The 'Times' devoted a leader in August 1886 to the theory, and the president of Section *D* at the British Association at Bath in the same month also criticised it.

A sharp discussion took place in the columns of 'Nature,' and it is characteristic of those who took the chief part in this controversy that their friendly relations remained undisturbed. Mr. Wallace criticised the theory in the 'Fortnightly,' and Mr.

Romanes wrote an article in the ' Nineteenth Century ' describing his beliefs on the subject. This theory was very close to his heart, and perhaps no part of his work was left unfinished with more keen regret.

He planned a course of experiments on plants in an alpine garden which, through the kindness of M. Correvon, Professor of Botany at Geneva, he was able to begin on a plot of ground near Bourg St. Pierre, on the great St. Bernard.

Other work diverted him a good deal from this, but Mr. Romanes had always large plans of work, looking forward through a course of years.

There were some experiments on the power dogs possess of tracking by scent, in the autumn of 1886.

With this year came the appointment to a Lectureship in the University of Edinburgh on ' The Philosophy of Natural History.'[1] This lectureship Mr. Romanes held for five years, and he enjoyed the fortnight's residence in Edinburgh it involved, and the meetings with Edinburgh people. He gave to his class a course on the History of Biology, and then proceeded to take them through a course of lectures on the Evidences of Organic Evolution, on the theories of Lamarck, of Mr. Darwin himself, and on post-Darwinian theories. These lectures he worked up into the three years' course he gave as Fullerian Professor at the Royal Institution, with many additions and alterations. The substance of them now appears in ' Darwin and after Darwin,' parts i. and ii. A third volume was to have been devoted to Physiological Selection, and enough was prepared in the form of notes to justify publication.

At the end of 1886 there fell on the Romanes family a bitter sorrow. Of the Geanies ' brotherhood,' the brightest and merriest, a remarkably handsome, joyous girl, absolutely unselfish and sweet,

---

[1] Through the kindness of Lord Rosebery.

most dearly loved and loving, was the first to die.
Her death was a terrible sorrow not only to her own
immediate circle of relations, but to the friends to
whom she had been as a very dear sister. On Mr.
Romanes this death, so sudden and so startling,
made a deep and lasting impression. From this
time more and more he turned in the direction of
faith, and his feelings found an outlet in poetry more
frequently and more effectually than before.

To Miss C. E. Romanes.

Edinburgh: Christmas Day, 1886.

My dearest Charlotte,—The time has come when
it is some relief to write, but how shall I begin to tell
the sadness of the saddest tragedy that has ever been
put together? First the hours of fluctuating hope,
and then the growing darkness of despair. She had
previously asked whether Ethel and G. J.[1] had come
down from London, and on being told that we were
in the house was so glad. We were admitted at night,
and only had to watch for three hours the peaceful
breathing, slower, slower, slower, until the last. Oh,
the unearthly beauty of that face! Nothing I have ever
seen in flesh or in marble—nothing I could have ever
conceived could approach it. But try to picture it
as you knew it in life changed into something so yet
more beautiful that it seemed no longer human, but
the face of the angel that she was. Then in one room
her little child, in another her mother, utterly broken
by illness. For my own part I have never had a
grief so great as this. Even in our sister's case there

---

[1] One of Mr. Romanes' numerous pet names.

were elements of mitigation ; but here absolutely none. Oh, it is bitter, bitter ; so much of life's happiness emptied out and Edith, our own Edith, no longer here !

In memory of this friend Mr. Romanes wrote a little poem called 'To a Bust,' and from this a few lines are given.

There is one point to which the writer of this memoir would like to call attention.

Mr. Romanes was incapable of exaggeration, of writing for effect, of insincerity. What he *wrote* he *felt*, and his very simplicity and sweetness of character, his childlike trust in the sympathy of others, made him unreserved to his friends, to those whom he loved.

> 'Upon that Christmas Eve
>   We saw thee pass away,
>
> .   .   .   .
>
> We heard the music of thy parting breath ;
>   We saw a light of angels in thy face—
> A beauty so ineffable, that Death
>   Was changed into a minister of Grace :
>
> .   .   .   .   .   .
>
>   The mountains in their autumn hues,
>   Of mountain reds and mountain blues,
>   With heather and with highland bells.
>   Await thy step on hills and fells ;
>   The spongy peat and dewy moss
>   Remember where we used to cross—
>   Remember how they loved thy tread,
>   Make for thy steps their softest bed :
>   The murmuring streams are calling thee.
>   The woodlands sigh in every tree ;
>   Yet when I walk upon the shore,
>   The waves are whispering—nevermore !
>
>   Mournfully, mournfully whispering, they,
>   Whispering, whispering every day,
>   Thy soul in their waters, thy breath in their spray,
>   Thy spirit still speaking in all that they say.

> They knew thee well, those weedy rocks,
> And now they rear their rugged blocks
>   When I pass by,
>   To ask me why
> They never feel thy tender hands ;
> And all the yellow of the sands
>   Is spread to greet
>   Thy tireless feet,
> Which loved to walk them when the tide was low.
>
>   Now when I walk alone,
>   To hear the ocean moan,
>   The sea-birds circling round
>   Sweep almost to the ground,
> And peep and pry above my head to know
>   Why thou dost never come,
>   To watch them flying home,
>   Upon the purple breast,
>   Where daylight sinks to rest.'

The Journal 1887, 1888, and 1889 is full of mention of pleasant dinners and meetings with interesting people. Young as Mr. Romanes was, he attained long before he died 'that which should accompany old age—honour, love, obedience, troops of friends,' and as one turns over the brief records of the Journal one is struck with the brightness of his outward life. He enjoyed constant pleasant intercourse with men and women differing widely in pursuits, in opinions, in social position ; he was full of plans for work, work which led him into many different phases of intellectual life, and he had every year an admixture of country life and country pursuits, and the love for music and for poetry, which increased each year, kept him from growing too absorbed in science, from being at all one-sided. He used sometimes to say he had too many interests, but be that as it may, these interests gave him much enjoyment and made him the most delightful of companions.

A dear friend wrote of him after his death that ' In the home few men have been more surrounded by love, or have better deserved it,' and few men have been more loved by those outside his home. He had an unlimited capacity for loyal, true-hearted friendship. As one most truly said, 'Romanes was the most loyal of friends.'

There was something womanly in the tenderness which he felt for anyone in trouble of mind or body, and he was—what perhaps is even more rare—always ready to put aside his own work to help other people. He never grudged time or trouble to write letters or testimonials ; he was always ready to go and see people who were sad or lonely ; he was never too busy to be kind. He was intensely loved by those who served him, and few have been better served. There were very few changes in his household, and no one was ever more unwilling to give needless trouble, to find fault without cause, than he, or more ready to be really grateful for the ungrudging and loving and devoted service he received. 'You were the nicest master I ever served,' wrote a gamekeeper. 'To think I have lived for fifteen years with him and never heard a cross word,' was said the day he was taken from his home. In money matters he was generous and almost lavish in readiness to give and also to lend.

In Mr. Romanes there was a certain chivalrous temper which could be roused to strong indignation where it was encountered by injustice and oppression, and the following letter to the 'Times' is one of many such :

To the Editor of the ' Times.'

Sir,—On several previous occasions I have been instrumental in obtaining remission of grievous sentences at the police-courts by simply drawing attention in your correspondence columns to the cases as they appear in your police reports. Adopting this course, I think that the following, which appeared in your issue of the 29th ult., requires some explanation :

'At Wandsworth, James Clarke, aged 17, a weakly-looking lad, residing at Byegrove Road, Mitcham, was charged with stealing two turnips, value 3*d.*, growing in a field belonging to Mr. H. Bunce, at Merton. The prosecutor having lost a quantity of produce, Police Constable Whitty was set to watch the property, and saw the prisoner pull the turnips and put them in his pocket. The accused said he had had nothing to eat all day, and being very hungry, he took the turnips ! A previous conviction was proved against him for felony, and he was now committed by Mr. Denman for six weeks' hard labour.'

One would like to possess a good large field of turnips, where each turnip can be fairly valued at $1\frac{1}{2}$*d.* But, taking this as the true value of the particular turnips in question, it appears that a starving man is now serving a week's hard labour for every half-penny's worth of the cheapest possible kind of food that he could steal. It is, of course, very right that he should have received some measure of punishment, if only as a warning to others in the neighbourhood; but the measure of punishment which he did receive seems, in the face of the matter, monstrous. We are not told what was the ' felony ' for which this ' weakly-looking lad ' was previously convicted ; but, at any rate, we do know that on the present occasion his theft was not for any purpose of gain. It must

have been, as he said, merely to alleviate the pains of
hunger, for otherwise he would have carried some
more capacious receptacle than either his pockets or
his stomach. On the whole, therefore, I say—and
say emphatically—this case demands some explanation.

I am, Sir, yours, &c.,

LL.D.

He was always ready to listen to what younger
men (and women) had to say, to talk to them about
his own subjects, his own work, to draw out their
abilities, to discuss their difficulties. What Mr.
Lionel Tollemache has written of Professor Owen is
not less applicable to him :

'His innate modesty enabled him, when speaking
upon his own subject, so to let himself down to the
level of the ordinary listeners that they not only felt
quite at their ease with him, but fancied for the
moment that they were experts like himself.'

Journal, Jan. 1888.—Met Mr. Burne-Jones at
the Humphry Wards', and had much interesting
talk anent Rossetti. Burne-Jones said Rossetti was
like an emperor; his voice was that of a king who
could *quell* his subjects. Also that he had a wonderful memory for metre, but that Swinburne's is
better still, inasmuch as he can remember prose.
On one occasion Swinburne recited to Burne-Jones
several pages of Milton's prose which he had read
once twenty years previously. Burne-Jones went on
to say that Rossetti worked a great deal at his poetry,
and added, 'That's what you can do with words,

worry them as much as you like, but you can't *tease*
a picture.'

March 9.—Mr. Leslie Stephen lectured on Cole-
ridge most admirably.

To Miss C. E. Romanes.

18 Cornwall Terrace : March 1, 1888.

My dearest Charlotte,—I find that neither of us
wrote yesterday, so I have two of your letters to
answer to-day.

You certainly seem to be having much the best
time of it as regards weather. Every week and every
day here is worse than the last—the month which
has just ended having been the most savage February
in the memory of living Londoners. You will have
seen that poor Cotter Morison has not survived it.
He died last Sunday, just too soon to see his son, who
had been telegraphed home from India. He had a
great desire to live long enough to have had this
meeting, and it seems hard that when he struggled
on so long and painfully at the end, that he should
just have missed it.

For Mr. Morison Mr. Romanes had a great regard,
and his death was a real sorrow.

Journal.—Sir F. Bramwell lectured on the ' Faults
of the Decimal System,' calling it a lecture without
a *point*. He was killingly amusing. Dinner at Sir
H. Thompson's, met Mr. J. Froude, Hannen, and
others.

We met the author of ' The New Antigone ' the other night at the Lillys'. He reviewed ' Mental Evolution in Man ' in a R.C. paper the other day : according to him it's the Gospel of Dirt ! Last Sunday we went to hear Spurgeon ; of *his* personal goodness there is no doubt.

May 14.—Stayed in Christ Church with the Pagets. G. had a most interesting talk with Aubrey Moore. Mr. Romanes had already, at the Aristotelian Society, met Mr. Aubrey Moore. Lunched on Sunday with the Max Müllers. He showed us a letter from Mr. Darwin most characteristic in its humility and sweetness.

May 20.—Very fine sermon from Mr. Scott-Holland on the Evidence of the Gospels. Tea at the Deanery, and G. had a little talk with the Dean.

There are frequent mentions now of Mr. Scott-Holland, whom Mr. Romanes often went to hear.

In 1888 appeared ' Mental Evolution in Man.'

To Miss C. E. Romanes.

Cornwall Terrace : May 18. 1888.

My own book is certain to make a ' commotion.' if not among ' the angels ' in heaven,[1] at least among ' the saints ' upon earth. One of these same saints has been behaving outrageously in print, and everybody is full either of jubilation or indignation at

---

[1] This is in allusion to a minister of a small country parish in Scotland, who prayed that there might be at this time, on account of this parish, ' a very great commotion among the angels.'

what he has been writing about Darwin and Darwinism. F. Darwin asked me to do the replying, and to-day I am returning proof of an article for the 'Contemporary Review.'

I am ashamed to have been so long in writing, but the truth is that, notwithstanding having put down *Finis* to my M.S., other things occurred to me to add, which required recasting some of the chapters, and so I have been fighting against time, and am still.

It will not be long now before you have the children.

They are looking forward with great glee to Dunskaith; but you must take care that they do not make it *too* lively. I never saw such nice children myself, but James may find them over-noisy when they are particularly high-spirited. His godson is the most comical chap that ever was born. He has a passion for what he calls 'loaded matches,' *i.e.* matches unused, and so ready to 'go off.' Yesterday his fingers were found to be burnt. Asked as to the cause, he said he had lighted some loaded matches and held his fingers in the flames so as to see if he could 'keep back crying.' This he seems to have done to his own satisfaction, and now wants to prove his prowess in public. Little Ethel was found bathed in tears a few days ago in a room by herself, and the grief turned out to have been on account of the death of the Emperor.[1]

You ask how the lectures are 'going on.' They are 'going on' rather too well. Owing to Schäfer

<hr>

[1] Of Germany.

having been taken ill with bronchitis, I agreed to relieve him of some engagements he had entered into for giving lectures to a Highgate Institution. Consequently I had to give two lectures on Tuesday (in the afternoon at the Institution, and in the evening at Highgate), and another yesterday, besides attending Council meetings, &c. The Institution lectures give much more satisfaction than I anticipated, as I thought the historical character of this year's course would appeal but to a small number of people. But the audience keeps up to between one hundred and two hundred very steadily (usually one hundred and fifty), and is in part made up of outsiders. But I shall not be sorry when they are over, as it will leave me more time for better work.

I am sorry that there still continue to be so many ups and downs in your daily reports.[1] The case is, indeed, dreadfully tedious. How would you like me to run down to see you after my lectures are over?

I enclose a photo which has just come from a man who is photographing the Royal Society.

We are all well and flying about in all directions. Such a time for dinners and concerts and all manner of things; it is a wonder that we are living at all, as old Jean[2] used to say.

To J. Romanes, Esq.

March 15, 1889.

I am glad you think so well of what I write, for it often seems to me that, amid so many distractions

---

[1] His brother was ill.　　　　[2] An old nurse.

and in so many directions, I work to very little purpose. The 'Guardian' reviewer[1] has written to me a private letter, from which it appears that he is a man I know very well. He is Aubrey Moore, of Oxford, and is considered one of the ablest men there. I enclose his letter, which I failed to send before.

It is indeed a change for you to like being nursed, and perhaps not altogether a bad one from the character point of view. The only 'explanation' I can give is that of the 'adaptation of the organism to *changed conditions* of life.'

About this time Mr. Romanes drew up a paper, which is given here, as it may interest some readers.

18 Cornwall Terrace, Regent's Park, London, N.W.

Dear Sir or Madam,—While engaged in collecting materials for a work on Human Psychology, I have been surprised to find the greatness of the differences which obtain between different races, and even between different individuals of the same race, concerning sentiments which attach to the thoughts of death. With the view, if possible, of ascertaining the causes of such differences, I am addressing a copy of the appended questions to a large number of representative and average individuals of both sexes, various nationalities, creeds, occupations, &c. It would oblige me if you would be kind enough to further the object of my inquiry by answering some or all of these questions, and adding any remarks

---

[1] Mr. Aubrey Moore reviewed *Mental Evolution in Man* in the *Guardian*.

that may occur to you as bearing upon the subject.

In order to save unnecessary trouble, I may explain that, in the event of your not caring to answer any of the questions, I shall not expect you to acknowledge this letter; and that, if you should reply, answers to many of the questions may be most briefly furnished by underlining the portion of each, which by its repetition would serve to convey your answer.

It is needless to add that the names of my correspondents will not be published.

I am yours very faithfully,
GEORGE J. ROMANES.

(1) Do you regard the prospect of your own death (A) with indifference, (B) with dislike, (c) with dread, or (D) with inexpressible horror?

(2) If you entertain any fear of death at all, is the cause of it (A) prospect of bodily suffering only, (B) dread of the unknown, (c) idea of loneliness and separation from friends, or (D) in addition to all or any of these, a peculiar horror of an indescribable kind?

(3) Is the state of your belief with regard to a future life that of (A) virtual conviction that there is a future life, (B) suspended judgment inclining towards such belief, (c) suspended judgment inclining against such belief, or (D) virtual conviction that there is no such life?

(4) Is your religious belief, if any, (A) of a vivid order, or (B) without much practical influence on your life and conduct?

(5) Is your temperament naturally of (A) a courageous or (B) of a timid order as regards the prospect of bodily pain or mental distress?

(6) More generally, do you regard your own disposition as (A) strong, determined, and self-reliant; (B) nervous, shrinking, and despondent; or (c) medium in this respect?

(7) Should you say that in your character the intellectual or the emotional predominates? Does your intellect incline to abstract or concrete ways of thought? Is it theoretical, practical, or both? Are your emotions of the tender or heroic order, or both? Are your tastes in any way artistic, and, if so, in what way, and with what strength?

(8) What is your age or occupation? Can you trace any change in your feelings with regard to death as having taken place during the course of your life?

(9) If ever you have been in danger of death, what were the circumstances, and what your feelings?

(10) Remarks.

(Signature.) [1]

This communication well exemplifies the spirit in which Mr. Romanes approached the problems of animal faculty. He spent, indeed, much time and labour in collecting and classifying the observations and anecdotes which he published in ' Animal Intelligence '; but he lost no opportunities of observing and experimenting for himself. In this, as in other departments of inquiry, his constant effort was to be in direct and immediate touch with facts. His observations on his own dogs, especially those which he published in his article [2] on ' Fetichism in Animals,' wherein he describes the effects on a terrier of the apparent coming to life of a dry bone which the dog had been playing with, and to which a fine thread

---

[1] I have not been able to discover any answer to these.

[2] *Nature*, vol. xvii. p. 168.

had been attached, and those which dealt with the power of tracking their master by scent,[1] further exemplify his careful methods and his resort, wherever possible, to experimental conditions. His observations, too, on the 'homing' of bees,[2] by which he showed that the insects find their way back to the hive through their experience of the topography and by knowledge of landmarks, rather than through any mysterious innate faculty or sense of direction, are the work of a scientific observer, and very different from the chance tales of a mere anecdotist.

The whole subject of comparative psychology had a special and peculiar fascination for Mr. Romanes, partly on account of its intimate connection with the theory of evolution, and partly from its bearing on those deeper philosophic problems which were never long absent from his thoughts. His treatment of the phenomena of instinct in 'Mental Evolution in Animals,' and elsewhere, was both comprehensive and exact, and still forms, in the opinion of competent authorities, the best general account of the subject that we have; though, had he lived to review and consolidate his work, some changes would probably have been introduced in view of later discussions on the nature and method of hereditary transmission. His arguments in 'Mental Evolution in Man,' in support of the essential similarity of the reasoning processes in the higher animals and in man, created a stir, at the time of their publication, which was in itself evidence that his critics felt that they had a writer and thinker that must be seriously and sharply met. He hoped by this work to win over the psychologists to the evolution camp; and he himself felt strongly that in some cases, when he failed fully to convince them of the adequacy of his

---

[1] *Nature*, vol. xxxvi. p. 273.   [2] *Nature*, vol. xxxii. p. 630.

method of treatment and of the arguments he adduced, it was rather in matters of definition than in matters of fact that the source of their differences lay. He was somewhat disappointed that his terms 'recept' and 'receptual' for mental products intermediate between the 'percept' and the 'concept' were not more generally accepted by psychologists, since, in his matured opinion, they and the conception they represent were eminently helpful in bridging the debatable space between the intellectual powers of man and the faculties of the lower animals.

It was Mr. Romanes' intention to continue the mental evolution series and to deal, in further instalments of his work, with the intellectual emotions, volition, morals, and religion. This intention, however, he did not live to fulfil. His further development of mental evolution in the light of his later conclusions in the region of philosophical and religious thought would have been profoundly interesting. But one's regret that this part of his life work remained incomplete is tempered by the recollection that what he did complete was so worthily done. For, in the words of Mr. Lloyd Morgan, which were quoted with approval by Dr. Burdon Sanderson in his Royal Society obituary notice: 'by his patient collection of data; by his careful discussion of these data in the light of principles clearly and definitely formulated; by his wide and forcible advocacy of his views; and, above all, by his own observations and experiments, Mr. Romanes left a mark in this field of investigation and interpretation which is not likely to be effaced.'

In 1889 Mr. Romanes attended the British Association which met that year at Newcastle. Here, he and Professor Poulton had a long discussion on the 'Inheritance of Acquired Characters'; he spoke so much, and was so much *en évidence*, at this Association that the Newcastle papers described him as a most belligerent person.

He wrote afterwards from Edinburgh :

Things progress as usual. After my lecture I played chess with Mrs. Butcher and dined with the Logans. Margaret, in telling me the pretty things she had heard, drew from her husband the rebuke that she was not judicious. So I told them your estimate of my merits, and Charles [1] was quite satisfied that I was in good keeping.

You have made a ' philosophical ' mistake about the dinner party to the R.'s which, of course, I imitated. Butcher has given me a MS. of his to read on the ' Psychology of the Ludicrous.' Seems very good.

To Professor Poulton.

Newcastle : Monday. September 1889.

My dear Poulton,—I am very glad to receive your long and friendly letter ; because, although I have the Ishmael-like reputation of finding my hand against every man, and every man's against mine. my blasto-genetic endowments are really of the peaceful order. Moreover, in the present instance the ' row ' was not one that affected me with any feelings of real opposi-tion, although it seemed expedient to point out that a somewhat hasty inference had not been judiciously stated. Therefore, I take it, we may now cordially, as well as formally, shake hands, and probably be better friends than ever. In token of which I may

---

[1] C. Logan, Esq., W.S., who had married Mr. Romanes' cousin.

begin by furnishing the explanation of what was
meant by the passage in the 'Contemporary Review'
to which you alluded.

I quite agree that Weismann's suggestion about
causes of variability is an admirable one. But it has
always seemed to me that it is comprised under
Darwin's general category of causes internal to the
organism (or, in his terminology, causes due to 'the
nature of the organism'). But besides this, he recognised the category of causes external to the organism
(or the so-called Lamarckian principles of direct
action of environment, *plus* inherited efforts of use
and disuse). Now, anyone who accepts this latter
category as comprising *veræ causæ*, obviously has a
larger area of causality on which to draw for his
theoretical explanations of variability, than has a
man who expressly limits the possibility of such
causes to the former category. This is all that I
had in my mind when writing the line in the 'Contemporary Review' which led you to suppose that I
was expounding W. without having read him; and
although I freely allow that the meaning was one
that required explanation to bring out, you may
remember that this meaning had nothing whatever
to do with the subject which I was expounding,
and therefore it was that I neglected to draw it out.
You will observe that, so far as the present matter
is concerned, it does not signify what views we
severally take touching the validity of Lamarckian
hypotheses. The point is, that anyone who sees
his way to entertaining them thereby furnishes
himself with a larger field of causality for explaining

variations than does a man who limits that field
to causes internal to organisms—even though, like
W., he suggests an extension of the latter.

And now about the ' Athenaeum.' I fear you think
I have been taking an unfair opportunity of giving
you a back-hander. In point of fact, however, I never
do such things ; and the more reason I have for anything like hitting back (which, however, is entirely
absent on the present occasion), the more careful
should I be to avoid any appearance of doing so in an
unsigned review. I neither wrote, nor have I read
the particular review in question.

Regarding articulation, read in my 'Mental
Evolution in Man,' Mr. Hales' admirable remarks on
children having probably been the constructors of all
languages, I believe this theory will prove to be the
true solution of the origin of *languages*, as distinguished from the faculty of *language*. What you say
about the latter being blastogenetic, requires you to
unsay what is said by W.

Please let me know whether there is anything
that you see in my ' cessation of selection ' different
from W.'s ' Panmixia.' The debate to-day failed to
furnish any opposition.

Yours very sincerely,
G. J. Romanes.

Geanies, Ross-shire, N.B. : October 21, 1889.

My dear Poulton,—Many thanks for your interesting letter. From it I quite understand your views
about the relation between reproduction and repair ;
are they those of Weismann or altogether your own ?

And have they, as yet, been published anywhere? If not, I suppose it is undesirable to allude to them in public? The theory is ingenious, but seems to sail rather near Pangenesis (as do many of the latter amendments of germplasm by W.); and I should have thought that the limbs of salamanders, &c., are too late products, both phylogenetically and ontogenetically, to fall within its terms.

I also see better what you mean about Sphex. But Darwin's letter in 'Mental Evolution in Animals' seems to me to meet (or rather to anticipate) the 'difficulty.' Of course, he did not suppose that the insects' knowledge of 'success' goes further than finding out and observing the best place to sting in order to produce the maximum effect. The analogy of Cymphs is apposite; but is it the fact that there is any species whose localisation is really comparable with that of Sphex? Contrasting Weismann's account with Fabre's, I should say not.

As for neuter insects (which you mentioned at Newcastle), Darwin allows that they constitute one of the most difficult cases to bring under natural selection, seeing that this has here to act at the end of a long lever of the wrong kind, so to speak. Read Perrier's preface to French translation of 'Mental Evolution in Animals,' and observe how good his suggestion is, on the supposition that Lamarckian principles have any applicability at all.

Lastly, at Newcastle you said something that seemed to imply a doubt upon such facts as Lord Morton's mare. Do you really doubt such facts? I cannot suppose it.

There are plenty of white stoats hereabouts, I believe, though I have never actually seen them, because I do not stay late enough in the year. I have told my keeper to try to catch some without injuring them, and, if he succeeds, to send them straight to the Zoo. The experiment would be a very interesting one. But the keeper says that even here the whiteness depends as to its intensity upon the amount of snow in different seasons. He is most positive about this; he says it depends upon snow, and not on cold. However, I do not quote him as an authority in science, although he certainly is an intelligent and observing man.

Regarding the Royal Institution, an after Easter course by you would be doubly interesting, because before Easter I have to give one on the 'Post-Darwinian Period,' which will be mainly concerned with Weismann. Your lectures might then serve as a counter-irritant, therefore I will do anything I can to bring them about, only, not being on the managing body, I can help merely by backing any application you may make. And, of course, there ought to be no difficulty about it. Only let me know if you should want backing.

Would it not be worth while to get also some mountain hares for observation at the Zoo? These, I think, I could get.

Yours very truly,
Geo. J. Romanes.

Geanies, Ross-shire, N.B.; October 15.

Would you mind sending me the part of your MS. dealing with Sphex? I do not know that I quite caught your objection to my difficulty, and want to allude to it in lectures which I am now preparing for my Edinburgh class.

Also, did I correctly understand you to say that you refused to acknowledge any fundamental identity between processes of reproduction and those of repair? For this identity is to my mind the most important of all objections to W.'s theory.

G. J. ROMANES.

18 Cornwall Terrace, Regent's Park, N.W.: December 3, 1889.

My dear Poulton,—I returned here a day or two ago, and now send you my copy of Perrier's remarks about the neuters of hymenopterous insects. But he said a good deal more in subsequent and private correspondence. His preface, however, will serve to show you the general tone of argument.

With regard to Panmixia, it occurs to me that very likely you have not seen all that I wrote upon it, as the three papers were scattered over several months in 'Nature.' The following are the references: Vol. ix. pp. 361, 440; vol. x. p. 164.

You will see that I took up a decided stand upon the principle of Panmixia not being able altogether to supersede that of disuse. This was for the reasons stated in my last letter; and I still see no further reason for changing the opinion that was then formed under the influence of Darwin's judgment.

With reference to the difference that you alluded to—and which, as far as I can see, is the only difference between Weismann's presentation of the principle and my own—I enclose an extract from the lecture which I have just been giving in Edinburgh. From this extract I think you will see that the one point of difference does not redound to the credit of Weismann's logic. After reading the extract in conjunction with the papers in ' Nature,' perhaps you will let me know whether you now understand my view any better, or still believe that the cessation of selection *alone* can reduce the average of a useless organ below fifty per cent. of its original size—so long, that is, as the force of heredity continues unimpaired.

G. J. ROMANES.

Some further letters to Mr. Thiselton Dyer and to Mr. F. Darwin follow.

To Professor Thiselton Dyer.

December 20, 1888.

Dear Dyer,—Would you mind sending me on a postcard the name of the genus of plants the constituent species of which you alluded to in the train as being mutually fertile, and also separated from one another topographically ? I want to get as many of such cases as I possibly can, so, if any others occur to you, please mention them likewise.

By reading pages 401 and 404 of my paper, you will see why such cases are of quite as much importance to me as the converse, viz. where closely allied species inhabiting *continuous* areas are more or less mutually sterile (see p. 392).

If you have hitherto failed to apply these converse tests to my theory, I cannot conceive by what other principle you have sought to test it. Pray read the passages referred to, which present the shortest summary of what I regard as the very backbone of my evidence.

If your large knowledge of geographical distribution should enable you to supply me with specific cases of the general principle mentioned by Darwin in the quotation given on page 392 (' Origin of Species,' 6th ed., pp. 134 5), I should much like to try experiments on the sterility which I should expect to find between these interlocking species.

It seems comical to ask a scientific opponent for assistance, but the fact of being able to do so proves the superiority of science to politics.

December 25, 1888.

It is very good of you to write such a long and suggestive letter.

As a result of attentively reading your letter, it appears to me that you think I suppose sterility in a high degree to be much more usual among allied species than I do suppose it. I well know the large amount of natural as well as artificial hybridisation that goes on. But, on the other hand, there are so many species which either will not cross at all, or produce sterile hybrids, that, taking a general view of all species together, mutual sterility does become by far the most generally distributed single peculiarity —*i.e.* is the one peculiarity which, more than any other that can be named, is common to numberless species.

Thus much for mutual sterility that is absolute,

either in first crosses or in their hybrid progeny.
But now, the most important thing for me is mutual
sterility that is *not* absolute (though, on my theory,
perhaps on its way to becoming so) but relative, *i.e.*
there being a *lower degree of fertility* between A × B
or B × A, than there is between A × A or B × B.

Hitherto very few experiments have been made
on these comparative degrees of fertility, yet it is
by such alone, it seems to me, that physiological
selections can be tested. Thus, *e.g.*, my point about
the 'interlocking' species (p. 392) is that in such
cases I should expect a higher degree of fertility in
A × A and B × B than crosswise. Indeed, my fear is
that when I shall have proved by experiment that
such is the general rule in such cases, naturalists
will turn round and say : 'Well, of course, on merely
a priori grounds you might have known that such
must have been the case ; for otherwise the two
interlocking species could never have existed as
separate species, they would have hybridised freely
along the whole frontier line and eventually blended
over the whole area.' And still more may this be
said in the case of allied species, not merely interlocking, but intermixed through common areas.
Therefore, as a believing F.R.S. said to me the other
day, 'Your letters in " Nature " will at least have the
effect of blunting the edge of such possible criticism
in the future.' Of course you will laugh at the
robustness of my faith in thus forecasting the line of
future opposition, but I would like to ask you this
much : Supposing, for the sake of argument, that
twenty years hence I publish one hundred instances

of allied species which grow intermixed in common areas, proving by experiment that in all the cases there is *some* comparative degree of sterility between them (if only due to pre-potency of their own pollen), would you regard this as making in favour of physiological selection?   Or are you already prepared to admit that such *must* be the case, since otherwise the species A and B could not exist without fusion into one? If you say that you are prepared to admit this, it seems to me that you have already accepted the theory of physiological selection on *a priori* grounds.

Again, if I should publish one hundred other instances of allied species topographically isolated from one another, all of which were proved by experiment to present no degree at all of mutual infertility (so that A × A and B × B are not more fertile than crosswise), would you allow that, taken in conjunction with the previous set of experiments, these finally prove the theory of physiological selection to be true?   If not, I do not see how it is possible to verify the theory at all : it is only by means of these two complementary lines of research that, as it seems to me, the theory can be experimentally tested.

In the former case—*i.e.* where allied species intermix in common areas—sometimes they inter-cross freely (e.g. *Primula vulgaris* and *veris*, *Geum urbanum* and *rivale*, *Rumex*, *Epilobium*, &c.), while in other instances they don't (e.g. *Ranunculus repens* and *bulbosus*, *Lepidium Smithii* and *campestre*, *Scrophularia nodosa* and *aquatica*, &c.).   Now, as regards the latter, I suppose you would not question that the 'physiological isolation' has to do with preventing the species from fusing? But, if so, by parity of reasoning, should we not expect to meet with *some degree* of the same thing in the other cases, which, although not here sufficiently pronounced to block off frequent hybridisation, is nevertheless sufficient to prevent the species from blending over their common area?

And here, I may say, I should not at all object to the charge of misunderstanding Darwin on any merely trivial point such as the one you mention. But in this instance it so happens that it is rather you who have misunderstood me. I know that 'a hybrid is not an intermediate form in his sense,' and this is just what constitutes my difficulty against his paragraphs quoted on p. 392 of my paper. For what I say is, these intermediate forms *ought* to be hybrids, *unless physiological selection, (i.e. mutual sterility) has been at work*. 'In his sense' I cannot conceive how such 'intermediate forms' can exist in the circumstances described, seeing that they are *not* hybrids, and yet that (in the absence of any hypothesis of physiological isolation for which I am contending) there is no reason given why the two interlocking species should not freely intercross.

Regarding sexual selection I certainly am very much in earnest about its parallel to p.s.[1] If you intend the meaning of n.s. so as to embrace s.s. it will at the same time embrace also p.s. For s.s., like p.s., has nothing to do with life-preserving characters:

[1] p.s.— physiological selection; s.s.—sexual selection; n.s.—natural selection.

yet, also like p.s., it has to do with the differentiation of specific forms. (There is no distinction to be drawn between 'the species of a cock' and 'the plumage of a cock': plumage is the most favourite part of a bird with ornithologists on which to found specific diagnoses.) Therefore, if p.s. is true at all—which, of course, is another question—even my celebrated powers of 'dialectical subtlety' are completely unable to perceive any difference between p.s. and s.s. in respect of their relation to n.s.

Lastly, as regards Nägeli, no doubt he is an out-and-out Lamarckian, but I did not see that this should make any difference touching his opinion on a matter of fact not more connected with Lism. than Dism. I will look up 'Nature' for 1870.

With best Christmas wishes and many thanks for botanical hints.

December 26, 1888.

It has occurred to me that if you know Churchill's address, I might save time by writing to him before seeing him when he comes in spring.

It has also occurred to me that I might perhaps put the argument on pp. 801-4 better before you thus:

If phys. sel. is true, it would follow that as between allied species, mutual sterility ought to occur in all degrees (from zero to absolute), and that there ought to be a correlation between these degrees of sterility and degrees of non-separation, topographically.

Now, you cannot possibly doubt that the first expectation is realised in nature; as between allied species sterility does occur in all degrees, from there being no such sterility at all in very many cases, to there being absolute sterility in other cases. Therefore, in stating this fact as a fact, I am not playing at 'heads I win and tails you lose,' nor 'begging the whole question at the outset.' Any 'question' really arises only with regard to the second expectation viz. whether there is a general correlation between degrees of mutual fertility and degrees of topographical isolation.

Now, this question I have not begged, but, on the contrary, stated as the question by an experimental answer to which my theory must stand or fall.

Thus, the cases which you mention obviously go to support the theory, inasmuch as they conform to the expectation above mentioned. What I want to do is to find as many genera as possible like binchona and begonia, where the constituent species are separated geographically or topographically, and (? in consequence) easily hybridise with one another.

Therefore, as a mere matter of method, I cannot see that I have begged any question; for the only question is not about the facts which I state, but about my suggested explanation of them. And this question can only be answered by ascertaining whether there is in nature any such general correlation between isolation and capability of hybridising (also, of course, between the absence of isolation and the absence of such capability) as my theory would require.

Yours very sincerely,
G. J. Romanes.

18 Cornwall Terrace, Regent's Park, N.W.: December 27, 1888.

I am most glad that in your last letter you deal with what I consider the real 'question'—viz. not whether degrees of sterility obtain among a large proportional number of species, but whether there is any such correlation between them and absence of isolation of other kinds as my theory would expect. And, in dealing with this question you hit upon precisely the two greatest difficulties which I have myself concluded lie against the theory. The first is about areas now discontinuous having been once continuous, and our being so often unable to say whether or not such has been the case. But this difficulty is one that lies against *verification* of the theory, not against the theory itself. It was in view of this difficulty that I mentioned oceanic islands as furnishing the best flora for trying experiments upon ; but since I published the paper, I have not been able to hear of any botanists visiting islands. Should you ever hear of any you might let me know.

The second difficulty is one that lies against the theory itself, and has always seemed to me most formidable. But as nobody else has ever mentioned it, I have not hitherto done so, as I want to work it out quietly. I allude to your remark about the extraordinary differences that obtain among different genera with regard to the capability of intercrossing exhibited by their constituent species. This, I confess, has from the first appeared a tremendous objection to my theory. On the other hand, I have taken comfort from the consideration that besides being a tremendous objection, it is also a tremendous mystery. For, as it must admit of some explanation, and as this explanation must almost certainly have to do with the sexual system, it becomes not improbable that when found the explanation may square with p.s. That the difference in question is functional and not structural (or physiological as distinguished from morphological) seems to be proved by the fact that in some cases it obtains as between the most closely allied genera, being, *e.g.*, most strongly pronounced of all between Geranium and Pelargonium. Even quite apart from my own theory, it seems to me that this is a subject of the highest importance to investigate.

As regards sexual selection I allow, of course, that the 'law of battle' is a form of natural selection. But where the matter is merely a pleasing of æsthetic taste, and the resulting structures therefore only ornamental, I can see nothing 'advantageous' in the sense of life-preserving. On the contrary, in most cases such structures entail considerable expenditure of physiological energy in their production. On this account Darwin says that nat. sel. must impose a check on sexual selection running beyond a certain point of injuriousness ('D. of M.,' p. 227). Now, physiological selection is never thus injurious; and although it is a 'form of isolation,' the isolation is neither so extreme nor of such long continuance as the ones you compare it with. Moreover, the environment (therefore all other or external conditions of life) remain the same, which is not the case under the other forms of isolation. Provided that the physiological change is not *in itself* injurious, I do not see why *physiologically* isolated forms should be less fit than those from which they have been separated, though I can very well see why this should be the case with such *geographically* isolated forms as you mention, for there the *schooling* is different. Lastly, physiological selection, if not in itself injurious, does not require that its children should be 'protected against the struggle for existence.' On the contrary, as I say in my paper, it is calculated to give this struggle a better chance than ever to develope adaptive character in the sexually isolated forms, because the swamping effects of intercrossing are diminished.

But I really did not intend to afflict you with another jaw of this kind. I am, however, very glad that we now understand each other better than we did. At all events on my side I think I now know exactly the points which I have to make good if Nature is so constituted as to admit of my theory. One thing only I have forgotten to say, viz. that nothing can be argued against the theory from the fact of hybridisation occurring in cases where, according to the theory, it ought not to occur. This argument only becomes valid where it is found that the resulting hybrids are *fertile*. In relation to the theory, a sterile hybrid is all the same as a failure to cross.

Yours very sincerely,
G. J. ROMANES.

P.S.—I forgot to ask you if there would be any facilities in spring at Kew for repeating Adam's graft of purple on yellow laburnum. I want to try this experiment in budding on a large scale because of its importance on Weismannism, should the result of any of the grafts go to corroborate Adam's account of the way in which he produced the hybrid. If you agree to the experiments being tried at Kew, perhaps you might let me know whether there are any purple laburnums already in the gardens, or whether I should get the material over from France. But in that case you might also let me know to whom in France or elsewhere I had best apply. However, do not bother to answer any other parts of this tremendous letter, these we can discuss in conversation hereafter. A postcard to answer this postscript. however, is desirable, as then it might be possible to get matters in train for next budding season.

G. J. R.

I should much like to meet Churchill. Will you remember to tell me when he comes?

To F. Darwin, Esq.

18 Cornwall Terrace, Regent's Park, N.W. : January 20. 1889.

Dear Darwin,—Many thanks for your long letter. I thought you might have had some notes or memories of conversations, to show in a general way what the 'line' would have been.[1] If so, of course I should not have said that my sayings were inspired. but should myself have known that I was not going astray.

The line I am going to take is :

[1] Of Mr. Darwin.

P

1st. Even assuming, for sake of argument, that heightened colour is correlated with increased vigour, Wallace everywhere fails to distinguish between brilliancy and ornament; yet it is the disposition of colours in patterns, &c., that is the chief thing to be explained.

2nd. In many cases (*e.g.* peacock's tail) the pattern is only revealed when unfolded during courtship. Besides natural selection could not be such a fool as to develope large (physiologically expressive) and weighty (impeding flight) structures like this—stags' antlers, &c., merely as correlates of vigour.

3rd. There is not much in Wallace's merely negative difficulty about our not knowing what goes on in the mind of a hen, when we set against that difficulty the positive fact that we can see what does go on in the mind of a cock—display, antics, song, &c.

4th. To say that 'each bird finds a mate under any circumstances' is merely to beg the whole question.

5th. There remains Wallace's jealousy of natural selection. He will not have any other 'factor,' and therefore says natural selection must eat up sexual selection like the lean kine have the fat kine. But natural selection alone does not explain all the phenomena of sexual colouring, courtship, &c., and sexual selection is exactly the theory that does. Wallace's jealousy, therefore, is foolish and inimical to natural selection theory itself, by forcing it into explanations which are plainly false.

My own belief is, that what Lankester calls the 'pure Darwinians' are doing the same thing in another direction. By endeavouring, with Wallace and Weismann, to make natural selection all in all as the sole cause of adaptive structure, and expressly discarding the Darwinian recognition of use and disuse, I think they are doing harm to natural selection theory itself.   Moreover, because I do not see any sufficient reason as yet to budge from the real Darwinian standpoint (Weismann has added nothing to the facts which were known to Charles Darwin), the post-Darwinians accuse me of moving away from Darwinian principles.   But it is they who are moving, and, because they see a change in our relative positions, affirm that it is I.   In point of fact, my position has never varied in the least, and my confession of faith would still follow, in every detail, that given on p. 421 of 'Origin,' 6th ed., which, it seems to me, might also be regarded as prophetic no less than retrospective.

If I did not say all this in my paper in physiological selection, it is only because I never conceived the possibility of my being accused of trying to undermine natural selection ; and, therefore, I only stated as briefly as possible what my relations were to it. Yet it seems to me that this statement was clear enough if Wallace had not come down with his preposterous 'Romanes *versus* Darwin.'   At all events, it is not in my power—or, I believe, in that of anybody else—to express more strongly than I now have in 'Nature,' in answer to Dyer, what I do hold about natural selection in its relation to physiological selection, sexual selection, and other subordinate principles. Of course, if there were a debate on these lines at the B.A., I should get my part of it published somewhere. As far as I can honestly see, my 'position' is absolutely identical with that in last editions of 'Origin' and 'Descent,' with, perhaps, a 'tendency' to lay more stress on levelling influence of Panmixia.

Re physiological selection. I have sent Correvon, of Geneva, £50 to help in founding a garden in the Alps, which will have the proud distinction of being the highest garden in the world. He is a splendid man for his knowledge of Alpine flora, and besides, is strongly bitten with a desire to test physiological selection. Of course I shall do the hybridising experiments myself, but he will collect the material from the different mountains—*i.e.* nearly allied species, topographically separated, and therefore, I hope, mutually fertile. The converse experiments of nearly allied species on common areas may be tried in England.

I am making arrangements for repeating on an extensive scale experiments on budding purple laburnum on yellow, to see if it is possible to reproduce 'Adam's eye' hybrid. If so, it would now be of more importance than ever in relation to Weismann. By the way, he is sorely put to it in the case of plants which reproduce themselves not only by cuttings, but even by leaves. Here he is bound to confess that his germ-plasma occupies all the cellular tissue of the entire plant. But if so, how in the world does his germ-plasma differ from gemmules?

There! I did not intend to write you anything of a letter when I began, but have gone on and on till it is well for you that the second sheet is coming to an end.

Yours ever,
G. J. ROMANES.

P.S.—Any contributions to Correvon's garden (however small) would be thankfully received by him. Possibly his garden may be of some use to English botanists ; if so, you might send the hat round, and collect any coppers that fall.

To Professor Thiselton Dyer.

18 Cornwall Terrace, Regent's Park, N.W. : January 7, 1889.

My dear Dyer,—Knowing what a busy man you are, I never expected you to answer my last letter, and therefore it has come as an agreeable surprise. For no doubt you will believe me when I say that I value much more communications which are opposed to physiological selection than those in its favour ; the former show me better what has to be done in the way of verification, as well as the general views which may be taken on the subject by other minds. And most of all is this the case when anyone like yourself gives me the benefit of opinions which are formed by a trained experience in botany, seeing that here I am myself such a sorry ignoramus. And I willingly confess that your strongly expressed opinion has seriously shaken my hopes for physiological selection, notwithstanding that some German botanists think otherwise. Nevertheless, I still think that it is worth while to devote some years to experimental testing, and then, if the results are against me—well, I shall be sorry to have spent so much time over a wild flower chase, and to have kicked up so much scientific dust in the process ; but I will not be ashamed to acknowledge that Nature has said No.

And now for your last letter. Read in the light of subsequent experience, I have no doubt that I ought to have expressed myself with more care while writing my paper. But, to tell the honest truth, it never once occurred to me that I of all men could be suspected of trying to undermine the theories of Darwin. I was entirely filled with the one idea of presenting what seemed to me 'a supplementary hypothesis,' which, while 'in no way opposed to natural selection,' would 'release the latter from the only difficulties' which to my mind it had ever presented. Therefore I took it for granted that everybody would go with me in recognising natural selection as the 'boss' round which every 'other theory' must revolve, without my having to say so on every page. So, of course, by 'other theory' I did not mean that physiological selection was in my opinion the *only* theory of the origin of species. Everywhere throughout the paper, from the title-page to the conclusion, I represented it as an 'additional suggestion,' a 'supplementary hypothesis,' &c., &c. Sexual selection is in my view (as it is also in Darwin's, Wallace's, and doubtless that of all evolutionists) one of the 'other theories that have been propounded on the origin of species.' So is Lamarck's theory, which was considered by Darwin as *more or less* 'supplementary' to natural selection; and this is all that I meant —or, I should say, could possibly be understood to mean in view of the title-page, &c.—by speaking of physiological selection as another theory of the origin of species. It certainly is not the *same* thing as natural selection or either of the 'other theories' just mentioned ; but no less certainly it is not *exclusive* of any of the three. Unquestionably it is as you say, and as I myself said, an *independent* theory—*i.e.* not identical with, but additional to, that of natural selection. But this is a widely different thing from saying that it is in itself an *exhaustive* theory, which must therefore swallow up all or any ' others.' In short, I abide by the closing statement of my introductory paragraph—viz. that the theory is an 'attempt at suggesting *another factor* in the formation of species, which, although quite *independent* of natural selection, is in no way *opposed* to natural selection, and may therefore be regarded as a factor *supplementary* to natural selection.' Statements to the same effect are indeed scattered through the entire paper ; but, of course, could I have foreseen the interpretations which afterwards arose, I should have reiterated such statements *ad nauseam*.

Sorry you cannot come to the B.A., or to dine, but certainly do not wonder.

Yours very sincerely,
G. J. ROMANES.

Lastly, about species not being able to exist as species without the physiological isolation of physiological selection (p. 403), the statement of course only applies to nearly allied species occupying common areas (see p. 404). If this statement is wrong, no one has yet shown me wherein it is so. I fancy you do not quite appreciate that by 'sterility' I always mean (unless otherwise expressly stated) sterility *in some degree*, and this not only with regard to the fertile hybrids. It is by no means enough to point to natural and fertile hybrids as cases opposed to physiological selection unless it has been shown by experiment through a generation or two that these hybrids are *fully* fertile—*i.e.* as fertile as their parent species. Now, experiments of this kind have rarely been carried through. If you assume that the result of carrying them through would be destructive of physiological selection by proving that fertile hybrids are, as a rule, fully fertile, and also (which is very important) that in any cases where experiment may show them to be so, further experiment would fail to show that isolation has not been effected in any other way (as by pre-potency, differences of insect fertilisation, &c.)—in short, if you assume that fertility is as complete between the two associated species as it is within each species, how is it conceivable that they should continue to be distinct? In this connection it is well to consult Gulick's paper already referred to (especially p. 259, paragraph 1st) on the theoretical side, and Jordan's papers and books on the practical side. I have repeated the latter's observations on poppies, and find that where any considerable number of individuals are concerned, natural selection is not nearly so great a power in this respect. (Even in cases where it happens that in-breeding is necessarily confined to single hermaphrodite individuals for numberless generations, the handicapping is not fatal: witness flowers which habitually fertilise themselves before opening—especially some species of orchids, which never seem to do otherwise, notwithstanding the elaborate pro-

visions for cross-fertilisation in other species.)   Now,
I believe most of all in what I have called 'collective
variation' of the reproductive system in the way
of physiological selection, whereby, owing to some
common influence acting on a large number of individuals similarly and simultaneously, they all become
sexually co-adapted *inter se* while physiologically
isolated from the rest.   This essential feature of the
theory seems to me entirely to remove the difficulty
about in-breeding, as well as that which Wallace
urged about the chances against a suitable meeting
of 'physiological complements.'

As for my having attributed too much to the
swamping effects of intercrossing (Panmixia), this, I
am convinced, is the one and only particular wherein
I have at all departed from the judgments of Darwin;
though, curiously enough, it is the particular on
which my critics have laid least stress when accusing
me of Darwinian heresy.   But it is too big a question
to treat in correspondence.   Gulick's recently published paper at the Linnean Society seems to me a
most important one in this connection, and I have
a large body of other evidence.

To F. Darwin, Esq.[1]

18 Cornwall Terrace, Regent's Park, N.W.: January 8, 1889.

Dear Darwin,—Hate you, indeed!   Why, I cannot imagine any better service than that of stopping
a fellow from making a fool of himself, and I most
cordially thank you for having done so in this case.

[1] Mr. F. Darwin had pointed out some erroneous conclusions in a pro-
jected scientific paper.

The business was so completely out of my line, that I did not know what was required. It seemed to me that if I got any evidence of bending towards the sparks, the only question I wanted to answer would be answered, and, therefore, that it did not matter a straw about temperature, moisture, and the rest. Moreover, the results did not seem to me to be of any importance, as they were just what might have been expected, and, therefore, I doubted whether it was worth while publishing a paper about them. Had they gone the other way, and proved that the plants would not bend to flashing light, I should have thought it much more interesting. · Lastly, the research was so expensive, costing £1 per day at the only place where I could get the requisite apparatus, and there they shut up at night.

Of course, I will withdraw this paper, and, if you think the thing is worth working out in all the details you suggest, will do so. In that case, it would be worth while to ascertain whether there would be any electrical apparatus at Cambridge which I could get the use of at a lower rate of profit to the owners. A good-sized induction coil is really all that is required, and they probably have this in the Cavendish. But there is not one available in any of the London workshops, and so I had to go to Appes, in the Strand. It is suggested that the debate in Section D at the British Association this year should be opened by me on the question of utility as universal. Before I agree, I should like to know what you think about the 'Nature' controversy which I have recently had with Dyer, and out of which the present suggestion has emanated. Perhaps we might arrange to meet somewhere soon to have a talk over the expediency of such a debate at all, and the lines on which, if held, it should run. Of course, physiological selection would be carefully kept out. My object would be to show the prime importance of natural selection as a theory which everywhere accounts for adaptations.

Yours very sincerely,

G. J. Romanes.

May 27, 1889.

Herewith I return, with many thanks, a pamphlet by Kerner, numbered 738.

In my experiments with electric spark illumination on plants, I notice that the seedlings, although so wonderfully heliotropic, never form chlorophyll, even if exposed to a continuous stream of sparks for 30 hours on end, while they will bend through 90° in seven hours to single sparks following one another at one per second. This proves that there is no connection at all between heliotropism and formation of chlorophyll, or *vice versa*—a point which I cannot find to have been hitherto stated. Do you happen to know if it has been? If you do not happen to remember anything bearing on this subject, do not trouble to search or to answer.

Wallace's book[1] strikes me as very able in many parts, though singularly feeble in others—especially the last chapter. He has done but scant justice to Gulick's paper. Had he read it with any care, he might have seen that it fully anticipates his criticism

[1] *Darwinism*, by Alfred Russell Wallace.

on mine. But I think he deserves great credit for
nowhere chuckling. From the first he has been consistent in holding natural selection the sole factor of
organic evolution—leaving no room for sexual selection, inheritance of acquired characters, &c., &c.
And now that he had lived to see an important
body of evolutionists adopting this view, there must
have been a strong temptation to ' I always told you
so.' Yet there is nowhere any note of this, or even
so much as an allusion to his previous utterances on
the subject.

To E. B. Poulton, Esq.

Geanies, Ross-shire : November 2, 1889.

My dear Poulton,—Continuing our antipodal correspondence, and taking the points in your last letter
seriatim, I quite saw that your theory of repair was
' the logical outcome of Weismann's ' (being, in fact, a
direct application of his views on phylogeny to the
case of repair) ; but I did not know whether the outcome had been traced by him or by yourself. Now, I
understand, I may allude to it as yours. Again, what
I meant about regeneration of entire limbs, &c., was
that, to meet such cases, your diagram would require
modification in the way that you now suggest. Has
it occurred to you as an argument in favour of this
suggestion (*i.e.* that the ' potentiality ' of somatic
germ-plasm may in such cases be arrested in its process of ontogenetic diffusion), that Darwin has shown,
or at least alleged, that all such cases may be traced
to special adaptation to special needs, dangers. &c.—

so that the arrest may have been brought about in these cases by natural selection?

If you deem the 'chief difference' between Darwin's and Weismann's theory of heredity to be 'that the one implies *material particles* and the other only *physical and chemical constitution*,' then, it seems to me, Weismann's theory will become identical with Herbert Spencer's—seeing that this is virtually the only respect in which Spencer's differs from Darwin's. But I think there is another and a much more important respect in which W.'s theory differs from both these predecessors. However, to proceed to the next point, I agree with you, that the sole object of the Sphex stinging the larvæ is *now* to cause them to 'keep,' and that natural selection must have worked upon this for perfecting the instinct. But the point is, what was the origin of the selective stinging? If merely chance congenital variations, would unity to billions express the chances against their ever arising? Get some mathematician to calculate—giving as data superficial area of caterpillar on the one hand and that of *nine* ganglia on the other. Even neglecting the consideration that the variation must occur many times to give unaided natural selection a chance to fix it as an instinct, the chances against its occurring only once would be represented by the following series, where x is the superficial area of the caterpillar *minus* that of eight ganglia, and unity is superficial area of one ganglia :

$$\frac{1}{x} \times \frac{1}{x} \times \frac{1}{x} \times \frac{1}{x} \times \frac{1}{x} \times \frac{1}{x} \times \frac{1}{x} \times \frac{1}{x} \times \frac{1}{x}$$

If, as I suppose, x may here be taken as $= 100,000$,

the chances against the variation occurring once would be written in figures expressing unity to one thousand million billion trillions. Of course I do not rely on calculations of this kind for giving anything like accurate results (mathematics in biology always seems to me like a scalpel in a carpenter's shop), but it makes no difference how far one cuts down such figures as these. Therefore, if Lamarck won't satisfy such facts, neither do I think that Darwin *minus* Lamarck can do so. We must wait for the next man.

I will send you ' Perrier ' on my return to town next month.

Lord Morton's experience is so universally that of all breeders of live stock, that I never knew anybody ever doubted it. But, if they do, there is no reason why they should not satisfy themselves on the point. For my part I do not feel that the fact requires any corroboration as regards mammals, though I have some experiments going on with birds. Lastly, the apparently analogous cases in plants are still worse for Weismann's theory, and they stand on the best authorities.

I enclose a letter received by same post that brought yours. It is from a former keeper of mine who is now more in the moorlands. Other applications are out, so I hope some of them will be successful. Very little doubt it will prove to be temperature. I found a dead stoat here to-day; it had not turned white at all, but then the season is very mild.

The Secretary of the R.I. is Sir F. Bramwell, Bart., F.R.S. You had better write to him. Also to his son-in-law, Victor Horsley, who is more of a biologist. Tell Bramwell, if you like, that I think he ought to jump at you.

Yours very truly,
G. J. ROMANES.

Geanies, Ross-shire, N.B. : November 6, 1889.

My dear Poulton,—Many thanks for your paper, which is the clearest exposition I have yet seen of Weismann's views. But how about your allusion to experiments in grafting ? As regards plants, there *is* a good deal of evidence as to the possibility of a graft-hybrid. As regards animals, fifteen years ago I spent an immensity of time in experimenting, and could not then find that there was any literature on the subject. Nobody who had grafted animal tissues had done so with any reference to the heredity question, nor do I know of any publications on the subject since then.

Yours very truly,
G. J. ROMANES.

Geanies, Ross-shire. N.B. : November 11, 1889.

My dear Poulton,—Although I spent more time and trouble than I like to acknowledge (even to my-self) in trying to prove Pangenesis between '73 and '80, I never obtained any positive results, and did not care to publish negative. Therefore there are no papers of mine on the subject, although I may fairly believe that no other human being has tried so many experiments upon it. No doubt you will think that I ought to regard this fact as so much negative evidence in favour of the new theory; and, up to a

certain point, I do, only the issue between Pangenesis
and Germ-plasm is not really or nearly so well defined
as Weismann represents, where the matter of experiments is concerned ; *e.g.* it is not the case that any
crucial test is furnished by the non-transmissibility of
mutilations ; Darwin did not set much store by them,
though Eimer and others have done so since. In
fact all the Germans on both sides, and all the
Englishmen on Weismann's side, seem to me unjust
to Darwin in this respect.

Regarding the cessation of selection, the motive
that prompted my question to you was not the paltry
one of claiming priority in the enunciation of an exceedingly obvious idea. My motive was to assure myself that this idea is exactly the same as Weismann's
Panmixia ; for, although I could see no difference, I
thought perhaps he and you did (from absence of
allusion to my paper, while priority is acknowledged
as regards a later one) ; and, if this were so, I wanted
to know where the difference lay. And the reason I
wanted to know this was because when my paper
was published, and Darwin accepted the idea with
enthusiasm, I put it to him in conversation whether
this idea might not supersede Lamarckian principles
altogether. (By carefully reading between the lines
of the paper itself, you will see how much this
question was occupying my mind at the time, though
I did not dare to challenge Lamarck's principles *in toto*
without much more full inquiry.) Then it was that
Darwin dissuaded me from going on to this point, on
the ground that there was abundant evidence of
Lamarck's principles apart from use and disuse of

structures—*e.g.* instincts—and also on the ground of his theory of Pangenesis. Therefore I abandoned the matter, and still retain what may thus be now a prejudice against exactly the same line of thought as Darwin talked me out of in 1873. Weismann, of course, has greatly elaborated this line of thought ; but what may be called the scientific axis of it (viz. possible non-inheritance of acquired characters) is identical, and all the more metaphysical part of it about the immortality, immutability, &c., of a hypothetical germ-plasm is the weakest part in my estimation.

Now, the point I am working up to is this. If there be no difference between Panmixia and Cessation of Selection, from what I have briefly sketched about it, it follows that, had Darwin lived till now, he would almost certainly have been opposed to Weismann. This is not a thing I should like to say in public, but one that I should like to feel practically assured about in my own mind.

Regarding the numerical calculations, I have not got a copy of the 'Nature' paper here, but, so far as I remember (and I think I am right), the idea was that ' Economy of Growth ' would go on assisting Cessation of Selection till the degenerating organ became ' rudimentary.' In other words, *reversal* of selection would co-operate with *cessation* of it.

This, as I understand it, is now exactly Weismann's view; only he thinks that thus the rudimentary organ would finally become extinguished. Here, however, it seems to me evident he must be wrong. The reasons are obvious, as I am going to show this week

to my Edinburgh class. Six lectures are to be devoted
entirely to Weismann, and when they are published
(as they will be this time next year), I think it will be
seen that Weismannism is not such very plain sailing
as Weismann himself seems to think. Vines has anticipated some of my points in his paper in 'Nature';
but I hope this may have the effect of letting me see
what answers can be given before I shall have to
publish.

Yours very truly,
G. J. ROMANES.

In the midst of these scientific labours and scientific controversies, Mr. Romanes found time for other
thoughts and for other work.

At the beginning of 1889 he delivered an address
at Toynbee Hall on the Ethical Teaching of Christ,
of which the following is an extract:

' The services rendered by Christ to the cause of
morality have been in two distinct directions. The
first is in an unparalleled change of moral conception, and the other in an unparalleled moral example,
joined with peculiar powers of moral exposition and
enthusiasm of moral feeling which have never before
been approached. The originality of Christ's teaching might in some quarters be over-rated, but the
achievement it was impossible to overrate. It is
only before the presence of Christ that the dry bones
of ethical abstraction have sprung into life. The
very essence of the new religion consists in re-
establishing more closely than ever the bonds between morality and religion. One important effect of

Christ's teaching and influence has been the carrying into effect of the doctrine of universalism, for previously the idea of human brotherhood can not be said to have existed. Again, in the exaltation of the benevolent virtues at the expense of the heroic, the change effected is fundamental and abrupt. Christ may be said to have created the virtues of self-abnegation, universal beneficence, unflinching humility—indeed, the divine supremacy of compassion. Whether Christ be regarded as human or divine, all must agree in regarding the work of His life as by far the greatest work ever achieved in the history of the human race. A topic of great importance is the influence of Christ's personality in securing the acceptance of His teaching. The personal character of Christ is of an order *sui generis*, and even the most advanced of sceptics have done homage to it. The more keen the intellectual criticism, the greater is the appreciation of the uniqueness of the personality. Men may cease to wonder at the effect of Christ's teaching; for, given the wonderful personality, all the rest must follow. Whatever answers different persons may give to the questions, " What think ye of Christ ?   Whose son is He ? " everyone must agree that " His name shall be called Wonderful ! " '

This brought on him two characteristic letters, one from an Agnostic lady, blaming him for attaching so much importance to Him whom she was pleased to call ' The Peasant of Nazareth,' the other from Dr. Paget :

Christ Church, Oxford: January 14. 1889.

My dear Romanes,—I hope you will not think me impertinent if I write a few words of gratitude for the happiness which I enjoyed in reading to-day even such an account of your address at Toynbee Hall as the 'Times' gave me. There is always a risk of impertinence in thanking a man for what he has said; for of course he has said it because he saw it, and thought he ought to say it, quite simply. But I may just thank you for the generous willingness with which you accepted such a task :—and for the light in which you looked at it :—as an opportunity for saying so ungrudgingly, so open-heartedly, that which is clear to you about our Lord. This must be, please God, a real bit of help to others ; and I trust and pray that it may return in help to you.

But how dark you were about it ! I should have been furious if I had been in London, and not there.

Please forgive me this letter ; and do not think it needs any answer.

Affectionately yours,
Francis Paget.

At the beginning of this year Mr. Romanes collected his various poems and had them privately printed. He writes to his sister :

February 1889.

Three weeks before the 11th I was wondering what I should get as a wedding-day present to mark the tenth anniversary. Ethel then chanced to say that she wished my poems were published, so that she could have them in type. This suggested to me the idea of putting them into type for private circulation, when they might serve at once as the required wedding-present, and as a preliminary to publication at any future time either by myself or, more probably, by her or someone else. So I got an estimate from the printer, and with an awful rush he set up the whole in a week. Proof corrections occupied another week, and the binding of a grand presentation copy the third week. Thus I only had my present ready a few hours before it had to be presented. Binding the other copies occupied the time till I sent you yours. In Ethel's copy (which is awfully swell) I have written a special sonnet, as I did in yours.

These poems, or rather a selection from them, will be published, in accordance with the author's wish.

Of his poetry, his sonnets (which were privately printed) seem the most successful. Various friends saw the privately printed book, and the present Professor of Poetry at Oxford gratified Mr. Romanes very much by his own kind words respecting them, and also by submitting them to Lord Tennyson, who spoke of them in kindly terms, as did also Dean Church, Mr. Edmund Gosse, Mr. George Meredith, and others. Two letters he received about his poems are here given :

From the Dean of St. Paul's.

Ettenheim, Torquay : February 26, 1889.

My dear Mr. Romanes,—Thank you very much for your kindness in thinking me worthy of your gift. I am always glad to see science and poetry go together

It was the way with the earliest efforts of natural science, as Empedocles and Lucretius; and when the strictest thinking of science is done, there is still something more of expression and meaning, of which poetry is the natural and only adequate interpreter.

My acquaintance with your volume is as yet only superficial. But I have been very much impressed by 'Charles Darwin,' and by the 'Dream of Poetry.' It is a very pleasant volume to open, and does not send one away empty and cold; which means that it is genuine poetry. We do not get on very fast; but we are better here than in London, and the place is pleasant.

Please remember us all to Mrs. Romanes. Mary sends a very special remembrance.

Yours faithfully,
R. W. Church.

From the Rt. Hon. W. E. Gladstone.

Hawarden.

Dear Mr. Romanes,—You have sent me an acceptable gift, and a most considerate note; considerate as regards me, but not, I fear, as respects yourself; for you have made your appeal to an incompetent judge. I do not think I possess, though I have always coveted, the gift of song, and I am not a qualified judge of those who have it.

But in your case there can surely be neither difficulty nor doubt. I came home on Saturday evening and found a book awaiting me with prior personal claims, which has taken up most of the short time since my arrival. It does not, however, I think, require much time to learn from your book whether you have or have not the poetic gift. Before many minutes had passed the affirmation, I will not say dawned, but glared, upon me.

I am very glad that you have proceeded to its further exercise. I can see no good reason why a man of science should not be a poet. Lord Bacon surely shows in his Essays that he had the poet in him. It all depends upon the way of going about it, and on the man's keeping himself, as man, above his pursuit, as Emerson well said long ago.

I do not quite apprehend your estimate of Darwin, nor of Darwin's works, in p. 119. This is no doubt due to my ignorance. I knew him little, but my slight intercourse with him impressed me deeply as well as pleasurably.

With sincere thanks, I remain, dear Mr. Romanes, faithfully yours,

W. E. GLADSTONE.

Mr. Romanes was an omnivorous reader of poetry, and this taste grew by what it fed on. On a holiday he read poetry in preference to anything else, and he was very fond of good anthologies, beginning first and foremost with the ' Golden Treasury.' Shakespeare, Milton, and, above all, Tennyson were the poets he most loved. For Byron he had had an early boyish enthusiasm, but this he seemed to outgrow ; at least Byron was not an author to whom in later years he turned. He grew more and more addicted to versifying in the later years of his life, and girl friends who grew into intimate acquaintances were sure to have sooner or later a sonnet sent to them on some special occasion.

As the years went on he became more interested in work amongst the poor, and longed to take up some special line. For a while he set up a small school in a slum near the Euston Road, in which he tried to attract the very poorest boys who had managed to elude the vigilance of the School Board. His plan was to have only morning school, and to give the children their dinner. The School Board officer came to his aid, and the school was maintained for one or two winters.

He visited the school regularly, and on one occasion, finding that a boy had been grossly rude to the mistress, he gave the young scamp a sound whipping.

For other people's interests in the way of work he had much sympathy; he several times went down to the Christ Church mission at Poplar when the Rev. H. L. Paget was in charge, and he lectured at Toynbee Hall and at the Oxford House.

Of the work of the clergy as a whole Romanes always spoke most warmly; of the peculiar dislike of and suspicion of 'black coats,' so often attributed to laymen in general and to scientific men in particular, he had no trace, and as years went on he used to be gently chaffed for his clerical tendencies and the way in which he was consulted as to the bearings of Science on Religion.

Two new correspondents were now added to Mr. Romanes' list, Professor Joseph Le Conte, of the University of California, and the Rev. J. Gulick, who was, and is still, an American missionary in Japan. Of Mr. Gulick's scientific attainments, Mr. Romanes entertained a very high opinion. Unfortunately, none of the letters to Mr. Gulick have come to hand.

Of Mr. Le Conte's book, ' Evolution and Religious

Thought,' Mr. Romanes thought very highly, and introduced it to the notice of various people, especially to Mr. Aubrey Moore.

He writes to Mr. Le Conte :

To Professor Le Conte.

Geanies, Ross-shire, N.B. : October 11, 1887.

Dear Sir,—I am much obliged to you for sending me a copy of your most interesting paper on Flora of the Coast Islands, &c.

If you are acquainted with my new theory of ' Physiological Selection ' (published in ' Journ. Lin. Soc.' 1886) you will understand why I regard your facts as furnishing first-rate material for testing that theory. If you cannot get access to my paper, I will send you a copy on my return to London in December.

My object in now writing—over and above that of thanking you for your paper—is to ask whether you yourself, or any other American naturalist whom you may know, would not feel it well worth while to try some experiments on the hybridisation of the peculiar species. Although I agree with you in thinking it probable that many of these species may be ' remnants,' I also think it abundantly possible that some of them may be merely evolved forms. A botanist on the spot might be able to determine, by intelligent comparison, which of the peculiar species are most probably of the last-mentioned character. These he might choose for his experiments on hybridisation. And I should expect him to find marked evidence of mutual sterility between closely allied unique species growing on the same island, with possibly unimpaired fertility between allied species growing on different islands. If this anticipation should be realised by experiment, the fact would go far to prove my theory.

Even if you do not happen to know of any botanist who would care to undertake this experimental research, you might possibly know of some one who would gather and transmit seeds for me to grow in hothouses here.

I shall be much interested to hear what you think of these proposals, and meanwhile remain

Yours truly,
G. J. ROMANES.

Geanies.

My dear Sir,—Your book I will look forward to with much interest, and certainly not least so to your treatment of that very comprehensive question —'What then?'

I will send you a copy of my paper on Physiological Selection as soon as I return to London, which will be about Christmas.

With many thanks for your kindness, I remain, yours truly,

G. J. ROMANES.

May 7, 1888.

My dear Sir,—Many thanks for sending me a copy of your book,[1] which seems to me everywhere admirable. Of course, I am particularly glad that you think with me so much on physiological selection, but

---

[1] *Evolution and Religious Thought.*

even apart from this, the work is, to my mind, one of the most clearly thought out that I have met with in Darwinian literature. I have sent it on to 'Nature' for review, understanding from the office that a copy had not then been received. But for your kind mention of myself, I should have reviewed it.

A most remarkable paper has been sent to the Linnean Society by a Mr. Gulick on 'Divergent Evolution,' for the publication of which in the 'Journal' you might look out.

G. J. ROMANES.

January 21, 1889.

My dear Sir,—I should like you to set your lucid wits to work upon the following questions, and let me know whether you can devise any answers.

On pp. 220–226 of your book, you state with extreme felicity, and much better than he does, Weismann's theory of the causes of variation. But it does not occur to him, and does not seem to have occurred to you, that there is a curious and unaccountable interruption in the ascending grades of sexual differentiation, for in the vegetable kingdom these do *not* follow the grades of taxonomic ascent ; but, on the contrary, and as a general rule, the *lower* the order of evolution, the *greater* is the tendency to bi-sexualism. Diœcious species (*i.e.* male and female organs on different plants) occur in largest proportion among the lower Cryptogams, less frequently among the higher, and more rarely still among Phanerogams. Monœcious species (*i.e.* male and female organs on the same plant, but locally distinct) occur chiefly among the higher Cryptogams and lower Phanerogams; Hermaphrodite species (*i.e.* male and female organs in the same flower) occur much more frequently among higher Phanerogams.

There is, besides, another difficulty. According to Weismann and yourself, it is natural selection that has brought about sexuality ' for the sake of better results in the offspring,' by making them more variable or plastic. But how can natural selection act prophetically? Unless the variability is of use to the individuals at each stage of its advance, it cannot come under the sway of natural selection, however advantageous it may *eventually* prove to the type. But, if one thinks about it, how can such variability be of any use to the individual? Observe, beneficial variability is quite different from beneficial variation. It is the *tendency to vary* that is in question, not the occurrence of this, that, and the other display of it. Now, I do not see how sexuality can have been evolved by natural selection for the purpose of securing their tendency *in the future,* when it can never be of any use to individuals *of the present.* Each individual of the present is an accomplished fact; the tendency to produce variable offspring is, therefore, of no use to it individually, and so natural selection would have no reason to pick it out for living and propagating. Such is my difficulty touching this point. Another is, why do we meet with such great differences between (sometimes) allied natural genera, and even whole natural orders, as to the facility with which their constituent species hybridise? For example, species of genus Geranium will hybridise almost better than any other, those of the Pelargonium scarcely at all.

I hope that at some time you will be able to get sent to me seeds of species peculiar to oceanic islands, should you hear of any botanists who are visiting such islands.

G. J. ROMANES.

I note that you have been good enough to pass my questions on to Mr. Greene, whose great kindness (already experienced by me) will, I trust, prevent him from thinking that the failure of the seeds to flower here was due to any negligence on my part.

Yes, it is the same Rev. Mr. Gulick whom you describe that wrote the paper on 'Divergent Evolution' to which I alluded, and which is a most remarkable paper in every way, though not at all easy to master. Wallace completely misunderstood it in his letter to 'Nature.' It was his work in shells that first led Mr. Gulick to study Isolation, and he has been at work upon the subject ever since. To the best of my judgment, he has demonstrated the necessity of what he calls 'segregate breeding' for 'polytypic evolution,' and in this connection has worked out the idea of physiological selection (which he calls segregate fecundity) much more fully than I have.

It is most astonishing to me with what a storm of opposition this idea has been met in England, and how persistent is the misunderstanding. In Germany and America it is being much more fairly treated, but meanwhile I intend to keep it as quiet as possible, till I shall be in a position to publish a large body of experimental observations. As far as time has hitherto allowed, the results are strongly corroborative of the theory.

I have now read your admirable book, and my only objection to it is that it seems in such large measure to anticipate the publication of my own course of lectures on the theory of Evolution which I am now giving at the Royal Institution. But, on the other hand, this will relieve me of the necessity of printing a good deal of my matter, as it will be sufficient to refer to your book in mine when the two cover common ground. It is needless to add that I am very glad to note you think so well of physiological selection.

Yours very truly,
G. J. ROMANES.

The theory of the Non-Inheritance of Acquired Characters, with which Professor Weismann's name is inseparably connected, was now coming to the front.

Mr. Romanes was, of course, intensely interested, and set himself *not* to dispute so much as to examine and to test it.

He devoted a large part of his last year at the Royal Institution to lecturing on Prof. Weismann's theory, which lectures he worked up into his book, 'An Examination of Weismannism,' published in 1892.

He devised many experiments to test that theory, experiments which have a pathetic interest for those who love him, for they occupied his mind up to the very day of his death.

Of this theory it may safely be said that since the promulgation of Mr. Darwin's great doctrine, no problem has interested the world of science so profoundly.

For the most part the younger English naturalists have accepted Professor Weismann's theory, which, by the way, had long ago been anticipated by Mr. Francis Galton, and Mr. Romanes was not much supported in his opposition, or, rather, his non-adherence to Weismannism.

Linnean Society, Burlington House, London, W.: March 21, 1890.

My dear Dyer,—I have come to the conclusion that anything published in ' Nature ' might as well never have been published at all; and therefore have come here to-day in order to look through the back numbers of ' Nature,' with a view to republishing as a small book the various things that I have contributed during the past twenty years. Thus it is I find that the explanation which I gave to Herbert Spencer *re* Panmixia and his articles on the ' Factors of Organic Evolution,' appeared in August 25, 1887, and showed that his whole argument was in the air.

I have also read my own article on Panmixia, written about two months ago, and published last week. The result is to satisfy me that your ' intelligent ' friends must have had minds which do not belong to the *a priori* order—*i.e.* are incapable of perceiving other than the most familiar relations. Such minds may do admirable work in other directions, but not in that of estimating the value of Darwinian speculations. A few years ago they would have thought the cessation of selection a very unimportant principle, and one which could not possibly sustain any such large question as that of the transmissibility of acquired character. And a few years hence they will wonder why they raised such an ado over the no less obvious principle of physiological selection.

Yours very truly,
G. J. Romanes.

He writes to his brother :

18 Cornwall Terrace, Regent's Park, N.W.: Sunday.

My dearest James,—This theory, of the Non-Inheritance of Acquired Characters, is that nothing that can happen in the lifetime of the individual exercises any influence on its progeny; effects of use or disuse, for example, cannot be inherited, nor, therefore, can any adaptation to external conditions which are brought about in individual organisms. Natural selection thus can only operate in spontaneous variations of germ-plasm, choosing those variations which, when ' writ large ' in the resulting organisms, are best suited to survive and transmit.

This is the most important question that has been raised in biology since I can remember, and one proof of an inherited *mutilation* would settle the matter against Weismann's theory. I am therefore also trying the mutilation of caterpillars at the Zoo, in the hope that a mutilation during what is virtually an embryonic period of life will be most likely to be transmitted, seeing that *congenital* variations are so readily transmissible, and that these are changes of a pre-embryonic kind.

All well and with much love, yours ever,
George.

Have you got the 'Contemporary Review' for June with my article on Darwinism? If not, I will send it.

Another bit of work was an investigation into the intelligence of the chimpanzee 'Sally' at the Zoological Gardens, which the following letter describes:

SAVAGE versus BRUTE.

To the Editor of the 'Times' (Sept. 19, 1888).

Sir,—In connection with the correspondence on the powers of counting displayed by savages, it may be of interest to narrate the following facts with regard to similar powers as displayed by brutes.

One often hears a story told which seems to show that rooks are able to count as far as five. The source of this story, however, is generally found to have been forgotten, and therefore the story itself is discredited. Now, the facts stand on the authority of a very accurate observer, and as he adds that they are 'always to be repeated when the attempt is made,' so that they are regarded by him as 'among the very commonest instances of animal sagacity,' we cannot lightly set them aside. The observer in question is Leroy, and the facts for which he personally vouches in his work on animal intelligence are briefly as follows:

'The rooks will not return to their nests during daylight should they see that anyone is waiting to shoot them. If to lull suspicion a hut is made below the rookery and a man conceal himself therein, he

R

will have to wait in vain, should the birds have ever been shot at from the hut on a previous occasion. Leroy then goes on to say: 'To deceive this suspicious bird, the plan was hit upon of sending two men into the watch-house, one of whom passed out while the other remained; but the rook counted and kept her distance. The next day three went, and again she perceived that only two returned. In fine, it was found necessary to send five or six men to the watch-house in order to throw out her calculation.'

Finding it on this testimony not incredible that a bird could count as far as five, I thought it worth while to try what might be done with a more intelligent animal in this connection. Accordingly, about a year ago, I began, with the assistance of the keeper, to instruct the chimpanzee at the Zoological Gardens in the art of computation. The method adopted was to ask her for one, two, three, four, or five straws, which she was to pick up and hand out from among the litter in her cage. Of course, no constant order was observed in making these requests, but whenever she handed a number not asked for her offer was refused. In this way the animal learnt to associate the numbers with their names. Lastly, if more than one straw were asked for she was taught to hold the others in her mouth until the required number was complete, and then to deliver the whole at once. This method prevented any possible error arising from her interpretation of vocal tones, an error which might well have arisen if each straw had been asked for separately.

After a few weeks' continuous instruction the ape

perfectly well understood what was required of her, and up to the time when I left town, several months ago, she rarely made a mistake in handing me the exact number of straws that I named. Doubtless she still continues to do so for her keeper. For instance, if she is asked for four straws she successively picks up three and puts them in her mouth, then she picks up a fourth and hands over all the four together. Thus, there can be no doubt that the animal is clearly able to distinguish between the numbers 1, 2, 3, 4, and 5, and that she understands the name for each. But as this chimpanzee is somewhat capricious in her moods, even private visitors must not be disappointed if they fail to be entertained by an exhibition of her learning, a caution which it seems desirable to add, as this is the first time that the attainments of my pupil have been made known to the public, although they have been witnessed by officers of the Society and other biological friends.

I have sent these facts to you, Sir, because I think that they bear out the psychological distinction which is drawn in your leading article of the 17th inst. Briefly put, this distinction amounts to that between sensuous estimation and intellectual notation. Any child, a year after emerging from infancy, and not yet knowing its numerals, could immediately see the difference between five pigs and six pigs, and therefore, as your writer indicates, it would be an extraordinary fact if a savage were unable to do so. The case, of course, is different where any process of calculation is concerned: e.g. 'each sheep must be paid for separately; thus, suppose two sticks of tobacco to be the rate of exchange for one sheep, it would sorely puzzle a Damara to take two sheep and give him four sticks.' (F. Galton, 'Tropical South Africa,' p. 213.) But if the savage had to deal with a larger number of pigs the insufficiency of his sensuous estimation would increase with the increase of numbers, until a point would be reached at which, if he were to keep count at all, he would be obliged to resort to some system of notation, *i.e.* to mark off each separate unit with a separate *nota*, whether by fingers, notches, or words. Similarly with the sense of hearing and the so-called muscular sense. We can tell whether a clock strikes 1, 2, 3, 4, or 5 without naming each stroke, and whether we have walked 1, 2, 3, 4, or 5 paces without naming each pace, but we cannot in this way be sure whether a clock has struck 11 or 12, or we ourselves have walked as many yards.

Thus there is counting and counting, distinguishing between low numbers by directly appreciating the difference between two quantities of sensuous perceptions, and distinguishing between numbers of any amount by marking each sensuous perception with a separate sign. Of course, in the above instance of animals counting it must be the former method alone that is employed, and, therefore, I have not sought to carry the ape beyond the number 5 lest I should spoil the results already gained. But a careful research has been made to find how far this method can be carried in the case of man. The experiments consisted in ascertaining the number of objects (such as dots on a piece of paper) which admit of being simultaneously estimated with accuracy. It was found that the number admits of being largely increased by practice, until, with an exposure to view of one second's duration, the estimate admits of being correctly made up to between 20 and 30 objects. (Preyer, 'Sitzungsber. d. Gesell. f. Med. u. Naturwiss.,' 1881.)   In the case of the ape it is astonishing over how long a time the estimate endures.   Supposing, for instance, that she is requested to find five coloured straws.   She perfectly well understands what is wanted, but as coloured straws are rare in the litter, she has to seek about for them, and thus it takes her a long time to complete the number; yet she remembers how many she has successively found and put into her mouth, so that when the number is completed she delivers it at once.   After having consigned them to her mouth she never looks at the straws, and therefore her estimate of their number must be formed either by the feeling of her mouth, or by retaining a mental impression of the successive movements of her arm in picking up the straws and placing them in her mouth.   Without being able to decide positively in which of these ways she estimates the number, I am inclined to think it is in the latter.   But, if so, it is surprising, as already remarked, over how long a time this estimate by muscular sense endures.   Should we trust Houzeau's statement, however (and he is generally trustworthy), it appears that computation by muscular sense may extend in some animals over a very long period.   For he says that mules used in the tramways at New Orleans have to make five journeys from one end of the route to the other before they are released, and that they make four of these journeys without showing any expectation of being released, but begin to bray towards the end of the fifth.[1]

From this letter it will, I hope, be apparent that so far as 'counting' by merely sensuous computation is concerned, the savage cannot be said to show much advance upon the brute. 'Once, while I watched a Damara floundering hopelessly in a calculation on one side of me, I observed Dinah, my spaniel, equally embarrassed on the other. She was overlooking half a dozen of her new-born puppies, which had been removed two or three times from her, and her anxiety was expressive as she tried to find out if they were all present, or if any were still missing. She kept puzzling and running her eyes over them, backwards and forwards, but could not satisfy herself. She evidently had a vague notion of counting, but the figure was too large for her brain. Taking the two as they stood, dog and Damara, the comparison reflected no great honour on the man.' (Galton, *loc. cit.*) But the case, of course, is quite otherwise when, in virtue of the greatly superior development of the sign-making faculty in man, the savage is enabled to employ the intellectual artifice of separate notation, whereby he attains the conception of number in the abstract, and so lays the foundation of mathematical science. Now, so far as I am aware, there is no trustworthy evidence of any race of savages who are without any idea of separate notation. Whether the system of notation be digital only, or likewise verbal, is, psychologically speaking, of comparatively little moment.

[1] *Fac. Ment. des Anim.* tom ii. p. 207.

For it is historically certain that notation begins by
using the fingers, and how far any particular tribe
may have advanced in the direction of naming their
numbers is a question which ought never to be confused with that as to whether the tribe can 'count'
i.e. notate.

GEORGE J. ROMANES.

Geanies, Ross-shire.

CHAPTER IV

OXFORD

LIFE had run very smoothly during these years from 1879 to 1890, only now and then fits of gout had shaken the belief Mr. Romanes had hitherto felt in his own strength, in his possession of perfect health.

But about the end of 1889 other signs of ill-health appeared in the shape of severe headaches; he began to weary of London and the distractions of London life.

By degrees his thoughts and inclinations turned strongly in the direction of Oxford. Oxford seemed to satisfy every wish. The beautiful city gratified his poetic sense; there were old friends already there to welcome him, and there seemed abundance of appliances and of facilities for scientific work.

Also the ease with which he could get into the country, the opportunities for constant exercise, the freedom he would obtain from councils and committees, were tempting. A beautiful old house opposite Christ Church was to be had, and this finally determined him. He fell absolutely in love with Oxford, and brief as his connection with her was to be, the University has had few more loyal sons, nor has she ever exercised more complete influence over any who have fallen under her sway.

It is surprising, as one looks back on the Oxford years, to realise how short a time Mr. Romanes spent there, and yet it is impossible not to realise also for how much that time counted in his life.

Many influences were working in him, a ripening judgment, a growth of character, a deepening sense of the inadequacy of scientific research, philosophical speculation, and artistic pleasures to fill 'the vacuum in the soul of man which nothing can fill save faith in God.'[1]   And now Oxford, with all the beauty still left to her, with all the associations which haunt her, with all the extraordinary witching spell which she knows so well how to exercise—Oxford, the home of 'lost causes' and also of forward movements, Oxford came to be for four brief years his home.

1890 opened with the death of Mr. Aubrey Moore. Only a very few weeks before his too early death, Mr. Moore had been present at the Aristotelian Society,[2] and had heard the joint papers contributed by Professor Alexander. the Rev. S. Gildea, and Mr. Romanes on the 'Evidences of Design in Nature.'

Here, again, Mr. Romanes showed how far he had receded from the materialistic point of view.   In his paper he quoted passages from Aubrey Moore's essay in 'Lux Mundi' (just published), and says :

Yet once more, it may be argued, as it has been argued by a member of this Society in a recently-published essay—and this an essay of such high ability that in my opinion it must be ranked among the very few of the very greatest achievements in the department of literature to which it belongs—it may, I say, be argued, as it recently has been argued by the Rev. Aubrey Moore, that 'the counterpart of the theological belief in the unity and omnipresence of God is the scientific belief in the unity of nature and the reign of

---

[1] Mr. Romanes had belonged for many years to the Aristotelian Society, and had contributed papers to the Journal of the Society.   He also once belonged to the Psychological Club, which used to meet at Professor Croom Robertson's house.   The other members of the club were Mr. Francis Galton, Mr. Sully, Mr. Shadworth Hodgson, Professor Edgeworth, Professor Dunstan, Mr. Edmund Gurney, Mr. Bryant. and one or two others.

[2] See *Thoughts on Religion*, p. 92.

law'; that 'the evolution which was at first supposed to
have destroyed teleology is found to be more saturated
with teleology than the view which it superseded ';
that ' it is a great gain to have eliminated chance, to
find science declaring that there must be a reason for
everything, even when we cannot hazard a conjecture
as to what the reason is '; that ' it seems as if in the
providence of God the mission of modern science was
to bring home to our unmetaphysical ways of thinking
the great truth of the Divine immanence in creation,
which is not less essential to the Christian idea of
God than to the philosophical view of nature.' But
on the opposite side it may be represented — as,
indeed, Mr. Aubrey Moore himself expressly allows—
that all these deductions are valid only on the pre-
formed supposition, or belief, ' that God is, and that
He is the rewarder of such as diligently seek Him.'
Granting, as Mr. Aubrey Moore insists, that a precisely analogous supposition, or belief, is required for
the successful study of nature—viz. ' that it is, and
that it is a rational (? orderly) whole which reason
can interpret,' still, where the question is as to
the existence of God, or the fact of design, it
constitutes no final answer to show that all these
deductions would logically follow if such an answer
were yielded in the affirmative. All that these
deductions amount to is an argument that there is
nothing in the constitution of nature inimical to the
hypothesis of design : beyond this they do not yield
any independent verification of that hypothesis. Innumerable, indeed, are the evidences of design in
nature if once a designer be supposed ; but, apart

from any such antecedent supposition, we are without
any means of gauging the validity of such evidence
as is presented.   And the reason of this is, that we
are without any means of ascertaining what it is that
lies behind, and is itself the cause of, the uniformity
of nature.   In other words, we do not know, and cannot discover, what is the nature of natural causation.

Nevertheless, I think it is a distinct gain, both to
the philosophy and the theology of our age, that
science has reduced the great and old-standing
question of Design in Nature to this comparatively
narrow issue.   Therefore, I have directed the purpose
of this paper to showing that, in view of the issue to
which science has reduced this question, it cannot be
answered on the lower plane of argument which Mr.
Alexander has chosen.   All that has been effected
by our recent discovery of a particular case of causality in the selection principle is to throw back the
question of design, in all the still outstanding pro-
vinces of Nature, to the question—What is the
nature of natural causation?   Or, again, to quote
Mr. Aubrey Moore, ' Darwinism has conferred upon
philosophy and religion an inestimable benefit by
showing us that we must choose between two alter-
natives : either God is everywhere present in Nature,
or He is nowhere.'   This, I apprehend, puts the issue
into as small a number of words as it well can be put.
And whether God is everywhere or nowhere depends
on what is the nature of natural causation.   Is this
intelligent or unintelligent?   Is it the mode in which
a Divine Being is everywhere simultaneously and
eternally operating; or is it but the practical expres-

sion of what we understand by a mechanical necessity ? In short, is it original or derived—final, and therefore inexplicable, because self-existing ; or is it the effect of a higher cause in the existence of a disposing Mind ?

Although I cannot wait to argue this, the ultimate question which we have met to consider, I may briefly state my own view with regard to it. This is the same view that the originator of the doctrine of natural selection himself used habitually to express to me in conversation—viz. to use his own words, ' I have long ago come to the conclusion that it is a question far beyond the reach of the human mind.' Such, of course, is the position of pure agnosticism.

At the end of this paper, Mr. Aubrey Moore remarked that he agreed with all Mr. Alexander's arguments, but disagreed with all his conclusions, and that he disagreed with all Mr. Gildea's arguments but agreed with his conclusions ; and as for Mr. Romanes, he could only leave him out, after the kind and flattering terms in which he had spoken of the essay in ' Lux Mundi.' At the end of his little speech he said aside to a friend, ' What a fellow Romanes is ! " Lux Mundi " has been out about three weeks, and he knows all about it.'

The friends are lying almost side by side in Holywell,[1] and it is impossible not to feel that their deaths have left places hard to fill. About Aubrey Moore, Mr. Romanes wrote some touching words in the ' Guardian ' (he was never afraid to express his admiration, to wear his heart upon his sleeve). The little notice has now been reprinted with two others as a Preface to the volume of Mr. Moore's Essays ' Science and the Faith.'

---

[1] The beautiful cemetery adjoining Holywell Church, Oxford.

18 Cornwall Terrace, Regent's Park, N.W.: January 27, 1890.

My dear Poulton,—Many thanks for your letter, with its very clear and cogent reasoning. But I am not sure that the latter does not hit Weismann harder than it hits me. For the cases you have in view are those where very recently acquired characters are concerned; and where, therefore, according to my views, 'the force of heredity' is weak and thus quickly 'worn out.' In such cases (as I say in the last passages of enclosed, which I return for you to hand me on Friday) 'cessation will (*quickly*) ensure the reduction of an unused organ below fifty per cent. of its original size, and so on down to zero; but this it does because it is now assisted by another and co-operating principle—viz. the eventual failure of heredity.'

Now it is just this co-operating principle that Weismann is debarred from recognising by his dogma about 'stability of germ-plasm.' And it is a principle that must act the more energetically (*i.e.* 'quickly') the shorter the time since the now degenerating organ was originally acquired. In the 'Nature' articles I was speaking of 'rudimentary organs' which in Darwin's sense are very old heirlooms. All this to make you reconsider whether there is any disagreement between us upon this point.

It is, indeed, a terrible thing about Aubrey Moore, and also a loss to Darwinism on its popular side.

G. J. R.

After receiving your letter this day a month ago, it occurred to me that I had better write an article in 'Nature' on Panmixia, pointing out the resemblances and the differences between Weismann's statement of the principle and mine. Shortly after sending it in, Weismann's answer to Vines appeared, and from this it seems that he has modified his views upon the subject. For while in his essays he says that 'the complete disappearance of a rudimentary organ can only take place by the operation of natural selection' (*i.e.* reversal of selection through economy, &c.), in 'Nature' he says, 'Organs no longer in use become rudimentary, and must finally disappear, solely by Panmixia.' Thus, the same facts are attributed at one time 'only' to the *presence* of selection, and at another time 'solely' to its *absence*.

Now, the latter view seems exactly the same as mine, if it means (as I suppose it must) that the cessation of selection ultimately leads to a failure of heredity. (How about stability of germ-plasm here?) The time during which the force of heredity will persist, when thus merely left to itself, will vary with the original strength of this force, which, in turn, will presumably vary with the length of time that the organ has previously been inherited. Thus, differences of merely *specific* value (to which you allude in your letter) will quickly disappear under cessation of selection, while 'vestiges' of *class* value are long-enduring. The point to be clear about is that the cessation of selection (in my view) entails *two* consequences, which are *quite distinct*. First, a comparatively small amount of reduction due to promiscuous variability round an average which, however, will be a continuously sinking average if the cessation is assisted by a reversal of selection; and second, later on, a failure of the form of heredity itself.

Touching the first of the two consequences you say that 'variations below or away from the standard would not be balanced by those above, because the standard was reached by the selection of such an extremely minute fraction of *all* variations which occurred.' But can variations in the matter of increase or decrease take place in more than two directions, up or down, smaller and larger, better or worse? (Read Wallace, 'Darwinism,' pp. 143–4.)

I write this in view of the lecture you say you are going to give, because I do not know when 'Nature' will bring out my article.

March 20. 1890.

It might perhaps be well for you to read the type-written reply which I have prepared to Wallace's criticism on 'physiological selection.' But this is for you to consider. He has fallen into some errors of great carelessness, not only with regard to my paper, but also to that of Mr. Gulick, whose theory of 'segregate fecundity' is the same as mine. On this account I am able to upset the whole criticism, and, bottom upwards, to show that it really supports the theory.

I see 'Nature' of this week contains my letter on Panmixia, and hope it will define in your and other minds the outs and ins of the matter.

Please return the enclosed, which I send as a fact that may interest you.

To Professor J. C. Ewart.

18 Cornwall Terrace, Regent's Park, N.W.: April 27. 1890.

As Ethel has already told you, I believe, we have taken a three years' lease of a charming old house, and let this one for a corresponding period. It is a very old house in Oxford, having been built by Cardinal Wolsey. It is immediately opposite Tom Tower of Christ Church, and full of old oak—walls, floors, and ceilings of the principal rooms being nothing else.

I do wish you could come up before we begin operations, to give us the benefit of your advice how so splendid an opportunity in the way of decoration should be utilised. We have to get out of this house, with all our furniture, on or before May 20. The children and servants will then go to Geanies, while my wife and I will go to Oxford to begin the decorations.

I am preparing my lectures on Darwinism for the press, so that they may be ready for publication on the last day of my course at Edinburgh in November. I suppose I have your permission to reproduce your R.S. pictures of electric organs? Also, could you send me for a day or two Haddon's book on Embryology?

I have just heard that Charles Lister (whom I think you met at Geanies) has died of fever in Brazil, where he was zoologising.

Yours ever sincerely,

GEO. J. ROMANES.

The move was made from London to Oxford in May 1890. Mr. Romanes incorporated with the University and became a member of Christ Church. This connection with 'the House' was a great pleasure to him.

For a little while during the early summer of 1890 Mr. Romanes was alone in Oxford, and he writes :

To Mrs. Romanes.

I called to-day on Mr. Dodgson, to sign my name in the Common Room, and signed my name in the book where the signatures go back to the foundation of the House. It is certainly the best thing I could have done to join Christ Church, and I am enjoying this return to my undergraduate days as something quite novel. Yesterday Liddon [1] graced the high table with his company. He was particularly gracious to me, remembering all about our meeting years ago, and hoping to be allowed to have the pleasure of calling upon us when we were settled in the 'almshouse.' [2] After dinner in the Common Room, seeing that the party was both elderly and reverend, all the other six being parsons, I started what seemed to me a suitable game, viz. who could best 'card wool' in opposite directions, or turn the right hand round and round one way, while at the same time turning the left hand round and round the other way. This innocent occupation at once became very popular—the Canon in particular being greatly interested in the peculiar difficulty which it presents. For my own part, I much enjoyed the spectacle of all these dons

[1] Dr. Liddon died in September 1890.

[2] The house which Mr. Romanes had taken was originally an almshouse.

winding their hands about, and this enjoyment reached its climax when Dr. Liddon ended by tilting his glass of claret off the table into his lap.

But there is a good deal of fun from behind his serious exterior, and he enjoyed this little catastrophe as much as the rest of us. So you see that the snares and temptations of University life do not dangerously assail your husband at the high table of Christ Church.

Yesterday we had our physiological picnic, starting in five boats, and taking tea on the river-bank near the old farmhouse. I took supper with the Sandersons, who had a party. The Victor Horsleys were at the picnic, and I have arranged that they will pay us a visit in October.

It is very jolly living in this house, but it is well we are both good sleepers, the noise of traffic is so great, even the foot-passengers sound like burglars.

But this will not affect the children in the other wing, and as for me, I could sleep if the carriages were driving through the rooms, with the burglars to boot.

I have only time to write a very few lines, as I am now momentarily expecting to be called on to give my exposition before the Physiological Society,[1] which has mustered in considerable force, and is now being regaled by Horsley[2] and Gotch[3] while I am watching my plants which are coming on next.

The dinner at Ch. Ch. yesterday was most enjoyable, though there were only four others besides myself at the high table. We had turtle soup and very good wine ; is that good for gout ?

---

[1] The Physiological Society has a yearly meeting at Oxford.
[2] Professor Victor Horsley, F.R.S., Univ. Coll. London.
[3] Professor of Physiology at Oxford.

St. Aldate's: July 1, 1890.

I have just come back from dinner. My next neighbour to-night was Liddon, and we had a long talk on the ethics of suicide regarded from the pre-Christian or purely 'secular' point of view.

I also improved the occasion in the interests of ——. It was clearly a new light to Liddon that —— should be so highly thought of by a man of science, and he appeared to have determined there and then to exert himself in getting a more suitable berth for ' a man now so greatly needed in the Church.'

Oxford.

Two bits of news. Dunstan [1] has a son and Liddon is seriously ill. Dr. John Ogle came yesterday afternoon from town to see him, and dined with us. There is great pain in the neck.

I lunched with the Sandersons, or rather with Mrs. Sanderson, as the Professor did not leave his room, but he is getting on very well.

Last night after dinner I looked in at the Poultons, and found them entertaining two Natural Science young ladies from Somerville Hall. A very agreeable party. Huxley is expected here this week. His article on ' Lux Mundi ' is very characteristic.[2]

It would be very enjoyable to go with you to Ober Ammergan, but I am sure I ought not. First, I should not enjoy it half so much as you; second, it would double the expense; third, it would run away with all the time I want to give to the book. So in

---

[1] Professor W. Dunstan, F.R.S.

[2] ' Lights of the Church and of Science.'

s 2

this case what is sauce for the goose is not sauce for the gander.

I wish I had some jokes to treasure up, but Oxford is not a joke-yielding place at present; Geanies must be jubilation itself compared with Oxford now.

I am the sole occupant of the laboratory as of the house. But I rather enjoy the exclusive privilege of my own company, save so far as it is relieved by guinea-pigs. I have written a letter to 'Nature' which will furnish a little joke for you on Friday next.

I am sorry to hear poor old Parker[1] is dead. You did not know him, but he was a real good fellow, and hearty friend to me.

I enjoyed my three days in London very much. Went twice to the theatre, and one of the plays was 'Judah.' Mr. H. A. Jones gave me a box. Saw a great deal of the Pollocks; met Scott,[2] who asked me to let him put me up for Royal Society Club; played chess with G. R. Turner.

I have now got to work on my plants and guinea-pigs.

To Professor Poulton.

Geanies. Ross-shire, N.B. : July 16, 1890.

My dear Poulton,—I went to the tennis ground yesterday week, but, as I expected, on account of the rain, found nobody there.

I now write to ask you if you would have any objection to my borrowing with acknowledgment figures from your book for mine, supposing the pub-

---

[1] Professor Kitchen Parker, F.R.S.   [2] Mr. R. Scott F.R.S.

lishers also consent. In particular figs. 1, 2, 6, 10, 40, and 41.

Having now read the book,[1] I may say how greatly it has delighted me. The whole is a wonderful story, and I congratulate you on the large share which you have had in adding to this chapter of Darwinism.

There is only one point I am not quite clear about, viz. pp. 213 215. It is doubtless an advantage to the parasites that the caterpillars should warn them off as having been already 'occupied.' But would not this be rather a *disadvantage* to the caterpillars —*i.e.* to their *species*? For in this way, it seems to me, a greater number of caterpillars would become infested than would be the case in the absence of such warning. Or is there any point about it which I do not understand ?

When is your next book coming out ? I should like you to read my reply to Wallace before it does. Also my re-statement of physiological selection, with discussion on the principles of Segregation and Divergence. I hope the whole will be in type before November. Can you wait till then, or shall I send type-written MSS.?

Yours very sincerely,
GEORGE J. ROMANES.

P.S.—Talking about hon. degrees the last time I saw you reminded me—but something again put it out of my head—that I had been wondering why

---

[1] *The Colours of Animals*, by E. B. Poulton, M.A., F.R.S. International Scientific Series, vol. lxviii.

Oxford or Cambridge does not offer one to F. Galton. Could you start a movement in that direction ? . . .

I am getting so convinced about physiological selection, that I do not care what is said at random, or without understanding the theory.

Later in the autumn he writes :

To Mrs. Romanes.

I hope to find letters from Ober Ammergau when I return to Geanies, with a dozen bottles of sulphur water and several pounds of heather honey. Went yesterday to see a waterfall, which was wonderfully beautiful ; on the way back met a pony with half a trap, and afterwards came on the other half with its previous occupants, Lord and Lady ——, cut about the face, but not seriously hurt. There is an awful row going on here in the Free Kirk, which bids fair to end in bloodshed locally, if not disruption generally.

I am so glad you do not repent going, and am longing to hear what you think of the play. I took Ethel and Ernest partridge-shooting, and had tea outside. The new hound, ' Dart,' has arrived. He is beautiful, and as gentle as a lamb with the children. This threw us off our guard, and at tea there was a horrible scene, ending in the murder of Sharpe.[1] The latter barked at him, and five minutes afterwards was a mangled misery. Have returned Dart with a civil note, for the sake of Norah and Jack,[2] the latter having only been saved by heroic measures on the part of Mytsie.

---

[1] A beautiful terrier.　　　　　　[2] Two more dogs.

Later in the autumn he wrote:

To Mrs. Henry Pollock.

Geanies: October 9, 1890.

My dear Mentor,—The lyric is certainly very pretty, but I am still—and much—more touched by the unrhymed, and perhaps unconscious, poetry that accompanies it. We have, indeed, many associations with Geanies in common;[1] and as neither the joys nor the sorrows of them can ever return into our lives as they were when they arose, it is perhaps better that they should be kept in our memories as they now are, without being overlaid by future experiences in the same moods and the same cliffs by the same sea. 'The water that has passed' has been beautiful, even in its sadness; and however long the wheel of life may still have to go, I do not think it could have done better work for any of us than during the years that it has gone at Geanies.

With my philosophic love to both of you, ever the same,

GEO. J. ROMANES.

My very dear Mentor,—You are quite too kind to me. The touching little present has just arrived, and I am smoking it now. It is just the kind that I like best. I wonder whether the vendor thought it was for yourself? Very many thanks.

Ethel sends her love, and tells me to ask you whether you want a copy of the photo group, where you do not look like a Mentor.

I enclose payment for the pipe in the form of son-

---

[1] This was the last summer at Geanies.

nets—although I am sure they are not so sweet—and remain, with love to Marion,

Ever yours most sincerely,

GEO. J. ROMANES.

This autumn Mr. Romanes delivered the last of his Edinburgh course of lectures. Giving the lectures had been a real pleasure, and he liked his Scotch students, who on their side were keenly appreciative and intelligent.

He was alone at Geanies for a few days before leaving for Edinburgh, and a letter written at this time shows for the first time a foreboding of failing health ; but when the headaches left him the foreboding vanished, and there was no real idea of serious mischief.

To his Wife.

Geanies: November 1890.

I really have three of your dear letters to answer. I did not write yesterday. I have had one continuous headache ; it is now nearly away, but the matter is getting serious, and I have written to Edward,[1] to send the 'home trainer' to Oxford, so that I may lose no time in giving his cure (exercise) a trial.

Don't get low about me ; I begin to doubt if these headaches are due to gout at all, and somehow or other I shall find a means of preventing them.

I am sorry for myself, my work, and most of all for you ; but we must take illness as it comes, and be glad it is no worse.

[1] Mr. E. B. Turner, F.R.C.S.

I will not disappoint you about the sonnet, which you expect to be in the vein of ' Weltschmerz,' and therefore send you the first of the series which I wrote in the small hours, after reading your favourite Psalm.[1] There was only one verse that remained appropriate to me, so I took it as a text.

The principal thing that has happened to-day is my having seen on the shore a sea otter. It was lying on a rock, and I came upon it at such close quarters I could have hit it with a stone. But it was so quick that I had not even time to fire my gun.

I may return the compliment as to letters. I did not intend to send the sonnet even to you when I wrote it, but afterwards thought I ought to have no secrets.

Fritz[2] and Ernest came out shooting. I am all right as to hitting ;[3] and my head is perfectly well. Jack[4] has been very Jackish. I told him we were all going to leave Geanies. He said, ' Geanies belongs to us.' I answered, ' No, it belongs to the Murrays.' ' Part of it belongs to me,' he continued. ' How is that ? ' said I. ' Because I was born here.' What would Victor Horsley say to this for early appreciation of rights conferred by birth ?

Ernest and Gerald are very happy. I allow them to play with the fire when they are with me, and this I find to be very popular.

[1] Psalm xxvii.   [2] A pet name for his daughter.
[3] He had slipped on the rocks and hurt his arm.
[4] His third son.

To Mrs. Romanes.

Edinburgh : November 23, 1890.

My lectures are now concluded, and I took an affectionate farewell of the class amid much enthusiasm on their side.

There is no news to give. I play chess with Mrs. Butcher and read MSS. which Professor Butcher lends me of his own; pay many calls, have sundry talks with professors that come to dine with Ewart, and so on.

Yesterday we had here what at Cambridge used to be called a 'Perpendicular,' twenty students to supper. Mrs. Butcher and Miss Trench came in to help to entertain them; the latter sang Irish songs.

I am going to give an additional lecture to the class on the controversy in 'Nature.'[1]

I send you a report of my lecture, that you may see how orthodox I was. Sellar[2] was at the lecture, and told me that I reminded him of some professor at St. Andrews, who had told him as a fact that he (the St. Andrews professor) always made a point of alluding to Providence in an introductory lecture, and afterwards 'threw him aside!'

The sonnet alluded to in one of the letters (p. 265) is so beautiful that it is inserted here. It shows better than any words could do the attitude of George Romanes' mind. Profoundly sincere, anxious, almost unduly anxious, to give no indulgence to his own

---

[1] On 'Physiological Selection.' See *Nature*, vol. xlii. pp. 5, 7, and vol. xliii. pp. 79 and 127.

[2] The late Professor Sellar.

longings, to state to himself and to others unsparingly, unflinchingly, what appeared to him the as yet irrefutable arguments against the Faith, when he was alone he relaxed and poured out his inmost heart.

> ' I ask not for Thy love, O Lord : the days
>   Can never come when anguish shall atone.
>   Enough for me were but Thy pity shown,
> To me as to the stricken sheep that strays.
> With ceaseless cry for unforgotten ways—
>   O lead me back to pastures I have known,
>   Or find me in the wilderness alone,
> And slay me, as the hand of mercy slays.
>
> I ask not for Thy love; nor e'en so much
>   As for a hope on Thy dear breast to lie ;
> But be Thou still my shepherd—still with such
>   Compassion as may melt to such a cry ;
> That so I hear Thy feet, and feel Thy touch,
>   And dimly see Thy face ere yet I die.'

In November Mr. Romanes came formally into residence, and at first nothing could have been happier than his Oxford life.

He simply revelled in the facilities for work which the splendidly equipped laboratories afforded, and he once said, ' that the laboratory alone had made the move from London to Oxford worth while ! '

He set to work on his book, ' Darwin, and after Darwin,' and on many experiments bearing on Professor Weismann's theories and on some other points.

He much wished to see established in Oxford what M. Giard has called an *Institut transformiste*, and wrote to many leading men of science on the subject. As yet the idea has come to nothing, but possibly it may be revived.

January 22, 1891.

My dear Poulton,—I am very sorry that, being already engaged for to-morrow, I cannot attend the meeting. But I should like to join the Society.[1] Only, please, postpone any suggestion about lecturing, as this term I shall be dreadfully busy, between the book and the experiments. H. has certainly been very successful over a very difficult experiment. I tried it in an elaborate way. But I lacked assistance for the mechanical performance, and so intended to do it here this term. Now I am saved the trouble, but have gained experience. This prevents me from regarding H.'s result as final, although, as you say, valuable. My scepticism is founded on a queer freak of heredity, which my own work showed me; but as I think I spoke too much about the experiments I was trying, in future I shall adopt Weismann's method of silence before publication.

Yours ever,
GEO. J. ROMANES.

About this time Mr. Romanes was much interested in a scheme for promoting the establishment of a garden or farm for the purpose of studying questions of hereditary transmission, or heredity. His object was to afford facilities which at present do not exist for observing the modifications produced in animals and plants by subjecting them during long periods and in successive generations to suitable external conditions, and for testing the transmissibility of the modifications so produced. He was anxious that such an Institution should be founded in connection with one of the Universities, and with this view, circulated the following memorandum.

[1] The Oxford Natural History Society.

' AN INSTITUT TRANSFORMISTE.'

In an English translation of a lecture which was recently delivered by M. Giard, as Professor of Evolutionary Biology in France, there occurs the following passage :

' If evolutionists must content themselves in most cases with experiments carried on in nature, or those of breeders, instead of applying themselves to verifications made with all the rigour of modern scientific precision, is it not because of the deplorable insufficiency of our laboratories ? It is astonishing that in no country, not even where science is held in greatest honour, does there yet exist an *Institut transformiste* devoted to the long and costly experiments now indispensable for the progress of evolutionary biology.'

That an institution of the kind in question would tend to promote the solution of problems in ' evolutionary biology,' it seems needless to argue. Many of the most desirable experiments in heredity and variation, for example, require such prolonged time and such constant attention, that it is practically impossible for individual workers to undertake them ; and, therefore, as M. Giard observes, they have never been undertaken. But if there were an *Institut transformiste* to which material might be sent from any part of the world, with directions as to its treatment, biologists of all countries would be furnished with an opportunity of experimentally testing any ideas which might occur to them in regard to these or kindred matters.

Again, it seems needless to remark that England ought to be regarded as the natural territory of an establishment of this character; that the establishment itself should be situated in the vicinity of others which are already devoted to the study of morphology and physiology; and that sufficient land should belong to the *Institut* to admit of plots of ground being set apart for researches on plants, as well as buildings for the accommodation of animals.

In order to satisfy all these conditions, the *Institut* ought to be established either in Oxford or Cambridge; and at least, one skilled naturalist, one competent gardener, and one trustworthy keeper ought to be resident. This would involve an annual expenditure of between 300*l*. and 400*l*. But the capital sum which would have to be sunk in the purchase of land and the erection of buildings would not be considerable; because, in the first instance, at all events, two or three acres of ground would probably be sufficient; while the animal houses would be chiefly —if not exclusively—required for the accommodation of small mammalia, birds, insects, and aquatic organisms.

Nevertheless, seeing that an initial expenditure of at least 1,000*l*. would be needed for the purposes just mentioned, as well as an annual income of at least 400*l*., and seeing that even this much money is not likely to be forthcoming for objects of a purely scientific nature, the scheme on behalf of which we solicit your opinion is the following.

From inquiries which we have made here, we think it is probable that the University would take up the matter, or, at any rate, render important assistance thereto, if the Hebdomadal Council were satisfied as to the desirability of the project from a scientific point of view. It is on this account that we have ventured to address you upon the subject. The appended memorial is being sent, together with this circular letter, to all the other leading biologists in this country; and if you could see your way to signing the former, you would render additional weight to the body of authoritative opinion which it will eventually convey to the University.

One of the experiments Mr. Romanes tried in the summers of 1891–93 was as to whether animals completely isolated would reproduce the *real* sounds natural to their kind. In other words, whether these vocal sounds were due to imitation. Through the kindness of Mr. Arthur Balfour, Mr. Romanes got the permission of the Trinity Brethren to try these experiments on lighthouses situated on lonely islands or rocks; he selected puppies, chickens, &c., but the results were not decisive. The puppies barked and the young cocks crowed, but Mr. Romanes was not able entirely to establish to his own satisfaction that the isolation had been complete.

Experiments were also carried on bearing on Heliotropism and on Seed Germination. Of these mention will be made later.

In the spring of 1891, he paid a visit to Paris and saw M. Pasteur and his laboratory, and also M. Brown-Séquard, in whose work he was specially interested.

And, apart from his work, Oxford and Oxford life were great sources of enjoyment. He made many new friends, and keenly enjoyed the institution, so characteristic of Oxford, of 'walks.'

Intimacies seemed to grow up quickly, and he

often spoke of the extreme kindliness, the 'pleasantness' which marked Oxford society.

Of all the friends made in these four years, Mr. Romanes undoubtedly was most drawn to the Rev. Charles Gore.

It is very difficult, very often misleading and even impertinent to speak of what one man owes to another in the way of direct or indirect intellectual or spiritual help. But those few persons who really watched and could see the workings of George Romanes' mind, saw that these Oxford years were, even before the first beginnings of fatal illness, years of rapid growth in what perhaps may be termed spiritual perception.

In 1891 Mr. Gore's famous Bampton Lectures were preached. Mr. Romanes heard them all, and was intensely interested by them; he wrote many notes on them for his own private use, notes by no means always in agreement with them, and in his 'Thoughts on Religion' he refers to them.

Many of his older friends were clergymen, and he was once much amused by hearing that a scientific friend in London had said, 'How on earth will Romanes stand the clerical atmosphere of Oxford?' Another time, a very eminent scientific man asked him his opinion of Liberal High Churchmen, 'Do you really think these people believe what they say?' to which Mr. Romanes replied that he knew several pretty intimately, and he was sure they would all go to the stake on behalf of their Faith.

In the spring of 1891 Mr. Romanes was elected by the committee a member of the Athenæum Club. The Journal notes:

Pleasant dinners at Merton, Keble, &c. Visit from the Gills,[1] which we much enjoyed. Lord and Lady Compton, from the 6th to the 8th of June. He delighted us with his magnificent singing.

---

[1] The Astronomer Royal at the Cape and his wife.

This summer, for the first time, Scotland and shooting were given up, and Mr. Romanes, accompanied by his wife and daughter, tried what the Engadine would do for his incessant headaches.

He enjoyed this tour, especially three weeks at Tarasp, in the lower Engadine, where he met his old friend Professor Joachim and also Professor Victor Carus. On the way back the Romanes stayed with Mr. H. Graham, M.P., at his lovely country home near Heidelberg, enjoying themselves much, but failing to see the famous ghost which is said to haunt the place. In the autumn, in spite of often-recurring headaches, he struggled on with his work and lectured in one or two provincial towns.

He says in one of his letters at this time: 'There is much excitement in Oxford to-day over the announcement that Paget is to be the new Dean of Christ Church. Of course we are greatly delighted. As he said to me to-day, 'We may now look forward to being close neighbours for not a few years to come.'

Journal, Nov., Birmingham Festival.—The 'Messiah' and Dvorak's 'Requiem,' Parry's 'Blest Pair of Sirens,' which one never hears too often. Went to Compton Wynyates, a splendid old house of temp. Henry VII. Only Lady Compton at home, but we much enjoyed our little visit. Went up to town and saw the Edmund Gosses and various other old friends. Saw Miss Rehan and her company in their last performance, 'A Last Word.' Poor play, but well acted.

It was during this autumn that Mr. Romanes resolved to found a lectureship at Oxford on the lines of the Rede Lectures at Cambridge, and after consulting various friends, chiefly the present Master of Pembroke,[1] the idea was submitted to the University and the offer was accepted. The preface, which is to be prefixed to the first volume of Lectures, gives the founder's ideas.

Founder's Preface.

The primary object of this Lectureship is to secure a perpetual series of discourses in the University of Oxford under the conditions laid down in the foregoing Statute. But seeing that these conditions are necessarily of a general character, I add the following suggestions with regard to certain matters of detail, in order that, as far as from time to time may seem expedient, the proceedings may be conducted in accordance with my wishes

(1) I desire that the selection of lecturers be irrespective of nationality, and determined with reference either (*a*) to general eminence in art, literature, or science, or (*b*) to special claims for discussing any particular subject of high interest at the time.

(2) I deem it desirable that foreigners, otherwise eligible, should not be disqualified from receiving invitations to lecture merely because they may not be able to do so in English. And, in order to meet such cases, I suggest that the translated addresses should be delivered before the University by some competent reader (to be selected by the Vice-Chancellor) in the presence of their authors.

(3) I further suggest that the same method of delivery should be adopted in cases where age or infirmity would render the voice of the lecturer

---

[1] The Rev. Bartholomew Price, D.D., F.R.S.

inaudible, or indistinct, to any portion of his audience. And I hope that neither age nor infirmity, any more than inability to speak the English language, will be deemed a hindrance to the issuing of invitations to the men of high distinction in their several departments. For, on the one hand, in order to have attained such distinction, it must often happen that such men will have attained old age, while, on the other hand, it is of more importance that they should be represented in these decennial volumes than that men of less eminence should be chosen in view of their superiority as lecturers.

G. J. ROMANES.

To the great satisfaction of the whole University, Mr. Gladstone most generously consented to give the first lecture, which consent he signified in the following letter :

Grand Hotel, Biarritz : December 18, 1891.

Dear Mr. Romanes,—Until I received your kind letter I reposed undoubtingly in the belief that the Vice-Chancellor had accepted my answer as the answer which best met the case.[1] I thought and think it right, for no one knows my poverty except myself. But Oxford is Oxford, and I think that if she desired me to climb up the spire of Salisbury, I should attempt it, or play the *Græculus esuriens* in any manner she desired. Your letter opens to me unexpectedly the fact that there is a desire, and that the proposal was not simply a courtesy.

---

[1] Mr. Gladstone had declined at first, but yielded to a second urgent request from the founder.

I therefore thankfully and respectfully accept; secretly relying a good deal, as I own, on the fact that there is (if I recollect the V.C.'s letter rightly) a good deal of time before me, and that the chances of intermediate reflection may bring up something to the surface which is not now there, for I own my perplexity continues as to the chance of making any presentation not wholly worthless. But enough of this : and let me thank you very much for the interest you, who have so high a title, have personally taken in bringing me to the front.

We are much delighted with this place ; more eminently, I think, a sea place than any other I happen to know.

I am sure, let me add, that you will make my apologies to the Vice-Chancellor; for I am sensible that the altered reply may seem less than respectful to the resident Head of the University.

Believe me, most faithfully yours,
W. E. GLADSTONE.

It had been arranged that the lectures (which the University, rather against the Founder's wish, decided should be called the 'Romanes Lectures') were to be given in the Trinity Term, but owing to the General Election of 1891, Mr. Gladstone postponed the delivery of his inaugural lecture until October 1892.

Journal, March 1892.—The Comptons have been here for Norman's baptism, which was a strikingly pretty ceremony in cathedral at evening service with the choir. Our Dean and the President of Magdalen, as well as Lady Compton, stood sponsors, so the boy

is well provided. The students at St. Hugh's Hall
decorated the font, and as the boy's second name is
Hugh, he is a special protégé of the little Hall.

April 1.--We spent a week at Malvern, in company with the Walter Hobhouses, and then went on
to Denton Manor,[1] where a company of the wise, including Ray Lankester, Professors Poulton and Shadworth
Hodgson, and Mr. Sully, were. Also others, including
Lady Cecil Scott Montagu, who walked abroad with
a divining rod, a real act of courage considering who
were among the party.

At Malvern Mr. Romanes wrote a sonnet which,
in the light of after years, was a sad prophecy.

MALVERN 1892

'To doze upon a sunny hill in June,
 And hear the lullaby that Nature lends;
 To drink the cup that sweet contentment blends
With sweetlier love of those whose hearts shall soon
Reverberate with joy, as they attune
 Their praise to praises that achievement sends:
 This is to feel that bounteous Nature bends
A mother's smile on manhood in its noon.

But when the shadows of the twilight come,
 And high Ambition needs must fold his wings,
While voices both of hearts and hills grow dumb,
 Can she still bring the smile that now she brings?
 Yea, by the memory of brighter things.
I'll trust her in the night that calls me home.'

Journal, May and June 1892.—Had a delightful
visit from the Butchers and Mr. H. Graham, later on
the Comptons, and Mr. Edmund Gosse, full of witty
and wise sayings. Lord Compton sang more divinely

[1] The home of Sir William and the Hon. Lady Welby-Gregory.

than ever, and the Principal of Brasenose played the piano. It was a real musical feast.

Professor Le Conte came to stay here, we had Mr. Gore and one or two others to meet him.

To Miss C. E. Romanes.

94 St. Aldate's, Oxford : June 10, 1892.

My dearest Charlotte,—I received your letter of the 6th inst., together with the pair of slippers ; the latter are the very thing that is required when occasion again arises.

Ever since you left we have been having Italian weather, the only objection to which being, that for my taste the sunshine is too continuous.

We have had staying with us Professor Palgrave and his daughter. I am going to take her to the Conversazione of the Royal Society on Wednesday next, as Ethel is going to stay behind for her political work. We have also had Lord Justice Fry, with his wife and daughter, staying with us for two or three days.

I have got a promise from Professor Huxley to give the second Romanes Lecture, provided he is able to do so next year. It will be an interesting occasion if he can, because he has not lectured for the last five or six years.

I am glad you like my book, which is selling off very well ; but, as you know, the second volume will be much more interesting.

We are all well, and, with united love to both, I remain yours ever the same,

GEO. J. ROMANES.

A new investigation is here described.

94 St. Aldate's, Oxford: March 27, 1892.

My dear Schäfer,—I think I have found a new ordinal character peculiar to the Primates—viz. a nude condition of the terminal phalanges. This does not occur in any other order of mammals that I have looked at, but in all species of primates from Lemurs to Man, as far, at all events, as I have been able to examine. Now I want to see whether hair-follicles, or vestiges thereof, can be found in the terminal phalanges of any species of the order. So I am making a number of sections of the skin of the backs of the terminal phalanges of fingers and toes, of man (adult and fœtal) apes, monkeys, baboons, and lemurs. Hitherto I cannot detect (nor can Kent) any signs or vestiges of follicles. But I should much like you to look over some of the specimens (a few would be enough), in order to see whether your trained eyes would be also unable to trace any rudiments of follicles. If you would care to do this, of course I should acknowledge my obligations in a paper which I am preparing on the subject.

Yours very truly,

G. J. Romanes.

'Darwin, and after Darwin' appeared in the spring of 1892.

It was a book which was written, so to speak, with the writer's life-blood, it was a great burden on him from the moment he commenced it, and one of his greatest sorrows was his inability to finish it.

It is curious to those who know Mr. Romanes' mind

intimately to note the exceeding severity, the almost harsh manner in which he treated the theological questions involved in the doctrines called, for convenience sake, 'Darwinism.' As more and more he found himself yielding on the side of emotion, of moral convictions, inducement, of spiritual need to the relinquished faith, so much the more did he resolve to be utterly true, to face every difficulty, to push no objection aside, to leave nothing unsaid—to be, in fact, absolutely and entirely honest. As a friend after his death, speaking of this very book, said, 'It was his *righteousness* which made him seem so hard.'

Yet there is a ring of hope of something which will one day turn to faith in the words which end the book :

'Upon the whole, then, it seems to me that such evidence as we have is against rather than in favour of the inference, that if design be operative in animate nature it has reference to animal enjoyment or well-being, as distinguished from animal improvement or evolution. And if this result should be found distasteful to the religious mind—if it be felt that there is no desire to save the evidences of design unless they serve at the same time to testify to the nature of that design as beneficent—I must once more observe that the difficulty thus presented to theism is not a difficulty of modern creation. On the contrary, it has always constituted the fundamental difficulty with which natural theologians have had to contend. The external world appears, in this respect, to be at variance with our moral sense ; and when the antagonism is brought home to the religious mind, it must ever be with a shock of terrified surprise. It has been newly brought home to us by the generalisations of Darwin, and therefore, as I said at the beginning, the religious thought of our generation has been more than ever staggered by the question—Where is now thy God? But I have endeavoured to show that the logical standing of the case has not been materially changed; and when this cry of reason pierces the heart of Faith it remains for Faith to answer now, as she always answered before—and answered with that trust which is at once her beauty and her life—Verily thou art a God that hidest Thyself.'

June 1892 brought the first warnings of serious illness. One day Mr. Romanes announced at lunch that he noticed a blind spot in one eye. He consulted his friend Mr. Doyne, the well-known oculist, who from the first thought seriously of the case.

He went up to town, and saw various doctors, and had some thoughts of taking a voyage. He was, however, well enough to attend the Conversazione at the Royal Society, and showed some experiments on rabbits and rats which bore on questions of acquired characters. He writes:

To Mrs. Romanes.

I have been thinking of you a great deal, and, with a somewhat literal application of a certain expletive addressed by a fast man to his eyes, am driven to address you through my goggles.

Nettleship has appointed to-morrow morning to see me, so I shall not be able to get home sooner than 6 train. Don't trouble to meet me, as I must take a cab for the rabbits and rats. The latter are now at the Royal Society, where ample space has been provided for their exhibition. The Zoological paper [1] went off very well, and Flower made a very good remark on it, the substance of which I will tell you when we meet, it had not previously occurred to me. Your letter to the Pollocks never reached them, so they had given me up. They were as enthusiastically kind as usual, and very sympathetic about my eyes.

He returned to Oxford, and was persuaded to rest, and not to go to London again to pay a promised visit to Professor Palgrave.

To Miss C. E. Romanes.

94 St. Aldate's, Oxford : June 18, 1892.

My dearest Charlotte,—Your little differences of opinion with regard to the rats are very amusing to me, and I quite see how the matter stands.

I am very glad to hear of your improvement in general health, and also of James' continued vigour. As regards myself I have no very satisfactory account to give. The headaches indeed are not worse —if anything they are better; but the gout is at work on other parts of this vile body, and the latest assault is a very serious one for a man of my pursuits. About ten days ago I found myself partially blind in the right eye—the upper half of the field of vision being totally obliterated. I have seen an Oxford

---

[1] On the work alluded to in a letter to Professor Schäfer.

and also a London oculist, who have both examined
the eye and pronounce the sudden seizure to be one of
serous effusion upon the retina. It seems probable
that the impairment of vision will be permanent, and
so prevent all operative work where any delicacy is
required. The blindness is so complete, that if I
look about an inch below the electric light placed at a
distance of a very few yards, I am not able to perceive any luminosity. Meanwhile, I have to wear
the darkest of possible goggles, and generally to live
the life of a blind man. *Per contra*, this may prove
a blessing in disguise, as it compels me to abstain
from work for some considerable time to come, and
I had been advised to this course on account of the
headaches. How I am to spend the six months'
rest which is prescribed I have not yet determined.
Shooting will be probably out of the question, as I
cannot use the left eye in any form of recreation.
My idea is rather to go to Egypt and Palestine, to
take a voyage to the Cape, or in some other such
way to break my usual habits without altogether
wasting time.

All the rest of the household are flourishing, and
with love to both,

I remain yours ever the same,

GEORGE.

In a day or two a second blind spot appeared, and
now the doctors took a very serious view of his case.
Life and sight alike were threatened, and instant
rest and quiet were ordered. For about three weeks
he remained in bed, until the extreme pulse tension
was reduced, and then it seemed as if hope might

be entertained of years of life, if only care were taken about diet, and work, and thought.

Now began the two years of quiet, steadfast, endurance; no one could realise from his quiet manner and cheerful talk how great was the inconvenience caused by the affection of his eyes, no one ever found him anything but unselfish and gentle. The one difficulty was to persuade him not to work, and this was almost impossible. He was almost feverishly anxious to finish his book, to work out experiments he had been planning; and as time went on, and he thought and pondered as he had ever done on the ultimate mysteries of life and being, other books were planned, other courses of reading mapped out.

Just then a letter came from Canon Scott-Holland which much touched the recipient.

Mr. Holland writes:

'I hear sad news of you through Philip Waggett.[1] You have passed under the sorest trial perhaps that could have been laid on your courage, your hopefulness, your peace.

I trust, indeed, that there is much to look for yet of recovered power and renewed work, but, for the moment, there must be anxiety, and the bitter strain of disappointment, and the rough curb of pain. You are assured of the deep sympathy of many warm-hearted friends to whom you have always shown most generous kindness, and I venture to rank myself among them. We shall remember you often and anxiously.

It is a tremendous moment when first one is called upon to join the great army of those who suffer.

---

[1] The Rev. Philip Napier Waggett, now of Cowley St. John, who was one of Mr. Romanes' most intimate friends. Mr. Waggett's scientific attainments made him a valuable as well as a much loved friend.

That vast world of love and pain opens suddenly to admit us one by one within its fortress.

We are afraid to enter into the land, yet you will, I know, feel how high is the call. It is as a trumpet speaking to us, that cries aloud—' It is your turn—endure.' Play your part. As they endured before you, so now, close up the ranks—be patient and strong as they were. Since Christ, this world of pain is no accident untoward or sinister, but a lawful department of life, with experiences, interests, adventures, hopes, delights, secrets of its own. These are all thrown open to us as we pass within the gates— things that we could never learn or know or see, so long as we were well.

God help you to walk through this world now opened to you as through a kingdom, regal, royal, and wide and glorious. My warmest sympathies to your wife.'

The first weeks of illness passed away, the physicians seemed more satisfied with his condition, and he was sent to Carlsbad, and after five weeks there, came the last bit of pleasant foreign travel. He and his wife travelled in the Tyrol and in the Bavarian Highlands, and Mr. Romanes was able to enjoy the glorious scenery with what seemed keener appreciation than ever ; he especially took a fancy to Parten Kirchen, in Bavaria, and planned a return to it another year with his children.

He got as far as Meran, and much enjoyed meeting Mr. and Mrs. Lecky (Mr. Lecky's works were among the very few historical books he read with any real pleasure). And on his return, Sir Andrew Clark was encouraging, holding out hopes of a return to health : ' You've made a bid for recovery,' he said in his genial way. It was thought best that Mr. Romanes should spend the winter in a warm climate, and Madeira was chosen.

Then came the first Romanes lecture, which was a great success in every way. Mr. Gladstone called it ' An Academic Sketch,' and nothing could have been a happier inauguration of the series. It was a memorable scene. The Prime Minister in his doctor's robes, the crowded Sheldonian theatre, the eloquent lecture, the inspiring words of which came like a trumpet call to Oxford's sons, ending with her motto, Dominus illuminatio mea.'

The few days of Mr. and Mrs. Gladstone's visit to Oxford were days of real enjoyment to Mr. Romanes. The Journal notes : 'We had a pleasant luncheon party for the Gladstones and Lord Acton, who was also in Oxford; also a breakfast party on the morning after the lecture, to which, among others, came the Principal of St. Edmund's Hall.[1] I put him next Mr. Gladstone, and the consequence was a Dante talk, to Lady Compton's great satisfaction. Mr. Gladstone's talk was wonderful, and no one would have suspected that he had any political cares whatsoever, or that the Election of 1892 was only just over.'

On the day of the lecture we had a delightful time before lunch. Mary Paget and Lord Compton sang for an hour, and put us in good humour.

It was with real regret that good-bye was said to the illustrious guests, with hopes of future meetings never to be realised.

Mr. Huxley accepted the invitation which the Vice-Chancellor permitted Mr. Romanes to give him privately. The following delightful letter gives his final decision : [2]

---

[1] The Rev. E. Moore, D.D.

[2] Since this letter has been in type the world has had to lament Mr. Huxley's death.

Hodeslea, Staveley Road, Eastbourne : November 1, 1892.

My dear Mrs. Romanes,—I have just written to the Vice-Chancellor to say that I hope to meet his disposition any time next May.

My wife is 'larking'—I am sorry to use such a word, but what she is pleased to tell me of her doings leaves me no alternative—in London, whither I go on Monday to fetch her back—in chains, if necessary. But I know, in the matter of being 'taken in and done for' by your hospitable selves, I may, for once, speak for her as much as myself.

Don't ask anybody above the rank of the younger son of a peer, because I shall not be able to go into dinner before him or her, and that part of my dignity is naturally what I prize most.

Would you not like me to come in my P.C.[1] suit? All ablaze with gold, and costing a sum with which I could buy, oh! so many books.

Only if your late experiences should prompt you to instruct your other guests not to contradict me—don't —I rather like it.

Ever yours very truly,
T. H. HUXLEY.

Bon voyage! You can tell Mr. Jones[2] that I will have him brought before the Privy Council, and fined as in the good old days, if he does not treat you properly.

Then came the departure for Madeira, which was a real trial, for never before had Christmas been spent

---

[1] Privy Councillor.   [2] The proprietor of an hotel in Madeira.

away from home.   But the change seemed to do him much good.   Save for occasional days of headache he was very bright and well, and worked at his book and wrote several articles for the ' Contemporary Review ' on Professor Weismann's theory.   But poetry he could not manage.

To Mrs. Henry Pollock.

Madeira : December 18, 1892.

My dear Mentor,—I fear you must have been thinking that I am either very ill or very heartless not to have written ere this.   Yet neither is the case. Ill I assuredly am, but not so much as to have prevented me from sending you a letter for the marriage day.   The fact is I have been trying to write a sonnet for that occasion ever since I came out here, and cannot.   Since my breakdown in June I have entirely lost the power of poetising ; I suppose it will come back if my general health should ever return, but still I did think that such an occasion ought to have inspired me.   Nothing further than rhymes, however, would come, so the day passed over without my intended contribution to its memorials.

So, dear Mentor, do not think hardly of me.   For indeed both you and Marion have been much in my thoughts ; and for you especially I know this time must be one of many and varied feelings of the kind that sink deepest into the heart.[1]   So not only my old affection, but a new sympathy, is with you—a sympathy in the joy as in the grief of it.

[1] Miss Pollock's marriage to Mr. Vernon Boys, F.R.S., is here referred to.

Ethel will have told you what little has to be told about our uneventful life here. As I have said to all my correspondents, it is the island that Tennyson must have had in view when he wrote his 'Lotus-eaters.' The description is so exact, that *I* need not write anything in the way of description, if you will only read *it*.

My headaches are growing less intense, although they still keep wonderfully persistent. I cannot foresee what is likely to happen in the end, as no one seems to know exactly what is the matter with me.

The last mail brought me a letter from the Master of my College at Cambridge, telling me that I had been unanimously elected to fill a vacancy in the list of Honorary Fellows. This seems to me very generous, seeing how I have played the prodigal and squandered my living on endowing the enemy.

Please give my very heartiest love and good wishes to the bride. Take also my Christmas greetings for all three of you, coupled with the congratulations that are so meet, and believe me to remain,

Yours ever affectionately,
GEO. J. ROMANES.

To James Romanes, Esq.

Madeira: 1892.

I suppose you will have seen in the newspapers, or have been told by Char.,[1] that Caius College has made me an Honorary Fellow.[2] This is a great pleasure to me, because I have always retained my first love for

---

[1] A pet name for his sister.

[2] A window to his memory is to be placed in Caius College Chapel.

Cambridge, and yet of late years I have so severed my connection with it. These coals of fire have therefore a heat about them which is all the more gratifying.

To Professor Ewart.

This would be a wonderful place for natural history if I were well enough to knock about.

I get fishermen, however, to bring any marine animals which they know to be rare. There is one fish which I never heard of before, and which seems to me remarkable on account of its curious combinations of character, for in all respects it seems to be a large dog-fish, excepting its teeth, which are those of a shark.

To Professor Poulton.

New Hotel, Madeira: December 2, 1892.

My dear Poulton,—I have now read the correspondence in 'Nature.' It seems to me that —— is quite absurdly 'aggressive,' even supposing that he proves to be right. But I send this to ask you about the grasshopper letter in last week's 'Nature,' just received here. I have noticed the same thing in grasshoppers, but do not remember to have seen any account of the changes of colour, or mechanism thereof, in them. Do you know if it has ever been worked at? If not, I might do so here.

The same question applies to lizards. It seems to me that those here vary their colours to suit those of *habitual* stations. I remember Eimer read a paper about the lizards in Capri, but forget details. He often alludes to it in his book translated by Cunningham. What are his main results?

G. J. R.

The Cambridge Fellowship was a great pleasure to Mr. Romanes. In the last months of his life he longed eagerly to visit his first University and his own college, and planned visits to Cambridge which, alas, were never paid.

Canon Isaac Taylor was in the same hotel at Madeira, and this considerably relieved the weariness of exile. Mr. Romanes was still full of fun and merriment; the headaches diminished; he played chess interminably, and even took part in a little play given one afternoon by a few people who formed themselves into an 'Oxford Brotherhood,' most of the members having some connection with the University of Oxford.

The members of the brotherhood were supposed to deliver lectures in turn, but the burden chiefly fell on Mr. Romanes. The lecturing, which in this particular case was simply talking, was never any trouble to him, and he used to deliver little impromptu discourses which apparently pleased his friendly audience. Canon Taylor kindly gave a discourse on the Aryans, and displeased one of his audience, a young lady, by remarking at the outset, 'My specimens (alluding to Romanes' scientific lectures) are before me, and I suppose we are all Aryans.' The young lady had imagined she was about to hear a lecture on Church history, and was not pleased at being dubbed an *Arian*.

Mr. Romanes' letters showed nearly always great brightness and increased feelings of health, although now and then he had 'bad days.'

To James Romanes, Esq.

Madeira : January 1, 1893.

This is the first letter which I write in 1893, and am writing it early in the morning before breakfast. New Year's Day is as glorious in sunshine and azure as all—or nearly all—the others have been since we came. I wish you many returns of them and happy, whether in cloud or sunshine.

January 31, 1893.

Your letter on the 15th has been a great treat to me; it rings true and deep, and the next best thing to having dear ones near is to receive expressions of their dearness.

Besides, I am all alone here, for but a few days, it is true, still the place seems dreary under present circumstances, therefore all you say is opportunely said.

For my own part I have always felt that the two most precious things in life are faith and love, and more and more the older that I grow. Ambition and achievement are a long way behind in my experience, in fact out of the running altogether. The disappointments are many and the prizes few, and by the time they are attained seem small.

The whole thing is vanity and vexation of spirit without faith and love.

Perhaps it is by way of compensation for having lost the former that the latter has been dealt to me in such full measure. I never knew anyone so well off in this respect. . . .

Although I have been very much in the world I have not a single enemy, unless it be the ———, who have entirely dropped out of my life.

On the other hand, I do not know anyone who has so many friends, not merely acquaintances, but men and women who are devoted with an ardent affection. . . .

Now, all this might sound very conceited to anyone who would not understand me as I know you will do. But I have been thinking the matter over in my solitude, and candidly I am wholly unable to account for it. Still, to be further candid, even love is not capable of becoming to me any compensation for the loss of faith. . . .

But it is time for me to go to bed and shut up this egotistic screed to post by to-morrow's mail.

I received a telegram yesterday announcing the arrival in England of my brace of Ethels, and to-morrow I expect the arrival here of Charlotte and Mytsie.[1] . . .

I forgot about the mesmerism article. You will have seen that the writer rather caved in at the end, so that one cannot well understand how much he himself supposes was genuine and how much imposture.

But quite apart from (this), there is no question in my mind that the facts, even as far as hitherto established, are very perplexing. But on this account there is all the more need for caution. I myself went over the Paris Salpêtrière two years ago, and saw the doctors' experiments on a number of girls, who were trotted out for my benefit.

---

[1] A favourite cousin, who died a few months after Mr. Romanes.

But there was such a lot of hocus pocus with magnets that I was much disappointed. Even if none of the girls were humbugging, I saw nothing that could not be explained by suggestion.

For the doctors made suggestions while performing the very experiments which were designed to exclude suggestion.

To Mrs. Vernon Boys.

New Hotel, Madeira: February 1, 1893.

My dear Marion,—If I have your husband's permission still to call you so—your kind letter has been a great solace to me, after my ineffectual efforts to supply a sonnet for the great occasion. For it shows me that your Laureate is forgiven, and my friend, what that friend has always been. Besides, I am now lonely—as my brace of Ethels has flown away—and therefore your affectionate words are all the more welcome.

This, however, is the last day of my solitude, as Charlotte and Mytsie ought to arrive in a few hours.

And now, having given you all my little news, let me pile up my congratulations as high as words can pile them. I heard all about the wedding from many different sources, and there was but one opinion as to the bride. I will not say what it was, but oh, had I been there to see. It is *so so* good of you to miss us in the middle of it all. But it may have been telepathy, because I was hard at work on my abortive sonnet all that day.

It is like northern breezes to read your account

of all the happy doings you have had on your wedding trip, and it makes me happy to feel that you have made so wise a choice in the greatest event of your life. Long may you live together in the cultivation of domestic bliss, although *of course* only in the moments snatched from the cultivation of science!

February 2.

Charlotte and Mytsie arrived last night at ten o'clock—twelve hours late. They had the roughest voyage which the boat has ever experienced. Poor Char.[1] is literally more dead than alive. But the weather here is beautiful, and I hope she may soon get to rights again.

With affectionate regards to my mentor, and to *yours*, I remain, ever the same,

PHILOSOPHER.

To James Romanes, Esq.

Madeira : March 8.

Charlotte enjoys this place amazingly, she is always saying, 'Just a very Paradise for James.' I quite agree with her. You liked Nice very much, but Nice is far from being up to this either in regard to sun, flowers, rocks, or mountains. It has certainly done me a lot of good. My headaches are virtually gone, and I can work a little again, which makes all the difference between Heaven and its antipodes.

March 13.

I am glad you are pleased about the lectureship foundation. The principal feature of the scheme is

See p. 289, above.

the perpetual publication of the lectures in volumes
of ten each through all time, or at least as long as
Oxford lasts.

I am better even since I last wrote to you. Even
my powers of work have, to a considerable extent,
returned. So I am answering H. Spencer's articles
on ' Weismannism.'

With warmest love, yours ever the same,

GEORGE.

To Mrs. G. J. Romanes.

Madeira.

I got your dear note soon after we went down
to the pier to see you start. Through the club
telescope I thought I saw you and Fritz. When you
got far out I came home. The Taylors joined our
table, which is very agreeable. The Canon told me
a good joke which came off to-day. Sir ' Gorgias '
told the Canon he had bought a second-hand book
which he thought Dr. Taylor might find interesting.

The Canon asked what the book was, and the
Knight replied it was by a man called Locke, and
was all about the Human Understanding.

February 2.

Char., Mytsie, and maid arrived ; they had a perfectly frightful passage. All passengers shut down
for two days, crockery broken, &c.

S—— presented a large wedding cake for the
Sunday tea of the Inner Brotherhood.

February 11.

This is the joyful day.[1] Your telegram was handed to me at lunch, so all the Inner Brotherhood had the benefit. The Canon said you ought to have used the comparative degree, so as to leave me an opportunity of returning the superlative.

What a journey you had, poor dears! It does not seem so certain after all that we should be safe for comfort on a long voyage. Mytsie and Char. had a worse passage than you, the wind was dead against them all the way.

It is indeed shocking about the Dean.[2] I heard it before you did. I will write to him by this mail.

So glad you had such a good concert. If you only knew how I was longing to enjoy it with you. . . .

An adagio movement has now followed the allegro, and I am looking forward to a presto home as a finale.

My news is not much. My cold was very bad from Saturday to Monday, but I slept most of the time straight on. If it were not for my eyes I should be almost as well as ever I was.

I read Walter Hobhouse's child story, and Mrs. —— capped it with another. A little girl she knew asked whether, when she got to heaven, she might 'have a little devil up to play with.' Mytsie's nephew, when three years old, had a much prettier idea. On M. telling him that something had happened before he was born, he said, 'Then that was

---

[1] His wedding-day.   [2] Dr. Paget had been very ill.

when I was still in heaven.' 'Yes,' answered M.,
'but what was heaven like?' 'Oh, there I played
with angels, and there was nothing but Christmas
trees.'

Are not the debates first-rate? It seems to me
I never read so many good speeches as those of
Balfour, Bryce, and Chamberlain. But the measure
itself is absurd.

We had a party on board the 'Royal Sovereign'
on Tuesday last. It was a dance on deck, and was
very pretty. Enormous profusion of flags and flowers
all over the ship. I asked one of the midshipmen
to dine with us at the 'round table;' he had shown
us over one of the ships on a previous day, as I told
you, and proved an awfully nice little fellow, curiously like P. N. W.[1] Suffers always horribly from
sea-sickness, and gave a dismal account of his life at
sea.

By the way, *à propos* of the B.A. I suppose you
have heard that Lord Salisbury is to be President
next year at Oxford. You had better be thinking
whom to invite as guests, leaving a margin in case
———— should redeem his promise. I shall meet
him between this and then somewhere and ascertain.

March 12.

There has been a most extraordinary change in
the weather. Up to yesterday we had three of the
calmest days that have been since I came. The sea
was without a ripple, and Char. and I were last night

---

[1] Mr. Waggett.

hoping it would be like that when we start, as it would be sure to last till we got home. When, lo and behold, this morning there is by far the highest wind and sea I have yet seen. The spray is flying right over the rocks, once up to where Fritz got over the wall by the bathing-place. Rain in sheets. The 'Drummond Castle' will have an awful time of it. No hope of a letter to-day.

March 16.

Letters, such jolly good gossip that I feel disposed to follow the example of the 'distinguished man' who lived apart from his wife because he so much enjoyed her letters. And yet I am like a hound straining at his leash to get away.

I *cannot* read what it is that York Powell is going to have designed for us, it looks like 'booky flash.'[1]

. . . . By the time you get this, it will only be another fortnight before you get me, and I believe you will get me in a wonderfully restored state of health.

March 17.

The weather is still the same. Tremendous wind and perpetual squalls of rain, 'the sea and the waves roaring,' also 'men's hearts failing them for fear,' for the occupants of the rooms we used to have never went to bed last night.

This morning an English man-of-war ran in for refuge, but had to run out again before the return salutes had been fired, as her anchors could not hold, and an odd accident happened. At the 18-minute

---

[1] It was 'book-plate.'

gun from the fort, one of the gunners somehow got
in front of the cannon and was blown to atoms. I
suppose they were all confused with the wind and the
spray.

The waterproof coat you sent me is in great
requisition. Moreover it is a source of great amusement to the Inner Brotherhood, as Miss Taylor has
discovered in it a close resemblance to a hassock—
no, I mean a cassock. She wants me to get a round
hat wherewith to ' cap ' it when I return to Oxford.
All the same, it is the best thing in the way of a
waterproof that I have met as yet.

March 19.

I have got Weismann's new book, ' The Germ-
Plasm.' It is a much more finished performance
than the ' Essays.' In fact, he has evidently been
consulting botanists, reading up English literature on
the subject, so he has anticipated nearly all the
points of my long criticisms. This is a nuisance.

Per contra, since coming here I have heard of no
less than three additional cases of cats which have
lost their tails afterwards having tailless kittens. I
wish to goodness I had been more energetic in getting on with my experiments about this, so I have
written to John to get me twelve kittens to meet me
on my return. It would be a grand thing to knock
down W.'s whole edifice with a cat's tail.

The monotony of life here is becoming intolerable.
There is nothing to write about.

You will have seen that Taine is dead. I was
just about to write to him, to ask if he would be the
Romanes lecturer.

Here is an odd thing. I find that Weismann in his new book has discussed all the points raised by Spencer. So Spencer and I have been hammering away at things which W. has already written upon. Luckily, he says about what I anticipated he would say (see my article), but how absurd a fiasco! I have written a postscript to go by the mail, hoping it may arrive in time to be bound up as a separate slip before the issue of April number, explaining that absence from England prevented me from getting W.'s new book until now. But S. ought to have known.

I have written to Weismann telling him that Bunting will send him a copy of the ' Cont. Review.' [1]

I have asked W. if he will give the Romanes Lecture some year. Love to you and the chicks. You will have to tell me which is which of the boys.

Unless he has already procured ordinary kittens, tell John [2] to get them either Angora or Persian. They will cost more, but will be much better.

I had a long innings with the doctor to-day; he says I am perfectly sound; believes my headaches are all gastric.

Your last letter just received is such a relief to me. I was just Ernest's age when I nearly died of whooping cough.

The home coming was very bright, and again Mr. Romanes set to work with renewed and, alas, too

---

[1] *Contemporary*, April 1892.

[2] His butler, an old and valued servant.

great vigour. Beyond absolutely refusing invitations to dine out at Oxford, and living as quietly as possible at home, there was no keeping him in order. The following letters show how irrepressible his spirits were whenever a day's health made him hopeful again.

To Mrs. G. J. Romanes.

Athenæum Club: May 10, 1893.

I was very sorry that I could not get home to-day, and hope you will have received my telegram. Everybody was at the Royal Society except Balfour, and I became wearied with congratulations on my improved appearance. I met Moulton,[1] who was awfully nice, and wanted me to dine and sleep at his house some day if I can, in order to talk over 'physiological selection.'

So I asked him to come and hear Huxley. He said he would try. . . . Galton asked me to join in an investigation of the French calculating boy at his house to-day, so I did. Oliver Lodge was there. The boy was most marvellous.

I am going to the Globe to-night and am very well. After the R.S. last night I went to a party at Lady Tenterden's. Very smart.

Yours ever lovingly,

GEORGE.

Journal: May.—Sir A. Clark is fairly encouraging. Dinner at Mrs. Pollock's; met the R. Palgraves and W. Flowers, who have blossomed out into K.C.B.'s since we left.

[1] F. J. Moulton, Esq., M.P., F.R.S.

20th.—The Huxleys' visit has been most delightful. He was most genial and 'mellow,' and his lecture has, of course, aroused great interest. Various people to meet them. Mr. Gore and Professor Froude one day to lunch. Somewhat heterogeneous elements. When the former had gone, Mr. Huxley suddenly awakened to the fact that it was the Principal of the Pusey House whom he had met.

Count and Countess Balzani have been here, and we had an 'historical' dinner for them.

This was the last bit of the old pleasant life which Mr. Romanes had so much enjoyed. He was busy arranging experiments on heliotropism and on the power of germination in dry seeds after precautions had been taken to prevent any ordinary processes of respiration, which were worked up into a Royal Society paper. He writes:

To F. Darwin, Esq.

St. Aldate's, Oxford: June 14.

My dear Darwin,—There has been no hurry about answering my letter because I cannot publish until I shall have ascertained what has already been done upon the subject, and for this purpose I have had to write to Germany. I am greatly obliged to you for the substantial assistance which your letter has given me.

My *modus operandi* was to give nine different kinds of seeds to Crookes,[1] to place them in one of his $\frac{1}{1000000}$ atmosphere vacuums for three months last year (viz. February, March, and April). He then

[1] Professor W. Crookes, F.R.S.

left one set undisturbed, whilst the other eight sets
were transferred to their respective gases (nine in
number), where they remained sealed up for a year.
On being planted last month they have all germinated
even better than those from the control packets of
seeds, which have been in air all the time.

I should have thought beforehand that at any rate
the seeds which have been in so high a vacuum for
fifteen months would have had any residual air extracted. But I will now try for next year, peeling
peas, beans, &c., as you suggest. Do you think it
would be well also to soak the seeds for a few hours
before sealing in Crookes' tubes?

Do not trouble to answer by letter, as I am going
to Cambridge on the 21st inst. for the day, and will
then see you if I can find you at home.

I am not exactly ' at work,' as I am not as yet
well enough to attempt it at anything like ordinary
pressure, but I am certainly better, and much obliged
to you for your kind inquiries upon the subject.

With our united kind regards to Mrs. Darwin and
yourself,

I remain, yours sincerely,

G. J. Romanes.

P.S. My illness has left me half blind, so I write
as much as possible by dictation. (What a bull!)

94 St. Aldate's, Oxford: June 15.

My dear Dyer,—Many thanks for your letter with
enclosures. The letter shows that ——'s opinion has
not altered since I last saw him. As I think I told

you at the Athenæum, he undertook some two or three years ago on my behalf to raise discussions in the papers, to which he alludes. Since that time he has sent me, I believe, copies of all the numberless letters which have been published in consequence. The result of our inquiry has been to confirm the opinion which he gave me at the first, and also to form my own in the same direction. (See my article in answer to Herbert Spencer in the 'Contemporary Review' for April.[1])

As regards the isolation of species I do not understand why you should suppose that the facts of hybridisation to which you allude should in any way modify my 'belief.' As fully set forth in 'Physiological Selection,' what I maintain is that the origin of species is in *all* cases due to isolation *of some kind*, but that only in the case of differential fertility can physo. sel. have been the kind of isolation at work. Therefore, it would be fatal to my views if all species were cross-sterile, because this would prove vastly too much. What the theory of phy. sel. requires is exactly what occurs, viz. cross-sterility between allied species in nearly all cases *where species have been differentiated on common areas* or identical stations, and more or less complete cross-fertility where they have been differentiated on different (discontinuous) areas, or else prevented from intercrossing by yet some other means of isolation.

I have collected a quantity of evidence in favour of both these otherwise inexplicable correlations.

[1] Mr. Herbert Spencer on 'Natural Selection,' *Contemporary Review*, April 1893.

But I should like to know the species of wild fowl which you have found to be hybridisable or cross-fertile, so that I may ascertain whether their natural breeding areas are, or are not, identical. Of course I should expect them not to be.

I have been told to save my eyes as much as possible, and therefore conduct most of my correspondence by dictation. But not being used to this process, I find it even more difficult than before to express my meaning with clearness, so I will tackle with my own hand what you say about Aquilegias.

I have looked up the group, and find that, with the exception of vulgaris (common columbine), all the European species seem to occupy restricted areas, or else well-isolated stations. Also, that the same seems to apply as a very general rule to other species all over the world, for, wherever mountains are concerned, stations are apt to be isolated by difference of altitude, &c.

Now if such be the case with the group in question, the fact of its constituent species being freely hybridisable when artificially brought together is exactly what my theory requires. For the specific differentiation has presumably been effected by geographical (or topographical) isolation, without physiological having had anything to do with it. In fact, as stated over and over again in my original paper, *this* correlation between geographical isolation and cross-fertility is *one* of my lines of verification, the *other* line being the correlation between identical stations and cross-sterility.

Now, as above stated, I have found both these

correlations to obtain in a surprisingly general manner.

I wish that, instead of perpetually misunderstanding the theory, you English botanists would help me by pointing out *exceptions* to these two rules, so that I might specially investigate them. It seems to me that the group you name goes to corroborate the first of them, while all Jordan's work, for instance, uniformly bears out the second. And whatever may be thought about him in other respects, I am not aware that anyone has ever refuted his observations and experiments so far as I am concerned with them.

Yours ever sincerely,

G. J. ROMANES.

94 St. Aldate's, Oxford : June 22.

Dear Dyer,—I received a letter from —— by the same post that brought yours of the 19th inst. From it I gather that his opinion on the subject of telegony has not changed in any material respect since our inquiry began. His opinion has always been such as you now quote ('atavism' on the one hand, with a small minority of ' dormant fertilisation ' cases on the other). His has likewise always been my own view (with the addition of coincidence), and has been corroborated by the result of these inquiries. So I think we are all three pretty well in agreement, because both —— and myself share in your doubts as to the minority of the cases being really due to dormant fertilisation—*i.e.* not to be ascribed to coincidence or mal-observation. Also, as I said before, I quite agree with you that ' neither view is any help to Herbert

Spencer.' In fact, I have somewhat elaborately sought to prove this in my 'Contemporary Review' article for April, and have been in private correspondence with him ever since, but without getting any 'forerder.'

But in this connection I should like to know whether you have any opinion upon the apparently analogous class of phenomena in plants which Darwin gives in the eleventh chapter of his ' Variation,' &c. Here, it seems to me, the evidence is much more cogent and of far more importance to the issue, Weismann *v.* Lamarck. Focke and Dr. Vris, however, seem to doubt the facts or their interpretation, although, as it seems to me, without presenting any adequate reasons for doing so. You need not bother with Dr. Vris, as he merely follows Focke, but I wish you would read Focke (' Die Pflanzen-Mischlinge,' p. 510, *et sq.*), and compare what he says with the evidence which Darwin presents.

As I do not know in what respects you have found one part of my previous letter not to ' tally ' with another, I cannot fully explain it; but I fancy that you will find they do, if, in reading the letter, you carry in your mind the simple proposition that, from the nature of the case, there can be no physiological selection except where differentiating varieties (' incipient species ') occur upon common areas and identical stations. I do not see any difficulty about willows, roses, brambles, &c., since Naudin's researches on *Datura* have shown how much variability, due to the hybridisation of any two species, may give rise to the *appearance* of there being many species. This, you will remember, is the view that Naudin himself takes with regard to willows &c.— although, of course, without any reference to phy. sel. If you will refer to p. 405 of the paper on phy. sel. you will find that from the first I have been aware of the difficulty about discontinuous areas to which you allude. But I think the converse line of evidence (viz. that of cross-sterility between incipient species on identical stations) will alone prove sufficient to verify the theory. At the same time I look for more corroboration from the cross-fertility of well differentiated species upon discontinuous areas where these are, as you say, oceanic islands, or, still better, mountainous districts where the allied species are severally peculiar to mountain tops and isolated valleys. For in these cases there must be much doubt, as a general rule, touching the species having been differentiated by topographical isolation upon the particular areas where they are now found. Moreover, and this I think quite as important, the consideration which Darwin adduces in another connection is obviated, viz. 'that if a species was rendered sterile with some one compatriot, sterility with other species would follow as a necessary contingency.'

Yours very sincerely,

G. J. ROMANES.

P.S.—From your first letter it would almost seem that you had supposed me to doubt the fact (or, at any rate, the frequency) of cross-fertility in general. And this after I had written the article on ' Hybridisation ' in the ' Ency. Brit.' !

In June Mr. Romanes took a small house for the summer months outside Oxford at Boar's Hill, a district well known to Oxford people, and it was hoped country air and quiet might do him much good.

He was rather headachy, and liked to lie on the grass in the garden and have novels read to him, but he was able to go up to London one day, and even planned to take a journey to Wiesbaden in order to consult an eminent oculist.

But on July 11 he was stricken down by hemiplegia. And now began the last year of patient endurance, for from that time the Shadow of Death was ever on him, and he knew it : from that July day he regarded himself as doomed. Sometimes the thought of leaving those whom he loved with such intense devotion, such wonderful tenderness, overwhelmed him ; sometimes the longing to finish his work was too great to be borne, but generally he was calm, and always, even when he was most sad, he was gentle and patient, and willing to be amused.

On July 13 Dr. Paget gave him the Holy Communion.

He slowly recovered from this attack, and there were hopes—not of perfect health, but of life, and of power to work. Now, more resolutely than ever, he set himself to face the ultimate problems of Life and Being, to face the question of the possibility of a return to Faith.

It is impossible here to tell of the inner workings of that pure and unselfish soul, of those longings and searchings after God, of the gradual growth in steadfast endurance in faith.

To one or two these are known, and the example of lofty patience and of single-heartedness is not one they are likely to forget. Of this more later.

It was almost pathetic to see how keen and vigorous his intellect was. In fact, the great difficulty was to keep the busy brain from thinking. Novels helped to some degree, and occasional visits from friends as he grew better. Dr. and Mrs. Burdon Sanderson, the President of Trinity and Mrs. Woods, the Dean, Mr. Gore, the President of Magdalen and Mrs. Warren, and Mr. Waggett, all helped, coming and paying brief visits, which did him good, for if he was not listening to reading or conversation, he would be planning experiments or pondering problems of theology, and ask by-and-by that his thoughts should be taken down from dictation, or that paper and pencil should be given him, or, worse than all, devising arrangements for finishing 'Darwin, and after Darwin.' He dictated some 'Thoughts on Things' in the very first days of his illness, and sent for Professor Lloyd Morgan, who came and received instructions about the unfinished books, instructions which he has carried out with unflagging diligence and never-failing kindness.

But still he grew better, and early in August he went back to Oxford, and by the first of September he was able to be present in the cathedral at the baptism by Dr. Talbot of his youngest son.

The fact that the Vicar of Leeds[1] and Mrs. Talbot were in Oxford during that August was a great pleasure to him, and he much enjoyed occasional talks with Dr. Talbot.

To Professor Ewart.

I do not know what account E. gave you of my illness, but it is much too serious an affair to admit of our going to the British Association. Indeed, I hardly anticipate being able to make any engage-

---

[1] Now Bishop of Rochester.

ments or do much work during the rest of my life,
which is not likely to be a long one. It is just
such an attack as I expected when walking with
you over Magdalen Bridge.[1]

Yours ever,
G. J. ROMANES.

By September he was able to listen to, and discuss, Dr. Sanderson's Presidential Address, which was
delivered in Nottingham at the British Association
of 1893.

It was one of the great disappointments of that
illness that he could not go to Nottingham. To be
at the Association when his dear friend and master
was president was a great wish of his, and early in
the summer a kind invitation from Lady Laura
Ridding, to stay with the Bishop of Southwell and
herself for it, had been accepted.

Nottingham and a visit to Denton, to which
Mr. Romanes had been looking forward, had to be
given up.

These things were real trials. It was not the
giving up particular bits of pleasure, but the realisation that he was too much of an invalid to do anything of the sort, which he found so hard to bear, and
which he did bear with ever-increasing patience.

His letters sometimes show how hard he felt his
trial.

To James Romanes, Esq.

Oxford: September 4.

My dearest James.—I have had two reasons for
not writing to Dunskaith since my letter about the
birth of Edmund.

[1] About eighteen months before, when a very temporary attack of
aphasia had come on.

I agree with all you say about Fritz and her numerous brothers, the last two of whom you have never seen.   But, although I have been so signally blest in my family . . . I am not disposed to fall in with your optimism in other respects.   Rather am I disposed to agree with the Scotch minister, that 'Man is a mi-ser-able worrm, craaling upon the airth;' for, both as regards the misery and the craaling I am now a type.

And this brings me to my two reasons for not writing before.   The first is, that I am almost unable to write; and the second is, that I did not want to let you and Charlotte know all the facts sooner than I could help.

The long and the short of it is that I believe I am dying.   I have been gradually getting worse and worse, . . . nor shall I be sorry when it comes. Such being the case, I should like to consult you about setting my house in order. . . . . .

The photos which the children brought with them of Dunskaith make me realise what splendid work the buildings are, and even although it is now improbable that I shall ever see them, I am glad to think that they will be in the family.[1]

I cannot write more now.   In fact I have not written so much since my attack.   But I send you the best love of a life-time's growth and that of your only brother.

GEORGE.

---

[1] His brother was making additions to the house at Dunskaith.

To W. T. Thiselton-Dyer, Esq.

94 St. Aldate's, Oxford: September 15, 1893.

Dear Dyer,—Many thanks for your letter with enclosures. As you say, there does not seem to be anything remarkable about the hybrid; but I am glad to see that both its parent species are well marked and presumably both of mountain origin. The case thus well accords with my views, as explained in my previous letters. I met with many such (*i.e.* hybrids between originally isolated species) in Madeira and the Canaries.

There are none so blind as those who will not see. Where can your powers of 'observation' have been when you can still remark that I ignore the facts of hybridisation? I can only repeat that from the first I have regarded them as evidence of the utmost importance as establishing a highly general correlation between *separate* origin of allied species and *absence* of cross-sterility. In fact, for the last five years I have had experiments going on in my Alpine garden, which I helped in founding for the very purpose of inquiring into this matter. And Focke, with whom I have been in correspondence from the first, and who *does* understand the theory, writes that in his opinion it will 'solve the whole mystery' of natural hybridisation in relation to artificial.

Since my last letter to you I have been at death's door. On July 11, I was struck down by paralysis of the left side, and am now a wreck. Not the least of my sorrow is that I fear I shall have to leave the verification of phys. sel. to other hands in larger measure than I had hoped. I have little doubt that it will eventually prevail; but more time will probably be needed before it does.

Yours very sincerely,
G. J. ROMANES.

Oxford: September 18, 1893.

Dear Dyer,—I am not a little touched by the kind sympathy expressed in your letter of the 16th. When one is descending into the dark valley, scientific squabbles seem to fade away in those elementary principles of good will which bind mankind together. And I am glad to think that in all the large circle of my friends and correspondents there is no vestige of ill will in any quarter, unless it be with —— and ——, who both seem to me half-crazy in their enmity, and therefore not of much count.

As for 'fortitude,' sooner or later the night must come for all of us; and if my daylight is being suddenly eclipsed, there is only the more need to work while it lasts. But, to tell the truth, I do not on this account feel less keenly the pity of it. With five boys—the eldest not yet in his teens and the youngest still in his weeks; with piles of note-books which nobody else can utilise, and heaps of experimental researches in project which nobody else is likely to undertake, I do bitterly feel that my lot is a hard one.

Looking all the facts in the face, I do not expect ever to see another birthday,[1] and therefore, like Job, am disposed to curse my first one. For I know that all my best work was to have been published in the

[1] He did see one more.

next ten or fifteen years; and it is wretched to think of how much labour in the past will thus be wasted.

However, I do not write to constitute you my confessor, but to thank you for your letter, and also to say that I am sending you a copy of my 'Examination of Weismannism,' just published by Longmans.

With our united kind regards to Mrs. Dyer and yourself. I remain, yours very sincerely,

GEO. J. ROMANES.

94 St. Aldate's, Oxford: September 26, 1893.

My dear Dyer,—This is one of my bad days, and I have just exhausted my little store of energy by answering a kind letter from Huxley. So please excuse brevity, as I cannot leave your highly appreciated benevolence without an immediate response.

I am much concerned to hear what you say about yourself, and it makes me doubly desirous of seeing you. On Monday next I am to try to go to town for the purpose of consulting doctors. But any day before that we should be truly glad if you could come as you so kindly propose. *Possibly* I might be able to drive out to Kew on Tuesday or Wednesday of next week, should you find it impracticable to run down here before then. But I fluctuate so much from day to day that I cannot make any engagements.

Most fully do I agree with all that you say regarding criticism. And, especially from yourself, I have never met with any but the fairest. Even the spice of it was never bitter, or such as could injure the gustatory nerves of the most thin-skinned of

men. I have, indeed, often wondered how you and
—— and —— can have so persistently misunderstood my ideas, seeing that neither on the Continent
nor in America has there been any difficulty in
making myself intelligible. But this, of course, is
quite another matter.

As regards Weismannism, I do not include under
this term the question of the inheritance of acquired
characters. That has been a question for me since
the publication of Galton's ' theory of heredity ' in
1875. Indeed, even before that, everybody knew the
contrast between congenital and acquired characters
in respect of heritability ; and you may remember,
the first time we met you gave me a lot of good
advice regarding my experiments on this subject.

Please remember both of us very kindly to your
wife when you write to her, and with our united best
wishes to yourself.

Believe me, ever yours sincerely,

G. J. ROMANES.

To Francis Darwin, Esq.

St. Aldate's. Oxford : October 8, 1893.

My dear Darwin,—Your very kind letter has been
one ray of light to me in my gloom. Yet you must
not think it is the only one.

.　　.　　.　　.　　.

It is comparatively easy to set our teeth and face
the inevitable with ' a grin ; ' but the ' highest
bravery ' is to hide our anguish with a smile. I do
think I make a decently good Stoic, but confess that

in times like this Christians have the pull. Nevertheless, I have often thought of the words, ' I am not in the least afraid to die,' [1] and wondered, when my time should come, I would be able to say them. But now I know that I can, and this even in the bitterness of feeling that one's work is prematurely cut short. . . . ' Somewhat too much of this,' however. What I want to tell you is that I managed to get to London on Friday for the purpose of consulting my doctors as to my prospects. They take a more hopeful view than I expected, *i.e.* notwithstanding that I have had three attacks in one year (in both eyes and now in the brain), it is not *inevitable* that I should have another for years to come, provided that I become a strict teetotaller, vegetarian, hermit, and abstainer from work. In short, ' that my rule of life,' ' the exemplar ' for my ' imitation,' is to be that of a tortoise. Hence it does not appear that there is any immediate necessity for saying farewell to my friends, and hence also I will not bother you by falling in with your kind proposal to come over from Cambridge to see me, much as I should like to see you in any case. But if you would care to pay a visit to Oxford any time between this and to-morrow week (16th), when I shall start for the vicinity of Nice, we should both be awfully glad to put you up. I think Dyer will probably be with us from Saturday to Monday (14 to 16).

With our united very kind regards to all,

Yours ever sincerely,

G. J. ROMANES.

---

[1] See *Life and Letters of C. Darwin*, vol. iii. p. 358.

Then came the journey to Costebelle, which he describes as follows :

To James Romanes, Esq.

Hôtel l'Ermitage, Costebelle : November 4, 1893.

My dearest James,—I ought to have answered long ago the kind letter which I received from you just as I was driving to the Oxford station, and read in the train. But I am still such a wretched invalid that I shrink from the smallest exertion, whether of body or mind. I caught a violent cold in crossing the Channel, which kept me in bed for three days at Amiens, and left me so weak that I had to further break the journey at Paris. Lyons, and Marseilles— finally arriving here with a still feverish temperature. But this has now subsided.

We found not only Paris but quite as much Lyons and Marseilles in a state of delirium over the Russian fleet officers, with whom we were muddled up all the way, greatly to our inconvenience. This was espe- cially the case on leaving Lyons, where the railway officials, after having put our luggage (containing our circular notes) in the railway station, locked the doors of the latter in our faces, when the police and military officials hurried us down the hill again in the town (in the rudest of ways) till the arrival of the Russians nearly an hour after our train was timed to depart. We had no doubt that our hand baggage had all been carried off in our railway carriage without us and without labels ; but on at last getting into the station found that our train had not started.

This is one of the most charming places I have ever seen. The hotel is situated on the top of a hill which slopes for a mile to the sea, and which is thickly clothed with pine and olive woods in all directions. The climate admits of our sitting out of doors without overcoats or shawls till sunset, amid the most wonderful profusion of aromas I have ever met with.

To the Dean of Christ Church.

Costebelle : November 28. 1893.

My dear Dean,—In the firmament of my friendships there is no such star as yourself, and I find it belongs to them all that the darker and the colder the night becomes, the more brightly do they shine.

It is quite certain that 'the South has not yet rendered its full service,' inasmuch as it has not rendered me any service at all. If anything I am worse than when I left Oxford. My muscular power, indeed, has somewhat improved, but my nervous exhaustion seems to be growing upon me, week by week; so that I am now able to walk but very little—to hope, not much, to think, not at all.

The truth is that my ailment, whatever it is, is not to be reached by climatic influences: it belongs to those mysterious internal changes, which Darwin ascribes to what he calls 'the nature of the organism ' —' variations which to our ignorance appear to arise spontaneously.' Hence, I am out of harmony with my environment, whatever the environment may be. And, as this Spencerianism applies to my spiritual.

no less than to my bodily organisation, it would seem that somehow or other I have been born into a wrong world—like those poor Porto Santo rabbits, which I took home with me last year, and the history of which I think I told you. However, I do not intend to grumble at the visible universe until I shall have had an opportunity of looking round the edge and seeing what is behind.

Most of our time is spent in sheer idleness, or rather, I should say, *all* of my time, and that proportion of my wife's which is spent in reading to me—chiefly novels, poetry, and history. Yesterday, we had Coppée's play 'Le Pater,' which I know you have read. For the length of it, I think it is as powerful a piece of dramatic writing as I have ever read.

Very few worries find their way to L'Ermitage. The worst at present is the choice of the next 'Romanes Lecturer.' Owing to his accident, Helmholtz has blocked the way for the last two months, but now promises a final reply in the course of a few days. If he does come, I hope the University will give him the D.C.L.

With our united kindest regards to Mrs. Paget, whose messages to me are of more benefit than all my doctor's drugs (now that is a thing I ' would rather have expressed otherwise ' !) and yourself.

I remain, ever your affectionate friend,

G. J. ROMANES.

For a while all went well, he liked the place, and was able to work a little, and to have many books read to him. He had taken out Dr. Martineau's ' Study of Religion,' and other philosophical books, and he also plunged into poetry, reading Wordsworth chiefly.

In December came what seemed to be a severe gastric attack, with other alarming symptoms, and for a few hours he seemed to be dying. But this passed off, and although he was kept in bed for three weeks he grew better, and in some ways there seemed grounds for fresh hope.

For a few days in January he was under the care of a cousin with two trained nurses, and his letters home were surprisingly bright.

His wife's maid, of whom he was very fond, was terribly ill in January, and he writes:

Give Jane my love, and tell her I never forget how good she was to me when I thought I was dying in her arms at Boar's Hill.

And again he wrote:

So glad to hear the operation has been successful. Congratulate her from me. Tell her I heartily wish I were in her place as to this, but that nevertheless I have not 'lost heart.' I am now certainly stronger, and if I could only submit my cranial cavity to Tom's[1] hands for removal of anything disagreeable, I should be comparatively joyful.

The weather is glorious. Marian is at mass, having read me one of Church's sermons.

Please tell John to send me a couple of hundred cigarettes (to prevent influenza!).

When you come out you will not find me a killjoy; the danger will rather be that of my scandalising you all by riotous conduct on Sunday.

[1] Mr. G. R. Turner, F.R.C.S., one of Mr. Romanes's dearest friends; a was also his brother, Mr. E. B. Turner, F.R.C.S.

And certainly he was astonishingly bright when his wife returned to him. It was on a Sunday afternoon, and his first proposition was, ' The church bell is tinkling, let's go to church.' It was the twenty-eighth of January, and the brightness and gladness of two of the Evening Psalms were oddly appropriate, and chimed in with feelings of a greater gladness dawning on him, for he was leaving the strange land in which for years he had not been able to sing ' The Lord's Song.'

And then began a time, often saddened by hours of intense physical exhaustion and physical depression, but also of what can only be called growth in holiness, in all that comes from nearness to God.

In the early autumn and winter there had been sad moments when still the clouds of darkness, of inability to grasp the Hand of God stretched out to meet him, hung over him, but in these months there had been the same growth.

One to whom he often spoke of the deepest things of life and of death will never forget his saying one day just after the attack of illness in December : ' I have come to see that cleverness, success, attainment, count for little : that goodness, or, as F. (naming a dear friend) would say, "*character*," is the important factor in life.'

For in early days Mr. Romanes had attached, so it seemed to some of those who knew him best, an undue importance to intellect, to cleverness, to intelligence, and the same person to whom he said the few words just quoted had often discussed with him the relative value of goodness and of intellect.

By goodness is meant perfect and complete goodness, not such as that of which it has been said, ' It is the business of the wise to rectify the mistakes of the good.'

And as weeks passed on he would often plan a

country house and a life in which 'good works' were
to have a share.

He had always had a high ideal of what Love and
Faith should bring about, and in the last months of his
life he said to one whom he dearly loved, 'Darling,
if you believe what you say you believe, why should
you mind so much?' With absolute resignation
he gave up all his ambitions, the old longing for
distinction, for greater fame, and yet he did not
lose for one moment the old interest in his scientific
work.

Two papers of his were read at the Royal Society
in October 1892. The first described experiments
undertaken by Mr. Romanes, the primary object of
which was to ascertain whether seeds which had been
kept out of contact with air for a lengthy period of time
still possessed the power of germination. The method
adopted was as follows : a certain number of seeds
were taken from each packet, mustard, cress, beans,
peas, &c., being the kinds employed, and having been
weighed in a chemical balance were sealed up in
tubes which had previously been exhausted of air,
and kept exposed to the vacuum for a period of
fifteen months. At the end of that time they were
removed from the tubes and sown in flower-pots
buried in moist soil. In some cases, after the seeds
had been in the vacuum tubes for three months,
they were transferred to other tubes charged with
pure gases, such as oxygen, nitrogen, hydrogen, car-
bon monoxide, or with aqueous or chloroform vapour,
and there kept for a further period of twelve months,
when they were sown as before.

In all cases the same number of seeds, of similar weights to those sealed up in the tubes, were
taken from each packet, kept in ordinary air for
the fifteen months, and then sown as control experiments.

The results clearly showed that the germinating power of the seeds was hardly, if at all, affected either by being exposed to the vacuum or to the atmospheres of the various gases and vapours. Further, in no single case, in the hundreds of seeds so treated, did the plants produced from them differ from the standard types grown from the control seeds even in the smallest degree.

The second paper described experiments in heliotropism, which had been undertaken by Mr. Romanes with the object of ascertaining whether plants would bend towards a light that is not continuous, but intermittent.

Mustard seedlings, grown in the dark until they were about one or two inches high, were used in all the experiments ; they were either placed in a dark room and exposed to flashes of light in the form of electric sparks passed at regular intervals, or they were put in a camera obscura, before which was placed a Swan burner or arc lamp, the light from which was rendered intermittent by the regular opening and shutting of the photographic shutter. The heliotropic effect on the seedlings was found in all cases to be very marked, the most vigorous ones beginning to bend towards the light ten minutes after the flashing began, bending through 45° in as many minutes, and often through another 45° in as many minutes more. By protecting half of the seedlings from the interrupted light, by means of a cardboard cap, then after the experiment uncovering them and exposing that half for the same duration of time to constant sunlight, Mr. Romanes found that the bending was less in this latter case, that is, when the light was continuous. This result was confirmed by placing two sets of plants under exactly similar conditions before a Swan burner, the light from which was constant for one set of seedlings, and rendered intermittent for the other set by working the flash shutter; in all cases the interrupted light caused the plants to start bending more quickly, and through a greater angle in a given time.

As regards the rate the flashes must succeed one another to produce this heliotropic effect, Mr. Romanes found that sparks passed at the rate of fifty in an hour would cause considerable bending in half an hour. It is of interest to note that in no single case was there any green colouring matter produced, the seedlings remaining colourless even when the sparks were passed at the rate of 100 per second continuously during forty-eight hours.

Dr. Sanderson writes :

Friday, November 17.

My dear Romanes,—There was a rather interesting discussion at the R.S. on your paper about the fresh experiments with seedlings. It was objected that there was no evidence that the effects were not due to one-sided drying of the stems of the seedlings, and —— wanted to know whether sufficient precautions were taken to guard against this. I suppose that he meant heat effects. I said that, under the conditions of this experiment, I could not see how any 'drying effect' could possibly take place.

My suggestion is that it would be worth while to add a note, if you think of the impossibility of any effect, excepting a light effect, being concerned. I asked Foster just now, and he agreed with me that it would be useful. I ought to add that it was admitted that the observation was a new one which promised to have very important bearings.

I am writing this in great haste. I trust that you are enjoying Costebelle.

Very truly yours,
T. Burdon Sanderson.

At this time Mr. Romanes had a very interesting correspondence with the Rev. G. Henslow, on the subject of the direct action of the environment on plant structures.

Ealing: October 19, 1893.

Dear Mr. Romanes,—If you are in town on November 16, I should be very glad indeed if you could come to the Linnean Society, and criticise my paper which I am going to read: 'On the origin of plant structures by self-adaptation to the environment, exemplified by desert and xerophyllous plants.'

In this and in subsequent letters Mr. Henslow explained the subject-matter of his paper, and as it formed the basis of the correspondence, a brief analysis, furnished by Mr. Henslow in a later letter, is here inserted.

The object of the paper is to show that the origin of varieties and species—as far as the vegetative organs are concerned—is solely due to climatic causes. For the acquired (somatic) characters become more or less hereditary if the same environment be maintained. But plants possess every degree in their capacities either of *reverting, changing,* or of *stability.*

The result is that I do not see any necessity for

natural selection at all in Nature, for the following reasons.

Variations are often *indefinite* in cultivation, especially after several years. Therefore to secure a useful race *artificial selection* is necessary. On the other hand, *variation* is *definite* in Nature, *all* the seedlings varying in one and the same direction, *i.e.* towards equilibrium with the environmental forces. Darwin knew of this fact, and you have abundantly described it. *But Darwin failed to see that this definite variation in Nature is the rule, and not the exception.* Hence, as he admits, natural selection is not wanted at all [*i.e. if* all variations are definite in Nature].

Moreover, it is contended that climatic variations are of no great, even of any useful importance. This may be so, for all I know, with animals; but it is *precisely the reverse with plants.* I took my illustrations from desert plants, and showed that their remarkable characteristics, which give the *facies* to desert plants, are on the one hand the direct results of the excessive drought, heat, light, &c. On the other, they are just those features which enable the plants to live under their extremely inhospitable environment. These characters are the minute leaves, hardening of woody tissues, thick cuticle, dense clothing of hair, wax, storage of water tissues, &c.; so that the whole economy of the plant, including its specific characters, is *all* climatically acquired. Although some may vary when the plants are grown in ordinary gardens, such is no more than one would expect on *a priori* grounds to be the case.

I would limit natural selection, as far as plants are concerned, to *three* things:

1. Mortality among seedlings with the survival of the *strongest*.

I do not say 'fittest,' because it is ordinarily understood to mean that the survivors have some *morphological features*, by which they are benefited, which lead on finally to specific characters.

I do not find this to be the case. Take an instance of great contrast. Sow 100 seeds of the water (submerged) *Ranunculus fluitans* in a garden. They *all* grow up as *aërial* plants, *i.e.* they vary as they grow precisely in the same way. It is only the *weakest* (from badly nourished seeds) which get crowded out of existence. Here, then, is *definite variation without the aid of natural selection. Ex uno disce omnes.*

2. *Delimitation of varieties and species* by the *non-reproduction* of intermediate forms.

It is generally said that if 'good species' are isolated, the intermediate forms have been killed off by natural selection. I maintain that they were *never reproduced.* Thus if A has passed by successive generations, A', A'', A''', &c., to A^n; A and A^n being now only in existence, then A', A'', &c., represented a *single generation* apiece, each offspring being one degree nearer to A^n, but could never be reproduced, as the environment was continually acting upon the whole series, urging each generation forwards till it became stable in A^n.

This is precisely what takes place in cultivating a wild plant like the parsnip. Each year the grower selects a slightly improved form, till the required type is fixed. The 'Student' is now A", a more or less permanently fixed form, each of the intermediate forms, lasting one year, having ceased to be reproduced.

3. The geographical distribution of varieties and species by *self-adaptation*.

That is, if a number of plants migrate to a new locality with new environmental conditions, half of them may die; because they cannot adapt themselves; the other half may live—change, and become fixed forms, by their power of adaptation. The final conclusion of the whole is that plants require nothing more than climatic influences, to which their protoplasm may respond. The result is new varietal or specific characters. Then, if the same environment lasts, these become gradually more and more fixed and hereditary, but one can never tell beforehand but that the oldest plant in creation may not change again as soon as it finds a new environment. . . . This is what a long study of plants and experiments has led me to; and it is not a conclusion arrived at solely by 'thinking out' or evolving from my own consciousness—like the German camel!

Hoping you are progressing,

Believe me, yours sincerely,

GEORGE HENSLOW.

Hôtel l'Ermitage, Costebelle, Hyères, France: October 29, 1893.

Dear Mr. Henslow,—You will correctly infer from this address that I shall not be able to attend the Linnean Society meeting on the 16th prox. For two or three years past my health has been breaking up, and several months ago I had a stroke of paralysis. So I have had to knock off all work, and have just arrived here to spend the winter—finding your letter, forwarded from Oxford, awaiting me.

It has interested me very much, and some time I should like to see the paper to which it refers, whether in MS. or print. As far as I can gather, you are spontaneously following in the footsteps of Asa Gray, Nägeli, and some other botanists. But, it seems to me, this self-adaptation doctrine is equivalent to an *a priori* abandoning of all hope to obtain any naturalistic explanation of the phenomena in question. It simply refers the facts of adaptation immediately to some theory of design, and so brings us back again to Paley, Bell, and Chalmers. As when a child asks why a flower closes at night, and we answer him: Because God has made it so, my dear. *C'est magnifique, mais ce n'est pas la science.*

But do not mistake me. My quarrel is with the term self-adaptation, which seems to imply causes of a non-naturalistic kind. Which, of course, is quite a different thing from doubting whether the naturalistic explanation given by Darwin is adequate to meet all the facts. I am myself more and more given to question 'the all-sufficiency of natural selection,' and this, whether or not use-inheritance is one of the supplementary factors. But that there are some hitherto undiscovered factors of this kind where many of the phenomena of adaptation are concerned, I am more and more disposed to suspect. Nevertheless I believe, in the light of analogy, that they will all prove to be natural causes, and therefore not correctly definable as due to 'self-adaptation.'

My hemiplegia has given me a terrible shake, so I cannot write much. Indeed, this is the longest of the few letters which I have written since my attack. So please excuse seeming bluntness, and believe me to remain,

Ever yours, very truly and most interestedly,

GEO. J. ROMANES.

P.S.—Of course you would not in any case expect to find so much variability of the *conspicuously indefinite* kind in nature as in cultivation. For, by hypothesis, natural selection is present in the one case (to destroy useless variations) while absent in the other. But I allow this does not apply to the examples you give me. Only remember the point in publishing your paper.

Hôtel Costebelle, Hyères: February 10, 1894.

Dear Mr. Henslow,—I am much indebted to you for all your most interesting letters, and also for prospect of receiving your books. Although forbidden to write letters myself, or to think about anything as yet, I must send a few lines, pending arrival of the books and papers, giving my general impression of your views as set out in your correspondence.

Briefly, it seems to me that your argument is perfectly clear up to a certain point, but then suddenly becomes a *petitio principii.* In other words, so far as your view is critical of natural selection considered as a *hypothetical cause* of adaptive evolution, I can well believe you have adduced a formidable array of facts. But I fail to follow, when you pass on to the constructive part of your case—or your suggested substitute for natural selection in self-adaptation. For self-adaptation, I understand, consists in results of *immediate response to stimuli supplied by environment.* But, if so, surely the statement that all the adaptive machinery of plant-organisation is due to self-adaptation is a mere begging of the question *against* natural selection *unless it can be shown how self-adaptation works in each case.* Now I do not find any suggestion as to this. And yet this is obviously the essential point; since, *unless it can be shown how self-adaptation works—i.e.* that it is a *vera causa,* and not a mere word serving to re-state the facts of adaptive evolution. We have got no further in the way of *explanation* than the physician, who said, that the reason why morphia produces sleep is because it possesses a soporific quality.

Observe, I purposely abstain from considering your criticism of natural selection, which, although perfectly lucid and possibly justifiable, yet certainly does admit of the answer that incipient variations of a *fortuitous* kind under nature *may* often be inconspicuous (while Wallace shows that in animals they are, as a matter of fact, usually considerable). But we need not go into this. The interesting point to all of us must be the constructive part of your work;

and I have tried to explain *my* difficulty with regard
to it. *Why should protoplasm be able to adapt itself*
into the millions of diverse mechanisms of nature by
converse with environment? The theory of natural
selection gives a logically possible, even if it be
a biologically inadequate answer. But I cannot see
that the theory of self-adaptation does, *unless it can
be shown that there is some sufficient reason why*, say
a *direct-environment should produce self-adaptation*
in the direction of hairs, a marine one in that of
fleshiness, &c. &c.

I have been very frank, because I know you, and
therefore that this is what you would prefer. But I
am too ill to make myself clear in a letter. I wish
you could stop here for a day on your way home, by
which time I shall probably have read your books,
and we might discuss the whole business before I
publish mine on the Post-Darwinian Theories.

With very many thanks,

I remain yours very truly,

G. J. ROMANES.

Hôtel Costebelle, Hyères: February 24, 1894.

Dear Mr. Henslow,—Nothing can be more clear
than are all your letters, and the last one, I take it,
sets at rest the only question which I had to ask. For
it expressly answers that, in your own view, hypothesis
of 'self-adaptation' is a *statement* rather than an
explanation of the facts. Nevertheless, it is also to
some certain extent advanced as an explanation on
Lamarckian lines, for in your books (for which I
much thank you) you attribute adaptive mechanism

in flowers to thrusts, strains &c. caused by insects
But here, if I may say so, it does not seem to me
that you sufficiently deal with an obvious criticism,
viz. How is it so much as conceivable that protoplasm should always respond to insect irritation
adaptively, when we look to the endless variety and
often great elaboration of the mechanism? Similarly
as regards the inorganic environment, Lamarck's
hypothesis of *use*-inheritance (*i.e.* mere increase and
decrease of parts as due to inherited efforts of greater
or less development by altered flow of nutrition) was
at least theoretically valid. But how can you extend
this to structures which, though *useful*, are never
active, so as to modify flow of nutrition, *e.g.* hard
shells of nuts, soft pulp of fruits, &c.? Here it is
that natural selection theory has the pull. And so
of adaptive *colours*, *odours*, and *secretions*? I confess that, even accepting inheritance of acquired
characters, I could conceive of 'self-adaptation'
alone producing all such innumerable and diversified
adjustments only by seeing with Newman (in his
'Apologia') an angel in every flower.

Besides, I do not see why you are shut up to
this, even on your own principles. For surely, be
there as much self-adaptation in Nature as ever you
please, it would still be those individuals (or *incipient
types*) *which best respond* to stimulation (*i.e.* most
adaptively do so) that, other things equal, would
survive in the struggle for existence, and so be
naturally selected. In other words, I do not see
why you should accept natural selection as regards
'vigour' of seedlings, and nowhere else.

I quite accept the validity of your criticism of my physiological selection in your book, supposing your 'self-adaptation' true to the extent you suppose. But otherwise what you say tells in favour of physiological selection, at least, excepting the statement as to new allied species originating as a rule on distant areas from parent types. This, however, is certainly an erroneous statement, though I should like to know how you came to make it.

I much wish I could write more or meet you. For, notwithstanding apparent bluntness (for brevity's sake), I see you are one of the few evolutionists who think for yourself.

With many thanks, yours very truly,
G. J. ROMANES.

I am not against your criticism of natural selection, for I have always thought there must be some other additional principle of adaptation at work.

Grand Hôtel, Costebelle, Hyères (Var): March 12.

Dear Mr. Henslow,—My husband has much enjoyed your long and clear letter which I have just read to him. He is too ill to reply himself, but he will dictate a few notes to me to send to you.

Yours very truly,
ETHEL ROMANES.

(A) I cry 'Peccavi' *as regards natural selection co-operating with self-adaptation.* Since you show that, even if it does, you are not concerned with this fact—*i.e.* of the *development of the adaptation*, but only with its origin.

(B) All the same, however, we must remember that where high elaboration of mechanism is concerned, the question as to the *causes of its development* become of more importance than those *of its origin*; *e.g.* even if self-adaptation be conceived capable of making a *first step* towards producing the exquisite mechanism of a bivalve shell, by discriminate variation, *how is it conceivable* that it should *go on* through *the odd millions of successive steps* of improvement needed to produce the perfect mechanism in which the great wonder of adaptation really occurs?

I can conceive of *no natural process to accomplish this development* even in one such case of mechanism *other than natural selection.* Let alone the 'endless variety' of elaborate mechanism elsewhere.

(c) Of course, if you could *prove* that indiscriminate variations have not occurred in wild plants, but only under cultivation, *you would destroy Darwinism —in toto.* But is the proposition credible *a priori*; or sustainable *a posteriori*, &c.?

I suppose you have read Wallace on the subject as regards wild animals, and if you were to make similar *measurements* with regard to *wild plants*, you would obtain analogous results.

I remember as a boy having a game of who could find most specimens of fern-leaved clover in a given time, or even two leaves of clover which would be exactly alike in all respects. But I have already

Z

discussed the matter of definite and indefinite variability in ' Darwin and after Darwin.'

(D) I will let the question of Use-Inheritance in relation to seemingly Passive Organs, go by default against me, as it is rather a side issue and would need much writing to discuss. The same applies to your remarks on Teleology. As regards both points I agree with your observations.

(E) Touching varieties as found in different areas from parent types, I suppose you heard how carefully Nägeli has gone into the subject, with the result that after making allowances for defects of isolation, change of environment, &c., only about *five per cent. of species of plants seem to have originated on distant areas*, while Wallace has shown that some such proportion applies to animals.

(F) As regards plants having been brought under cultivation, and yielding variations that prove heredity, I knew there were innumerable cases where artificial selection had been brought into play. But of course they are all out of court until the question on which you are engaged has been decided in your favour, *i.e.* until you have succeeded in *disproving natural selection* as analogous or parallel to artificial. It was for this reason I mentioned the case of parsnips, where the hereditary variations seem to have taken place in the *first generation* after transplanting, and therefore without leaving time for selection of any kind to have come into play.

Hôtel Costebelle, Hyères: March 29.

Dear Mr. Henslow,—I am still terribly ill and cannot write much. We must have a talk. Could you come to Oxford any day you like and be our guest? I think we might derive mutual benefit. I shall be there from the middle of April till I do not know when. Why not come on May 2, to hear Weismann give his lecture in the afternoon?

I much wish you would save seed of any fixed local varieties of plants you may find to be in seed, while you are in Malta (or bulbs), in order to see whether plants grown from them in England will or will not prove fully fertile. This is in relation to my own theory of physiological selection, according to which isolation produces segregation of type; in the same way as it does that of a language—viz. by prevention of intercourse with the parent type and consequently with an independent history of variation. Where the isolation is due to physical barriers (as at Malta) there is no need for any sexual differentiation to originate a species. But on common areas, sexual differentiation is the only means of securing the isolation. Therefore (I say) we can see why Jordan's French varieties all prove sterile with their parent forms, and I should expect your Malta varieties to prove fertile with *theirs* elsewhere.

G. J. R.

Costebelle: April 15, 1894.

Dear Mr. Henslow,—Yes, please write when you get back, suggesting any time you may find convenient for spending a day or two with us at

94 St. Aldate's, Oxford (immediately opposite Christ Church). I cannot talk long at a time, but I think the meeting will be of use to both.

Of course ' Isolation *produces* segregation of type,' is only a short-hand expression, meaning—*indiscriminate variation being supposed*—isolation supplies a necessary condition to segregation of type by upsetting the previous stability that was due to free inter-crossing.

I quite agree that Darwin *very greatly* over-estimated the *benefit* of inter-crossing, as I am showing in my forthcoming book on ' Physiological Selection.' But this is quite a different thing from his having *made too much of inter-crossing* as a condition to stability of type; I do not think that this *can* be made too much of. Indeed, how is it conceivable that there ever can be *divergence* of type without *isolation* of some kind having first occurred at the origin, and throughout the growth of every branch? Moreover, I agree with you about self-fertilisation, but see in it a form of physiological selection; it is one kind of sexual isolation, or prevention of inter-crossing with neighbouring individuals. So that the more perfectly it obtains in any given type, the better chance there is for that type to become a new species by independent variability—and this whether or not the *independent* variability is likewise *indiscriminate* (or in *your* terminology ' indefinite ').

In my last letter I referred to the works of Jordan and Nägeli for any number of '*facts* in *Nature* of varieties *arising among* the type forms.' I will show you the passages when we meet. But even in cases of 'local varieties,' where a variety has a habitat of its own *surrounded by the type-form*, I should expect experiment would often (though by no means always) show some degree of *cross-infertility* between the two, pointing to prepotency (*i.e.* early stages of physiological selection) being the origin of the divergence.

Before we meet I wish you would try to think of any plants which can be propagated by cuttings (or otherwise asexually) which are known to be modifiable by changed conditions of life in the first generation. I understand you that in some cases the seed of such a plant *will not revert*—when sown in its natural environment, though, of course, the rule is that it does. Well, in either case, I should much like to try whether a cutting &c. from the transplanted (and therefore modified) tubers &c. would revert to its ancestral character. When retransplanted to its natural environment, much would follow from result of such an experiment as regards Weismannism.

Yours very and always truly,
G. J. ROMANES.

P.S.—Of course in saying 'on common areas, sexual differentiation is the only means of securing the isolation,' I did not include self-fertilising plants —any more, *e.g.* than insect fertilising where changes in the instincts of insects may cause sexual isolation.

I leave for Oxford to-morrow.

These months were made very happy to him by the fact that three friends, Mrs. and Miss Church and the Rev. R. C. Moberly,[1] were staying in the same hotel. He often alludes in his letters to the intense pleasure these friends gave him, and speaks of how much he owed to their tenderness and sympathy, and to their perception when to come and when to stay away.

Many books were heard and read by him. Mr. Gore's Bampton Lectures were read aloud to him, and he liked them even better than when he heard them preached. Several other theological books were read, and of all these the one which bears marks of most careful study is Pascal's 'Pensées.' He used Mr. C. Kegan Paul's translation. The copy he had at Costebelle, which used to lie by his bedside, is marked and annotated. It is the last book he read to himself in his own careful and student-like fashion. He also wrote some notes of advice to his boys.

At this time he began to make notes for a work which he intended to be a supplement or an answer to the 'Candid Examination of Theism.' As he went on, his notes grew—so it seemed to one who read them—increasingly nearer Faith, but of them the world can now judge.

He said one day, while scribbling down notes, 'If anything happens to me before I can work them up into a book, give them to Gore. He will understand.'

Nothing can be more erroneous than to suppose that the change in point of view was sudden, or due to any fear of death, or that it caused mental suffering to the author of 'Thoughts on Religion,' or that he was influenced by anyone, priest or layman.

There will always be unconscious influence, and it probably was not altogether in vain that two or three

[1] Regius Professor of Pastoral Theology at Oxford.

of Mr. Romanes' greatest and most intimate friends were Christian as well as intellectual men. But of influence and argument and persuasion, as most people imagine them, there was nothing. Discussions many, during the past years, but to these he owed little.

It is written, that those who seek find, and to no one do these words more fitly apply.

During these months Mr. Romanes read many books of a religious nature; particularly and pre-eminently he liked to have Dean Church read aloud, and he also liked Mr. Holland's 'City of God' and Mr. Illingworth's sermons, particularly one on 'Innocence,' which he asked for more than once. He also read much poetry, Miss Rossetti and Archbishop Trench being especial favourites at this time.

To himself he read or had read to him the Bible and Thomas à Kempis, and he liked Dr. Bright's Ancient Collects, and in part Bishop Andrewes' Devotions. He never would read or have anything read to him which did not ring true to him and which he could not appreciate; for instance, the Pleadings of Our Lord's Physical Sufferings in Andrewes' Devotions for Friday were very distasteful to him.

He often went to the English Church for short services, and on Easter Monday Dr. Moberly gave him Holy Communion, for which he had asked and for which he wished.

In the week before Easter he felt very ill, and said, 'I wish Moberly (who had gone away for a few days) were here, and we could have that Celebration I don't think I shall live till Easter.' But this passed away, and on Easter Day he was peculiarly bright, and in the evening said, 'I have written this poem to-day.'

It is impossible to resist the wish to insert it here :

HEBREWS xi. 10 (*or* ii. 10).

' Amen, now lettest Thou Thy servant, Lord,
    Depart in peace, according to Thy Word:
    Although mine eyes may not have fully seen
    Thy great salvation, surely there have been
    Enough of sorrow and enough of sight
    To show the way from darkness into light;
And Thou hast brought me, through a wilderness of pain,
To love the sorest paths if soonest they attain.

' Enough of sorrow for the heart to cry—
    " Not for myself, nor for my kind, am I : "
    Enough of sight for Reason to disclose,
    " The more I learn the less my knowledge grows."
    Ah ! not as citizens of this our sphere,
    But aliens militant we sojourn here,
Invested by the hosts of Evil and of Wrong,
Till Thou shalt come again with all Thine angel throng.

' As Thou hast found me ready to Thy call,
    Which stationed me to watch the outer wall,
    And, quitting joys and hopes that once were mine,
    To pace with patient steps this narrow line,
    Oh ! may it be that, coming soon or late,
    Thou still shalt find Thy soldier at the gate,
Who then may follow Thee till sight needs not to prove,
And faith will be dissolved in knowledge of Thy love.'

From the manuscript it is difficult to determine what was the motto of the poem, Hebrews xi. or Hebrews ii.; the latter is more probable, at least so it seems to the present writer.

On the 28th Mr. Romanes wrote a letter to the Dean of Christ Church, which, besides some items of personal interest, and of expressions of affection too intimate to be given, contains the following :

Costebelle : March 28, 1894.

My dear Paget,—I have had to abandon letter writing for several weeks past, as the least effort,

even in the way of conversation, produces exhaustion
in a painful degree. So, as usual, I had to ask my
wife to answer your kind letter yesterday. But this
morning I feel a little bit better, so I should like to
have a try. She has gone to church, and therefore,
as I could not even hear her read the letter which
she posted to you yesterday, there is likely to be
some repetition.

     .   .   .

Oddly enough for my time of life, I have begun to
discover the truth of what you once wrote about
logical processes not being the only means of research
in regions transcendental. It is too large a matter
to deal with in a letter, but I hope to have a conversation with you some day, and ascertain how far
you will agree with a certain 'new and short way
with the Agnostics.'

    .   .   .   .

Yours ever sincerely and affectionately,
GEO. J. ROMANES.

He had all his old interest in psychical research,
and a friend, Mrs. Crawfurd, of Auchinames, who
shared this interest, used to beguile many weary
hours with ghost stories, and he and she used to
'cap' each other's narratives.

There were pleasant people in the hotels around,
and the bright sunshine and balmy air were
great sources of enjoyment to him. Dr. Bidon, of
Hyères, was unfailing in constant kindness, and it
would be ungrateful not to say how much was owed
to the kind landlord, M. Peyron, and to Madame
Peyron.

The journey to England was apparently borne without undue fatigue, and the home coming was very bright, with joyous meeting with his children and with various friends. The only difficulty was to keep him quiet enough. It was said one day, 'When you go home you must not see too many people.' 'Oh, no,' he replied, 'I only want to see Paget, and Dr. Sanderson, and Gore, and Philip (Waggett), and Mrs. Woods, and Ray Lankester, and——' but he stopped, laughing, the list was already so long and would soon have been doubled. For a few days his wife was away, and during this brief absence a very dear friend, Miss Rose Price, the daughter of the Master of Pembroke, died.

He writes:

To Mrs. Romanes.

How glad I am you are still mine! I have just returned from Rose's funeral, which was all but too much for me. As you know, I have seen other such things on a grander scale, but never any approach to this one in point of beauty and pathos. The College Chapel was completely filled with members of the University, with wives and daughters, yet all personal friends of hers, including all members of the family, the poor Master separated from the rest in his official seat. All the undergraduates of Pembroke were present, each provided with a lovely wreath, carried in procession to the grave. The whole of the east end was one mass of white flowers, the coffin with its own flowers being placed in the middle of the aisle. The procession walked first all round the quad, and then through Christ Church Meadows, being met at Holywell by the choir.[1]

[1] Of St. Giles's Parish Church.

This is the last letter I shall write. All well here, and the Interlopers[1] know me now. Weismann accepts invitation to lecture, and is on his way on purpose. I have obtained an invitation from the Royal Society for him to the 'soirée.'

Four weeks more, and the writer of this letter was also borne through Christ Church Meadow, and laid to rest near the young girl whom he had made his friend, and whose death he deeply mourned.

It was thought at this time that a country home would be possibly better for him. Many drives were taken in search of houses or of possible sites for building, and he was often positively boyish and merry during these expeditions.

He began to devise experiments again, and also set to work to arrange his papers and manuscripts in the most methodical way. As has been said he had already arranged that if he died before completing 'Darwin, and after Darwin,' Professor Lloyd Morgan should finish it and publish it, and any other scientific papers, an arrangement to which Mr. Lloyd Morgan most kindly consented. To Mr. Gore were bequeathed the fragmentary notes now published under the title 'Thoughts on Religion.'

On May 3 came the third Romanes Lecture. It was given by Professor Weismann, and was a worthy successor to the two which had preceded it.

Mr. Romanes was glad to meet Professor Weismann, and enjoyed the pleasant talk he and his distinguished opponent had in his house after the lecture.

On the seventh of May he went to London to consult doctors, and for the last time he stayed with his two dear friends, Sir James and Lady Paget.

[1] A pet name for the two babies.

He saw one or two people and was, as one friend said, 'just his dear merry old self, chaffing and being chaffed.'

He enjoyed music as much as ever, and on the nineteenth of May he went to a concert given by the Ladies' Orchestral Society.

He was often at the Museum, and he wrote frequently of the experiments he was devising, all bearing on Professor Weismann's theory : in these he was assisted by Dr. Leonard Hill.

He wrote several times to Professor Schäfer, and on May 19, four days before his death, in the midst of a long letter too technical to be given, he says, ' All I can do now for science is to pay.'

He still took much interest in Oxford life, and one of the last things he did was to vote against the introduction of the English Language and Literature School.

Cathedral was more than ever a pleasure to him, and he used often to slip in for bits of the service, particularly if some particular service or anthem was going to be given. Especially he loved a few special anthems ; Brahms' ' How lovely are Thy dwellings fair ' being a great favourite.

He used to go down to the ' Eights ' when they began, and on almost the very last day of his life he was with difficulty dissuaded from writing a letter to the ' Times,' strongly supporting the Christ Church authorities whose proceedings in some disturbances in the College had been criticised. On Whit Sunday, for the last time, he went to the University Sermon, which happened to be preached by the Bishop of Lincoln, and which greatly impressed Mr. Romanes, brought as he was for the first time under the spell of one who has influenced more than one generation of Oxford men.

And as the days went on, there was a curious

feeling of preparation for some change. He made all his arrangements and was quite calm, quite gentle, even merry at times; now and then the weary fits of physical lassitude or of headache would prostrate him, but when these were past he would placidly begin some bit of work.

On Thursday in Whit week he went to the eight o'clock Celebration of Holy Communion in the Latin Chapel of Christ Church, and in the course of that day he said, 'I have now come to see that faith is intellectually justifiable.' By-and-by he added, 'It is Christianity or nothing.'

Presently he added, 'I as yet have not that real inward assurance; it is with me as that text says, "I am not able to look up," but I feel the service of this morning is a means of grace.'

This was almost the last time he ever spoke on religious subjects.

With Mr. Philip Waggett there had been in these last days some talks, and the two friends, united as they had been in earlier years by their common interest in science, and in those problems which all who think at all must sooner or later face, now found themselves in closer and fuller agreement than either could at one time have believed possible.

Sunday, the twentieth of May, was his birthday and that of his eldest son, and had always been a family festa. He was bright and merry, went to Magdalen to see Mrs. Warren, saw for the last time Dr. Paget, and had a little talk about his 'Thoughts on Religion' with Mr. Gore, whom he went to hear preach in one of the Oxford churches. And on Monday he keenly enjoyed a small luncheon party, consisting of the Master of Balliol, Mr. Gore, and Miss Wordsworth, saying that Poetry, Science, Theology, Philosophy were all represented, and that he would have such-like little parties

every now and then, they were so refreshing and did
not tire him.

One or two special friends came in to see him on
these last days, and he had planned to go and stay at
a country house belonging to the President of Trinity,
which had been with characteristic kindness put at
his disposal.

On Wednesday, May 23, he seemed particularly
well; he wrote a letter to the Editor of the 'Contemporary Review' and did some bits of work. It was
Sir James and Lady Paget's Golden Wedding day,
and he despatched a telegram of congratulation to
them. (The very last bit of shopping he ever did was
to buy a present for that Golden Wedding, which
reached those for whom it was intended after he was
dead.)

He came into his study about twelve, and asked
that the book in which he was then interested, 'Some
Aspects of Theism,'[1] might be read aloud: but before
the reading began he changed his mind, and said he
would lie down in his bedroom and be read to there.
On lying down he complained of feeling very ill, said
a few loving words to one who was with him, and
became unconscious. His children and the Dean
came to him, but he did not recover enough to know
them, and passed away in less than an hour: *Ex
umbris et imaginibus in veritatem.*

Five days later he was laid to rest in Holywell
Cemetery, after an early Celebration in Christ Church,
the first part of the service being said in the cathedral which he had loved so much, and which had
brought him so much comfort in the last weeks of life.

His favourite hymn, 'Lead, kindly Light,' was
sung, and the service was said in part by the friend
who had been with him on his wedding day, given

---

[1] By Professor Knight of St. Andrews.

him his first Communion after the illness began, and who had been bound up with many joys and sorrows ;[1] and in part by Mr. Philip Waggett, who had been to him as a young brother, more and more loved, during the seven years in which they had walked and talked as friends, the friend known as 'Carissime.' (One other special friend, Mr. Gore, was prevented by illness from coming.)

Looking back over these two years of illness, it is impossible not to be struck by the calmness and fortitude with which that illness was met. There were, as has been said, moments of terrible depression and of disappointment and of grief. It was not easy for him to give up ambition, to leave so many projects unfulfilled, so much work undone.

But to him this illness grew to be a mount of purification,

> Ove l' umano spirito si purga,
> E di salire al ciel diventa degno.[2]

More and more there grew on him a deepening sense of the goodness of God. No one had ever suffered more from the Eclipse of Faith, no one had ever been more honest in dealing with himself and with his difficulties.

The change that came over his mental attitude may seem almost incredible to those who knew him only as a scientific man ; it does not seem so to the few who knew anything of his inner life. To them the impression given is, not of an enemy changed into a friend, antagonism altered into submission ; rather is it of one who for long has been bearing a heavy burden on his shoulders bravely and patiently, and who at last has had it lifted from him, and lifted so gradually that he could not tell the exact moment when he found it gone, and

---

[1] The Dean of Christ Church.   [2] Dante's *Purgatorio*, I.

himself standing, like the Pilgrim of never to be forgotten story, at the foot of the Cross, and Three Shining Ones coming to greet him.

It was recovery, to some extent discovery, which befell him, but there was no change of purpose, no sudden intellectual or moral conversion.

He had always cared more for Truth, for the knowledge of God, than for anything else in the world. In the years most outwardly happy he was crying out in the darkness for light, with a soul athirst for God, and, as was said before, he did most truly re-echo St. Augustine's words, ' *Fecisti nos ad Te, et inquietum est cor nostrum, donec requiescat in Te.*'

It is difficult for anyone who has lived in closest intimacy with him to speak of him in words which will not to those who did not know him seem exaggerated, nay, extravagant; to those who knew and loved him, cold, inadequate, lifeless: for he bore ' the white flower of a blameless life ' from boyhood onwards, and in heart and life he was unstained, pure, unselfish, unworldly in the truest sense.

When the Shadow of Death lay on him, and the dread messenger was drawing near, and he looked back on his short life, he could reproach himself only for what he called sins of the intellect, mental arrogance, undue regard for intellectual supremacy.

No one better understood him than the friend [1] who wrote:

When a man has lived with broad and strong interest in life, neither discarding nor slighting any true part of it in home, or society, or work, the various aspects of his character and career are likely to be many and suggestive. And so there may be

---

[1] The Dean of Christ Church.

some warrant for an attempt to disengage one line of
advance in the life, one trait in the example, and to
concentrate attention upon that, while the other and
perhaps more widely recognised elements are for the
moment left unnoticed. There was one such line of
advance in the life of George Romanes, of which it
may be hard to speak, but wrong, perhaps, to be
wholly silent. Few men have shown more finely
the simplicity and patience in sustained endeavour
which are the conditions of attainment in the quest
of truth. It is easy to see how the training and
habits of a mind devoted to natural science may
render faith more difficult, and cross or check the
venture of the soul towards the things eternal and
unseen. But there is one quality proper to such a
mind which should have a different effect, and act as
a safeguard against a fault that often checks or mars
the growth of faith. That quality is tenacity of un-
correlated fragments ; the endurance of incomplete-
ness ; the patient refusal to attenuate or discard a
fact because it will not fit into a system ; the determined hope that whatsoever things are true have
further truth to teach, if only they are held fast
and fairly dealt with. The sincerely scientific mind
shows such tenacity as that under every trial of its
faith and patience, howsoever long and unpromising
and unrelieved ; for it knows itself responsible not for
attainment, but for perseverance ; not for conquest,
but for loyalty. It resists even the temptation to dislike the untidy scraps of observation or experience
which will match nothing and go nowhere ; for it
suspects and reveres in all the possibility of new light.

And surely there is a like excellence of thought, rare, and high, and exemplary, in regard to the things unseen, the things that are spiritually discerned. Scattered up and down the world, coming one way or another within the ken of all men, there are facts of plain experience which will not really fit, unmutilated, undisfigured, into any scheme or view of life that leaves God out of sight. They are facts, it may be, of which a full account can hardly, if at all, be given. They are fragmentary, isolated, imponderable; clearer at one time than at another; largely dependent, for anything like due recognition, upon the individual mind, and heart, and will. Yet there they are, flashing out at times with an intensity which makes all else seem pale and cold; disclosing, or ready to disclose, to any quietness of thought, great hints of worlds unrealised and possibilities of overwhelming glory.

And it is on loyalty, on justice to such fragments of truth, unaccounted for and unarranged, that for many men the trial of faith may turn. All is not lost, and everything is possible, so long as the mind refuses to doubt the reality of the light that has come, perhaps, as yet only in broken rays. Of such justice and loyalty George Romanes set a very high example. The strength and simplicity and patience of his character appeared in nothing else more remarkably, more happily, than in his undiscouraged grasp of those unseen realities which invade this world in the name and power of the world to come. The love of precision and completeness never dulled his care for the things that he could neither define, nor label, nor arrange; in their fragmentariness he treasured them, in their reserve he trusted them, waiting faithfully to see what they might have to show him. And they did not fail him. This is not the place in which to try to speak of the graces and the gladness which from such loyal sincerity passed into his life, nor of the clearer light that grew and spread before his wistful, hopeful gaze. But it hardly can be wrong to have said thus much of so noble and so timely a pattern of allegiance to all truth discerned: and of this great lesson in a life which seemed even here to have the earnest of that promise—' He that seeketh, findeth '—a life which seemed to be moving steadily towards the blessing of the pure in heart, the vision of Almighty God.[1]

F. P.

A letter from Mr. Gladstone cannot be omitted, and seems to come in fittingly at this place:

1 Carlton Gardens: June.

Dear Mrs. Romanes.—My present circumstances are not very favourable to direct personal communication, and my personal intercourse with Mr. Romanes was so scanty in its quantity as hardly to warrant my present intrusion, but I cannot help writing a few words for the purpose of conveying my deep sympathy on the heavy bereavement you have sustained, and further of saying how deep an impression he left upon my mind in the point of character not less than of capacity. He was one of the men whom the age

---

[1] Reprinted from the *Guardian* of June 6.

specially requires for the investigation and solution of its especial difficulties, and for the conciliation and harmony of interests between which a factitious rivalry has been created.

Your heavy private loss is then coupled in my view with a public calamity; but while I can rejoice in your retrospect of his labour, I also trust it may please God in His wisdom to raise up others to fill up his place and carry forward his work May you enjoy the abundance of the Divine consolations in proportion to your great need.

Believe me, most truly yours,
W. E. Gladstone.

Not much remains to be said. The life here described would seem to have been cut short, but, as was said by a friend, 'in a short time he fulfilled a long time,'[1] and few have won for themselves more love in the home and beyond it. He left no enemy, and those who loved him and to whom his loss has left a blank and desolation of which it is not well to speak, can only be thankful for what he was and for what he is. Not indeed that one would forget those words of Dean Church quoted in the beautiful preface to his Life : [2]

'I often have a kind of waking dream : up one road, the image of a man decked and adorned as if for a triumph, carried up by rejoicing and exulting friends, who praise his goodness and achievements; and, on the other road, turned back to back to it, there is the very man himself, in sordid and squalid apparel, surrounded not by friends but by ministers of

----

[1] Wisdom, iv. 13.
[2] Preface to *Life and Letters of Dean Church*, p. xxiv.

justice, and going on, while his friends are exulting,
to his certain and perhaps awful judgment. That
vision rises when I hear, not just and conscientious
endeavours to make out a man's character, but when
I hear the loose things that are said—often in kindness and love—of those beyond the grave.

But there have been men and women who have
lifted the minds and the hearts of those who knew
and loved them to increasing love for goodness, to increasing loftiness of ideal, and for these, whom now
no praise can hurt, no blame can wound, one can but
lift one's heart in ever growing thankfulness for
the gifts and graces which made them what they
were, and which will grow and increase in them until
the Perfect Day.

Beati mundo corde, quoniam ipsi Deum videbunt.

May 23, 1895.

INDEX

PRINTED BY
SPOTTISWOODE AND CO., NEW-STREET SQUARE
LONDON

A Classified Catalogue

OF WORKS IN

GENERAL LITERATURE

PUBLISHED BY

LONGMANS, GREEN, & CO.

39 PATERNOSTER ROW, LONDON, E.C.

15 EAST 16TH STREET, NEW YORK, AND 32 HORNBY ROAD, BOMBAY.

INDEX OF AUTHORS.

<h1 style="text-align:center">CONTENTS.</h1>

History, Politics, Polity, Political Memoirs, &c.

Abbott.—*A HISTORY OF GREECE.* By EVELYN ABBOTT, M.A., LL.D.
Part I.—From the Earliest Times to the Ionian Revolt. Crown 8vo., 10s. 6d.
Part II.—500-445 B.C. Crown 8vo., 10s. 6d.

Acland and Ransome.—*A HANDBOOK IN OUTLINE OF THE POLITICAL HISTORY OF ENGLAND TO 1894.* Chronologically Arranged. By A. H. DYKE ACLAND, M.P., and CYRIL RANSOME, M.A. Crown 8vo., 6s.

ANNUAL REGISTER (THE). A Review of Public Events at Home and Abroad, for the year 1894. 8vo., 18s.
Volumes of the *ANNUAL REGISTER* for the years 1863-1893 can still be had. 18s. each.

Armstrong.—*ELIZABETH FARNESE;* The Termagant of Spain. By EDWARD ARMSTRONG, M.A. 8vo., 16s.

Arnold (THOMAS, D.D.), formerly Head Master of Rugby School.
INTRODUCTORY LECTURES ON MODERN HISTORY. 8vo., 7s. 6d.
MISCELLANEOUS WORKS. 8vo., 7s. 6d.

Bagwell.—*IRELAND UNDER THE TUDORS.* By RICHARD BAGWELL, LL.D. (3 vols.) Vols. I. and II. From the first invasion of the Northmen to the year 1578. 8vo., 32s. Vol. III. 1578-1603. 8vo. 18s.

Ball.—*HISTORICAL REVIEW OF THE LEGISLATIVE SYSTEMS OPERATIVE IN IRELAND,* from the Invasion of Henry the Second to the Union (1172-1800). By the Rt. Hon. J. T. BALL. 8vo., 6s.

Besant.—*THE HISTORY OF LONDON.* By WALTER BESANT. With 74 Illustrations. Crown 8vo., 1s. 9d. Or bound as a School Prize Book, 2s. 6d.

Brassey (LORD).—PAPERS AND ADDRESSES.
NAVAL AND MARITIME. 1872-1893. 2 vols. Crown 8vo., 10s.

Brassey (LORD).—PAPERS AND ADDRESSES—*Continued.*
MERCANTILE MARINE AND NAVIGATION, from 1871-1894. Crown 8vo., 5s.
IMPERIAL FEDERATION AND COLONISATION FROM 1880 to 1894. Cr. 8vo., 5s.
POLITICAL AND MISCELLANEOUS. 1861-1894. Crown 8vo 5s.

Bright.—*A HISTORY OF ENGLAND.* By the Rev. J. FRANCK BRIGHT, D.D.
Period I. *MEDIÆVAL MONARCHY*: A.D. 449 to 1485. Crown 8vo., 4s. 6d.
Period II. *PERSONAL MONARCHY.* 1485 to to 1688. Crown 8vo., 5s.
Period III. *CONSTITUTIONAL MONARCHY.* 1689 to 1837. Crown 8vo., 7s. 6d.
Period IV. *THE GROWTH OF DEMOCRACY.* 1837 to 1880 Crown 8vo., 6s.

Buckle.—*HISTORY OF CIVILISATION IN ENGLAND AND FRANCE, SPAIN AND SCOTLAND.* By HENRY THOMAS BUCKLE. 3 vols. Crown 8vo., 24s.

Burke.—*A HISTORY OF SPAIN* from the Earliest Times to the Death of Ferdinand the Catholic. By ULICK RALPH BURKE, M.A. 2 vols. 8vo., 32s.

Chesney.—*INDIAN POLITY:* a View of the System of Administration in India. By General Sir GEORGE CHESNEY, K.C.B., With Map showing all the Administrative Divisions of British India. 8vo., 21s.

Creighton.—*HISTORY OF THE PAPACY DURING THE REFORMATION.* By MANDELL CREIGHTON, D.D., LL.D., Vols. I. and II., 1378-1464. 32s. Vols. III. and IV., 1464-1518, 24s. Vol. V., 1517-1527, 8vo., 15s.

Curzon.—*PERSIA AND THE PERSIAN QUESTION.* By the Hon. GEORGE N. CURZON, M.P. With 9 Maps, 96 Illustrations, Appendices, and an Index. 2 vols. 8vo., 42s.

History, Politics, Polity, Political Memoirs, &c.—*continued*.

De Tocqueville.—*DEMOCRACY IN AMERICA*. By ALEXIS DE TOCQUEVILLE. 2 vols. Crown 8vo., 16s.

Dickinson.—*THE DEVELOPMENT OF PARLIAMENT DURING THE NINETEENTH CENTURY.* By G. LOWES DICKINSON, M.A. 8vo., 7s. 6d.

Ewald.—*THE HISTORY OF ISRAEL.* By HEINRICH EWALD. 8 vols., 8vo., Vols. I. and II., 24s. Vols. III. and IV., 21s. Vol. V., 18s. Vol. VI., 16s. Vol. VII., 21s. Vol. VIII., 18s.

Fitzpatrick. — *SECRET SERVICE UNDER PITT.* By W. J. FITZPATRICK. 8vo., 7s. 6d.

Froude (JAMES A.).

THE HISTORY OF ENGLAND, from the Fall of Wolsey to the Defeat of the Spanish Armada.

   Popular Edition. 12 vols. Cr. 8vo. 3s. 6d. each.

   Silver Library Edition. 12 vols. Cr. 8vo. 3s. 6d. each.

THE DIVORCE OF CATHERINE OF ARAGON. Crown 8vo., 6s.

THE SPANISH STORY OF THE ARMADA, and other Essays.
   Silver Library Edition, Cr. 8vo., 3s. 6d.

THE ENGLISH IN IRELAND IN THE EIGHTEENTH CENTURY.
   Cabinet Edition. 3 vols. Cr. 8vo., 18s.
   Silver Library Ed. 3 vols. Cr. 8vo., 10s. 6d.

ENGLISH SEAMEN IN THE SIXTEENTH CENTURY. Cr. 8vo., 6s.

SHORT STUDIES ON GREAT SUBJECTS. 4 vols. Cr. 8vo., 3s. 6d. each.

CÆSAR : a Sketch. Cr. 8vo., 3s. 6d.

Gardiner (SAMUEL RAWSON, D.C.L., LL.D.).

HISTORY OF ENGLAND, from the Accession of James I. to the Outbreak of the Civil War, 1603-1642. 10 vols. Crown 8vo., 6s. each.

A HISTORY OF THE GREAT CIVIL WAR, 1642-1649. 4 vols. Cr. 8vo., 6s. ea.

A HISTORY OF THE COMMONWEALTH AND THE PROTECTORATE. 1649-1660. Vol. I. 1649-1651. With 14 Maps. 8vo., 21s.

THE STUDENT'S HISTORY OF ENGLAND. With 378 Illust. Cr. 8vo., 12s.
   Also in Three Volumes, price 4s. each.
   Vol. I. B.C. 55–A.D. 1509. 173 Illus.
   Vol. II. 1509-1689. 96 Illustrations.
   Vol. III. 1689-1885. 109 Illustrations.

Greville.—*A JOURNAL OF THE REIGNS OF KING GEORGE IV., KING WILLIAM IV., AND QUEEN VICTORIA.* By CHARLES C. F. GREVILLE, formerly Clerk of the Council. 8 vols. Crown 8vo., 6s. each.

Hearn. *THE GOVERNMENT OF ENGLAND: its Structure and its Development.* By W. EDWARD HEARN. 8vo., 16s.

Herbert.—*THE DEFENCE OF PLEVNA,* 1877. Written by One who took Part in it. By WILLIAM V. HERBERT. With Maps. 8vo., 18s.

Historic Towns.—Edited by E. A. FREEMAN, D.C.L., and Rev. WILLIAM HUNT, M.A. With Maps and Plans. Crown 8vo., 3s. 6d. each.

Bristol. By Rev. W. Hunt.
Carlisle. By Mandell Creighton, D.D., Bishop of Peterborough.
Cinque Ports. By Montague Burrows.
Colchester. By Rev. E. L. Cutts.
Exeter. By E. A. Freeman.
London. By Rev. W. J. Loftie.
Oxford. By Rev. C. W. Boase.
Winchester. By G. W. Kitchin, D.D.
York. By Rev. James Raine.
New York. By Theodore Roosevelt.
Boston (U.S.) By Henry Cabot Lodge.

Joyce.—*A SHORT HISTORY OF IRELAND,* from the Earliest Times to 1608. By P. W. JOYCE, LL.D. Crown 8vo., 10s. 6d.

Lang. *ST. ANDREWS.* By ANDREW LANG. With 8 Plates and 24 Illustrations in the Text by T. HODGE. 8vo., 15s. net.

Lecky (WILLIAM EDWARD HARTPOLE, M.P.).

HISTORY OF ENGLAND IN THE EIGHTEENTH CENTURY.
   Library Edition. 8 vols. 8vo., £7 4s.
   Cabinet Edition. ENGLAND. 7 vols. Crown 8vo., 6s. each. IRELAND. 5 vols. Crown 8vo., 6s. each.

HISTORY OF EUROPEAN MORALS FROM AUGUSTUS TO CHARLEMAGNE. 2 vols. Crown 8vo., 16s.

HISTORY OF THE RISE AND INFLUENCE OF THE SPIRIT OF RATIONALISM IN EUROPE. 2 vols. Crown 8vo., 16s.

THE EMPIRE : its value and its Growth. An Inaugural Address delivered at the Imperial Institute, November 20, 1893. Cr. 8vo., 1s. 6d.

History, Politics, Polity, Political Memoirs, &c.—*continued.*

Macaulay (LORD).

COMPLETE WORKS.

Cabinet Edition. 16 vols. Post 8vo., £4 16s.
Library Edition. 8 vols. 8vo., £5 5s.

HISTORY OF ENGLAND FROM THE ACCESSION OF JAMES THE SECOND.

Popular Edition. 2 vols. Cr. 8vo., 5s.
Student's Edition. 2 vols. Cr. 8vo., 12s.
People's Edition. 4 vols. Cr. 8vo., 16s.
Cabinet Edition. 8 vols. Post 8vo., 48s.
Library Edition. 5 vols. 8vo., £4.

CRITICAL AND HISTORICAL ESSAYS, WITH LAYS OF ANCIENT ROME, in 1 volume.

Popular Edition. Crown 8vo., 2s. 6d.
Authorised Edition. Crown 8vo., 2s. 6d., or 3s. 6d., gilt edges.
Silver Library Edition. Cr. 8vo., 3s. 6d.

CRITICAL AND HISTORICAL ESSAYS.

Student's Edition. 1 vol. Cr. 8vo., 6s.
People's Edition. 2 vols. Cr. 8vo., 8s.
Trevelyan Edition. 2 vols. Cr. 8vo., 9s.
Cabinet Edition. 4 vols. Post 8vo., 24s.
Library Edition. 3 vols. 8vo., 36s.

ESSAYS which may be had separately price 6d. each sewed, 1s. each cloth.

Addison and Walpole.	Frederick the Great.
Croker's Boswell's Johnson.	Ranke and Gladstone.
Hallam's Constitutional History.	Milton and Machiavelli.
	Lord Byron.
Warren Hastings. 3d. sewed, 6d. cloth.	Lord Clive.
	Lord Byron, and The
The Earl of Chatham (Two Essays).	Comic Dramatists of the Restoration.

MISCELLANEOUS WRITINGS

People's Edition. 1 vol. Cr. 8vo., 4s. 6d.
Library Edition. 2 vols. 8vo., 21s.

MISCELLANEOUS WRITINGS AND SPEECHES.

Popular Edition. Crown 8vo., 2s. 6d.
Cabinet Edition. Including Indian Penal Code, Lays of Ancient Rome, and Miscellaneous Poems. 4 vols. Post 8vo., 24s.

SELECTIONS FROM THE WRITINGS OF LORD MACAULAY. Edited, with Occasional Notes, by the Right Hon. Sir G. O. Trevelyan, Bart. Crown 8vo., 6s.

May.—*THE CONSTITUTIONAL HISTORY OF ENGLAND* since the Accession of George III. 1760-1870. By Sir THOMAS ERSKINE MAY, K.C.B. (Lord Farnborough). 3 vols. Cr. 8vo., 18s.

Merivale (THE LATE DEAN).

HISTORY OF THE ROMANS UNDER THE EMPIRE.

Cabinet Edition. 8 vols. Cr. 8vo., 48s.
Silver Library Edition. 8 vols. Crown 8vo., 3s. 6d. each.

THE FALL OF THE ROMAN REPUBLIC: a Short History of the Last Century of the Commonwealth. 12mo., 7s. 6d.

Montague.—*THE ELEMENTS OF ENGLISH CONSTITUTIONAL HISTORY.* By F. C. MONTAGUE, M.A. Crown 8vo., 3s. 6d.

Moore.—*THE AMERICAN CONGRESS:* a History of National Legislation and Political Events, 1774-1895. By JOSEPH WEST MOORE. 8vo., 15s. net.

O'Brien.—*IRISH IDEAS. REPRINTED ADDRESSES.* By WILLIAM O'BRIEN. Cr. 8vo. 2s. 6d.

Richman.—*APPENZELL: PURE DEMOCRACY AND PASTORAL LIFE IN INNER-RHODEN.* A Swiss Study. By IRVING B. RICHMAN, Consul-General of the United States to Switzerland. With Maps. Crown 8vo., 5s.

Seebohm (FREDERIC).

THE ENGLISH VILLAGE COMMUNITY Examined in its Relations to the Manorial and Tribal Systems, &c. With 13 Maps and Plates. 8vo., 16s.

THE TRIBAL SYSTEM IN WALES: Being Part of an Inquiry into the Structure and Methods of Tribal Society. With 3 Maps. 8vo., 12s.

Sharpe.—*LONDON AND THE KINGDOM:* a History derived mainly from the Archives at Guildhall in the custody of the Corporation of the City of London. By REGINALD R. SHARPE, D.C.L., Records Clerk in the Office of the Town Clerk of the City of London. 3 vols. 8vo. 10s. 6d. each.

Sheppard.—*MEMORIALS OF ST. JAMES'S PALACE.* By the Rev. EDGAR SHEPPARD, M.A., Sub-Dean of H.M. Chapels Royal. With 41 Full-page Plates (8 Photo-Intaglio) and 32 Illustrations in the Text. 2 vols. 8vo., 36s. net.

Smith.—*CARTHAGE AND THE CARTHAGINIANS.* By R. BOSWORTH SMITH, M.A. With Maps, Plans, &c. Cr. 8vo., 3s. 6d.

History, Politics, Polity, Political Memoirs, &c.—*continued.*

Stephens.—*A HISTORY OF THE FRENCH REVOLUTION.* By H. MORSE STEPHENS. 3 vols. 8vo. Vols. I. and II. 18s. each.

Stubbs.—*HISTORY OF THE UNIVERSITY OF DUBLIN*, from its Foundation to the End of the Eighteenth Century. By J. W. STUBBS. 8vo., 12s. 6d.

Sutherland.—*THE HISTORY OF AUSTRALIA AND NEW ZEALAND*, from 1606 to 1890. By ALEXANDER SUTHERLAND, M.A., and GEORGE SUTHERLAND, M.A. Crown 8vo., 2s. 6d.

Taylor.—*A STUDENT'S MANUAL OF THE HISTORY OF INDIA.* By Colonel MEADOWS TAYLOR, C.S.I., &c. Cr. 8vo., 7s. 6d.

Todd.—*PARLIAMENTARY GOVERNMENT IN THE BRITISH COLONIES.* By ALPHEUS TODD, LL.D. 8vo., 30s. net.

Wakeman and Hassall.—*ESSAYS INTRODUCTORY TO THE STUDY OF ENGLISH CONSTITUTIONAL HISTORY.* By Resident Members of the University of Oxford. Edited by HENRY OFFLEY WAKEMAN, M.A., and ARTHUR HASSALL, M.A. Crown 8vo., 6s.

Walpole (SPENCER).

HISTORY OF ENGLAND FROM THE CONCLUSION OF THE GREAT WAR IN 1815 TO 1858. 6 vols. Crown 8vo., 6s. each.

THE LAND OF HOME RULE: being an Account of the History and Institutions of the Isle of Man. Crown 8vo., 6s.

Wolff.—*ODD BITS OF HISTORY:* being Short Chapters intended to Fill Some Blanks. By HENRY W. WOLFF. 8vo., 8s. 6d.

Wood-Martin.—*PAGAN IRELAND: AN ARCHÆOLOGICAL SKETCH.* A Handbook of Irish Pre-Christian Antiquities. By W. G. WOOD-MARTIN, M.R.I.A. With 512 Illustrations. Crown 8vo., 15s.

Wylie.—*HISTORY OF ENGLAND UNDER HENRY IV.* By JAMES HAMILTON WYLIE, M.A., one of H. M. Inspectors of Schools. 3 vols. Crown 8vo. Vol. I., 1399-1404, 10s. 6d. Vol. II., 15s. Vol. III., 15s. Vol. IV. [*In the press.*

Biography, Personal Memoirs, &c.

Armstrong.—*THE LIFE AND LETTERS OF EDMUND J. ARMSTRONG.* Edited by G. F. ARMSTRONG. Fcp. 8vo., 7s. 6d.

Bacon.—*THE LETTERS AND LIFE OF FRANCIS BACON, INCLUDING ALL HIS OCCASIONAL WORKS.* Edited by JAMES SPEDDING. 7 vols. 8vo., £4 4s.

Bagehot.—*BIOGRAPHICAL STUDIES* By WALTER BAGEHOT. Crown 8vo., 3s. 6d.

Blackwell.—*PIONEER WORK IN OPENING THE MEDICAL PROFESSION TO WOMEN:* Autobiographical Sketches. By Dr. ELIZABETH BLACKWELL. Cr. 8vo., 6s.

Boyd (A. K. H., D.D., LL.D., Author of 'Recreations of a Country Parson,' &c.).

TWENTY-FIVE YEARS OF ST. ANDREWS. 1865-1890. 2 vols. 8vo. Vol. I. 12s. Vol. II. 15s.

ST. ANDREWS AND ELSEWHERE: Glimpses of Some Gone and of Things Left. 8vo., 15s.

Buss.—*FRANCES MARY BUSS AND HER WORK FOR EDUCATION.* By ANNIE E. RIDLEY. With 5 Portraits and 4 Illustrations. Crown 8vo, 7s. 6d.

Carlyle.—*THOMAS CARLYLE:* A History of his Life. By JAMES ANTHONY FROUDE.
1795-1835. 2 vols. Crown 8vo., 7s.
1834-1881. 2 vols. Crown 8vo., 7s.

Erasmus.—*LIFE AND LETTERS OF ERASMUS.* By JAMES ANTHONY FROUDE. Crown 8vo., 6s.

Fox.—*THE EARLY HISTORY OF CHARLES JAMES FOX.* By the Right Hon. Sir G. O. TREVELYAN, Bart.
Library Edition. 8vo., 18s.
Cabinet Edition. Crown 8vo., 6s.

Halford.—*THE LIFE OF SIR HENRY HALFORD, BART., G.C.H., M.D., F.R.S.,* President of the Royal College of Physicians, Physician to George III., George IV., William IV., and to Her Majesty, Queen Victoria. By WILLIAM MUNK, M.D., F.S.A. 8vo., 12s. 6d.

Hamilton.—*LIFE OF SIR WILLIAM HAMILTON.* By R. P. GRAVES. 3 vols. 15s. each. ADDENDUM. 8vo., 6d. sewed.

Havelock.—*MEMOIRS OF SIR HENRY HAVELOCK, K.C.B.* By JOHN CLARK MARSHMAN. Crown 8vo., 3s. 6d.

Luther.—*LIFE OF LUTHER.* By JULIUS KÖSTLIN. With Illustrations from Authentic Sources. Translated from the German. Crown 8vo., 7s. 6d.

Biography, Personal Memoirs, &c.—*continued*.

Macaulay.—*THE LIFE AND LETTERS OF LORD MACAULAY.* By the Right Hon. Sir G. O. TREVELYAN, Bart., M.P.
Popular Edition. 1 vol. Cr. 8vo., 2s. 6d.
Student's Edition. 1 vol. Cr. 8vo., 6s.
Cabinet Edition. 2 vols. Post 8vo., 12s.
Library Edition. 2 vols. 8vo., 36s.

Marbot. — *THE MEMOIRS OF THE BARON DE MARBOT.* Translated from the French. Crown 8vo., 7s. 6d.

Seebohm.—*THE OXFORD REFORMERS—JOHN COLET, ERASMUS AND THOMAS MORE*: a History of their Fellow-Work. By FREDERIC SEEBOHM. 8vo., 14s.

Shakespeare. — *OUTLINES OF THE LIFE OF SHAKESPEARE.* By J. O. HALLIWELL-PHILLIPPS. With Illustrations and Fac-similes. 2 vols. Royal 8vo., £1 1s.

Shakespeare's *TRUE LIFE.* By JAMES WALTER. With 500 Illustrations by GERALD E. MOIRA. Imp. 8vo., 21s.

Stephen.—*ESSAYS IN ECCLESIASTICAL BIOGRAPHY.* By Sir JAMES STEPHEN. Crown 8vo., 7s. 6d.

Turgot.—*THE LIFE AND WRITINGS OF TURGOT*, Comptroller-General of France, 1774-1776. Edited for English Readers by W. WALKER STEPHENS. 8vo., 12s. 6d.

Verney. —*MEMOIRS OF THE VERNEY FAMILY.*
Vols. I. & II., *DURING THE CIVIL WAR.* By FRANCES PARTHENOPE VERNEY. With 38 Portraits, Woodcuts and Fac-simile. Royal 8vo., 42s.
Vol. III., *DURING THE COMMONWEALTH.* 1650-1660. By MARGARET M. VERNEY. With 10 Portraits, &c. Royal 8vo., 21s.

Walford. — *TWELVE ENGLISH AUTHORESSES.* By L. B. WALFORD. Crown 8vo., 4s. 6d.

Wellington.—*LIFE OF THE DUKE OF WELLINGTON.* By the Rev. G. R. GLEIG, M.A. Crown 8vo., 3s. 6d.

Wolf. —*THE LIFE OF JOSEPH WOLF, ANIMAL PAINTER.* By A. H. PALMER. With 53 Plates and 14 Illustrations in the Text. 8vo., 21s.

Travel and Adventure, the Colonies, &c.

Arnold (SIR EDWIN, K.C.I.E.).
SEAS AND LANDS. With 71 Illustrations. Cr. 8vo., 3s. 6d.
WANDERING WORDS. With 45 Illustrations. 8vo., 18s.

AUSTRALIA AS IT IS, or Facts and Features, Sketches, and Incidents of Australia and Australian Life with Notices of New Zealand. Crown 8vo., 5s.

Baker (SIR S. W.).
EIGHT YEARS IN CEYLON. With 6 Illustrations. Crown 8vo., 3s. 6d.
THE RIFLE AND THE HOUND IN CEYLON. With 6 Illus. Cr. 8vo., 3s. 6d.

Bent (J. THEODORE, F.S.A., F.R.G.S.).
THE RUINED CITIES OF MASHONALAND: being a Record of Excavation and Exploration in 1891. With Map, 13 Plates, and 104 Illustrations in the Text. Crown 8vo., 3s. 6d.
THE SACRED CITY OF THE ETHIOPIANS: being a Record of Travel and Research in Abyssinia in 1893. With 8 Plates and 65 Illustrations in the Text. 8vo., 18s.

Bicknell.—*TRAVEL AND ADVENTURE IN NORTHERN QUEENSLAND.* By ARTHUR C. BICKNELL. With 24 Plates and 22 Illustrations in the Text. 8vo, 15s.

Brassey (THE LATE LADY).
THE LAST VOYAGE TO INDIA AND AUSTRALIA IN THE 'SUNBEAM'. With Charts and Maps, and 240 Illus. 8vo., 21s.
A VOYAGE IN THE 'SUNBEAM;' OUR HOME ON THE OCEAN FOR ELEVEN MONTHS.
Library Edition. With 8 Maps and Charts, and 118 Illustrations. 8vo. 21s.
Cabinet Edition. With Map and 66 Illustrations. Crown 8vo., 7s. 6d.
Silver Library Edition. With 66 Illustrations. Crown 8vo., 3s. 6d.
Popular Edition. With 60 Illustrations. 4to., 6d. sewed, 1s. cloth.
School Edition. With 37 Illustrations. Fcp., 2s. cloth, or 3s. white parchment.
SUNSHINE AND STORM IN THE EAST.
Library Edition. With 2 Maps and 141 Illustrations. 8vo., 21s.
Cabinet Edition. With 2 Maps and 114 Illustrations. Crown 8vo., 7s. 6d.
Popular Edition. With 103 Illustrations. 4to., 6d. sewed, 1s. cloth.
IN THE TRADES, THE TROPICS, AND THE 'ROARING FORTIES.'
Cabinet Edition. With Map and 220 Illustrations. Crown 8vo., 7s. 6d.
Popular Edition. With 183 Illustrations. 4to., 6d. sewed, 1s. cloth.
THREE VOYAGES IN THE 'SUNBEAM'.
Popular Edition. With 346 Illustrations. 4to., 2s. 6d.

Travel and Adventure, the Colonies, &c.—*continued.*

Brassey.—*VOYAGES AND TRAVELS OF LORD BRASSEY, K.C.B., D.C.L., 1862-1894.* Arranged and Edited by Captain S. Eardley-Wilmot. 2 vols. Cr. 8vo., 10s.

Froude (JAMES A.).

OCEANA: or England and her Colonies. With 9 Illustrations. Crown 8vo., 2s. boards, 2s. 6d. cloth.

THE ENGLISH IN THE WEST INDIES: or, the Bow of Ulysses. With 9 Illustrations. Crown 8vo., 2s. boards, 2s. 6d. cloth.

Howitt.—*VISITS TO REMARKABLE PLACES.* Old Halls, Battle-Fields, Scenes, illustrative of Striking Passages in English History and Poetry. By WILLIAM HOWITT. With 80 Illustrations. Crown 8vo., 3s. 6d.

Knight (E. F.).

THE CRUISE OF THE 'ALERTE': the Narrative of a Search for Treasure on the Desert Island of Trinidad. With 2 Maps and 23 Illustrations. Crown 8vo., 3s. 6d.

WHERE THREE EMPIRES MEET: a Narrative of Recent Travel in Kashmir, Western Tibet, Baltistan, Ladak, Gilgit, and the adjoining Countries. With a Map and 54 Illustrations. Cr. 8vo., 3s. 6d.

Lees and Clutterbuck. B.C. 1887; *A RAMBLE IN BRITISH COLUMBIA.* By J. A. Lees and W. J. Clutterbuck. With Map and 75 Illustrations. Crown 8vo., 3s. 6d.

Murdoch.—*FROM EDINBURGH TO THE ANTARCTIC:* an Artist's Notes and Sketches during the Dundee Antarctic Expedition of 1892-93. By W. G. Burn-Murdoch. With 2 Maps and numerous Illustrations. 8vo., 18s.

Nansen (FRIDTJOF).

THE FIRST CROSSING OF GREENLAND. With numerous Illustrations and a Map. Crown 8vo., 3s. 6d.

ESKIMO LIFE. With 31 Illustrations. 8vo., 16s.

Peary.—*MY ARCTIC JOURNAL:* a year among Ice-Fields and Eskimos. By JOSEPHINE DIEBITSCH-PEARY. With 19 Plates, 3 Sketch Maps, and 44 Illustrations in the Text. 8vo., 12s.

Quillinan.—*JOURNAL OF A FEW MONTHS' RESIDENCE IN PORTUGAL,* and Glimpses of the South of Spain. By Mrs. QUILLINAN (Dora Wordsworth). New Edition. Edited, with Memoir, by EDMUND LEE, Author of "Dorothy Wordsworth," &c. Crown 8vo. 6s.

Smith.—*CLIMBING IN THE BRITISH ISLES.* By W. P. HASKETT SMITH. With Illustrations by ELLIS CARR, and Numerous Plans.

Part I. *ENGLAND.* 16mo., 3s. 6d.
Part II. *WALES AND IRELAND.* 16mo., 3s. 6d.
Part III. *SCOTLAND.* [In preparation.

Stephen. *THE PLAY-GROUND OF EUROPE.* By LESLIE STEPHEN. New Edition, with Additions and 4 Illustrations. Crown 8vo., 6s. net.

THREE IN NORWAY. By Two of Them. With a Map and 59 Illustrations. Crown 8vo., 2s. boards, 2s. 6d. cloth.

Whishaw (FRED. J.).

OUT OF DOORS IN TSARLAND: a Record of the Seeings and Doings of a Wanderer in Russia. Crown 8vo., 7s. 6d.

THE ROMANCE OF THE WOODS: Reprinted Articles and Sketches. Crown 8vo., 6s.

Veterinary Medicine, &c.

Steel (JOHN HENRY).

A TREATISE ON THE DISEASES OF THE DOG. With 88 Illustrations. 8vo., 10s. 6d.

A TREATISE ON THE DISEASES OF THE OX. With 119 Illustrations. 8vo., 15s.

A TREATISE ON THE DISEASES OF THE SHEEP. With 100 Illustrations. 8vo., 12s.

OUTLINES OF EQUINE ANATOMY: a Manual for the use of Veterinary Students in the Dissecting Room. Cr. 8vo., 7s. 6d.

Fitzwygram.—*HORSES AND STABLES.* By Major-General Sir F. Fitzwygram, Bart. With 56 pages of Illustrations. 8vo., 2s. 6d. net.

"Stonehenge."—*THE DOG IN HEALTH AND DISEASE.* By "STONEHENGE". With 78 Wood Engravings. 8vo., 7s. 6d.

Youatt (WILLIAM).

THE HORSE. Revised and Enlarged by W. WATSON, M.R.C.V.S. With 52 Wood Engravings. 8vo., 7s. 6d.

THE DOG. Revised and Enlarged. With 33 Wood Engravings. 8vo., 6s.

Sport and Pastime.
THE BADMINTON LIBRARY.

Edited by the DUKE of BEAUFORT, K.G., assisted by ALFRED E. T. WATSON.

Crown 8vo., price 10s. 6d. each Volume.

ARCHERY. By C. J. LONGMAN, Col. H. WALROND, Miss LEGH and Viscount DILLON. With 195 Illustrations.

ATHLETICS AND FOOTBALL. By MONTAGUE SHEARMAN. With 51 Illus.

BIG GAME SHOOTING. By C. PHIL-LIPPS-WOLLEY, Sir SAMUEL W. BAKER, W. C. OSWELL, F. C. SELOUS, &c.
Vol. I. Africa and America. With 77 Illustrations.
Vol. II. Europe, Asia, and the Arctic Regions. With 73 Illustrations.

BILLIARDS. By Major W. BROAD-FOOT, R.E. With Illustrations, and Diagrams. [*In the Press.*

BOATING. By W. B. WOODGATE. With 49 Illustrations and 4 Maps.

COURSING AND FALCONRY. By HARDING COX and the Hon. GERALD LASCELLES. With 76 Illustrations.

CRICKET. By A. G. STEEL, the Hon. R. H. LYTTELTON, ANDREW LANG, R. A. H. MITCHELL, W. G. GRACE, and F. GALE. With 64 Illustrations.

CYCLING. By the EARL OF ALBE-MARLE and G. LACY HILLIER. With 63 Illustrations.

DANCING. By Mrs. LILLY GROVE, F.R.G.S., &c. With 131 Illustrations.

DRIVING. By the DUKE OF BEAU-FORT. With 65 Illustrations.

FENCING, BOXING, AND WRESTLING. By WALTER H. POLLOCK, F. C. GROVE, C. PREVOST, E. B. MITCHELL, and WALTER ARMSTRONG. With 42 Illustrations.

FISHING. By H. CHOLMONDELEY-PENNELL, the MARQUIS OF EXETER, HENRY R. FRANCIS, G. CHRISTOPHER DAVIES, R. B. MARSTON, &c.
Vol. I. Salmon, Trout, and Grayling. With 158 Illustrations.
Vol. II. Pike and other Coarse Fish. With 133 Illustrations.

GOLF. By HORACE G. HUTCHIN-SON, the Rt. Hon. A. J. BALFOUR, M.P., Sir W. G. SIMPSON, Bart., LORD WELL-WOOD, H. S. C. EVERARD, ANDREW LANG, and other Writers. With 89 Illustrations.

HUNTING. By the DUKE OF BEAU-FORT, K.G., MOWBRAY MORRIS, the EARL OF SUFFOLK AND BERKSHIRE, Rev. E. W. L. DAVIES, DIGBY COLLINS, GEORGE H. LONGMAN, &c. With 53 Illustrations.

MOUNTAINEERING. By C. T. DENT, Sir F. POLLOCK, Bart., W. M. CONWAY, DOUGLAS FRESHFIELD, C. E. MATHEWS, &c. With 108 Illustrations.

RACING AND STEEPLE-CHASING. By the EARL OF SUFFOLK AND BERKSHIRE, W. G. CRAVEN, ARTHUR COVENTRY, and A. E. T. WATSON. With 58 Illustrations.

RIDING AND POLO. By Captain ROBERT WEIR, J. MORAY BROWN, the DUKE OF BEAUFORT, K.G., &c. With 59 Illustrations.

SEA FISHING. By JOHN BICKER-DYKE, W. SENIOR, A. C. HARMSWORTH, and Sir H. W. GORE-BOOTH, Bart. With 197 Illustrations.

SHOOTING. By LORD WALSING-HAM, Sir RALPH PAYNE-GALLWEY, Bart., LORD LOVAT, LORD C. LENNOX KERR, the Hon. G. LASCELLES, and A. J. STUART-WORTLEY.
Vol. I. Field and Covert. With 105 Illustrations.
Vol. II. Moor and Marsh. With 65 Illustrations.

SKATING, CURLING, TOBOGGANING, ICE-SAILING, AND BANDY. By J. M. HEATHCOTE, C. G. TEBBUTT, T. MAX-WELL WITHAM, the Rev. JOHN KERR. With 284 Illustrations.

SWIMMING. By ARCHIBALD SIN-CLAIR and WILLIAM HENRY. With 119 Illustrations.

TENNIS, LAWN TENNIS, RACKETS AND FIVES. By J. M. and C. G. HEATH-COTE, E. O. PLEYDELL-BOUVERIE, A. C. AINGER, &c. With 79 Illustrations.

YACHTING.
Vol. I. Cruising, Construction, Racing Rules, Fitting-Out, &c. By Sir EDWARD SULLIVAN, Bart., LORD BRASSEY, K.C.B., C. E. SETH-SMITH, C.B., &c. With 114 Illustrations.
Vol. II. Yacht Clubs, Yachting in America and the Colonies, Yacht Racing, &c. By R. T. PRITCHETT, the EARL OF ONSLOW, G.C.M.G., &c. With 195 Illustrations.

Sport and Pastime—*continued.*
FUR AND FEATHER SERIES.
Edited by A. E. T. WATSON.
Crown 8vo., price 5s. each Volume.

THE PARTRIDGE. Natural History by the Rev. H. A. MACPHERSON; Shooting, by A. J. STUART-WORTLEY; Cookery, by GEORGE SAINTSBURY. With 11 Illustrations and various Diagrams in the Text.

THE GROUSE. Natural History by the Rev. H. A. MACPHERSON; Shooting, by A. J. STUART-WORTLEY; Cookery, by GEORGE SAINTSBURY. With 13 Illustrations and various Diagrams. in the Text.

THE HARE AND THE RABBIT. By the Hon. GERALD LASCELLES, &c.
[*In preparation.*

THE PHEASANT. Natural History by the Rev. H. A. MACPHERSON; Shooting, by A. J. STUART-WORTLEY; Cookery, by ALEXANDER INNES SHAND. With 10 Illustrations and various Diagrams.

WILD FOWL. By the Hon. JOHN SCOTT-MONTAGU, M.P., &c.
[*In preparation.*

THE RED DEER. By CAMERON OF LOCHIEL, LORD EBRINGTON, &c.
[*In preparation.*

Bickerdyke.—*DAYS OF MY LIFE ON WATERS FRESH AND SALT;* and other Papers. By JOHN BICKERDYKE. With Photo-Etched Frontispiece and 8 Full-page Illustrations. Crown 8vo., 6s.

Campbell-Walker.—*THE CORRECT CARD;* or, How to Play at Whist; a Whist Catechism. By Major A. CAMPBELL-WALKER, F.R.G.S. Fcp. 8vo., 2s. 6d.

DEAD SHOT (THE): or, Sportsman's Complete Guide. Being a Treatise on the Use of the Gun, with Rudimentary and Finishing Lessons on the Art of Shooting Game of all kinds. By MARKSMAN. Crown 8vo., 10s. 6d.

Ellis.—*CHESS SPARKS:* or, Short and Bright Games of Chess. Collected and Arranged by J. H. ELLIS, M.A. 8vo., 4s. 6d.

Falkener.—*GAMES, ANCIENT AND ORIENTAL, AND HOW TO PLAY THEM.* By EDWARD FALKENER. With numerous Photographs, Diagrams, &c. 8vo., 21s.

Ford.—*THE THEORY AND PRACTICE OF ARCHERY.* By HORACE FORD. New Edition, thoroughly Revised and Re-written by W. BUTT, M.A. With a Preface by C. J. LONGMAN, M.A. 8vo., 14s.

Francis.—*A BOOK ON ANGLING:* or, Treatise on the Art of Fishing in every Branch; including full Illustrated List of Salmon Flies. By FRANCIS FRANCIS. With Portrait and Coloured Plates. Crown 8vo., 15s.

Gibson.—*TOBOGGANING ON CROOKED RUNS.* By the Hon. HARRY GIBSON. With Contributions by F. DE B. STRICKLAND and 'LADY-TOBOGANNER'. With 40 Illustrations. Crown 8vo., 6s.

Hawker.—*THE DIARY OF COLONEL PETER HAWKER,* Author of 'Instructions to Young Sportsmen.' 2 vols. 8vo., 32s.

Lang.—*ANGLING SKETCHES.* By ANDREW LANG. With 20 Illustrations. Cr. 8vo., 3s. 6d.

Longman.—*CHESS OPENINGS.* By FREDERICK W. LONGMAN. Fcp. 8vo., 2s. 6d.

Maskelyne.—*SHARPS AND FLATS:* a Complete Revelation of the Secrets of Cheating at Games of Chance and Skill. By JOHN NEVIL MASKELYNE, of the Egyptian Hall. With 62 Illustrations. Crown 8vo., 6s.

Payne-Gallwey (SIR RALPH, Bart.).
LETTERS TO YOUNG SHOOTERS (First Series). On the Choice and use of a Gun. With 41 Illustrations. Crown 8vo., 7s. 6d.
LETTERS TO YOUNG SHOOTERS (Second Series). On the Production, Preservation, and Killing of Game. With Directions in Shooting Wood-Pigeons and Breaking-in Retrievers. With Portrait and 103 Illustrations. Crown 8vo., 12s. 6d.

Pole (W., F.R.S.).
THE THEORY OF THE MODERN SCIENTIFIC GAME OF WHIST. Fcp. 8vo., 2s. 6d.
THE EVOLUTION OF WHIST: a Study of the Progressive Changes which the Game has undergone. Cr. 8vo., 6s.

Proctor (RICHARD A.).
HOW TO PLAY WHIST: WITH THE LAWS AND ETIQUETTE OF WHIST. Cr. 8vo., 3s. 6d.
HOME WHIST: An Easy Guide to Correct Play. 16mo., 1s.

Ronalds.—*THE FLY-FISHER'S ENTOMOLOGY.* By ALFRED RONALDS. With 20 coloured Plates. 8vo., 14s.

Wilcocks.—*THE SEA FISHERMAN:* Comprising the Chief Methods of Hook and Line Fishing in the British and other Seas, and Remarks on Nets, Boats, and Boating. By J. C. WILCOCKS. Illustrated. Cr. 8vo., 6s.

Mental, Moral, and Political Philosophy.
LOGIC, RHETORIC, PSYCHOLOGY, ETC.

Abbott.—*THE ELEMENTS OF LOGIC.* By T. K. ABBOTT, B.D. 12mo., 3s.

Aristotle.

THE POLITICS: G. Bekker's Greek Text of Books I., III., IV. (VII.), with an English Translation by W. E. BOLLAND, M.A.; and short Introductory Essays by A. LANG, M.A. Crown 8vo., 7s. 6d.

THE POLITICS: Introductory Essays. By ANDREW LANG (from Bolland and Lang's ' Politics '). Crown 8vo., 2s. 6d.

THE ETHICS: Greek Text, Illustrated with Essay and Notes. By Sir ALEXANDER GRANT, Bart. 2 vols. 8vo., 32s.

THE NICOMACHEAN ETHICS: Newly Translated into English. By ROBERT WILLIAMS. Crown 8vo., 7s. 6d.

AN INTRODUCTION TO ARISTOTLE'S ETHICS. Books I.-IV. (Book X. c. vi.-ix. in an Appendix). With a continuous Analysis and Notes. By the Rev. EDW. MOORE, D.D., Cr. 8vo. 10s. 6d.

Bacon (FRANCIS).

COMPLETE WORKS. Edited by R. L. ELLIS, JAMES SPEDDING and D. D. HEATH. 7 vols. 8vo., £3 13s. 6d.

LETTERS AND LIFE, including all his occasional Works. Edited by JAMES SPEDDING. 7 vols. 8vo., £4 4s.

THE ESSAYS: with Annotations. By RICHARD WHATELY, D.D. 8vo., 10s. 6d.

THE ESSAYS. Edited, with Notes, by F. STORR and C. H. GIBSON. Crown 8vo., 3s. 6d.

THE ESSAYS: with Introduction, Notes, and Index. By E. A. ABBOTT, D.D. 2 Vols. Fcp. 8vo., 6s. The Text and Index only, without Introduction and Notes, in One Volume. Fcp. 8vo., 2s. 6d.

Bain (ALEXANDER, LL.D.).

MENTAL SCIENCE. Cr. 8vo., 6s. 6d.

MORAL SCIENCE. Cr. 8vo., 4s. 6d.

The two works as above can be had in one volume, price 10s. 6d.

SENSES AND THE INTELLECT. 8vo., 15s.

EMOTIONS AND THE WILL. 8vo., 15s.

LOGIC, DEDUCTIVE AND INDUCTIVE. Part I. 4s. Part II. 6s. 6d.

PRACTICAL ESSAYS. Cr. 8vo., 3s.

Bray (CHARLES).

THE PHILOSOPHY OF NECESSITY: or, Law in Mind as in Matter. Cr. 8vo., 5s.

THE EDUCATION OF THE FEELINGS: a Moral System for Schools. Cr. 8vo., 2s. 6d.

Bray.—*ELEMENTS OF MORALITY,* in Easy Lessons for Home and School Teaching. By Mrs. CHARLES BRAY. Crown 8vo., 1s. 6d.

Davidson.—*THE LOGIC OF DEFINITION,* Explained and Applied. By WILLIAM L. DAVIDSON, M.A. Crown 8vo., 6s.

Green (THOMAS HILL).—THE WORKS of. Edited by R. L. NETTLESHIP.

Vols. I. and II. Philosophical Works. 8vo., 16s. each.

Vol. III. Miscellanies. With Index to the three Volumes, and Memoir. 8vo., 21s.

LECTURES ON THE PRINCIPLES OF POLITICAL OBLIGATION. With Preface by BERNARD BOSANQUET. 8vo., 5s.

Hodgson (SHADWORTH H.).

TIME AND SPACE: A Metaphysical Essay. 8vo., 16s.

THE THEORY OF PRACTICE: an Ethical Inquiry. 2 vols. 8vo., 24s.

THE PHILOSOPHY OF REFLECTION. 2 vols. 8vo., 21s.

Hume.—*THE PHILOSOPHICAL WORKS OF DAVID HUME.* Edited by T. H. GREEN and T. H. GROSE. 4 vols. 8vo., 56s. Or separately, Essays. 2 vols. 28s. Treatise of Human Nature. 2 vols. 28s.

Justinian.—*THE INSTITUTES OF JUSTINIAN:* Latin Text, chiefly that of Huschke, with English Introduction, Translation. Notes, and Summary. By THOMAS C. SANDARS, M.A. 8vo., 18s.

Kant (IMMANUEL).

CRITIQUE OF PRACTICAL REASON, AND OTHER WORKS ON THE THEORY OF ETHICS.. Translated by T. K. ABBOTT, B.D. With Memoir. 8vo., 12s. 6d.

FUNDAMENTAL PRINCIPLES OF THE METAPHYSIC OF ETHICS. Translated by T. K. ABBOTT, B.D. (Extracted from ' Kant's Critique of Practical Reason and other Works on the Theory of Ethics.') Crown 8vo., 3s.

INTRODUCTION TO LOGIC, AND HIS ESSAY ON THE MISTAKEN SUBTILTY OF THE FOUR FIGURES.. Translated by T. K. ABBOTT. 8vo., 6s.

Killick.—*HANDBOOK TO MILL'S SYSTEM OF LOGIC.* By Rev. A. H. KILLICK, M.A. Crown 8vo., 3s. 6d.

Mental, Moral and Political Philosophy—*continued*.

Ladd (GEORGE TRUMBULL).

PHILOSOPHY OF MIND: An Essay on the Metaphysics of Psychology. 8vo., 16s.

ELEMENTS OF PHYSIOLOGICAL PSYCHOLOGY. 8vo., 21s.

OUTLINES OF PHYSIOLOGICAL PSYCHOLOGY. A Text-book of Mental Science for Academies and Colleges. 8vo., 12s.

PSYCHOLOGY, DESCRIPTIVE AND EXPLANATORY: a Treatise of the Phenomena, Laws, and Development of Human Mental Life. 8vo., 21s.

PRIMER OF PSYCHOLOGY. Cr. 8vo., 5s. 6d.

Lewes.—*THE HISTORY OF PHILOSOPHY*, from Thales to Comte. By GEORGE HENRY LEWES. 2 vols. 8vo., 32s.

Max Müller (F.).

THE SCIENCE OF THOUGHT. 8vo., 21s.

THREE INTRODUCTORY LECTURES ON THE SCIENCE OF THOUGHT. 8vo., 2s. 6d.

Mill.—*ANALYSIS OF THE PHENOMENA OF THE HUMAN MIND.* By JAMES MILL. 2 vols. 8vo., 28s.

Mill (JOHN STUART).

A SYSTEM OF LOGIC. Cr. 8vo., 3s. 6d.

ON LIBERTY. Crown 8vo., 1s. 4d.

ON REPRESENTATIVE GOVERNMENT. Crown 8vo., 2s.

UTILITARIANISM. 8vo., 2s. 6d.

EXAMINATION OF SIR WILLIAM HAMILTON'S PHILOSOPHY. 8vo., 16s.

NATURE, THE UTILITY OF RELIGION, AND THEISM. Three Essays. 8vo., 5s.

Romanes.—*MIND AND MOTION AND MONISM.* By the late GEORGE JOHN ROMANES, LL.D., F.R.S. Cr. 8vo., 4s. 6d.

Stock.—*DEDUCTIVE LOGIC.* By ST. GEORGE STOCK. Fcp. 8vo., 3s. 6d.

Sully (JAMES).

THE HUMAN MIND: a Text-book of Psychology. 2 vols. 8vo., 21s.

OUTLINES OF PSYCHOLOGY. 8vo., 9s.

THE TEACHER'S HANDBOOK OF PSYCHOLOGY. Crown 8vo., 5s.

STUDIES OF CHILDHOOD. 8vo., 12s. 6d.

Swinburne.—*PICTURE LOGIC*: an Attempt to Popularise the Science of Reasoning. By ALFRED JAMES SWINBURNE, M.A. With 23 Woodcuts. Crown 8vo., 5s.

Thomson.—*OUTLINES OF THE NECESSARY LAWS OF THOUGHT*: a Treatise on Pure and Applied Logic. By WILLIAM THOMSON, D.D., formerly Lord Archbishop of York. Crown 8vo., 6s.

Whately (ARCHBISHOP).

BACON'S ESSAYS. With Annotations. 8vo., 10s. 6d.

ELEMENTS OF LOGIC. Cr. 8vo., 4s. 6d.

ELEMENTS OF RHETORIC. Cr. 8vo., 4s. 6d.

LESSONS ON REASONING. Fcp. 8vo., 1s. 6d.

Zeller (Dr. EDWARD, Professor in the University of Berlin).

THE STOICS, EPICUREANS, AND SCEPTICS. Translated by the Rev. O. J. REICHEL, M.A. Crown 8vo., 15s.

OUTLINES OF THE HISTORY OF GREEK PHILOSOPHY. Translated by SARAH F. ALLEYNE and EVELYN ABBOTT. Crown 8vo., 10s. 6d.

PLATO AND THE OLDER ACADEMY. Translated by SARAH F. ALLEYNE and ALFRED GOODWIN, B.A. Crown 8vo., 18s.

SOCRATES AND THE SOCRATIC SCHOOLS. Translated by the Rev. O. J. REICHEL, M.A. Crown 8vo., 10s. 6d.

History and Science of Language, &c.

Davidson.—*LEADING AND IMPORTANT ENGLISH WORDS:* Explained and Exemplified. By WILLIAM L. DAVIDSON, M.A. Fcp. 8vo., 3s. 6d.

Farrar.—*LANGUAGE AND LANGUAGES:* By F. W. FARRAR, D.D., F.R.S. Crown 8vo., 6s.

Graham. — *ENGLISH SYNONYMS,* Classified and Explained : with Practical Exercises. By G. F. GRAHAM. Fcp. 8vo., 6s.

Max Müller (F.).

THE SCIENCE OF LANGUAGE.—Founded on Lectures delivered at the Royal Institution in 1861 and 1863. 2 vols. Crown 8vo., 21s.

BIOGRAPHIES OF WORDS, AND THE HOME OF THE ARYAS. Crown 8vo., 7s. 6d.

Max Müller (F.)—*continued.*

THREE LECTURES ON THE SCIENCE OF LANGUAGE, AND ITS PLACE IN GENERAL EDUCATION, delivered at Oxford, 1889. Crown 8vo., 3s.

Roget.—*THESAURUS OF ENGLISH WORDS AND PHRASES.* Classified and Arranged so as to Facilitate the Expression of Ideas and assist in Literary Composition. By PETER MARK ROGET, M.D., F.R.S. Recomposed throughout, enlarged and improved, partly from the Author's Notes, and with a full Index, by the Author's Son, JOHN LEWIS ROGET. Crown 8vo. 10s. 6d.

Whately.—*ENGLISH SYNONYMS.* By E. JANE WHATELY. Fcp. 8vo., 3s.

Political Economy and Economics.

Ashley.—*ENGLISH ECONOMIC HISTORY AND THEORY.* By W. J. ASHLEY, M.A. Crown 8vo., Part I., 5s. Part II. 10s. 6d.

Bagehot.—*ECONOMIC STUDIES.* By WALTER BAGEHOT. Crown 8vo., 3s. 6d.

Barnett.—*PRACTICABLE SOCIALISM.* Essays on Social Reform. By the Rev. S. A. and Mrs. BARNETT. Crown 8vo., 6s.

Brassey.—*PAPERS AND ADDRESSES ON WORK AND WAGES.* By Lord BRASSEY. Edited by J. POTTER, and with Introduction by GEORGE HOWELL, M.P. Crown 8vo., 5s.

Devas.—*A MANUAL OF POLITICAL ECONOMY.* By C. S. DEVAS, M.A. Cr. 8vo., 6s. 6d. (*Manuals of Catholic Philosophy.*)

Dowell.—*A HISTORY OF TAXATION AND TAXES IN ENGLAND,* from the Earliest Times to the Year 1885. By STEPHEN DOWELL, (4 vols. 8vo.) Vols. I. and II. The History of Taxation, 21s. Vols. III. and IV. The History of Taxes, 21s.

Macleod (HENRY DUNNING).

BIMETALISM. 8vo., 5s. net.

THE ELEMENTS OF BANKING. Cr. 8vo., 3s. 6d.

THE THEORY AND PRACTICE OF BANKING. Vol. I. 8vo., 12s. Vol. II. 14s.

Macleod (HENRY DUNNING)—*continued.*

THE THEORY OF CREDIT. 8vo. Vol. I., 10s. net. Vol. II., Part I., 10s. net. Vol. II., Part II., 10s. 6d.

A DIGEST OF THE LAW OF BILLS OF EXCHANGE, BANK-NOTES, &c. [*In the press.*

Mill.—*POLITICAL ECONOMY.* By JOHN STUART MILL.

Popular Edition. Crown 8vo., 3s. 6d.

Library Edition. 2 vols. 8vo., 30s.

Symes.—*POLITICAL ECONOMY:* a Short Text-book of Political Economy. With Problems for Solution, and Hints for Supplementary Reading. By Professor J. E. SYMES, M.A., of University College, Nottingham. Crown 8vo., 2s. 6d.

Toynbee.—*LECTURES ON THE INDUSTRIAL REVOLUTION OF THE 18TH CENTURY IN ENGLAND:* Popular Addresses, Notes and other Fragments. By ARNOLD TOYNBEE. With a Memoir of the Author by BENJAMIN JOWETT, D.D. 8vo., 10s. 6d.

Webb.—*THE HISTORY OF TRADE UNIONISM.* By SIDNEY and BEATRICE WEBB. With Map and full Bibliography of the Subject. 8vo., 18s.

Evolution, Anthropology, &c.

Babington. — *FALLACIES OF RACE THEORIES AS APPLIED TO NATIONAL CHARACTERISTICS.* Essays by WILLIAM DALTON BABINGTON, M.A. Crown 8vo., 6s.

Clodd (EDWARD).

THE STORY OF CREATION: a Plain Account of Evolution. With 77 Illustrations. Crown 8vo., 3s. 6d.

A PRIMER OF EVOLUTION: being a Popular Abridged Edition of 'The Story of Creation'. With Illustrations. Fcp. 8vo., 1s. 6d.

Lang. — *CUSTOM AND MYTH*: Studies of Early Usage and Belief. By ANDREW LANG. With 15 Illustrations. Crown 8vo., 3s. 6d.

Lubbock. — *THE ORIGIN OF CIVILISATION*, and the Primitive Condition of Man. By Sir J. LUBBOCK, Bart., M.P. With 5 Plates and 20 Illustrations in the Text. 8vo., 18s.

Romanes (GEORGE JOHN, LL.D., F.R.S.).

DARWIN, AND AFTER DARWIN: an Exposition of the Darwinian Theory, and a Discussion on Post-Darwinian Questions.
Part I. THE DARWINIAN THEORY. With Portrait of Darwin and 125 Illustrations. Crown 8vo., 10s. 6d.
Part II. POST-DARWINIAN QUESTIONS: Heredity and Utility. With Portrait of the Author and 5 Illus. Cr. 8vo., 10s. 6d.

AN EXAMINATION OF WEISMANNISM. Crown 8vo., 6s.

Classical Literature, Translations, &c.

Abbott. — *HELLENICA.* A Collection of Essays on Greek Poetry, Philosophy, History, and Religion. Edited by EVELYN ABBOTT, M.A., LL.D. 8vo., 16s.

Æschylus. — *EUMENIDES OF ÆSCHYLUS.* With Metrical English Translation. By J. F. DAVIES. 8vo., 7s.

Aristophanes. — *THE ACHARNIANS OF ARISTOPHANES,* translated into English Verse. By R. Y. TYRRELL. Crown 8vo., 1s.

Becker (PROFESSOR).

GALLUS: or, Roman Scenes in the Time of Augustus. Illustrated. Post 8vo., 3s. 6d.

CHARICLES: or, Illustrations of the Private Life of the Ancient Greeks. Illustrated. Post 8vo., 3s. 6d.

Cicero. — *CICERO'S CORRESPONDENCE.* By R. Y. TYRRELL. Vols. I., II., III., 8vo., each 12s. Vol. IV., 15s.

Farnell. — *GREEK LYRIC POETRY*: a Complete Collection of the Surviving Passages from the Greek Song-Writing. Arranged with Prefatory Articles, Introductory Matter and Commentary. By GEORGE S. FARNELL, M.A. With 5 Plates. 8vo., 16s.

Lang. — *HOMER AND THE EPIC.* By ANDREW LANG. Crown 8vo., 9s. net.

Mackail. — *SELECT EPIGRAMS FROM THE GREEK ANTHOLOGY.* By J. W. MACKAIL, Fellow of Balliol College, Oxford. Edited with a Revised Text, Introduction, Translation, and Notes. 8vo., 16s.

Rich. — *A DICTIONARY OF ROMAN AND GREEK ANTIQUITIES.* By A. RICH, B.A. With 2000 Woodcuts. Crown 8vo., 7s. 6d.

Sophocles. — Translated into English Verse. By ROBERT WHITELAW, M.A., Assistant Master in Rugby School; late Fellow of Trinity College, Cambridge. Crown 8vo., 8s. 6d.

Tyrrell. — *TRANSLATIONS INTO GREEK AND LATIN VERSE.* Edited by R. Y. TYRRELL. 8vo., 6s.

Virgil.

THE ÆNEID OF VIRGIL. Translated into English Verse by JOHN CONINGTON. Crown 8vo., 6s.

THE POEMS OF VIRGIL. Translated into English Prose by JOHN CONINGTON. Crown 8vo., 6s.

THE ÆNEID OF VIRGIL, freely translated into English Blank Verse. By W. J. THORNHILL. Crown 8vo., 7s. 6d.

THE ÆNEID OF VIRGIL. Books I. to VI. Translated into English Verse by JAMES RHOADES. Crown 8vo., 5s.

Wilkins. — *THE GROWTH OF THE HOMERIC POEMS.* By G. WILKINS. 8vo., 6s.

Poetry and the Drama.

Acworth.—*BALLADS OF THE MARA-THAS.* Rendered into English Verse from the Marathi Originals. By HARRY ARBUTHNOT ACWORTH. 8vo., 5s.

Allingham (WILLIAM).

IRISH SONGS AND POEMS. With Frontispiece of the Waterfall of Asaroe. Fcp. 8vo., 6s.

LAURENCE BLOOMFIELD. With Portrait of the Author. Fcp. 8vo., 3s. 6d.

FLOWER PIECES; DAY AND NIGHT SONGS; BALLADS. With 2 Designs by D. G. ROSSETTI. Fcp. 8vo., 6s. large paper edition, 12s.

LIFE AND PHANTASY: with Frontispiece by Sir J. E. MILLAIS, Bart., and Design by ARTHUR HUGHES. Fcp. 8vo., 6s.; large paper edition, 12s.

THOUGHT AND WORD, AND ASHBY MANOR: a Play. Fcp. 8vo., 6s.; large paper edition, 12s.

BLACKBERRIES. Imperial 16mo., 6s.

Sets of the above 6 vols. may be had in uniform Half-parchment binding, price 30s.

Armstrong (G. F. SAVAGE).

POEMS: Lyrical and Dramatic. Fcp. 8vo., 6s.

KING SAUL. (The Tragedy of Israel, Part I.) Fcp. 8vo., 5s.

KING DAVID. (The Tragedy of Israel, Part II.) Fcp. 8vo., 6s.

KING SOLOMON. (The Tragedy of Israel, Part III.) Fcp. 8vo., 6s.

UGONE: a Tragedy. Fcp. 8vo., 6s.

A GARLAND FROM GREECE: Poems. Fcp. 8vo., 7s. 6d.

STORIES OF WICKLOW: Poems. Fcp. 8vo., 7s. 6d.

MEPHISTOPHELES IN BROADCLOTH: a Satire. Fcp. 8vo., 4s.

ONE IN THE INFINITE: a Poem. Crown 8vo., 7s. 6d.

Armstrong.—*THE POETICAL WORKS OF EDMUND J. ARMSTRONG.* Fcp. 8vo., 5s.

Arnold (Sir EDWIN, K.C.I.E.).

THE LIGHT OF THE WORLD: or the Great Consummation. Cr. 8vo., 7s. 6d. net.

POTIPHAR'S WIFE, and other Poems. Crown 8vo., 5s. net.

ADZUMA: or the Japanese Wife. A Play. Crown 8vo., 6s. 6d. net.

THE TENTH MUSE, and other Poems. Crown 8vo., 5s. net.

Beesly. — *BALLADS AND OTHER VERSE.* By A. H. BEESLY. Fcp. 8vo., 5s.

Bell.—*CHAMBER COMEDIES:* a Collection of Plays and Monologues for the Drawing Room. By Mrs. HUGH BELL. Cr. 8vo., 6s.

Cochrane.—*THE KESTREL'S NEST,* and other Verses. By ALFRED COCHRANE. Fcp. 8vo., 3s. 6d.

Goethe.

FAUST, Part I., the German Text, with Introduction and Notes. By ALBERT M. SELSS, Ph.D., M.A. Crown 8vo., 5s.

FAUST. Translated, with Notes. By T. E. WEBB. 8vo., 12s. 6d.

Ingelow (JEAN).

POETICAL WORKS. 2 vols. Fcp. 8vo., 12s.

LYRICAL AND OTHER POEMS. Selected from the Writings of JEAN INGELOW. Fcp. 8vo., 2s. 6d. cloth plain, 3s. cl. gilt.

Kendall.—*SONGS FROM DREAMLAND.* By MAY KENDALL. Fcp. 8vo., 5s. net.

Lang (ANDREW).

BAN AND ARRIÈRE BAN: a Rally of Fugitive Rhymes. Fcp. 8vo., 5s. net.

GRASS OF PARNASSUS. Fcp. 8vo., 2s. 6d. net.

BALLADS OF BOOKS. Edited by ANDREW LANG. Fcp. 8vo., 6s.

THE BLUE POETRY BOOK. Edited by ANDREW LANG. With 100 Illustrations. Crown 8vo., 6s.

Special Edition, printed on India paper. With Notes, but without Illustrations. Crown 8vo., 7s. 6d.

Lecky.—*POEMS.* By W. E. H. LECKY, M.P. Fcp. 8vo., 5s.

Lytton (THE EARL OF), (OWEN MEREDITH).

MARAH. Fcp. 8vo., 6s. 6d.

KING POPPY: a Fantasia. With 1 Plate and Design on Title-Page by ED. BURNE-JONES, A.R.A. Cr. 8vo., 10s. 6d.

THE WANDERER. Cr. 8vo., 10s. 6d.

LUCILE. Crown 8vo., 10s. 6d.

SELECTED POEMS. Cr. 8vo., 10s. 6d.

Macaulay.—*LAYS OF ANCIENT ROME, &c.* By Lord MACAULAY.

Illustrated by G. SCHARF. Fcp. 4to., 10s. 6d.

———————————— Bijou Edition. 18mo., 2s. 6d. gilt top.

———————————— Popular Edition. Fcp. 4to., 6d. sewed, 1s. cloth.

Illustrated by J. R. WEGUELIN. Crown 8vo., 3s. 6d.

Annotated Edition. Fcp. 8vo., 1s. sewed, 1s. 6d. cloth.

Poetry and the Drama—*continued*.

Murray (Robert F.).—Author of 'The Scarlet Gown'. His Poems, with a Memoir by Andrew Lang. Fcp. 8vo., 5s. net.

Nesbit.—*Lays and Legends*. By E. Nesbit (Mrs. Hubert Bland). First Series. Crown 8vo., 3s. 6d. Second Series. With Portrait. Crown 8vo., 5s.

Peek (Hedley) (Frank Leyton).

Skeleton Leaves: Poems. With a Dedicatory Poem to the late Hon. Roden Noel. Fcp. 8vo., 2s. 6d. net.

The Shadows of the Lake, and other Poems. Fcp. 8vo., 2s. 6d. net.

Piatt (Sarah).

An Enchanted Castle, and Other Poems: Pictures, Portraits, and People in Ireland. Crown 8vo., 3s. 6d.

Poems: With Portrait of the Author. 2 vols. Crown 8vo., 10s.

Piatt (John James).

Idyls and Lyrics of the Ohio Valley. Crown 8vo., 5s.

Little New World Idyls. Cr. 8vo., 5s.

Rhoades.—*Teresa and other Poems*. By James Rhoades. Crown 8vo., 3s. 6d.

Riley (James Whitcomb).

Old Fashioned Roses: Poems. 12mo., 5s.

Poems: Here at Home. Fcp. 8vo., 6s. net.

Shakespeare.—*Bowdler's Family Shakespeare*. With 36 Woodcuts. 1 vol. 8vo., 14s. Or in 6 vols. Fcp. 8vo., 21s.

The Shakespeare Birthday Book. By Mary F. Dunbar. 32mo., 1s. 6d.

Sturgis.—*A Book of Song*. By Julian Sturgis. 16mo., 5s.

Works of Fiction, Humour, &c.

Anstey (F., Author of 'Vice Versâ').

The Black Poodle, and other Stories. Crown 8vo., 2s. boards, 2s. 6d. cloth.

Voces Populi. Reprinted from 'Punch'. First Series. With 20 Illustrations by J. Bernard Partridge. Crown 8vo., 3s. 6d.

The Travelling Companions. Reprinted from 'Punch'. With 25 Illust. by J. Bernard Partridge. Post 4to., 5s.

The Man from Blankley's: a Story in Scenes, and other Sketches. With 24 Illustrations by J. Bernard Partridge. Fcp. 4to., 6s.

Arnold.—*The Story of Ulla*, and other Tales. By Edwin Lester Arnold. Crown 8vo., 6s.

Astor.—*A Journey in Other Worlds*: a Romance of the Future. By John Jacob Astor. With 10 Illustrations. Cr. 8vo., 6s.

Baker.—*By the Western Sea*. By James Baker, Author of 'John Westacott'. Crown 8vo., 3s. 6d.

Beaconsfield (The Earl of).

Novels and Tales. Cheap Edition. Complete in 11 vols. Cr. 8vo., 1s. 6d. each.

Vivian Grey. | Henrietta Temple.
The Young Duke, &c. | Venetia.   Tancred.
Alroy, Ixion, &c. | Coningsby.   Sybil.
Contarini Fleming, &c. | Lothair.   Endymion.

Novels and Tales The Hughenden Edition. With 2 Portraits and 11 Vignettes. 11 vols. Crown 8vo., 42s.

Boulton.—*Josephine Crewe*. By Helen M. Boulton. Crown 8vo., 6s.

Carmichael.—*Poems*. By Jennings Carmichael (Mrs. Francis Mullis). Crown 8vo., 6s. net.

Clegg.—*David's Loom*: a Story of Rochdale life in the early years of the Nineteenth Century. By John Trafford Clegg. Cr. 8vo., 2s. 6d.

Deland.—*Philip and His Wife*. By Margaret Deland, Author of 'John Ward'. Crown 8vo., 6s.

Dougall (L.).

Beggars All. Cr. 8vo., 3s. 6d.

What Necessity Knows. Crown 8vo., 6s.

Works of Fiction, Humour, &c.—*continued.*

Doyle (A. CONAN).

MICAH CLARKE: A Tale of Monmouth's Rebellion. With 10 Illustrations. Cr. 8vo., 3s. 6d.

THE CAPTAIN OF THE POLESTAR, and other Tales. Cr. 8vo., 3s. 6d.

THE REFUGEES: A Tale of Two Continents. With 25 Illus. Cr. 8vo., 3s. 6d.

THE STARK MUNRO LETTERS. Cr. 8vo, 6s,

Farrar (F. W., DEAN OF CANTERBURY).

DARKNESS AND DAWN: or, Scenes in the Days of Nero. An Historic Tale. Cr. 8vo., 7s. 6d.

GATHERING CLOUDS: a Tale of the Days of St. Chrysostom. 2 vols., 8vo., 28s.

Fowler.—*THE YOUNG PRETENDERS.* A Story of Child Life. By EDITH H. FOWLER. With 12 Illustrations by PHILIP BURNE-JONES. Crown 8vo., 6s.

Froude.—*THE TWO CHIEFS OF DUNBOY:* an Irish Romance of the Last Century. By JAMES A. FROUDE. Cr. 8vo., 3s. 6d.

Gerard.—*AN ARRANGED MARRIAGE.* By DOROTHEA GERARD. Crown 8vo., 6s.

Gilkes.—*THE THING THAT HATH BEEN:* or, a Young Man's Mistakes. By A. H. GILKES, M.A. Crown 8vo., 6s.

Haggard (H. RIDER).

JOAN HASTE. With 20 Illustrations. Crown 8vo., 6s.

THE PEOPLE OF THE MIST. With 16 Illustrations. Crown 8vo., 6s.

MONTEZUMA'S DAUGHTER. With 24 Illustrations. Crown 8vo., 6s.

SHE. With 32 Illustrations. Crown 8vo., 3s. 6d.

ALLAN QUATERMAIN. With 31 Illustrations. Crown 8vo., 3s. 6d.

MAIWA'S REVENGE: Crown 8vo., 1s. boards, 1s. 6d. cloth.

COLONEL QUARITCH, V.C. Cr. 8vo. 3s. 6d.

CLEOPATRA. With 29 Illustrations, Crown 8vo., 3s. 6d.

BEATRICE. Cr. 8vo., 3s. 6d.

ERIC BRIGHTEYES. With 51 Illustrations. Crown 8vo., 3s. 6d.

NADA THE LILY. With 23 Illustrations. Crown 8vo., 3s. 6d.

ALLAN'S WIFE. With 34 Illustrations. Crown 8vo., 3s. 6d.

THE WITCH'S HEAD. With 16 Illustrations. Crown 8vo., 3s. 6d.

Haggard (H. RIDER).—*continued.*

MR. MEESON'S WILL. With 16 Illustrations. Crown 8vo., 3s. 6d.

DAWN. With 16 Illustrations. Cr. 8vo., 3s. 6d.

Haggard and Lang.—*THE WORLD'S DESIRE.* By H. RIDER HAGGARD and ANDREW LANG. With 27 Illustrations. Crown 8vo., 3s. 6d.

Harte.—*IN THE CARQUINEZ WOODS* and other stories. By BRET HARTE. Cr. 8vo., 3s. 6d.

Hornung.—*THE UNBIDDEN GUEST.* By E. W. HORNUNG. Crown 8vo., 3s. 6d.

Lemon.—*MATTHEW FURTH.* By IDA LEMON. Crown 8vo., 6s.

Lyall (EDNA).

THE AUTOBIOGRAPHY OF A SLANDER. Fcp. 8vo., 1s. sewed.

Presentation Edition. With 20 Illustrations by LANCELOT SPEED. Crown 8vo., 2s. 6d. net.

DOREEN. The Story of a Singer. Crown 8vo., 6s.

Matthews.—*HIS FATHER'S SON:* a Novel of the New York Stock Exchange. By BRANDER MATTHEWS. With 13 Illustrations. Cr. 8vo. 6s.

Melville (G. J. WHYTE). WORKS BY

The Gladiators.	Holmby House.
The Interpreter.	Kate Coventry.
Good for Nothing.	Digby Grand.
The Queen's Maries.	General Bounce.

Crown 8vo., 1s. 6d. each.

Oliphant (MRS).

MADAM. Cr. 8vo., 1s. 6d.

IN TRUST. Cr. 8vo., 1s. 6d.

Prince.—*THE STORY OF CHRISTINE ROCHEFORT.* By HELEN CHOATE PRINCE. Crown 8vo., 6s.

Payn (JAMES).

THE LUCK OF THE DARRELLS. Cr. 8vo., 1s. 6d.

THICKER THAN WATER. Cr. 8vo., 1s. 6d.

Phillipps-Wolley.—*SNAP:* a Legend of the Lone Mountain. By C. PHILLIPPS-WOLLEY. With 13 Illustrations. Crown 8vo., 3s. 6d.

Quintana.—*THE CID CAMPEADOR:* an Historical Romance. By D. ANTONIO DE TRUEBA Y LA QUINTANA. Translated from the Spanish by HENRY J. GILL, M.A., T.C.D. Crown 8vo, 6s.

Rhoscomyl.—*THE JEWEL OF YNYS GALON:* being a hitherto unprinted Chapter in the History of the Sea Rovers. By OWEN RHOSCOMYL. Cr. 8vo., 6s.

Works of Fiction, Humour, &c.—*continued*.

Robertson.—*NUGGETS IN THE DEVIL'S PUNCH BOWL*, and other Australian Tales. By ANDREW ROBERTSON. Cr. 8vo., 3s. 6d.

Sewell (ELIZABETH M.).

A Glimpse of the World.	Amy Herbert.
Laneton Parsonage.	Cleve Hall.
Margaret Percival.	Gertrude.
Katharine Ashton.	Home Life.
The Earl's Daughter.	After Life.
The Experience of Life.	Ursula. Ivors.

   Cr. 8vo., 1s. 6d. each cloth plain. 2s. 6d. each cloth extra, gilt edges.

Stevenson (ROBERT LOUIS).

   STRANGE CASE OF DR. JEKYLL AND MR. HYDE. Fcp. 8vo., 1s. sewed. 1s. 6d. cloth.

   MORE NEW ARABIAN NIGHTS—THE DYNAMITER. Crown 8vo., 3s. 6d.

Stevenson and Osbourne.—*THE WRONG BOX.* By ROBERT LOUIS STEVENSON and LLOYD OSBOURNE. Cr. 8vo., 3s. 6d.

Suttner.—*LAY DOWN YOUR ARMS* (*Die Waffen Nieder*): The Autobiography of Martha Tilling. By BERTHA VON SUTTNER. Translated by T. HOLMES. Cr. 8vo., 1s. 6d.

Trollope (ANTHONY).

   THE WARDEN. Cr. 8vo., 1s. 6d.

   BARCHESTER TOWERS. Cr. 8vo., 1s. 6d.

   TRUE (A) RELATION OF THE TRAVELS AND PERILOUS ADVENTURES OF MATHEW DUDGEON, GENTLEMAN: Wherein is truly set down the Manner of his Taking, the Long Time of his Slavery in Algiers, and Means of his Delivery. Written by Himself, and now for the first time printed. Cr. 8vo., 5s.

Walford (L. B.).

   MR. SMITH: a Part of his Life. Crown 8vo., 2s. 6d.

   THE BABY'S GRANDMOTHER. Cr. 8vo., 2s. 6d.

   COUSINS. Crown 8vo., 2s. 6d.

   TROUBLESOME DAUGHTERS. Cr. 8vo., 2s. 6d.

   PAULINE. Crown. 8vo., 2s. 6d.

   DICK NETHERBY. Cr. 8vo., 2s. 6d.

   THE HISTORY OF A WEEK. Cr. 8vo. 2s. 6d.

   A STIFF-NECKED GENERATION. Cr. 8vo. 2s. 6d.

   NAN, and other Stories. Cr. 8vo., 2s. 6d.

   THE MISCHIEF OF MONICA. Cr. 8vo., 2s. 6d.

   THE ONE GOOD GUEST. Cr. 8vo. 2s. 6d.

   '*PLOUGHED,*' and other Stories. Crown 8vo., 6s.

   THE MATCHMAKER. Cr. 8vo., 6s.

West (B. B.).

   HALF-HOURS WITH THE MILLIONAIRES: Showing how much harder it is to spend a million than to make it. Cr. 8vo., 6s.

   SIR SIMON VANDERPETTER, and MINDING HIS ANCESTORS. Cr. 8vo., 5s.

   A FINANCIAL ATONEMENT. Cr. 8vo.

Weyman (STANLEY).

   THE HOUSE OF THE WOLF. Cr. 8vo., 3s. 6d.

   A GENTLEMAN OF FRANCE. Cr. 8vo., 6s.

   THE RED COCKADE. Cr. 8vo., 6s.

Popular Science (Natural History, &c.).

Butler.—*OUR HOUSEHOLD INSECTS.* An Account of the Insect-Pests found in Dwelling-Houses. By EDWARD A. BUTLER, B.A., B.Sc. (Lond.). With 113 Illustrations. Crown 8vo., 6s.

Furneaux (W.).

   THE OUTDOOR WORLD; or The Young Collector's Handbook. With 18 Plates 16 of which are coloured, and 549 Illustrations in the Text. Crown 8vo., 7s. 6d.

   BUTTERFLIES AND MOTHS (British). With 12 coloured Plates and 241 Illustrations in the Text. Crown 8vo., 12s. 6d.

Graham.—*COUNTRY PASTIMES FOR BOYS.* By P. ANDERSON GRAHAM. With 252 Illustrations from Drawings and Photographs. Crown 8vo., 6s.

Hartwig (DR. GEORGE).

   THE SEA AND ITS LIVING WONDERS. With 12 Plates and 303 Woodcuts. 8vo., 7s. net.

   THE TROPICAL WORLD. With 8 Plates and 172 Woodcuts. 8vo., 7s. net.

   THE POLAR WORLD. With 3 Maps, 8 Plates and 85 Woodcuts. 8vo., 7s. net.

   THE SUBTERRANEAN WORLD. With 3 Maps and 80 Woodcuts. 8vo., 7s. net.

Popular Science (Natural History, &c.)—*continued.*

Hartwig (Dr. George).—*continued.*

The Aerial World. With Map, 8 Plates and 60 Woodcuts. 8vo., 7s. net.

Heroes of the Polar World. 19 Illustrations. Cr. 8vo., 2s.

Wonders of the Tropical Forests. 40 Illustrations. Cr. 8vo., 2s.

Workers under the Ground. 29 Illustrations. Cr. 8vo., 2s.

Marvels Over our Heads. 29 Illustrations. Cr. 8vo., 2s.

Sea Monsters and Sea Birds. 75 Illustrations. Cr. 8vo., 2s. 6d.

Denizens of the Deep. 117 Illustrations. Cr. 8vo., 2s. 6d.

Volcanoes and Earthquakes. 30 Illustrations. Cr. 8vo., 2s. 6d.

Wild Animals of the Tropics. 66 Illustrations. Cr. 8vo., 3s. 6d.

Hayward.—*Bird Notes.* By the late Jane Mary Hayward. Edited by Emma Hubbard. With Frontispiece and 15 Illustrations by G. E. Lodge. Cr. 8vo., 6s.

Helmholtz.—*Popular Lectures on Scientific Subjects.* By Hermann von Helmholtz. With 68 Woodcuts. 2 vols. Cr. 8vo., 3s. 6d. each.

Hudson.—*British Birds.* By W. H. Hudson, C.M.Z.S. With a Chapter on Structure and Classification by Frank E. Beddard, F.R.S. With 16 Plates (8 of which are Coloured), and over 100 Illustrations in the Text. Crown 8vo., 12s. 6d.

Proctor (Richard A.).

Light Science for Leisure Hours. Familiar Essays on Scientific Subjects. 3 vols. Cr. 8vo., 5s. each.

Chance and Luck: a Discussion of the Laws of Luck, Coincidence, Wagers, Lotteries and the Fallacies of Gambling, &c. Cr. 8vo., 2s. boards. 2s. 6d. cloth.

Rough Ways made Smooth. Familiar Essays on Scientific Subjects. Silver Library Edition. Cr. 8vo., 3s. 6d.

Pleasant Ways in Science. Cr. 8vo., 5s. Silver Library Edition. Cr. 8vo., 3s. 6d.

The Great Pyramid, Observatory, Tomb and Temple. With Illustrations. Cr. 8vo., 5s.

Nature Studies. By R. A. Proctor, Grant Allen, A. Wilson, T. Foster and E. Clodd. Cr. 8vo., 5s. Silver Library Edition. Crown 8vo., 3s. 6d.

Proctor (Richard A.).—*continued.*

Leisure Readings. By R. A. Proctor, E. Clodd, A. Wilson, T. Foster and A. C. Ranyard. Cr. 8vo., 5s.

Stanley.—*A Familiar History of Birds.* By E. Stanley, D.D., formerly Bishop of Norwich. With Illustrations. Cr. 8vo., 3s. 6d.

Wood (Rev. J. G.).

Homes without Hands: A Description of the Habitation of Animals, classed according to the Principle of Construction. With 140 Illustrations. 8vo., 7s., net.

Insects at Home: A Popular Account of British Insects, their Structure, Habits and Transformations. With 700 Illustrations. 8vo., 7s. net.

Insects Abroad: a Popular Account of Foreign Insects, their Structure, Habits and Transformations. With 600 Illustrations. 8vo., 7s. net.

Bible Animals: a Description of every Living Creature mentioned in the Scriptures. With 112 Illustrations. 8vo., 7s. net.

Petland Revisited. With 33 Illustrations. Cr. 8vo., 3s. 6d.

Out of Doors: a Selection of Original Articles on Practical Natural History. With 11 Illustrations. Cr. 8vo., 3s. 6d.

Strange Dwellings: a Description of the Habitations of Animals, abridged from 'Homes without Hands'. With 60 Illustrations. Cr. 8vo., 3s. 6d.

Bird Life of the Bible. 32 Illustrations. Cr. 8vo., 3s. 6d.

Wonderful Nests. 30 Illustrations. Cr. 8vo., 3s. 6d.

Homes under the Ground. 28 Illustrations. Cr. 8vo., 3s. 6d.

Wild Animals of the Bible. 29 Illustrations. Cr. 8vo., 3s. 6d.

Domestic Animals of the Bible. 23 Illustrations. Cr. 8vo., 3s. 6d.

The Branch Builders. 28 Illustrations. Cr. 8vo., 2s. 6d.

Social Habitations and Parasitic Nests. 18 Illustrations. Cr. 8vo., 2s.

Works of Reference.

Longmans' *GAZETTEER OF THE WORLD.* Edited by GEORGE G. CHISHOLM, M.A., B.Sc. Imp. 8vo., £2 2s. cloth, £2 12s. 6d. half-morocco.

Maunder's (Samuel) Treasuries.

BIOGRAPHICAL TREASURY. With Supplement brought down to 1889. By Rev. JAMES WOOD. Fcp. 8vo., 6s.

TREASURY OF NATURAL HISTORY: or, Popular Dictionary of Zoology. With 900 Woodcuts. Fcp. 8vo., 6s.

TREASURY OF GEOGRAPHY, Physical, Historical, Descriptive, and Political. With 7 Maps and 16 Plates. Fcp. 8vo., 6s.

THE TREASURY OF BIBLE KNOWLEDGE. By the Rev. J. AYRE, M.A. With 5 Maps, 15 Plates, and 300 Woodcuts. Fcp. 8vo., 6s.

TREASURY OF KNOWLEDGE AND LIBRARY OF REFERENCE. Fcp. 8vo., 6s.

Maunder's (Samuel) Treasuries— *continued.*

HISTORICAL TREASURY. Fcp. 8vo., 6s.

SCIENTIFIC AND LITERARY TREASURY. Fcp. 8vo., 6s.

THE TREASURY OF BOTANY. Edited by J. LINDLEY, F.R.S., and T. MOORE, F.L.S. With 274 Woodcuts and 20 Steel Plates. 2 vols. Fcp. 8vo., 12s.

Roget. — *THESAURUS OF ENGLISH WORDS AND PHRASES.* Classified and Arranged so as to Facilitate the Expression of Ideas and assist in Literary Composition. By PETER MARK ROGET, M.D., F.R.S. Crown 8vo., 10s. 6d.

Willich.—*POPULAR TABLES* for giving information for ascertaining the value of Lifehold, Leasehold, and Church Property, the Public Funds, &c. By CHARLES M. WILLICH. Edited by H. BENCE JONES. Crown 8vo., 10s. 6d.

Children's Books.

Crake (REV. A. D.).

EDWY THE FAIR; or, The First Chronicle of Æscendune. Cr. 8vo., 2s. 6d.

ALFGAR THE DANE; or, The Second Chronicle of Æscendune. Cr. 8vo. 2s. 6d.

THE RIVAL HEIRS: being the Third and Last Chronicle of Æscendune. Cr. 8vo., 2s. 6d.

THE HOUSE OF WALDERNE. A Tale of the Cloister and the Forest in the Days of the Barons' Wars. Crown 8vo., 2s. 6d.

BRIAN FITZ-COUNT. A Story of Wallingford Castle and Dorchester Abbey. Cr. 8vo., 2s. 6d.

Lang (ANDREW).—EDITED BY.

THE BLUE FAIRY BOOK. With 138 Illustrations. Crown 8vo., 5s.

THE RED FAIRY BOOK. With 100 Illustrations. Crown 8vo., 6s.

THE GREEN FAIRY BOOK. With 99 Illustrations. Crown 8vo., 6s.

THE YELLOW FAIRY BOOK. With 104 Illustrations. Cr. 8vo., 6s.

THE BLUE POETRY BOOK. With 100 Illustrations. Cr. 8vo., 6s.

THE BLUE POETRY BOOK. School Edition, without Illustrations. Fcp. 8vo., 2s. 6d.

Lang (ANDREW).—EDITED BY—cont.

THE TRUE STORY BOOK. With 66 Illustrations. Cr. 8vo., 6s.

THE RED TRUE STORY BOOK. With 100 Illustrations. Crown 8vo., 6s.

Meade (L. T.).

DADDY'S BOY. With Illustrations. Crown 8vo., 3s. 6d.

DEB AND THE DUCHESS. With Illustrations. Cr. 8vo., 3s. 6d.

THE BERESFORD PRIZE. Cr. 8vo., 3s. 6d.

Molesworth—*SILVERTHORNS.* By Mrs. MOLESWORTH. With Illustrations. Cr. 8vo., 5s.

Stevenson.—*A CHILD'S GARDEN OF VERSES.* By ROBERT LOUIS STEVENSON. Fcp. 8vo., 5s.

Upton. *THE ADVENTURES OF TWO DUTCH DOLLS AND A 'GOLLIWOG'.* Illustrated by FLORENCE K. UPTON, with Words by BERTHA UPTON. With 31 Coloured Plates and numerous Illustrations in the Text. Oblong 4to., 6s.

Wordsworth.—*THE SNOW GARDEN, AND OTHER FAIRY TALES FOR CHILDREN.* By ELIZABETH WORDSWORTH. With 10 Illustrations by TREVOR HADDON. Crown 8vo., 5s.

Longmans' Series of Books for Girls.

Price 2s. 6d. each.

ATELIER (THE) DU LYS: or, an Art Student in the Reign of Terror.

BY THE SAME AUTHOR.

MADEMOISELLE MORI: a Tale of Modern Rome.

IN THE OLDEN TIME: a Tale of the Peasant War in Germany.

THE YOUNGER SISTER.

THAT CHILD.

UNDER A CLOUD.

HESTER'S VENTURE

THE FIDDLER OF LUGAU.

A CHILD OF THE REVOLUTION.

ATHERSTONE PRIORY. By L. N. COMYN.

THE STORY OF A SPRING MORNING, etc. By Mrs. MOLESWORTH. Illustrated.

THE PALACE IN THE GARDEN. By Mrs. MOLESWORTH. With Illustrations. Crown 8vo., 2s. 6d.

NEIGHBOURS. By Mrs. MOLESWORTH.

THE THIRD MISS ST. QUENTIN. By Mrs. MOLESWORTH.

VERY YOUNG; AND QUITE ANOTHER STORY. Two Stories. By JEAN INGELOW.

CAN THIS BE LOVE? By LOUISA PARR.

KEITH DERAMORE. By the Author of ' Miss Molly '.

SIDNEY. By MARGARET DELAND.

LAST WORDS TO GIRLS ON LIFE AT SCHOOL AND AFTER SCHOOL. By Mrs. W. GREY.

STRAY THOUGHTS FOR GIRLS. By LUCY H. M. SOULSBY, Head Mistress of Oxford High School. 16mo., 1s. 6d. net.

The Silver Library.

CROWN 8vo. 3s. 6d. EACH VOLUME.

Arnold's (Sir Edwin) Seas and Lands. With 71 Illustrations. 3s. 6d.

Bagehot's (W.) Biographical Studies. 3s. 6d.

Bagehot's (W.) Economic Studies. 3s. 6d.

Bagehot's (W.) Literary Studies. With Portrait. 3 vols, 3s. 6d. each.

Baker's (Sir S. W.) Eight Years in Ceylon. With 6 Illustrations. 3s. 6d.

Baker's (Sir S. W.) Rifle and Hound in Ceylon. With 6 Illustrations. 3s. 6d.

Baring-Gould's (Rev. S.) Curious Myths of the Middle Ages. 3s. 6d.

Baring-Gould's (Rev. S.) Origin and Development of Religious Belief. 2 vols. 3s. 6d. each.

Becker's (Prof.) Gallus: or, Roman Scenes in the Time of Augustus. Illustrated. 3s. 6d.

Becker's (Prof.) Charicles: or, Illustrations of the Private Life of the Ancient Greeks. Illustrated. 3s. 6d.

Bent's (J. T.) The Ruined Cities of Mashonaland. With 117 Illustrations. 3s. 6d.

Brassey's (Lady) A Voyage in the ' Sunbeam '. With 66 Illustrations. 3s. 6d.

Clodd's (E.) Story of Creation: a Plain Account of Evolution. With 77 Illustrations. 3s. 6d.

Conybeare (Rev. W. J.) and Howson's (Very Rev. J. S.) Life and Epistles of St. Paul. 46 Illustrations. 3s. 6d.

Dougall's (L.) Beggars All: a Novel. 3s. 6d.

Doyle's (A. Conan) Micah Clarke. A Tale of Monmouth's Rebellion. 10 Illustrations. 3s. 6d.

Doyle's (A. Conan) The Captain of the Polestar, and other Tales. 3s. 6d.

Doyle's (A. Conan) The Refugees: A Tale of Two Continents. With 25 Illustrations. 3s. 6d.

Froude's (J. A.) Short Studies on Great Subjects. 4 vols. 3s. 6d. each.

Froude's (J. A.) Thomas Carlyle: a History of his Life.

1795-1835. 2 vols. 7s.

1834-1881. 2 vols. 7s.

Froude's (J. A.) Caesar: a Sketch. 3s. 6d.

Froude's (J. A.) The Spanish Story of the Armada, and other Essays. 3s. 6d.

Froude's (J. A.) The Two Chiefs of Dunboy: an Irish Romance of the Last Century. 3s. 6d.

Froude's (J. A.) The History of England, from the Fall of Wolsey to the Defeat of the Spanish Armada. 12 vols. 3s. 6d. each.

Froude's (J. A.) The English in Ireland. 3 vols. 10s. 6d.

Gleig's (Rev. G. R.) Life of the Duke of Wellington. With Portrait. 3s. 6d.

Haggard's (H. R.) She: A History of Adventure. 32 Illustrations. 3s. 6d.

Haggard's (H. R.) Allan Quatermain. With 20 Illustrations. 3s. 6d.

Haggard's (H. R.) Colonel Quaritch, V.C. : a Tale of Country Life. 3s. 6d.

Haggard's (H. R.) Cleopatra. With 29 Full-page Illustrations. 3s. 6d.

Haggard's (H. R.) Eric Brighteyes. With 51 Illustrations. 3s. 6d.

Haggard's (H. R.) Beatrice. 3s. 6d.

Haggard's (H. R.) Allan's Wife. With 34 Illustrations. 3s. 6d.

Haggard's (H. R.) The Witch's Head. With 16 Illustrations. 3s. 6d.

Haggard's (H. R.) Mr. Meeson's Will. With 16 Illustrations. 3s. 6d.

Haggard's (H. R.) Nada the Lily. With 23 Illustrations. 3s. 6d.

Haggard's (H. R.) Dawn. With 16 Illusts. 3s. 6d.

Haggard's (H. R.) and Lang's (A.) The World's Desire. With 27 Illustrations. 3s. 6d.

Harte's (Bret) In the Carquinez Woods and other Stories. 3s. 6d.

Helmholtz's (Hermann von) Popular Lectures on Scientific Subjects. With 68 Illustrations. 2 vols. 3s. 6d. each.

Hornung's (E. W.) The Unbidden Guest. 3s. 6d.

Howitt's (W.) Visits to Remarkable Places. 80 Illustrations. 3s. 6d.

The Silver Library—*continued.*

Jefferies' (R.) **The Story of My Heart:** My Autobiography. With Portrait. 3s. 6d.

Jefferies' (R.) **Field and Hedgerow.** With Portrait. 3s. 6d.

Jefferies' (R.) **Red Deer.** 17 Illustrations. 3s. 6d.

Jefferies' (R.) **Wood Magic:** a Fable. With Frontispiece and Vignette by E. V. B. 3s. 6d.

Jefferies (R.) **The Toilers of the Field.** With Portrait from the Bust in Salisbury Cathedral. 3s. 6d.

Knight's (E. F.) **The Cruise of the 'Alerte':** the Narrative of a Search for Treasure on the Desert Island of Trinidad. With 2 Maps and 23 Illustrations. 3s. 6d.

Knight's (E. F.) **Where Three Empires Meet:** a Narrative of Recent Travel in Kashmir, Western Tibet, Baltistan, Gilgit. With a Map and 54 Illustrations. 3s. 6d.

Lang's (A.) **Angling Sketches.** 20 Illustrations. 3s. 6d.

Lang's (A.) **Custom and Myth:** Studies of Early Usage and Belief. 3s. 6d.

Lees (J. A.) **and Clutterbuck's (W. J.) B. C. 1887, A Ramble in British Columbia.** With Maps and 75 Illustrations. 3s. 6d.

Macaulay's (Lord) **Essays and Lays of Ancient Rome.** With Portrait and Illustration. 3s. 6d.

Macleod's (H. D.) **Elements of Banking.** 3s. 6d.

Marshman's (J. C.) **Memoirs of Sir Henry Havelock.** 3s. 6d.

Max Müller's (F.) **India, what can it teach us?** 3s. 6d.

Max Müller's (F.) **Introduction to the Science of Religion.** 3s. 6d.

Merivale's (Dean) **History of the Romans under the Empire.** 8 vols. 3s. 6d. each.

Mill's (J. S.) **Political Economy.** 3s. 6d.

Mill's (J. S.) **System of Logic.** 3s. 6d.

Milner's (Geo.) **Country Pleasures:** the Chronicle of a Year chiefly in a Garden. 3s. 6d.

Nansen's (F.) **The First Crossing of Greenland.** With Illustrations and a Map. 3s. 6d.

Phillipps-Wolley's (C.) **Snap:** a Legend of the Lone Mountain. 13 Illustrations. 3s. 6d.

Proctor's (R. A.) The Orbs Around Us. 3s. 6d.

Proctor's (R. A.) The Expanse of Heaven. 3s. 6d.

Proctor's (R. A.) **Other Worlds than Ours.** 3s. 6d.

Proctor's (R. A.) Rough Ways made Smooth. 3s. 6d.

Proctor's (R. A.) Pleasant Ways in Science. 3s. 6d.

Proctor's (R. A.) Myths and Marvels of Astronomy. 3s. 6d.

Proctor's (R. A.) Nature Studies. 3s. 6d.

Rossetti's (Maria F.) **A Shadow of Dante.** 3s. 6d.

Smith's (R. Bosworth) **Carthage and the Carthaginians.** With Maps, Plans, &c. 3s. 6d.

Stanley's (Bishop) **Familiar History of Birds.** 160 Illustrations. 3s. 6d.

Stevenson (R. L.) and Osbourne's (Ll.) The Wrong Box. 3s. 6d.

Stevenson (Robert Louis) and Stevenson's (Fanny van de Grift) More New Arabian Nights.—The Dynamiter. 3s. 6d.

Weyman's (Stanley J.) **The House of the Wolf:** a Romance. 3s. 6d.

Wood's (Rev. J. G.) Petland Revisited. With 33 Illustrations. 3s. 6d.

Wood's (Rev. J. G.) **Strange Dwellings.** With 60 Illustrations. 3s. 6d.

Wood's (Rev. J. G.) **Out of Doors.** 11 Illustrations. 3s. 6d.

Cookery, Domestic Management, Gardening, etc.

Acton.—*MODERN COOKERY.* By ELIZA ACTON. With 150 Woodcuts. Fcp. 8vo., 4s. 6d.

Bull (THOMAS, M.D.).

HINTS TO MOTHERS ON THE MANAGEMENT OF THEIR HEALTH DURING THE PERIOD OF PREGNANCY. Fcp. 8vo., 1s. 6d.

THE MATERNAL MANAGEMENT OF CHILDREN IN HEALTH AND DISEASE. Fcp. 8vo., 1s. 6d.

De Salis (MRS.).

CAKES AND CONFECTIONS À LA MODE. Fcp. 8vo., 1s. 6d.

DOGS: A Manual for Amateurs. Fcp. 8vo., 1s. 6d.

DRESSED GAME AND POULTRY À LA MODE. Fcp. 8vo., 1s. 6d.

DRESSED VEGETABLES À LA MODE. Fcp. 8vo., 1s. 6d.

DRINKS À LA MODE. Fcp. 8vo., 1s. 6d.

ENTRÉES À LA MODE. Fcp. 8vo., 1s. 6d.

De Salis (MRS.).—WORKS BY—*continued.*

FLORAL DECORATIONS. Fcp. 8vo., 1s. 6d.

GARDENING À LA MODE. Fcp. 8vo. Part I., Vegetables, 1s. 6d. Part II., Fruits, 1s. 6d.

NATIONAL VIANDS À LA MODE. Fcp. 8vo., 1s. 6d.

NEW-LAID EGGS. Fcp. 8vo., 1s. 6d.

OYSTERS À LA MODE. Fcp. 8vo., 1s. 6d.

PUDDINGS AND PASTRY À LA MODE. Fcp. 8vo., 1s. 6d.

SAVOURIES À LA MODE. Fcp. 8vo., 1s. 6d.

SOUPS AND DRESSED FISH À LA MODE. Fcp. 8vo., 1s. 6d.

SWEETS AND SUPPER DISHES À LA MODE. Fcp. 8vo., 1s. 6d.

TEMPTING DISHES FOR SMALL INCOMES. Fcp. 8vo., 1s. 6d.

WRINKLES AND NOTIONS FOR EVERY HOUSEHOLD. Crown 8vo., 1s. 6d.

Cookery, Domestic Management, &c.—*continued*.

Lear.—*MAIGRE COOKERY*. By H. L. SIDNEY LEAR. 16mo., 2s.

Poole.—*COOKERY FOR THE DIABETIC*. By W. H. and Mrs. POOLE. With Preface by Dr. PAVY. Fcp. 8vo., 2s. 6d.

Walker.—*A BOOK FOR EVERY WO-MAN*. Part I., The Management of Children in Health and out of Health. By JANE H. WALKER, L.R.C.P.I., L.R.C.S., M.D. (Brux). Crown 8vo., 2s. 6d.

Walker.—*A HANDBOOK FOR MO-THERS*: being Simple Hints to Women on the Management of their Health during Pregnancy and Confinement, together with Plain Directions as to the Care of Infants. By JANE H. WALKER, L.R.C.P.I., L.R.C.S., and M.D. (Brux). Crown 8vo., 2s. 6d.

Miscellaneous and Critical Works.

Allingham.—*VARIETIES IN PROSE*. By WILLIAM ALLINGHAM. 3 vols. Cr. 8vo., 18s. (Vols. 1 and 2, Rambles, by PATRICIUS WALKER. Vol. 3, Irish Sketches, etc.)

Armstrong.—*ESSAYS AND SKETCHES*. By EDMUND J. ARMSTRONG. Fcp. 8vo., 5s.

Bagehot.—*LITERARY STUDIES*. By WALTER BAGEHOT. With Portrait. 3 vols. Crown 8vo., 3s. 6d. each.

Baring-Gould.—*CURIOUS MYTHS OF THE MIDDLE AGES*. By Rev. S. BARING-GOULD. Crown 8vo., 3s. 6d.

Battye. — *PICTURES IN PROSE OF NATURE, WILD SPORT, AND HUMBLE LIFE*. By AUBYN TREVOR BATTYE, F.L.S., F.Z.S. Crown 8vo., 6s.

Baynes. — *SHAKESPEARE STUDIES*, and other Essays. By the late THOMAS SPENCER BAYNES, LL.B., LL.D. With a Biographical Preface by Professor LEWIS CAMPBELL. Crown 8vo., 7s. 6d.

Boyd (A. K. H.) ('A.K.H.B.').
And see Miscellaneous Theological Works, p. 24.

AUTUMN HOLIDAYS OF A COUNTRY PARSON. Crown 8vo., 3s. 6d.

COMMONPLACE PHILOSOPHER. Cr. 8vo., 3s. 6d.

CRITICAL ESSAYS OF A COUNTRY PARSON. Crown 8vo., 3s. 6d.

EAST COAST DAYS AND MEMORIES. Crown 8vo., 3s. 6d.

LANDSCAPES, CHURCHES, AND MORA-LITIES. Crown 8vo., 3s. 6d.

LEISURE HOURS IN TOWN. Crown 8vo., 3s. 6d.

LESSONS OF MIDDLE AGE. Crown 8vo., 3s. 6d.

OUR LITTLE LIFE. Two Series. Crown 8vo., 3s. 6d. each.

Boyd (A. K. H.) ('A.K.H.B.').—*continued*.

OUR HOMELY COMEDY: AND TRA-GEDY. Crown 8vo., 3s. 6d.

RECREATIONS OF A COUNTRY PARSON. Three Series. Crown 8vo., 3s. 6d. each. Also First Series. Popular Edition. 8vo., 6d.

Butler (SAMUEL).

EREWHON. Crown 8vo., 5s.

THE FAIR HAVEN. A Work in De-fence of the Miraculous Element in our Lord's Ministry. Cr. 8vo., 7s. 6d.

LIFE AND HABIT. An Essay after a Completer View of Evolution. Cr. 8vo., 7s. 6d.

EVOLUTION, OLD AND NEW. Cr. 8vo., 10s. 6d.

ALPS AND SANCTUARIES OF PIED-MONT AND CANTON TICINO. Illustrated. Pott 4to., 10s. 6d.

LUCK, OR CUNNING, AS THE MAIN MEANS OF ORGANIC MODIFICATION? Cr. 8vo., 7s. 6d.

EX VOTO. An Account of the Sacro Monte or New Jerusalem at Varallo-Sesia. Crown 8vo., 10s. 6d.

Gwilt.—*AN ENCYCLOPÆDIA OF AR-CHITECTURE*. By JOSEPH GWILT, F.S.A. Illustrated with more than 1100 Engravings on Wood. Revised (1888), with Alterations and Considerable Additions by WYATT PAPWORTH. 8vo., £2 12s. 6d.

James.—*MINING ROYALTIES*: their Practical Operation and Effect. By CHARLES ASHWORTH JAMES, of Lincoln's Inn, Barrister-at-Law. Fcp. 4to., 5s.

Miscellaneous and Critical Works - *continued.*

Jefferies.—(RICHARD).

FIELD AND HEDGEROW: last Essays. With Portrait. Crown 8vo., 3s. 6d.

THE STORY OF MY HEART: my Autobiography. With Portrait and New Preface by C. J. LONGMAN. Crown 8vo., 3s. 6d.

RED DEER. With 17 Illustrations by J. CHARLTON and H. TUNALY. Crown 8vo., 3s. 6d.

THE TOILERS OF THE FIELD. With Portrait from the Bust in Salisbury Cathedral. Crown 8vo., 3s. 6d.

WOOD MAGIC: a Fable. With Frontispiece and Vignette by E. V. B. Crown 8vo., 3s. 6d.

THOUGHTS FROM THE WRITINGS OF RICHARD JEFFERIES. Selected by H. S. HOOLE WAYLEN. 16mo., 3s. 6d.

Johnson.—*THE PATENTEE'S MANUAL*: a Treatise on the Law and Practice of Letters Patent. By J. & J. H. JOHNSON, Patent Agents, &c. 8vo., 10s. 6d.

Lang (ANDREW).

LETTERS TO DEAD AUTHORS. Fcp. 8vo., 2s. 6d. net.

BOOKS AND BOOKMEN. With 2 Coloured Plates and 17 Illustrations. Fcp. 8vo., 2s. 6d. net.

OLD FRIENDS. Fcp. 8vo., 2s. 6d. net.

LETTERS ON LITERATURE. Fcp. 8vo., 2s. 6d. net.

COCK LANE AND COMMON SENSE. Fcp. 8vo., 6s. 6d. net.

Laurie.—*HISTORICAL SURVEY OF PRE-CHRISTIAN EDUCATION.* By S. S. LAURIE, A.M., L.L.D. Crown 8vo., 12s.

Leonard.—*THE CAMEL*: Its Uses and Management. By Major ARTHUR GLYN LEONARD, late 2nd East Lancashire Regiment. Royal 8vo., 21s. net.

Max Müller (F).

INDIA: *WHAT CAN IT TEACH US?* Crown 8vo., 3s. 6d.

CHIPS FROM A GERMAN WORKSHOP.

Vol. I. Recent Essays and Addresses. Crown 8vo., 6s. 6d. net.

Vol. II. Biographical Essays. Crown 8vo., 6s. 6d. net.

Vol. III. Essays on Language and Literature. Crown 8vo., 6s. 6d. net.

Vol. IV. Essays on Mythology and Folk Lore. Crown 8vo., 8s. 6d. net.

Macfarren. *LECTURES ON HARMONY.* By Sir GEORGE A. MACFARREN. 8vo., 12s.

Milner (GEORGE).

COUNTRY PLEASURES: the Chronicle of a Year chiefly in a Garden. Cr. 8vo., 3s. 6d.

STUDIES OF NATURE ON THE COAST OF ARRAN. With 10 Full-page Copperplates and 12 Illustrations in the Text by W. NOEL JOHNSON. Cr. 8vo., 6s. 6d. net.

Poore. *ESSAYS ON RURAL HYGIENE.* By GEORGE VIVIAN POORE, M.D., F.R.C.P. With 13 Illustrations. Crown 8vo., 6s. 6d.

Proctor (RICHARD A.).

STRENGTH AND HAPPINESS. With 9 Illustrations. Crown 8vo., 5s.

STRENGTH: How to get Strong and keep Strong, with Chapters on Rowing and Swimming, Fat, Age, and the Waist. With 9 Illustrations. Crown 8vo., 2s.

Richardson.—*NATIONAL HEALTH.* A Review of the Works of Sir Edwin Chadwick, K.C.B. By Sir B. W. RICHARDSON, M.D. Crown 8vo., 4s. 6d.

Rossetti. *A SHADOW OF DANTE*: being an Essay towards studying Himself, his World and his Pilgrimage. By MARIA FRANCESCA ROSSETTI. With Frontispiece by DANTE GABRIEL ROSSETTI. Cr. 8vo., 10s. 6d. Cheap Edition, 3s. 6d.

Solovyoff. *A MODERN PRIESTESS OF ISIS (MADAME BLAVATSKY).* Abridged and Translated on Behalf of the Society for Psychical Research from the Russian of VSEVOLOD SERGYEEVICH SOLOVYOFF. By WALTER LEAF, Litt.D. With Appendices. Crown 8vo., 6s.

Stevens. *ON THE STOWAGE OF SHIPS AND THEIR CARGOES.* With Information regarding Freights, Charter-Parties, &c. By ROBERT WHITE STEVENS, Associate-Member of the Institute of Naval Architects. 8vo., 21s.

Van Dyke. *A TEXT-BOOK OF THE HISTORY OF PAINTING.* By JOHN C. VAN DYKE, of Rutgers College, U.S. With Frontispiece and 110 Illustrations in the Text. Crown 8vo., 6s.

West.—*WILLS, AND HOW NOT TO MAKE THEM.* With a Selection of Leading Cases. By B. B. WEST, Author of "Half Hours with the Millionaires". Fcp. 8vo., 2s. 6d.

Miscellaneous Theological Works.

. *For Church of England and Roman Catholic Works see* MESSRS. LONGMANS & CO.'s
Special Catalogues.

Balfour. — *THE FOUNDATIONS OF BELIEF:* being Notes Introductory to the Study of Theology. By the Right Hon. ARTHUR J. BALFOUR, M.P. 8vo., 12s. 6d.

Boyd (A. K. H.).

OCCASIONAL AND IMMEMORIAL DAYS: Discourses. Crown 8vo., 7s. 6d.

COUNSEL AND COMFORT FROM A CITY PULPIT. Crown 8vo., 3s. 6d.

SUNDAY AFTERNOONS IN THE PARISH CHURCH OF A SCOTTISH UNIVERSITY CITY. Crown 8vo., 3s. 6d.

CHANGED ASPECTS OF UNCHANGED TRUTHS. Crown 8vo., 3s. 6d.

GRAVER THOUGHTS OF A COUNTRY PARSON. Three Series. Crown 8vo., 3s. 6d. each.

PRESENT DAY THOUGHTS. Crown 8vo., 3s. 6d.

SEASIDE MUSINGS. Cr. 8vo., 3s. 6d.

'*TO MEET THE DAY*' through the Christian Year: being a Text of Scripture, with an Original Meditation and a Short Selection in Verse for Every Day. Crown 8vo., 4s. 6d.

De la Saussaye. — *A MANUAL OF THE SCIENCE OF RELIGION.* By Professor CHANTEPIE DE LA SAUSSAYE. Translated by Mrs. COLYER FERGUSSON (*née* MAX MULLER). Crown 8vo., 12s. 6d.

Kalisch (M. M., Ph.D.).

BIBLE STUDIES. Part I. Prophecies of Balaam. 8vo., 10s. 6d. Part II. The Book of Jonah. 8vo., 10s. 6d.

COMMENTARY ON THE OLD TESTAMENT: with a New Translation. Vol. I. Genesis. 8vo., 18s. Or adapted for the General Reader. 12s. Vol. II. Exodus. 15s. Or adapted for the General Reader. 12s. Vol. III. Leviticus, Part I. 15s. Or adapted for the General Reader. 8s. Vol. IV. Leviticus, Part II. 15s. Or adapted for the General Reader. 8s.

Macdonald (GEORGE, LL.D.).

UNSPOKEN SERMONS. Three Series. Crown 8vo., 3s. 6d. each.

THE MIRACLES OF OUR LORD. Crown 8vo., 3s. 6d.

A BOOK OF STRIFE, IN THE FORM OF THE DIARY OF AN OLD SOUL: Poems. 18mo., 6s.

10,000/12/95.

Martineau (JAMES, D.D., LL.D.).

HOURS OF THOUGHT ON SACRED THINGS: Sermons, 2 vols. Crown 8vo., 7s. 6d. each.

ENDEAVOURS AFTER THE CHRISTIAN LIFE. Discourses. Crown 8vo., 7s. 6d.

THE SEAT OF AUTHORITY IN RELIGION. 8vo., 14s.

ESSAYS, REVIEWS, AND ADDRESSES. 4 Vols. Crown 8vo., 7s. 6d. each. I. Personal; Political. II. Ecclesiastical; Historical. III. Theological; Philosophical. IV. Academical; Religious.

HOME PRAYERS, with *TWO SERVICES* for Public Worship. Crown 8vo., 3s. 6d.

Max Müller (F.).

HIBBERT LECTURES ON THE ORIGIN AND GROWTH OF RELIGION, as illustrated by the Religions of India. Cr. 8vo., 7s. 6d.

INTRODUCTION TO THE SCIENCE OF RELIGION: Four Lectures delivered at the Royal Institution. Crown 8vo., 3s. 6d.

NATURAL RELIGION. The Gifford Lectures, delivered before the University of Glasgow in 1888. Crown 8vo., 10s. 6d.

PHYSICAL RELIGION. The Gifford Lectures, delivered before the University of Glasgow in 1890. Crown 8vo., 10s. 6d.

ANTHROPOLOGICAL RELIGION. The Gifford Lectures, delivered before the University of Glasgow in 1891. Cr. 8vo., 10s. 6d.

THEOSOPHY, OR PSYCHOLOGICAL RELIGION. The Gifford Lectures, delivered before the University of Glasgow in 1892. Crown 8vo., 10s. 6d.

THREE LECTURES ON THE VEDÂNTA PHILOSOPHY, delivered at the Royal Institution in March, 1894. 8vo., 5s.

Phillips. — *THE TEACHING OF THE VEDAS.* What Light does it Throw on the Origin and Development of Religion? By MAURICE PHILLIPS, London Mission, Madras. Crown 8vo., 6s.

Romanes. — *THOUGHTS ON RELIGION.* By GEORGE J. ROMANES, LL.D., F.R.S. Crown 8vo., 4s. 6d.

SUPERNATURAL RELIGION: an Inquiry into the Reality of Divine Revelation. 3 vols. 8vo., 36s.

REPLY (A) TO DR. LIGHTFOOT'S ESSAYS. By the Author of 'Supernatural Religion'. 8vo., 6s.

THE GOSPEL ACCORDING TO ST. PETER: a Study. By the Author of 'Supernatural Religion'. 8vo., 6s

Thom. — *A SPIRITUAL FAITH.* Sermons. By JOHN HAMILTON THOM. With a Memorial Preface by JAMES MARTINEAU, D.D. With Portrait. Crown 8vo, 5s.